Near Death

GLENN COOPER

PROLOGUE
THREE DAYS

I t was a familiar backdrop for a TV news story with religious overtones. The Duomo in Milan was ornate and spiky, a forest of ecclesiastical pinnacles and spires beautifully set against a pale sky.

RAINEWS 24 reporter Moreno Stasi carefully brushed his thick hair while peering into a mirror held by his producer, Daniela Persano. This late March was unseasonably warm. He'd chosen the wrong jacket for the day and he was sweating and irritable.

He looked around the square at the tourists gawking at the camera setup. "Just keep them out of my shot," he growled.

"Yeah, yeah," she replied. They'd been together for years. She knew his moods.

They'd already recorded interviews with enough locals and tourists to fill the piece. All that was needed was a setup and a wrap.

"We're ready when you are," Persano said.

He clutched the microphone, looked directly into the lens and started when the videographer raised his finger.

"This is Moreno Stasi in Milano speaking with ordinary people about the crisis sweeping through this city, this country, and much of the world. Is there a better place than the Duomo—this ancient symbol of religion and culture, where people come to pray and meditate—to discuss the upheavals we are facing, this cataclysm?" He stopped and asked, "Is that okay? Too melodramatic?"

"No, it's good," Persano said, trying to be positive. "Keep going."

He cleared his throat. "This clock, this Internet clock of which everyone is aware, is ticking down to only three days left. Until what? That's the issue on everyone's mind. So here, today, I'm asking people these questions: Have you taken Bliss? Has a friend or loved one? And what do you think is going to happen to the world on the last day?"

He lowered the microphone and handed it to Persano. "Give me a second." He lit a cigarette and puffed a few times before stubbing it out on his sole and parking it on a stone by his foot. "Okay, let's do the wrap."

"Start when you want," she said.

He wet his lips and adjusted his facial expression to match where he'd left off. "So, outside this great cathedral, we've heard from people who are scared, people who are hopeful, and people who are simply bewildered. No one knows what will happen Sunday afternoon but one thing is sure. A great many people will be attending mass that morning, praying to God, because never in our recent history has God been so important. This is Moreno Stasi reporting from Milano."

"Okay," Stasi said, relighting his cigarette. "Get it over to Antonio to edit."

"Antonio?" his producer said, shocked.

"Why not?"

"I thought you knew?"

He shook his head, suddenly afraid.

"Antonio killed himself last night."

Stasi took another deep drag. "Jesus, not another one."

1

MONTHS EARLIER

The dogs smelled them coming. They started to bay and howl when the men were well down the corridor with three sets of locked doors still to navigate. By the time the two of them entered the suite of cages, the beagles were in a frenzy, straining on hind limbs, pushing their black fleshy noses against the mesh, filling the bare room with frantic high-pitched yelps.

The smaller man clamped his hands over his ears, grimaced, and raised his voice. "Can you make them stop?"

The taller one addressed the animals earnestly with hands on hips. "My friend Thomas would like you to stop barking." The adenoidal Liverpool accent was mellowed by years in America.

His words had no effect.

He shrugged. "No, I can't. They'll settle down."

He unlocked another door and led Thomas into the next suite. These rooms were soundproofed and the barking became muffled. Thomas relaxed a little when the fluorescent lights flickered on and he was able to absorb familiar landmarks: a stainless steel surgical table; anesthesia gear; cardiac monitor; sterile surgical packs; meds.

"See?" Alex said. "I told you it was a proper operating room."

"The table's too small."

"I'll make myself fit."

Thomas took off his jacket and began an inventory, collecting the items he needed from shelves and drawers and laying them out on a cart.

Alex followed the balding, gracile man with his eyes, attracted especially to his long effeminate fingers. He'd noticed them before, reminiscent of the hands of a pianist who could stretch at least a tenth. "Everything's there, right?"

"Hang on," Thomas said. "Where's the spinal tray?"

He pointed to a cabinet.

Thomas broke the sterile seal, unwrapped it, and donned a pair of surgical gloves to inspect the skinny Quinke needle.

"It's a large-animal kit," Alex grimly offered. "It should work, no?"

"It's the right size."

"Good. Let's hurry. I'll get the tubes ready."

While Thomas finished organizing his work space, Alex collected specimen tubes and labeled them with a black Sharpie. On the first one he wrote, A.W. BASELINE, the second one, A.W. 2:00 MINUTES. The next four were labeled in fifteen-second increments, the last one, A.W. 3:00 MINUTES. He envisioned himself in his lab the next morning, processing six precious tubes of his own bodily fluids.

Thomas had finished his prep but he stood there motionless, staring at the cart.

"Are we ready?" Alex asked.

"I guess so."

"What's the matter?"

"Look, Alex …"

"It'll be fine. Don't worry." The words flipped off his tongue, more command than emollient. "Only my shirt, okay?"

Thomas nodded.

Alex stripped to the waist. He was tall and lean, his ribcage prominent. He saw that Thomas was fixated on the large geographic patch of heaped-up skin on his shoulder and back. "Didn't I tell you about my burns?"

"No."

"Some other time." He collected his shoulder-length hair in his fist and twisted an elastic band around it. "Ready?"

Thomas covered the surgical table with a green sheet. "I need you turned toward the door, on your right side."

Alex saw he'd be facing the large clock with a sweeping second hand. "Good."

The table was not meant for people and he had to balance himself precariously, his head teetering off the end. With his knees drawn up tightly to his chest he was secure, not particularly comfortable, but comfort wasn't at the top of his agenda. Thomas stuck cardiac electrodes onto his chest and the monitor came to life, pleasantly beeping with each heartbeat. When he started describing what he was about to do, Alex cut him off. He didn't want a running commentary but rather to retreat to an internal space.

Control your breathing.

Find your center.

You're a speck in the universe, dust in the wind.

He felt the iodine swabbed onto his back, shockingly cold, the sterile drapes positioned over his torso. Thomas couldn't help talking. "You're going to feel a pinch."

The sharp pain of the lidocaine needle in the small of his back lasted a few seconds then dissipated.

"I need you to tighten your fetal position: knees up, chin on your chest. I'm going to insert the needle between L3 and L4."

"Bloody hell, Thomas. Spare me. I've done more of these than you." He inhaled deeply, held it for a few seconds then blew the breath out. "Go on."

He felt pressure but no pain and the curious realization that a four-inch needle was being pushed between his vertebrae on its way to his spinal cord. There was a perceptible *pop* as the tough dura sheath surrounding the cord was punctured.

Thomas pulled out the stylet and a drop of Alex's crystal-clear spinal fluid welled from the base of the needle, suspended there by surface tension. "I'm collecting the baseline now." Viscous drops slid into a plastic tube. "You okay?"

"Never better," he grunted.

Thomas reinserted the stylet into the lumen of the needle to staunch the flow. He told him, "I've got the sample."

Alex took a deep breath and when he let it out it sounded like a sigh. "Okay, showtime." He fumbled for the front pocket of his jeans, extending one leg a little to let his hand dig into the pocket, careful to keep his pierced back as motionless as possible. "I should have taken these out before," he said.

He had two things in his hand, a clear plastic bag and a roll of electrical tape.

Thomas was behind him so Alex couldn't see his face—but he could hear the small man forcing air through his nose with the hesitancy of a horse that didn't want to leave its stall. He sensed the man needed more words. "Are you ready, Thomas?"

"I don't want to do it."

"We've talked through this. We've gone this far."

"I know but I'm scared."

"Don't be. It'll be all right."

"I'm having second thoughts."

"I've already paid you."

"You can have the money back."

He could hear the weakness in Thomas's voice and it repulsed him. He hated that quality in a man but he understood that showing anger might blow things up. "I promise you this will be okay. I'm strong and healthy. I can tolerate three minutes easily. Four would be a problem."

"What if something goes wrong?"

"Nothing will! Just make sure you get the first sample at two minutes, then every fifteen seconds until three minutes. Then pull me out and we'll go have a beer. We're making a little history, tonight, you and I. Doesn't that excite you?"

"I don't know. Maybe."

"Good! Let's get this over with. Just stay cool and watch the clock."

He didn't wait for an answer. *Better to press ahead and force the matter to its conclusion.* The clock's second hand was approaching the top of the circle. Without another thought Alex pulled the plastic bag over his head and tightly sealed it around his neck with loops of tape. The second hand swept the twelve. Through the bag he shouted, "Time zero!"

The bag immediately clouded with condensation.

Thomas stepped to the head of the table so he could watch Alex's face and the cardiac monitor simultaneously. What he saw horrified him, the sight of a gasping head, plastic sucking into an open mouth, blowing out and sucking back in.

"Are you sure you want to do this?" Thomas shouted.

He nodded. He was sure.

Twenty-three years.

This was twenty-three years coming. He could still see the flames and hear the hiss of burning plastic.

It was harder than he imagined, fighting the panic of air starvation. He had to stay calm, stay motionless—make himself succumb.

The terror was overwhelming. The hot wet plastic sucked into his mouth. All the air was gone from the bag. His body was programmed to survive, to reach up and rip the bag open, but his mind was stronger. He had to go through with it. He *had* to know.

Through the cloudy plastic he had a fleeting glimpse of Thomas looking as wild-eyed and panicked as he. He heard distant shouts but the words didn't register. He was close, he could feel it coming.

Stay strong.

There was a fade to gray as if a dimmer switch was being turned and then the terror receded.

Blackness. Pure blackness without a photon of light.

It enveloped him, he floated in it. He was a fetus again and the blackness was his amniotic fluid.

He was aware of breathing, of light. He reached up and touched his forehead. His face and hair were wet. The bag was gone. He was on his back, his long legs dangling off the table. He felt utterly lost, confused, and then he saw Thomas, sitting on a stool beside him, distraught, tearful, an oxygen mask in his lap.

"Did you get the samples?"

Thomas was silent.

"Did you get them?" He sat up. His head was pounding. His mind shouldn't have been as blank as it was. Something was wrong.

"No."

He was incredulous. "What do you mean *no*?"

Thomas was crying. "I couldn't go through with it. I thought you were going to die."

"How long was I out?"

"Forty seconds, maybe fifty."

"That's all?"

"I'm sorry. I couldn't. I cut the bag off, I gave you oxygen."

He stood on shaky legs, towering over the slight man.

"Are you telling me I went through this hell for nothing?"

"I thought you were going to die!"

He felt the greatest surge of rage he'd ever experienced: overwhelming, murderous rage. He'd never struck a man but he felt his fist automatically balling up and his arm arching backward. His fist swung forward with all his weight behind it and caught Thomas on the side of his face, square on the cheek. The pain of impact shot up his arm and brought him to his senses.

What have I done?

Thomas let out a sick sound of surprise as he toppled from the stool, surrendering to gravity. The opposite side of his head was the first body part to hit. It caught the rounded corner of a lab bench hard. There was a nauseating sound of bone letting go, he uttered a simple *Ugh*, then crumpled to the floor. He convulsed for no more than ten seconds then lay motionless.

Alex knelt beside him and called his name, then shook him by the shoulders. The body was lifeless. One of his pupils was already fully dilated, a cold black saucer. The other was following suit, an expanding mass of blood choking his brainstem.

The pulse at the neck was thready. He could start CPR but he'd need help. He had his cell phone. His thumb hovered over the 9 in 911. Then he saw the clock and found himself subtracting off the approximate number of seconds since the head blow. His anger returned. He hated this pathetic creature dying at his knees.

He rose and found the spinal needle on the cart, still glistening with his own fluids. He drew up a syringe of saline, flushed the needle twice then collected his unused specimen tubes, all the while keeping the clock in his sight lines.

One minute gone, one minute to go.

He turned Thomas on his side and pulled up his shirt. His back-bones were spiky like the tail of a reptile. He felt the space between two vertebrae and pushed the needle through the skin.

He promptly hit something hard. Bone. He tried again—and again. He couldn't get the lifeless body into enough of a curl to open up the intervertebral space. He tried again. Another dry tap. His hands started to shake.

The second hand was approaching the two-minute mark. He desperately tried again then gave up in disgust.

There—a plastic case on one of the benches. He opened it. The stainless-steel tool with its battery pack was heavy in his hand.

He stood over Thomas, thinking ferociously, at war with his emotions.

Two minutes ten seconds. He was running out of time.

He pulled the trigger of the surgical drill and it whirred to life, making his hand vibrate and feel vital. He lowered himself onto his haunches and let the drill bit hover an inch from Thomas's skull.

Do it.

He closed his eyes and pressed down hard.

2

Cyrus O'Malley felt like a stranger. It wasn't his church. He sat in a rear pew at the aisle so he could make a gentle exit if he had a change of heart. It was an older crowd, pale wrinkled ladies in veils and well-fed men with bellies spilling over their belts. There were very few children. This was old school: medieval old.

He still wasn't sure what instinct had grabbed hold and made him find a church that did a Tridentine mass, rare these days. Vatican II had all but nailed that coffin shut. Now Sunday mass was a progressive thing done in the local vernacular to the strains of folk guitars; too watered down. He needed stronger medicine.

Sitting there, the Latin echoing around the old church, the woodwork perfumed with age, he felt plugged into the ancient religion and it soothed his nerve endings like butter on a burn. The priest was surprisingly young, his voice almost womanly, his body ample and round.

"Pater noster, qui es in coelis, sanctificetur nomen tuum: adveniat regnum tuum: fiat voluntas tua, sicut in coelo et in terra panem nostrum quotidianum da nobis hodie; et dimitte nobis debita nostra, sicut et nos dimittimus debitoribus nostris: et ne nos inducas in tentationem." *(Our Father, who art in heaven, hallowed be thy name: thy kingdom come; thy will be done on earth as it is in heaven. Give us this day our daily bread: and forgive us our trespasses, as we forgive them that trespass against us. And lead us not into temptation.)*

And Cyrus and the congregation intoned as one, "Sed libera nos a malo." *(But deliver us from evil.)*

Deliver Tara from evil, he thought. *Deliver her, Lord. Deliver her.*

Outside, the crisp autumn morning was suffused with the orange of an ascending sun. He lingered, unconnected to the parishioners but nonetheless taking comfort being in their midst, listening to old-folk conversations about lunch plans. He had no such plans. The rest of his empty Sunday lay before him. His thin-walled apartment sickened him. He supposed he'd try to read but the Pats were playing and the game would be filtering in from both sides. No point asking his neighbors to tone it down; for them it was the big event of the week. Headphones only helped to a point. Their foot-stomping and shouting came through anyway. It would have been a good afternoon to take Tara to a movie and get ice cream but it wasn't his weekend. He'd probably just climb in his car, pick a compass point and burn some gas. Maybe stop in a bookstore then find a quiet coffee shop.

The priest looked up and broke away from a knot of congregants. He had noticed the athletic stranger, a man close to his age, late thirties, forty at most, too handsome and well-hinged to be drifting alone on the stairs of an unfamiliar church. Yet there was also a melancholy about him that beckoned the priest to missionary work.

Though Cyrus was a large man, he seemed smaller than his physical presence, compacted by mood, his heavy shoulders drooping in a tan blazer, hooded brown eyes cast down, mouth curled in a half-frown. The priest approached him with an open-faced curiosity, his white chasuble billowing in the breeze.

"Hello there, I'm Father Donovan."

"Cyrus O'Malley, Father. Pleased to meet you."

The priest leaned in, in a friendly way, his breath smelling of sacramental wine. "Any relation to Bob O'Malley from Needham?"

"Not that I know of."

"We haven't seen you here before."

"It's my first time." He hesitated and found a two-word explanation. "The Latin."

"I'm glad you appreciate it. It's not for everyone."

"Forsitan non, tamen ego utor Latin," Cyrus answered.

The priest was taken aback. "I haven't met someone with a conversational knowledge of Latin since seminary. Are you a scholar?"

Cyrus smiled at the question. "Hardly. I'm an FBI agent."

"Well, I confess that surprises me. Our first encounter and I'm confessing to you! Do you regularly attend somewhere else, Cyrus?"

"I'm in between. I used to go to St. Anselm's in Sudbury."

"Father Bonner. He gives a good sermon. So you like the Latin mass. You seem awfully youthful for that."

"Childhood memories."

"From where?"

"In Brighton. St. Peter."

"A local boy. Well, we'd love to see you here again, Cyrus." He waved his arms at his departing flock. "You'd bring our average age down considerably."

Cyrus's phone chirped.

"You get that," the priest said, touching him on the shoulder. "It was good talking to you."

The caller ID read AVAKIAN. He pictured Pete's hairy forearms bulging from the sleeves of his golf shirt.

"How're you hitting them?" Cyrus answered.

"Long and left. Fairways hit: zero. Where are you?"

"Praying."

"Me too. Over my putts."

"What do you want?" For them, blunt equaled friendly.

"Just a heads up. Stanley's got something new for us. He's rolling it out tomorrow."

"I don't want it."

"I told him you wouldn't. He's a shitty golfer but he's not a bad guy. He's sympathetic."

"But ..."

"But, it's a done deal, Cy. He said he's been protecting you but he's got no choice. Our number's up."

Cyrus sighed loud enough for Avakian to hear it over the clamor of his foursome ordering breakfast burritos at the half-way canteen. "How bad is it?"

"It looks like it could be a big case."

3

"What's it going to be tonight, honey?"

She delivered the question as if she were taking an order from behind a deli counter. The man in the car looked back at her with a blank expression. "I don't know ... the usual."

"There's no such thing," she said impatiently. "I'm not a mind reader." She was a white girl, early twenties, a little overweight, a lot of foundation makeup filling in burned-out acne craters. Both stockings had ladders disappearing up her skirt. Her cologne had dissipated hours earlier. She smelled of cigarettes.

"A blow job maybe." "It's fifty dollars. You okay with that?"

He wavered, a few beats too long for her comfort. "Yes."

"What?" she demanded. She gave her john another once-over. She'd judged him safe enough to climb in after leaning into his car window and studying his face for signs of trouble as she purred her rote introduction in a faux-sexy voice. He was clean-looking, a big handsome face with prominent landmarks: arching cheekbones, high forehead, large hazel eyes and a smooth jutting jaw, long brown hair pulled into a ponytail. Then his hands: dirt-free, not a brute's. He looked brainy, not her standard street trade. She had a habit of checking out backseats. Nothing good came from a backseat littered with fast-food wrappers and old clothes, greasy tools, hidden lumpy things under blankets. His was barren.

"Nothing, no problem," he insisted, pulling away from the curb after checking his mirrors and signaling with the caution of a kid taking his road test.

At 2 A.M. Mass Ave was traffic-free. The streets were slicked from an evening shower. She pulled her jacket around herself for warmth. He seemed to notice and like a gentleman, turned up the heater. "Where're we going?" she asked.

"I don't want to park on the street. A friend of mine has a lock-up garage in Cambridge. I don't want to pull a Hugh Grant."

"Who's he?"

"A British actor. Caught in the act in his car."

"You sound like you're from there. Or at least not from here."

"Yeah," he answered. "People tell me that."

"I know places to park that are safe," she said. "We don't need to go all the way to Cambridge."

"It's not far. It's just over the bridge."

She screwed up her mouth defiantly. "I don't like the sound of a lock-up garage."

He stopped at a light and smiled weakly. "I understand. The thing is, I've got an important job and I can't risk getting busted. I'll do a hundred. But if you're uncomfortable, I'll let you out here, no harm, no foul."

She fumbled for a cigarette and didn't ask for permission to light up. "Okay, but don't get weird on me. Tomorrow's my birthday."

He pulled money out of his shirt pocket and politely handed it to her. "You can trust me." He opened his window to let out smoke then drove toward the river.

She noticed his knuckles. They were white from gripping the steering wheel too tightly. She'd seen that before. Some of the johns were coiled springs, only letting their guard down a few moments before coming.

Soon, they left Memorial Drive for the tight, protected grid of Cambridgeport. Cars with pasted-on overnight parking permits lined both sides of the narrow streets. The residential neighborhood was a claustrophobic jumble of triple-deckers, single-family houses, and low, squat apartment blocks, mostly dark except for the students and insomniacs whose lights were still blazing. He made a couple of lefts and a right then slowed to a crawl in front of a two-story house with white siding. The windows were black.

"This it?" the girl asked.

He nodded, pulled into the stubby driveway, and told her he'd be back in a second.

He left the car idling and slid open the garage door. When he returned, the girl said, "You couldn't do that where I live."

"Do what?"

"Leave a garage unlocked."

"It's a safe neighborhood."

It was more of a shed than a garage, too narrow to park at the midline if you wanted to open the driver's side door without bumping. She noticed right away that the wall was hugging her passenger side and there was no way out. While she nervously lit another cigarette, the john wriggled out his side, flicked an overhead light switch and shut the garage door.

When he got back in he said, "There." He seemed more relaxed.

She rested the cigarette in the ashtray.

"You smoke a lot," he said.

She ignored him and reached for his crotch.

He told her to wait.

"Why?"

"I want to talk first."

"You want to talk?"

"Yes."

"About what?"

"Anything."

She pouted. "Time's money. I need to get back to my block."

He had another hundred in twenties, folded and ready, as if this were planned out. She suspiciously took the money and quickly put it away in her purse. "So, start talking," she said like a wiseacre.

He evenly told her that he was paying and he wanted *her* to talk. She shrugged and asked for a topic. To her surprise, he mentioned her birthday.

The suggestion made her uneasy. "What about it?"

"Tell me about the best birthday you ever had."

She retrieved the cigarette from the ashtray and took a deep drag. "You're weird, you know that?"

"Any age," he said smoothly, "the best one you can remember, that's what I want to hear about."

She accepted the assignment and went quiet for a while, sorting through memories until she signaled she'd found the item by resolutely pressing her lips together. "My birthdays were always all mixed up with Halloween, their being so close to each other. When I was eight, up in Bangor, you know, my aunt and uncle had a barn back behind their place and after dinner my parents told me I was going to get cake at my aunt's house. But instead of going inside, they took me up to the barn. And my mama opened the door and inside it was dark except that it was filled with jack-o-lanterns, all carved up with smiley faces, glowing from candles inside. And there was a big sign, Happy Birthday, Carla, and my aunt and uncles and cousins were there. And a cake too."

He startled her by saying her name, "Carla." Then, "How did that make you feel?"

She welled up. "It made me feel like they loved me."

"What's the matter?" he asked.

"My mama died a few years after that."

He said he was sorry then mumbled he was cold as he slipped on leather gloves. She hardly noticed and took a diaphragm-deep hit off her cigarette. A large cloud of exhaled smoke hit the dash and blew back into her eyes. She closed them, waiting for the irritation to pass, and in that moment of darkness she saw the magical barn and her beaming mother again. Lost in thought, happy and sad, she reluctantly blinked and returned to the passenger seat of her john's car.

She reopened her eyes the instant before his hands clamped down on her neck.

She felt her larynx being painfully crushed beneath his digging thumbs.

This isn't happening.

This isn't how it's supposed to end.

The panic of air hunger set in, crowding out the pain. She couldn't breathe in or out.

And then, she decided to give up without mounting any fight, any resistance.

She felt her arms go limp.

She was almost bewildered at the way she was abandoning her life so easily until she realized she was captive to his voice, his hypnotic voice, soothing her as he was killing her, uttering through the strain of his exertion, "Carla, listen to me. Don't be mad and don't be scared. Right now you are being loved as much as you've ever been loved. As much as the day you told me about. I'm loving you, little girl. I'm loving you. Your mother is loving you. I know you can hear me. I want you to go to her now."

She could see the strain in his bulging eyes, almost empathize with the exquisite pain he must be feeling in his shuddering hands, and in her final moments she was aware he was doing his best to make the last words she'd hear sound silky.

"Go to her. Go to her. Go to her."

Then, in her last moments, she saw a man suddenly gripped by something exquisitely wonderful, something that made his face go soft and his eyes moist. "You're the lucky one," he said dreamily.

What are you thinking, she wondered as she slipped into unconsciousness.

4

ENGLAND, 1988

Alex was huddled beside his older brother in the backseat of the family's Vauxhall Cavalier. Neither dared open their mouths. He was beyond disappointment, but his father was in a different state of angry, mute agony. His mother had remained uncomfortably stiff-bodied since the moment Dickie snapped at her twenty miles back. Her crime: meekly offering her husband a packed sandwich as the dusk was overtaking them on the northbound carriageway of the M6.

The warm spring day had begun with all the hope and promise of a glorious and certain outcome. When Dickie Weller stamped into the boys' bedroom before dawn they were already decked out in a kit of Liverpool red and white and were chafing to get on the road for the long journey to Wembley to see mighty Liverpool, league champions, go up against lowly Wimbledon for the FA Cup title. *Wimbledon* for God's sake! Complete joke, that! How they'd managed to beat Luton to get to the finals was anybody's guess, but the matchup's result was a foregone conclusion.

Still, the Wellers and scores of Liverpool supporters weren't itching for drama. They were happy with the certainty of biding their time till their lads were cleanly victorious and forever in the record books at the end of regulation play.

In the Liverpool stands before match time, the boys had shouldered against each other, straining on their toes to get a good view of the beautiful green pitch. They listened with delight to the catcalls and opprobrium raining down on the pathetic Wimbledon blues massed on the other side of the vast, roaring, heaving stadium. Their father, big and brawny in his red cap, had waved his arm like a general surveying the opposing army and shouted loudly enough for them to hear, "Proud of your Dad, then?" and they were. "You won't forget this day anytime soon!" he yelled.

He'd scored the four coveted midfield tickets from Boddingtons for pulling more pints of Cain's best bitter than any other Merseyside bar owner. His Publican of the Year award hung over the mantel at the Queen's Arms, beside the photo of a smiling brewery executive from Manchester handing him the tickets envelope. The boys always enjoyed the butter-churn frothiness of living over their wildly popular pub, and in the run-up to Wembley they had sparked from the electricity of their father's celebrity status.

As halftime approached, ten-year-old Alex stooped to pick up his dropped pennant just as Wimbledon's Sanchez headed in a free kick from Wise to take a 1–0 lead. Alex jerked at the roar and saw his father's water-freezing look of rage and his mother's hen-clucking pout. His brother, Joe, five years senior, punched him hard in the shoulder as if the goal were his fault for looking away.

In the nervy second half, at the one-hour point, Wimbledon's Beseant secured a place in history as the first keeper in cup finals to block a penalty shot. That was the killer. Instead of reaching a momentum-grabbing tie, Liverpool faltered and couldn't mount enough pressure in the remaining half hour to avoid a bone-crushing loss.

At the final whistle, his father's fists were clenched in furious disbelief at how a perfect day for the Weller clan had been perfectly and inexorably cocked up. During the long painful walk back to the car park, Alex's eyes burned with tears. He hated the look of despair in his father's flushed face and the brittleness of his mother's quietude. And he resented his brother for being able to let the loss slide off him easily enough to turn the full bore of his attention to chatting up a pair of blondies in red jerseys.

Just north of Birmingham, Alex was resting his head on the window and sleepily staring at the hypnotic chain of headlights coming at them across the divided motorway. Suddenly, he felt deceleration as his father was forced to adjust his speed to accommodate a slow-moving truck that had lumbered onto the left-hand lane from an entrance ramp. Just behind the truck, a Volvo estate car slowed and flashed its brake lights and his father pumped his own brakes a few times to keep off the Volvo's rear end. He swore under his breath and checked his sideview mirror to see if it was safe to pull into the middle lane but it was not. A Yamaha motorcycle was ripping past their car before pulling even with the Volvo.

The driver of the Volvo had the same thought of overtaking the truck but the motorcycle must have been in his blind spot because as he changed lanes he merged directly into the bike and set off the first link in a fateful chain reaction that would ripple through time and unexpectedly alter the world—strangely.

The door panel of the Volvo kissed the rear wheel of the bike, sending the little machine careening into the fast lane and onto the median where the rider fell off and snapped his neck. The Volvo driver reacted instinctively to the contact by sharply turning his wheel to the left. He reentered the slow lane and caught the front end of Dickie Weller's Vauxhall hard at a catastrophic angle.

At the moment of impact, Dickie saw what was happening and loudly swore, *"Bugger me!"*

Alex experienced the next several seconds in a weird slow motion. He'd once been on a plane to a family holiday in Tenerife and the sensation of the car going airborne reminded him of the moment of takeoff. His father always thought seat belt laws were an insidious part of the nanny state and none of them were belted as they began their barrel roll.

At first Alex was more fascinated than alarmed. The weightlessness and down-is-up feeling inside the spiraling cabin felt like an amusement park ride. It was only the sickening crunch of contact with the paved shoulder that jolted him into terror and then there was nothing.

Until—

The car was righted, wheels back on ground.

He was aware of pain—a brutal pain—in his left leg and a fuzzy throbbing in his head. His mother's bucket seat had collapsed onto his lap and he felt the weight of the seat and her body pinning him down. She was moaning, a low primitive vibration that scared him. He saw her right arm limply hanging down between the seats, blood streaming onto her pretty charm bracelet. There was no sound at all from his father. Dickie's head was pitched forward resting against the steering wheel, his Liverpool cap miraculously in place.

For some reason all Alex could think about was his brother, who incongruously wasn't in the car anymore.

"Joe! Joe!"

The back window was blown out and fresh night air whistled through.

The fire began with a *pop* that lifted the whole car a few inches into the air and set it bouncing back on its tires.

Petrol from the ruptured fuel lines had ignited somewhere under the driver's seat and had spread retrograde to the tank. After the terrible rumble of the explosion, Alex felt the heat and his lungs began to fill with stinking plumes of burning gas.

Then the awful yellow and blue flames.

He tried to wriggle free but his legs were pinned and his lower body seemed fixed in concrete. The plastic on the dash and kick panels started to sizzle like a load of bubble and squeak on the breakfast griddle.

He felt the flames licking his back, heard the sickening crinkle of his polyester jumper melting away, the sulfurous smell of vaporizing hair and a moment after the searing anguish began, everything changed.

He was no longer in the car.

He was no longer in pain.

He was floating above the motorway, looking down with an overwhelming sense of childhood curiosity.

The good old family car was pretty well bashed up and flames were licking through it. Joe was on the grassy verge, crawling away from danger. "Go on Joe!" he wanted to shout. "You can make it!" Cars were stopping and men were approaching.

The scene below blurred and went dark as if a fog had rolled in. Now he was hovering over a two-dimensional, perfectly circular disc of blackness that became three-dimensional at once. Though he could see nothing, nothing at all, he had no fear—remarkable, since he still needed a night-light to fall asleep. There was a sense of movement and narrowing, as though he were flowing through a long funnel, like motor oil during a top-up.

Now his ten-year-old body was moving with incredible speed, or maybe he was stationary and the black tunnel was moving around him. There was a sound of whooshing wind akin to a winter gale whipping in from the Irish Sea. He blinked in wonder as the indistinct walls of the tunnel began to come alive with brilliant flashes, redolent of light glinting off embedded clusters of polished diamonds.

A pinpoint of real light ahead grew larger and larger into another perfect circle, until finally he was spit out into a soft landing of pure whiteness—as comforting as emerging from a bubble bath into one of his mom's oversized fluffy towels fresh from the dryer.

Whiteness faded into translucency and he found himself on an expanse of green terrain that seemed to yield slightly to his footsteps, though he was quite sure it wasn't grass. The sky, if that's what it was, was the palest blue, as though an artist had mixed a thimbleful of azure into a gallon of white.

He heard something evocative.

With a sense of excitement reminiscent of rushing down stairs on Christmas morning he moved toward the beckoning sound of gurgling water.

It didn't look like any river he'd ever seen. In fact, it didn't look like it was even made of water—more like rapidly moving streams of shimmery light broken into whirlpools and jetties by a path of shiny stepping-stones. The stones stretched from bank to bank, traversing a span of fifteen yards or so, about the distance of Liverpool's tragically blocked penalty kick.

When he first glanced across the opposite bank he saw nothing but a limitless plain of cool greenness merging with that pale-blue sky.

Though featureless, it seemed to possess infinite promise and he was drawn to the other side with rising excitement.

On his second glance, he saw a man.

A big man, waving his arms wildly and happily.

"Dad?"

"Alex!" He could just hear his name over the sound of the rushing river.

"What's happening, Dad?"

"I'm dead, son."

"What?" He cupped his ear to better hear the reply.

"Dead!"

The word didn't strike him as scary. He made his hands into a megaphone. "What shall I do?"

"Come over! Come to me, lad!"

Dickie was waving his arms as he had done when the boy took his first clumsy steps on the sitting room carpet or his first wobbly pedals without training wheels.

The stepping-stones snaked across fast-moving light beams. They looked slippery but he was certain he could make it and wanted nothing more than to be enveloped in his father's waiting arms. He gingerly and eagerly placed his left foot onto the first stone.

His father looked so happy at that moment, as though Liverpool had come back to pull off a 2–1 victory. And he felt happy too, overwhelmed by a feeling of pure bliss more powerful than anything he'd experienced in all his young life.

He was about to transfer his weight and push his right foot off the bank but he couldn't.

He was being pulled backward, away from the river.

"Hey!"

Everything reversed with stunning speed. He was back in the tunnel, zooming in the opposite direction, back to the motorway, back to the crash, back to the burning car and when he got there, he was aware of being dragged out the passenger side rear door by the shoulders, feeling violent pain all over and being racked by wicked paroxysms of coughing.

Men were shouting.

He was looking into the face of a bearded stranger. "Can you hear me, boy?"

The coughing stopped long enough for him to sputter, "Please let me go back." He didn't want to be here. He desperately wanted to be *there*.

The stranger looked confused. "The only place you're going is to hospital. The ambulance'll be here soon enough. Lie still. Put your head on my jacket."

He coughed some more and rasped, "I want to go to back to my Dad."

The man looked at the gaggle of Samaritans standing over his father's broken corpse, shaking their heads. Others were kneeling over his mother arguing about mouth-to-mouth technique. Nearby, at a safe enough distance, the car was fully engaged by fire. There were shouts as someone discovered his brother crawling through the woods.

"I'm sorry, son," the man said tremulously. "You're safe now. You'll be okay."

He defiantly tried to sit up. "I want to go back!"

"You're not going anywhere! Just lie still and wait for the ambulance to come."

At that, the boy lay back down on the ground, turned his head away and began to sob. "I want to go back."

5

Cyrus held the crime scene photo in his hand and studied it before setting it down on a growing pile. Avakian kept them coming: dozens of shots of a fully clothed Caucasian girl in a roadside ditch, attractive as corpses go, discovered by a highway crew, her flesh nicely preserved by the chilled autumn air. In some angles, she looked like she could have been woken with a good prodding. If the family had wanted an open casket it was definitely doable.

He sat at the little round conference table shoehorned into Avakian's office, a meager symbol of the older man's seniority. His own office was even more of a nutshell; his ex-wife's walk-in closet was larger. He looked away from the photos for a moment and glanced out the window onto the moonscape of Government Center, an ugly expanse of municipal concrete made grayer by the steady rain. He sighed, unavoidably breathing in the other man's cologne, that sickly spicy smell, day after day, month after month, year after year. Avakian was a creature of repetition: same striped ties, same bagged lunch every day, same deprecating stories about the wife and kids. He was shiny-bald and powerful, the physical embodiment of a bullet with a flat pugnacious boxer's nose and a black Vandyck neatly trimmed and smattered with gray.

The two shared over a decade of history. The office didn't have a formal partner system but as the Counterterrorism and Counterintelligence Divisions had expanded post–9/11, Major Thefts and Violent

Crimes had shrunk. Cyrus had always been able to avoid a transfer to another squad. The FBI had a boatload of specialists among their ranks: accountants, lawyers, computer jocks, internationalists. He was more of a glorified cop and so was Avakian. With a dwindling supply of special agents to do battle against ordinary villains, Cyrus found himself working with Avakian most of the time. Not that he minded it. Avakian was many things to him, most of them agreeable.

"The last set is from her autopsy."

In the best of times, Cyrus wasn't wild about seeing snaps of a young woman cut open on a slab and these weren't the best of times. He hardened his jaw and reluctantly stuck out his hand. The first photo showed her head on its side. She had a nice profile, a pleasing upturn to her nose, a good chin. A neat rectangle of bleached hair had been shaved from her right temple by the coroner's assistant and a steel metric rule was laid out on her scalp. In the pale-flesh center of the shaved patch was a small, perfectly round, perfectly black hole. The next photo was an extreme close-up that made the black hole look unanatomical, infinitely deep, and unspeakably evil.

He tried to detach himself from the image by asking a pedestrian question. "What is that, three-sixteenths? Eighth of an inch?"

Avakian had the report. "It's the same as the others. Eighth-of-an-inch drill bit. Nothing distinctive about it. Same as you can get in any hardware store."

Minot slipped in behind them and watched them work for a moment. The fabric of his clothes was permeated with aromatic pipe tobacco and both men turned at the sensory cue. He asked them how it was going.

Avakian deadpanned they'd have it wrapped up by lunch.

There was an air of academia about Minot; it was difficult to imagine he'd ever qualified on the pistol range or the obstacle course at Quantico. He was borderline emaciated, blessed or cursed by a rapid metabolism that gave him the lipid profile of a youngster but left him so perpetually cold that he always wore a sweater vest under his suit jacket, even in summer. His thinning but carefully combed hair drained of color and his pink-tinged plastic bifocals that framed lachrymal eyes suggested an aging Boston banker, not someone with a holster in his desk and a badge in his pocket.

He touched Cyrus's arm the same way the priest had done earlier and asked, "How's your daughter?"

"She's home. Everything's status quo."

Minot gestured at the files. "I wish I didn't have to give this to you."

Cyrus shrugged to signal he understood.

"It's a weird case, isn't it?" Minot mused.

Avakian handed him the photo of the punctured skull, then followed suit with other autopsy photos of two young black women with the same wound.

"This is a sick guy," he clucked. "Didn't Jeffrey Dahmer drill his victims?"

Cyrus knew the details; he remembered these kinds of things. "He injected their frontal lobes with acid. He wanted to turn them into sex zombies but he wasn't a great scientist. All of them died."

"Anything similar going on here?"

"No one thinks foreign substances were introduced," Avakian said.

"What then?"

He rubbed his bald head, fingers splayed like a man who still had tousled hair. "To be determined, Stanley."

After lunch they took a drive. They had to start somewhere so they decided to begin with the latest victim, Carla Louise Goslinga, a twenty-one-year-old prostitute from Boston whose body was found the previous Friday up in Hooksett, New Hampshire. Her probable interstate transport put the crime on the federal map. The case was shaping up to be a jurisdictional hash anyway: the first victim was found on state-owned land on the banks of the Charles in Newton, so the Massachusetts State Police had it; the second victim was discovered in a vacant lot in Columbia Point not far from the JFK Library, so that case was owned by Boston Homicide. Now that the third case triggered the FBI's involvement, everyone was rushing to dump off their databases and let the feds have the headache and expense of a serial killing investigation.

It was a straight shot out of Boston, north on I-93. Avakian drove one of the pool cars, his attention moronically glued to a sports radio station while Cyrus wearily rested his hands on his knees and stared through the beating wiper blades at the dull highway scenery. Despite that peak foliage was only a week or so past, the wet afternoon and gloomy light muted the palette of the woodlands. Avakian was babbling to the radio, calling one of the talk-show guys an idiot, but Cyrus was able to tune out, only distantly aware of a stream of logorrhea.

When they crossed the state line, Cyrus pulled out the report from the New Hampshire State Police with the precise location of Goslinga's body. They had to drive right past the spot, so a quick tramp through the crime scene was on the agenda even if it meant soaking trousers.

When they passed the Route 3A exit, Cyrus reached over and turned off the radio, prompting Avakian to swear at him. "Three miles," he said in response. "There's a large pond. Let's not overshoot it."

"I can drive and listen to the radio, it's not that advanced," Avakian grumbled.

"This crap makes you crazy," he replied, referring to football.

"Our running game sucks. We need more balance."

"No, *you* need more balance."

"Yeah, right," Avakian countered. "My egghead partner's telling me *I* need balance. I like red-blooded American sports, you like libraries. Tell me which one of us is normal and which one needs professional help."

He guided Avakian off the road onto the shoulder as soon as he glimpsed the edge of Pinnacle Pond through the misty trees.

Finding the location where her body had been discovered was a piece of cake because a knot of yellow police tape remained on a nearby tree. Cyrus had a wide-angle photo showing the body in a roadside depression: he and Avakian thus were able to stand over the precise spot, close to the grassy verge, down a natural slope in a shallow piece of ground puddled with runoff.

Cyrus pointed to the highway. "All he had to do was pull off the shoulder, park there, pull her body out of the car, drag it three feet and push it down the slope. He's in and out in under a minute."

"They couldn't get any tire tracks," Avakian said. "The grass is too thick and it was dry last week."

"No witnesses either," Cyrus added. "He was probably here late at night when the traffic's thin." They were getting drenched.

"Okay, we've seen it," Avakian said, making a move back to the car. Cyrus wasn't following. He was trying to decide whether to jump down into the wet ditch. "They went over the place," Avakian implored. "You think you're going to find the perp's wallet down there? Let's go, for Christ's sake."

Back in the car while Avakian dried his scalp with his pocket handkerchief, Cyrus offered up his assessment. "He picked her up in Boston off her usual beat, probably *didn't* have sex with her, strangled her, drilled her head for whatever reason, drove her up here, pulled off the highway at a random place when there weren't any headlights in his rearview mirror, dumped her just far enough off the road so she wouldn't be spotted immediately, took the next exit and turned tail back to Massachusetts."

"Why no sex?"

"Because he made no attempt to conceal the body by burying it, covering it up, dragging it another twenty yards and throwing it into the pond. That tells me he's confident we wouldn't find his DNA on her body. Just like the other two." He seemed to second-guess himself for being so opinionated and he abruptly adopted a less certain tone. "I could be wrong. He could've used a condom."

Avakian grunted and turned the radio back on. "You keep thinking, I'll keep driving." He turned the volume up. "No ego problems here."

The rain was coming down too hard for Avakian to deign to use the parking lot. He pulled up to the covered entrance of the Holiday Inn in Concord, got out and showed his badge to the attendant. The young man didn't give him any lip and ran off excitedly to tell his buddies that a couple of FBI agents were on the premises.

The assistant deputy medical examiner who'd conducted the girl's autopsy over the weekend was attending a conference, and he agreed to meet with the FBI agents on short notice only if he could see them at the hotel. All the medical examiners in southern New Hampshire, along with their support staffs, were holed up for the day at an off-site meeting to get in-serviced on new database software that was supposed to make their lives easier. Dr. Ivan Himmel nevertheless had grumbled over the phone in a stream-of-consciousness way that there was nothing wrong with the software they already had and that the state of New Hampshire never got anything right.

The doctor seemed beyond grateful when someone from the conference staff pulled him out of the hotel ballroom. He approached Cyrus and Avakian like a puppy then happily led them over to a table near the afternoon coffee setup. "First dibs on the baked goods," he exulted. "Load up. On me."

Himmel was one of those older men who never seemed to grow out of adolescence, and even though he was a portly sixty-five decked out like a period piece in a red bow tie and suspenders and short-sleeved white shirt, he had juvenile mannerisms, dunking his chocolate chip cookies into his coffee and wiping the crumbs off his puffy lips with the back of liver-spotted hands.

He slurped his coffee and apologized again for the venue before launching into a tirade on the inefficiencies of state government. Cyrus grounded him at the first polite moment. "The cause of death was strangulation, right?"

"Yeah. Her larynx was crushed. It was manual, from the front. The bruises were consistent with a pair of thumbs. It's not so easy to kill someone like that unless they were drugged or passed-out drunk."

"You don't have the tox back yet, right?" Avakian asked.

"Hello? This is New Hampshire. Have you seen our budget? The idiot bureaucrats are spending money on software we don't need instead of nuts and bolts."

Cyrus jumped in, heading off a tangent. "Which came first, the strangulation or the head wound?"

"Look, if she was conscious at the time of the assault, I'd say a hundred percent she was strangled then drilled." He turned his hand into a power drill, pointed a finger against his skull and made a long drawn-out *brrrrrrr* sound with his throat, causing the two agents to blink in disbelief at his antics. "You can't sink a drill bit into someone's skull without them putting up a little bitty fight and there aren't any signs of bondage. If she was drugged first, then all bets are off on the sequence. If she still had a beating heart the drilling would have produced a real gusher. There wasn't any blood at the crime scene but she was certainly killed somewhere else. There also wasn't a lot of blood on her hair and scalp so she was probably dead or fibrillating when she got trephined. We'll know more when the labs come back, but like I said, it'll take a while."

Avakian squinted at him. "Trephined?"

"Hole made in head," Himmel said slowly, as if Avakian were a child. Cyrus could tell his partner wanted to sock the guy in the nose.

"Talk to us about the head drilling," Cyrus said quickly.

"I've been at this for a long time and this is unique. It's more than a trephination, you know. I'm sure you saw it on my report, there was a tract I probed, maybe two to three millimeters in diameter, extending from the hole in the parietal bone through the entire left parietal lobe into the left lateral ventricle." Himmel sat back and waited for their murmurs of interest.

"Help me out, Doc," Cyrus begged.

"The ventricles. The chambers at the middle of the brain where the cerebrospinal fluid is formed then circulates around the outside of the brain and spinal cord. The fluid cushions the brain, like shock absorbers."

"Is the killer making a deposit or a withdrawal?" Avakian asked.

"Good question." He seemed surprised. "We'll need to get our tox samples back and all the fixed tissue sections, but grossly, I didn't see any dramatic evidence of injection of a foreign substance, like a caustic agent."

"Just like the other cases," Avakian said.

"What other cases?"

Cyrus thought he'd mentioned the others on the phone but maybe he hadn't. He got irritated at himself for not remembering; it wasn't like him.

His mobile rang. He pulled it from his inside pocket and saw it was from Marian. He put it on vibrate, stuffed it back in his pocket and let it hum into his ribs for a few more seconds. "In the past six weeks, two other prostitutes were found in Massachusetts, strangled with eighth-of-an-inch holes drilled through their heads," he said, retrieving a folder from his briefcase. "Both of them had what's been described as needle tracts into the center of their brains. I've got pictures from their autopsies if you want to see them."

Himmel greedily grabbed the photomicrographs and began to pore over them just as the afternoon session broke and his colleagues started pouring from the ballroom. One man walked an arthritic line to their table and sat down without invitation. He was about the same age as Himmel, thinner, a pinched face, another gray-haired relic nearing retirement. "Aren't you going to get coffee?" Himmel asked him.

The other man reached for one of Himmel's cookies. "Is Stanley Minot still at the Boston office?"

"He's our boss," Cyrus replied.

"Tell him Lennie Adler said hello."

Himmel said to the agents, "I told him the FBI was going to visit me. He's already introduced himself in his maladroit way. I'm embarrassed to say he's my oldest friend. I'm in charge of Merrimack County. Lennie does Rockingham County. Get your own cookies, Lennie."

Adler ignored him and looked at the scattered photos on the table. "What are these?"

Himmel grinned, showing large coffee-stained teeth. "It looks like I'm in the middle of a very interesting serial killing case," he bragged. "I got my victim on Friday. These are from the other cases in Massachusetts. Are you jealous?"

Adler snorted, picked up one of the glossies and dug for his reading glasses. He studied a blown-up microscopic view of the cross section of a long slender needle tract plunging through the straw-yellow substance of a human brain. When he tossed the photo down he said, "Tell me there wasn't a hole drilled through the parietal bone."

Cyrus stiffened. He felt weirdly disoriented, as if he were the target of a cunning parlor trick. "How could you know that?"

"Because two months ago I had a case just like this."

"What? A strangled hooker?" Avakian asked, equally startled.

"No, no. It was a young man with a fractured skull, a male nurse. He was found off of I-95, just over the state line. The Seabrook police have nothing. Bupkis." Adler stole another cookie and smugly looked around the table at the slack mouths. "It looks like you fellows might be interested."

Cyrus's phone started buzzing again. He fished it out, glanced at the caller ID and saw it was a repeat from Marian. He thought better of ignoring her for a second time and announced to the table, "Hang on. I've got to take this."

As he listened to her, his breathing got faster, his throat constricted. "Why didn't you call me when it happened?" Then, an existential *"Damn it."* Then, "I'm an hour away. I'm coming."

6

Cyrus automatically made his way through the twisty corridors like a lab rat that had mastered a complex maze. At the Neurology Ward on the ninth floor he was immediately recognized at the nurse's station from past visits. He felt his stomach knot, sickened by the all-too-familiar smell of body fluids masked by lemony disinfectants. "Where is she?" he asked.

The nurse wasn't put off by his brusqueness; she understood and just said, "Nine nineteen."

Outside her door he recognized it as one of the isolation rooms; in fact, he vividly recalled she'd been in that exact room several months ago. There was a sealed anteroom where one could hang a coat and don a mask, gloves, shoe covers and a paper gown. He began the ritual and tried to sneak a wave through the glass but a gowned woman blocked the head of the bed. The woman was too slight to be Marian—just another in an endless stream of doctors, nurses, med school students.

The woman finished whatever she was doing and when she left Tara's bedside, the girl spied him through the glass and weakly waved her hand in a sad little "I'm here again" kind of gesture.

The woman entered the anteroom and removed her mask.

"Hi," she said. "Are you Tara's dad?"

He nodded and kept balancing on one leg, sliding on a shoe cover. He didn't recognize her. He was sure he would have remembered that face.

"I'm Doctor Frost," she said with a light, faintly musical twang. She was older and more self-confident than a med student or resident but still a young woman. She pulled off her gloves and started to untie her gown as he was tying his. There was something oddly intimate about a man and a woman dressing and undressing together in a small room.

"What are you, neurology? Infectious diseases?" Cyrus asked.

"Psychiatry."

He was startled. "What's the matter with her?"

"Well, you know she had a seizure this morning and was readmitted with low blood counts and fever."

"Mentally," he pressed. "I mean mentally."

"Emotionally, nothing beyond the obvious."

"Then why are you here?"

"I've seen Tara before. Her mother requested a consult during her last hospitalization."

"A consult for what?"

She looked at him square on and said, "I'm helping her with her fears."

With her gown off he could see she was petite and small-waisted. The photo ID hanging off her pocket showed her even younger, a tyro with long hair disappearing behind her shoulders. It was short now, businesslike but the same color as in the picture—of light passing through ancient amber. She had a natural kind of beauty requiring only a dusting of makeup, so unlike Marian, who habitually plastered layer upon layer. She met his now evident fury with luminous blue eyes and a disarming blend of firmness and fragility in the way she set her small jaw.

Still, he angrily towered over her, a threatening presence in the tight confines of the gowning room. He snapped the surgical mask around his face in rage. "What the hell do you mean by fears?" he said too loudly, quickly dialing it back for Tara's sake. "Are you talking about dying?"

She held her ground and said softly, "Your daughter has end-stage brain cancer. She's young but she knows the score. In my experience it helps kids to talk about their feelings and their fears."

"I've got news for you," he spat through the mask in a whispered shout, "She's not going to die! I don't want you seeing her anymore."

She had shucked and binned the last of her sterile gear, maintaining her composure. She replied evenly, professionally, "I think you and Tara's mom should talk about this."

"We're divorced."

"That doesn't mean you can't make a responsible decision about your daughter. You might want to talk to Tara too. My only interest is her well-being." Her hand was on the door. "By the way, it was nice meeting you. Tara talks about you all the time."

As soon as he entered her room, his daughter, a sliver of an eight year old, scolded him in a birdlike voice. "Why were you shouting at Emily?"

"Is that her name?"

"Emily Frost," the small voice replied. "Like Jack Frost."

"I wasn't shouting."

There was an infusion tube dripping blood into her arm and a spent bag of antibiotics. She looked limp. Her skin was translucent, white and fine as rice paper. But even when she was sick, even without her silky hair, her small pouting angel face looked pretty. Freddy the Teddy, the omnipresent pink bear, was lying beside her, tucked under the sheet. She was a bit old for a stuffed animal but her illness knocked her back a few years. She set Cyrus on his heels by declaring, "She's my dying doctor."

He was grateful he was wearing the mask. "You don't need that kind of doctor!" he exclaimed, stooping to caress her, a frustrating barrier of latex between his fingers and her skin. He started spinning out mundane questions: When did she start feeling ill, how did she feel now—anything to change the subject; but she came back to it with innocent insistence.

"Why did you tell Emily she couldn't see me anymore?"

"You heard me say that?"

She nodded as emphatically as she could, lifting her head from the pillow.

"I'll talk about it with Mom. Where is she?"

"She left when Emily came. She said you were coming to stay with me. Do you have your pen?"

He nodded.

"Do you have paper?"

"I can find some. What for?"

"Tic-tac-toe?" Her favorite game and he was happy to shut up and play.

When she finally drifted off to sleep, the page filled with *X*s and *O*s, he crept out and silently shed his gown. At the nurse's station, he left a message for Tara's mother to find him in the cafeteria.

He grabbed a tray of food without giving the choices much thought and found an isolated table. He didn't want to listen to young doctors and nurses talking about their patients or hear the nervous whispers of families in crisis.

What he did hear was the distinctive cadence of Marian's high heels spiking the cafeteria tiles. He didn't have to look up. He knew that urgent walk cold. She had always moved fast with self-important small quick steps, the swing of her legs constrained by her hip-hugging skirts. He looked up from his soup and instead of the plaintive eyes of a worried mother he saw a hot anger he had come to expect.

He knew how her mind worked: every time Tara had a relapse or a complication it was *his* fault. There was cancer on *his* side of the family. His cousin's son had brain cancer. The bad genes were from *his* bloodlines. Everything he had ever done had consistently fallen short of her expectations and now he was killing their daughter. Many child brain cancers were curable; hers wasn't. The tumor was too high grade. One debulking operation slowed the inexorable course but the tumor was growing again. Chemotherapy was buying time now, but at a cost. She was sustained by transfusions and antibiotics. *All this horror because of my inferior O'Malley gene pool.*

Of course, if he'd ever vocalized these thoughts she'd accuse him of being delusional and have her lawyer file another motion with the court questioning his fitness to maintain joint custody, but he could tell from those damned eyes of hers burning like little hot coals that *she* was the crazy one.

Marty, the new husband, was dutifully at her side, looking his usual prosperous self, every inch the successful in-town commercial banker. They made a nice couple, Cyrus scornfully noted—both spent a lot of time on personal grooming and wardrobes. Since Tara was often too ill to return to his apartment for custody visits, his lawyer was able to wrest a court-ordered accommodation allowing Cyrus to spend the occasional evening or weekend day staying with Tara at their house while Marian and Marty stepped out for a few hours. While his daughter napped, Cyrus would wander around their five-bedroom, plush carpeted spread as though he were at a crime scene, prurient, checking out their lives. Marty had a lot of nice clothes, a closet full of Italian suits and cashmere sweaters.

But it was the guy's sink and bathroom cupboards that really got Cyrus going. Marty certainly used a lot of product! A real metrosexual's trove: with as many tubes and bottles for his skin and hair as Marian. She'd always been irked by Cyrus's spare grooming habits—a bar of soap, a stick of deodorant, toothpaste—that was pretty much it. With Marty, she'd landed herself a real spa hound, just what she'd always wanted.

Good for her.

Marty was ten years older than she, graying temples, fairly fit, a good tennis player but Cyrus chuckled the first time he saw a Viagra prescription in his medicine cabinet. He seemed to refill it regularly.

Good for her.

"Care to join me?" Cyrus asked.

Marian shook her head vigorously. She had so much spray, her shiny black hair didn't rustle. "How can you eat?" she asked contemptuously.

"I could use a bite," Marty said hopefully but she shot him down with a scowl. Cyrus almost felt sorry for the bastard.

She was clutching her expensive handbag too hard, squashing one of her breasts. "You didn't tire her out, did you? She was out like a light."

"Took her roller skating."

She ignored him. "You left a message. What did you want?"

"I met Doctor Frost. I don't want Tara to see her again."

"She's top notch. Doctor Thorpe recommended her."

"She doesn't need that kind of doctor."

"The experts say otherwise. Are you an expert?"

"I'm her father."

"And I'm her mother!"

Marty retreated to the safety of his iPhone while the two old adversaries glowered at each other.

"We're supposed to make joint decisions about these things," Cyrus insisted.

"This isn't even controversial. I'm told it's standard for patients like her."

"Which means what?"

"Don't make me say it." She began to cry and pulled out a Kleenex before her mascara could run.

Cyrus pushed his tray away and stood up. All he said back to her was, "Joint decisions."

Marty piped up, lamely trying to mediate. "Tara seems to like the lady."

"I say no."

Marian's tears stopped, so abruptly it defied normal physiology. "Then you'd better have Allan talk to Jan about taking it to Judge Sugarman."

"Fine, I'll do that. I'm going back up to say good-bye. Give me ten minutes and I'll be gone."

Every call to his lawyer cost him dearly, financially and emotionally, but he might have to fight Marian hard on this one. He didn't want Tara talking about it, didn't want her thinking about it.

He didn't want death anywhere near his little girl.

7

The FedEx boxes sat on the floor and their contents littered his desk. The Seabrook, New Hampshire police had made quick work of bundling and shipping all their files and evidence bags on the murder of Thomas Quinn, white male, age thirty-four.

For the sake of speed, Cyrus and Avakian had decided to divide and conquer. Avakian took the two Massachusetts cases, and Cyrus, the two New Hampshire murders. To coordinate, they only had to liaise with each other, which meant drinks at the end of the day at the Kinsale Pub in Government Center. Avakian limited himself to a couple of beers before hitting the Pike to get back home for dinner. Cyrus had no such constraints. He would linger over a third vodka then walk the narrow lamplit streets of Beacon Hill until he figured he was safe enough to drive back to his dark apartment with its over-worked microwave that smelled of popcorn and frankfurters whenever he popped the door.

Aside from the obvious differences between Thomas Quinn and the three prostitutes, Cyrus had no doubt they were dealing with a single killer. In the Quinn case, the police hadn't publicly disclosed head drilling so there was no template for a copycat crime. The timescale and proximity of the four murders together with their signature brain piercings made the linkages undeniable.

Quinn's body had been spotted by a motorist who had pulled off the highway to change a flat. He was already the subject of a missing person report after he failed to show up for his shift in Boston as a nurse anesthetist at the Beth Israel Deaconess Hospital. Local police had gone to his Hampton Falls house in southern New Hampshire where they had forced entry and found nothing amiss. His postmortem showed cause of death to be a massive subdural hematoma caused by a depressed skull fracture, and had it not been for Dr. Leonard Adler's obsessive technique, the drill wound on the opposite side of his head might have gone unnoticed. This grotesque detail was kept from the press to preserve the integrity of the investigation.

The police had done a workmanlike job fleshing out the high points of Quinn's life. He was single and homosexual. He was not in a steady relationship. He was solvent and up to date on his mortgage and financial obligations. He had no police record and to their knowledge was uninvolved in drug use or trafficking. None of his friends or family could point to soured relationships or lurking dangers. He wasn't shy about his sexuality and was a fixture at a few gay nightclubs in Boston. The working hypothesis was that he had strayed into a random sexual encounter with a homicidal psycho.

The police had focused on his mobile phone records, particularly the last calls he had made on his putative day of death, a Thursday. He had worked a full day shift in the OR doing orthopedic procedures. His phone was inactive throughout the day but at three o'clock it came to life with a flurry of calls between two numbers, a mobile phone belonging to a graduate student at Boston University named Davis Fox and a landline at Harvard Medical School assigned to a researcher named Alex Weller.

Both men had been interviewed by the police. Fox described a brief affair with Quinn a year earlier. The relationship had cooled but they had remained friends. Weller apparently had no romantic connections with the victim. Instead, they had some common intellectual interests that Fox also shared. Police reports were vague about the details; egghead stuff. Neither Fox nor Weller had seen Quinn that Thursday afternoon or evening and neither had any theories as to his fate. The police had canvassed Quinn's usual haunts in Boston but he hadn't been seen at any of them since the previous Saturday night.

Cyrus arranged to meet Davis Fox at the BU Student Union during the heart of the lunch hour. The place was packed with kids coming and going and he wondered how he'd be able to pick one young man out of the crowd. Beneath the hanging food court sign, he shifted his weight from foot to foot, absorbing the din generated by students living a life he dimly remembered, unencumbered by those things that were making his own existence as oppressive as the air in a malarial jungle.

As it happened, it was easier for Fox to find *him* since Cyrus was the lone short-haired clean-shaven adult in a suit and overcoat. A pale-skinned African-American youth in skinny jeans tucked into boots and a bright woolly scarf flamboyantly draped around his sweater approached and asked, "You the FBI guy?" He had the flowing manner of an effete trendy, the body of a dissipated male model. He was not quite handsome, his eyes too narrow, mouth too large.

They found a table for two and no sooner sat down when Fox's mobile rang. "Yeah, I'm with him now. I'll call you later."

Cyrus immediately wanted to know who was calling but shelved his curiosity. He began with small, procedural questions. Fox told him he'd been interviewed a month earlier, that he'd told the police everything he knew, et cetera, et cetera. Cyrus let him go unprompted until he talked himself out. He liked to see where people would wander, unguided. Over the years, if he had a hundred dollars for every time this approach was useful he'd be living in a better zip code.

Cyrus began to probe deeper and studied the young man's face as he responded. It was contemporary hirsute with carefully shaped hair, long sideburns, uniform stubble and a neat tuft between his chin and lower lip. He had multiple small gold loops piercing each earlobe, which Cyrus found off-putting. He tried not to look at them.

When Fox talked about Thomas Quinn, Cyrus sensed a lack of guile; he'd been at the game long enough to trust his intuition. As to the details of the crime, Fox knew, as widely reported, that Quinn's head had been caved in. If he had any knowledge of the more macabre aspects of the case, he certainly didn't volunteer it.

Fox was a second-year grad student in experimental psychology. He'd known Quinn for a little under two years. They'd met through a mutual friend, Alex Weller. Cyrus grunted at the name—his next appointment. Fox told him that Quinn had seemed his normal self during their last phone conversation, maybe a little tired and stressed from a busy day. If he had plans for that evening, he never shared them.

"When was the last time you saw him?" The hall was noisy; Cyrus almost felt he was shouting.

"At Alex's house, the previous Saturday night."

"Tell me about Alex."

"He's a great guy, an amazing guy, a really brilliant research doctor. When I was an undergrad I read one of his papers and e-mailed him. We got to know each other."

"He's at Harvard Med, isn't he?" Cyrus asked, aware of the answer.

"Yeah. And at Children's Hospital. I wouldn't be shocked if he gets the Nobel Prize one day for his work on brain injury."

"Brain injury," Cyrus repeated. "Lot of that going around. What were you doing at his house?"

For the first time the young man stiffened. "A bunch of people meet at his place in Cambridge a couple of times a month to talk about science and philosophy. Alex is sort of the focal point."

He wanted to know more but Fox was hesitant. "You're going to be talking to Alex. He'll tell you about it."

"How come you know I'm talking to him?"

"He told me."

"Was that him on the phone?"

Nodding, Fox tried to avoid sounding unhelpful. "Look, it's not a big mystery or anything. It's just that Alex likes to keep the group's discussions private for a lot of reasons. If you've got any questions after you've seen him—any whatsoever—call me and I'll be happy to help you out but really, Alex is in the best position to give you the low-down." Whenever Fox talked about Weller, Cyrus noticed he lowered his eyes and spoke a little more softly. What was it? Was he in awe of the guy? Something else?

If Fox's intent was to put him at ease, the conversation had the opposite effect. Cyrus was satisfied Fox was telling the truth about his relationship with Thomas Quinn. In his gut he believed the kid probably didn't have information on the murder. But this Weller character made his antennae vibrate like crazy and he hadn't even met him. The police report on Weller's interview was two-dimensional, minimalist and uninteresting. The real story was bound to be richer.

When he was ready to leave he flipped a business card on the table and worried the kid by sternly saying, "Since your friend Alex is so interested in my whereabouts, let him know I'm on my way over to his lab."

As he drove down Longwood Avenue past Children's Hospital, Cyrus stared unswervingly at the bumper of the car in front of him, refusing to look at the buildings. If there was a place on earth he loathed more, he hadn't yet found it. Tara was still there. He'd visit her later. For now he tried to block it out.

Down the street, he pulled into a handicapped spot in front of Vanderbilt Hall, the med school dorm, and put his FBI OFFICIAL BUSINESS placard on the dash.

Across Longwood Avenue, the entrance to the Harvard Medical campus, long ago dubbed the Great White Quadrangle, was festooned with a pair of oversized stoneware urns. He sighed heavily at the imposing sight of five large marble buildings surrounding a central green crisscrossed with students walking purposefully, to this day self-conscious about his own academic credentials.

His start had been auspicious: a scholarship at Boston College, which took care of a good piece of the financial burden. A couple of campus jobs and a modest contribution from his parents had covered the rest. Sad to say, he considered his two years at BC his life's high-water mark. The ivy-crept campus, the library books that smelled of past generations, the lofty ideas; the hours spent reading beautiful sentences. Thinking about those years made him ache.

Then, in the summer before his junior year, his father got into the kind of trouble that blights a family for generations: accusations of sexual impropriety involving a woman at a traffic stop at midnight—on the surface way out of character for an old family man like Sergeant O'Malley. But then a first transgression was compounded by a bigger one: he threatened her. The woman got it on tape, and with the speed of the self-inflicted bullet that would soon end his life his career as a Boston cop was over.

As the oldest son, Cyrus was the responsible male. He'd take a year off, get a job, help with the bills, help his younger brothers and sisters and a shell-shocked mother who'd cloistered herself at their church. A year turned to two, then three. He wasn't ever going to return to the shaded campus. His books would stay in cardboard boxes. He'd need a better job with higher pay to keep supporting his brothers and sisters. His father's pals greased the skids. He aced the qualifying exams with perfect scores, and he became a Boston cop. He didn't really want it, he never wanted it, but that's what he did.

With grim determination he decided if he was going into police work he might as well do it well, better than his old man.

Smart cops became detectives. Smart detectives sometimes went to the FBI.

Yet he always felt he'd left a part of himself on the BC campus and was forever reminded of his academic cleft. His ex-wife had gone to Wellesley, his former neighbors on both sides were Harvard men, Stanley Minot actually wore his Phi Beta Kappa pin from Columbia, special agents with Ivy League degrees were all over the Boston bureau; even Avakian was a bigtime U Mass alum. He tried to be philosophical about his truncated collegiate life but such moments as these brought back unpleasant memories, bitter ones that puckered his mouth like a shot of unsweetened espresso.

The grandiosity of the quadrangle dazzled and depressed at once. He imagined how it might feel to be one of these students, treading on a lawn covered in gold maple leaves the color of success, hurrying to afternoon lectures in deep-welled lecture halls steeped in a century of tradition.

In another life, he thought, not this one.

Alex looked out his office window down onto the quadrangle and spotted the man who surely had be the FBI agent. He took a sip from a water bottle to wet his throat that was acidic with fear. He had a minute or two to compose himself: with everything to lose and nothing to gain, what choice did he have but go through the motions, try to be helpful, act clueless, and then in a worst-case scenario, feign indignation?

Why wouldn't they leave him alone? If they only understood what the stakes were, they'd let him finish his work in peace. Throughout history great minds were always persecuted. He was close but he needed time.

Just a little more time.

Down a long echo-chamber hall, Cyrus passed a dozen closed doors until he found Weller's nameplate. He rapped his knuckles against frosted glass and entered. Three lab workers bathed in harsh fluorescents looked up from their benches and one of them, a man only in his twenties with a long white lab coat and bad skin, asked harshly, "In the right place?" He had an incongruous townie accent and a coiled toughness that didn't fit the profile of a plummy academic laboratory.

"I'm looking for Alex Weller."

The man had his name stitched onto his lab coat in red thread: *Frank Sacco.* "You expected?"

Cyrus sent him scurrying to a closed office at the rear by tersely telling him he was from the FBI. The others, young Chinese women, put their heads down and minded their own business.

The lab was an old-world space on one of the floors that had so far escaped renovation, a turn-of-the-century room with period floorboards and dated soapstone countertops; but it was packed with twenty-first-century electronics and analytical instruments. Cyrus involuntarily sniffed at the acetone vapors hanging in the air. Every few seconds he was startled by a harsh vibratory whir when one of the women pressed a test tube against a mechanical agitator.

Sacco returned and pointed mutely toward the rear. Alex Weller stood at his corner office door, arms folded, forcing a smile. He was tall and lanky, late thirties, hair pulled into a hippie ponytail, casual in jeans, pullover and running shoes. To Cyrus's ear he had an unvarnished British accent, like Ringo's. He launched into a voluble barrage. "Davis Fox passed along your message. Welcome. Should I call you Mister O'Malley, Agent O'Malley, or Cyrus?"

Cyrus bristled at the way Weller was trying to take charge. "It's Special Agent O'Malley."

The tall man shrugged in a suit-yourself way. "Well, I'm more informal. I'm just Alex."

Alex closed the door, offered a chair and squeezed back behind his desk. The airless office was impossibly small, so jammed with journals and papers as to be almost comical.

"Sorry for the mess," he said, resting his feet on the one bare patch of desktop. The sneaker soles were worn from serious roadwork. "I don't know how I can help. As I said, I already spoke with the police."

Cyrus awkwardly stripped off his overcoat without standing up and let it drape back over the chair. "You were the last person to speak with Thomas Quinn on his mobile. I'm hoping you can be of further assistance to the investigation."

"Has there been any progress?"

"I'd say yes," he replied enigmatically, trying to ferret out some kind of response, verbal or nonverbal; but Alex was impassive. "I want you to walk me through your last phone calls with Thomas. That Thursday you spoke with him at three-fifteen for about a minute and again at five-twenty for three minutes."

Cyrus detected a smirk of sorts. "Glad to; but first, I'm curious why the FBI would be involved. I grew up in Britain so perhaps I don't understand these things as well as I should."

He wasn't about to humor him so he replied curtly, "The police asked for our help. The phone calls?"

Alex shrugged again and told him that both calls involved planning for their next Saturday meeting. Thomas helped organize biweekly salons at his house. They had discussed who was coming, the ever important matter of refreshments, and whether they would have a guest speaker. As memory served him, their first call was interrupted when Thomas had to take care of something in the recovery room, and the second call, a continuation of the first occurred during Thomas's evening commute.

Had he seen Thomas in person at any time on Thursday or Friday? Alex said no, emphatically.

Cyrus looked at his notepad. He had written the word *salon* in capital letters and had underlined it twice. "Tell me about these salons. What are they?"

Alex gestured grandly as if he were about to impart a great teaching. "Well, a salon is a gathering of like-minded intellectuals who meet to—"

Cyrus cut him off irritably. "*Your* salons. What do *you* like-minded intellectuals discuss at *your* house?"

Alex innocently smiled back. "My friends and I are interested in all manner of topics relating to philosophy, religion, and biology. Specifically, we share a fascination in cultural concepts of the afterlife. It's a subject I've been toying with ever since my university days. Several years ago I founded a small private society, the Uroboros Society—no more than an informal salon, really—to stimulate discussions."

"What does that mean, *Uroboros?*"

"It's an ancient mythological symbol, the serpent swallowing its own tail. It represents eternal return, life after death, self-renewal; immortality. It may sound pretentious, I know—and believe me, I'm not a pretentious bloke—but it encapsulates the scope of our interests."

"Immortality and life after death. Is that what neuroscientists think about in their spare time?"

"This one does. The intersection between science, philosophy, and religion is blurred but fascinating. I'm immersed in that intersection."

"What kind of research do you do?"

Alex wet his lips with his tongue. "I study the stressed brain … the brain in trauma, in oxygen deprivation, at the boundary between life and death."

"Is this theoretical? Practical?"

"Well, this is a medical school. I'm a pediatric neurologist. I split my time between patient care and research. My grant funding points toward the discovery of new drugs for brain injury; but it is fundamental thanatobiology—the biology of death—that really gets my motor running. Death isn't instantaneous, you know. We're complex machines, and when we shut down, a lot happens in specific sequences at a cellular and molecular level. By understanding death, maybe we'll get a better understanding of life."

Cyrus raised his eyebrows. "If you say so. What kind of people go to your salon?"

"All types: biologists, psychologists, philosophy students, dilettantes, a theologian or two."

"Thomas was a nurse. What did he bring?"

"Thomas was an interesting man, very astute. He wasn't all that book smart, yet his line of work made him a keen observer of life and death. He held his own in debates with PhDs."

"What is it you debate about?"

"This is relevant to Thomas's murder, how?" Cyrus was staring back at him icily, prompting Alex to add, "I'm just asking."

"I'm not sure it is, I'm not sure it isn't," Cyrus said evenly. "A guy's got a fascination with death, his last cell phone call is to another guy who's got the same interest and he winds up dead. I don't know ... call me crazy for being curious."

"Just as long as you don't think I had anything to do with it," Alex said with forced cheeriness. "We debate many things: What should we read into the differences in cross-cultural beliefs in life after death? Does God exist—that's a biggie. Why are so-called near death experiences so similar by description across multiple cultures? Is there a biological basis for them or should we be looking toward spirituality? We ask large questions and after lively discussion, we come up with small answers, which guarantees we'll be talking for a very long time."

Cyrus slipped into a higher gear and asked a series of rapid-fire questions. Did Thomas have any serious conflicts with members of the group? Could he get a list of members? Did Thomas have any enemies? Did Alex know whether he engaged in illicit activities? What did he know about Thomas's relationship with Davis Fox?

Alex's short, bland answers added nothing. Then Cyrus caught him off guard with, "Do you know any prostitutes?"

Alex finally pulled his feet off the desk. "What?"

"Prostitutes. Know any? Use any?"

For the first time, Alex got surly. "Absolutely not! I've got a girl-friend. Why are you asking me that?"

Cyrus's mobile rang. He was going to ignore it but the caller ID said MARIAN so he picked up, listened to her then said, "I'm just down the street from Children's. I can meet you there in ten minutes."

He put the phone away. "I've got to take off. Thank you for your time, Doctor Weller. I may need to talk with you again."

Alex rose, momentarily towering over him until Cyrus stood himself. Alex's anger over the last question seemed to have dissipated and he said in a quiet, almost pastoral voice, "You're going to Children's Hospital?"

Cyrus put his coat back on and didn't answer.

"Do you have a sick child?"

Cyrus found himself nodding. There was an odd expression on Weller's face. He reached into the breast pocket of a white lab coat hanging on a nearby hook. There was a stack of three-by-five cards stamped with names and scribbled with notes. He rifled through them like he was looking for jokers in a deck before plucking out one card. Cyrus couldn't imagine what he was up to.

"Your daughter's name isn't Tara O'Malley, is it?"

It was like getting hit in the gut by a thick piece of wood. Cyrus felt sick. His ears rang. He nodded again.

"Her surgeon, Bill Thorpe, asked me to see her. I've been adjusting her seizure medications. I've met your wife."

"*Ex*-wife," Cyrus said automatically, fishing for something else to say.

"Well, this is a bit awkward, isn't it?" Alex said. "Would you like me to walk over with you?"

Cyrus reached for the doorknob. He wanted to get out of the building into the cold air. "She just had another seizure."

"Let me call over and make sure one of the other attendings sees her right away. Perhaps, under the circumstances, I should transfer her care to a colleague."

Cyrus swallowed and nodded. "That would be good."

"Let me say this," Alex added. "She's a lovely girl. A perfectly lovely little girl."

8

It was late and the neurology ward was quiet. When Alex was a young boy in England staying with his grandparents in the village of Gressingham, he and his brother used to sneak into the parish church around midnight. The heavy oak door in the old Norman tower was always unlocked so they really weren't being delinquent but it felt naughty and dangerous and that's why they were drawn to it. The dark, narrow nave was full of musty dead air. He'd touch the smooth pulpit and nervously whisper to his brother about an imagined noise coming from the large tomb in the chapel. These were the things he remembered, walking through the ward that night.

Standing outside Room 919 he looked around to see if anyone was in the corridor. It was still deserted. He went inside and quietly put on a sterile gown, gloves, and mask.

Tara O'Malley was asleep. Though another neurologist had taken over her case, he was drawn to her in a new context: no longer his patient, she was the daughter of a man who was pursuing him.

He picked up her chart and flipped through it. She'd been seizure-free for several days. Her blood counts were coming back, her infection clearing. She'd be going home soon; but her last MRI was disturbing. The tumor was on the prowl.

He stood over her. Her plump lips parted with each breath. *Pretty as a china doll*, he thought. Cyrus O'Malley was going to miss her.

9

The last leaves of the season were whipping past the big windows and settling onto the quadrangle. That Saturday, Alex was alone in his lab, his skin prickling with anticipation. He liked being the only one there, uninhibited, flitting from bench to bench, reagent to reagent, machine to machine, humming, singing snippets of pop tunes stuck in his head, waiting for the LC-mass spec to spit out his data. No prying eyes. No small talk. No seemingly innocent questions to answer.

He was on the brink.

He could feel it.

It was neither guesswork nor intuition: he was a very good scientist, plain and simple. He likened his quest to one of those big, concentric circle mazes where you start on the outside and draw your way in until your pencil stops dead center. There was heaviness in the air and lightness in his head. Would today be the day he was going to reach the center?

Every set of samples inched him closer. Every experiment had chipped away at the mantle of rock, exposing more of the crystal gemstone at its kernel.

Poor Thomas Quinn had not died in vain. He took comfort in that, he really did. The two-minute sample of Thomas's cerebrospinal fluid had revealed a small telltale spike at 854.73 *m/z*. At three minutes, the value was off the charts.

854.73.

To Alex, there was no more important number in the world, the mass-to-charge ratio: the precise peak on his mass spectrometry instrument where his beautiful unknown showed itself over and over. He had first laid eyes on that peak two years earlier when a brilliantly simple experiment in mice yielded the same result time after time. The idea had come to him in a *eureka*-type of flash, so obvious in retrospect that he was pained it had taken him so long to think of it. Emboldened, he started to climb the evolutionary ladder. Rats had the same peak. Cats. Dogs. Monkeys.

And man?

A subject was needed.

Who else but himself? At least that was the plan. He'd need Thomas's help to be sure; Thomas was the ideal partner for an ethically challenged experiment. He was adept, discreet, part of Alex's inner circle.

Following that terrible night in the dog lab, he had spent two weeks in a state of alternating despair and ecstasy. He had murdered a man. From his limited knowledge of the law it could have been manslaughter, but Thomas nevertheless was dead and he had caused it. His anxiety skyrocketed when the body was found. Every day the articles in the papers would send him into a panic—then the agonizing phone call from the police and the interview with a simpleton detective that had meandered and mercifully sputtered.

Yet, the data was so perfect, so validating, that it almost liberated him from guilt and sent him soaring. Thomas had the peak too: just as predicted; but this was only the beginning. What molecule was lurking at 854.73 *m/z*? What was its chemistry, its biology? Was it his Holy Grail? There was no point trying to isolate it from lower species. He eventually had to go to man anyway …

To really know.

At night, lying awake next to Jessie's slumbering warmth, so much heat from so small a body, he would turn his mind into a rollicking debating society, arguing the pros and cons of his next steps. He wasn't a murderer, he was a biologist. He wasn't Mengele—he was a scientist. Should a few be sacrificed for the greater good? Could the end justify the means? Even if it did, could he stomach the act?

Could he live with himself?

Still, he couldn't make the decision. In a madly detached way he felt he had to delegate it to someone else. Then, one night, staring at the dark ceiling, he found the decision transcendently taken out of his hands. He felt like a marionette, his movements controlled by invisible wires. He shifted to an altered consciousness whereby he became external observer, passively watching himself get dressed, drive to the lab, sign in at the security desk, pick up his sample tubes and instruments, sneak out a rear exit, hop into his car and cruise the streets.

The black girl was plump and unattractive: perversely, that had helped. He heard himself invite her into the car and observed the drive across the river to his garage. He watched himself strangle her, enduring her blows until she stopped fighting. Then he dispassionately viewed the medical procedures—the piercing of the skull, penetration of the ventricles, the satisfying rush of clear cerebrospinal fluid filling the barrel of the syringe.

When it was done he waited for the trembling to start but it didn't. He remained cool. There was a body to dump, tubes to process at the lab. Only when he was back in bed next to Jessie did his body start to shake uncontrollably. Jessie awakened and probably thought he was having one of his nightmares because she held him, cooing and soothing until she regained sleep while he fought it, staying awake until the morning for fear of replaying the killing in his dreams.

It got easier.

The next two murders took on the quality of smoothly replicated experiments and he was able to quickly blot them from his mind and pay less attention to the newspaper stories that followed. Each new set of samples moved the ball farther down the field. He was learning more and more about his mystery peak, refining his methodologies, working out how to fractionate the samples. He felt like a hunter closing in on his prey, slowly, painstakingly flushing it from the thick undergrowth until he had it in his sights, a finger curled around the cold hard trigger.

He had learned so much from Thomas and the first two women. He had high hopes that the samples from the third prostitute, the pumpkin girl, would allow him to fractionate his mystery peak into a pure aliquot—and from there, a structure; then from structure to synthesis, synthesis to biology, and, finally, from biology to real answers. *Yes*, he told himself again and again, *the end does justify the means*.

The pumpkin girl was the youngest and that was exciting. Thomas was in his late thirties. The first two prostitutes were in their late twenties and their mystery peaks were even more abundant. He'd seen the same things in animals and had tucked the observation away. Younger animals had bigger peaks. The pumpkin girl was the youngest yet, twenty-two.

Cyrus O'Malley, this inconsequential man, had interrupted his reverie and pulled him back into the world of fear and hazard. O'Malley had clearly connected the dots between Thomas and the others, but that was inevitable. He had nothing concrete, he was fishing; otherwise, he would have played his cards already. Alex had been as careful as he could: gloves to prevent DNA transfer, leather car seats and plastic floor mats to avoid fibers. The drill bit and needles obsessively autoclaved. The syringes, melted into plastic globs. He was sure he was safe, at least for the time being, especially if the pumpkin girl was the last.

He prayed she was the last.

And what of the exquisite irony, that his pursuer's daughter was his patient? This was a triangle, he thought; no, a circle! Like the Uroboros! O'Malley had the power of the FBI over him, he had the power of a doctor over Tara, and she had the power of a sick child over her father. *A serpent swallowing its tail: it was meant to be*, he thought. All this was meant to happen.

His Agilent LC-MS system was a state-of-the-art instrument purchased under his last NIH grant. It could separate unknown compounds in complex mixtures and then identify them through mass spectrometry analysis. Throughout the afternoon he followed the instrument's progress via its graphical interface and drew closer to the bench when he saw that fraction 6 was being processed. He stopped humming and stood silent before the monitor, watching the countdown to readout as if he were watching a rocket launch. Thirty seconds. Fifteen. Ten … he held his breath. Three seconds.

854.73.
The fraction was pure. No other peaks.
And it was lavishly abundant.
He had a large, pure sample of his beautiful unknown.
He could see the pumpkin girl's face in his mind.
The younger the better.
He exhaled and felt gloriously light-headed.
The killings could stop.

10

Alex pushed the living room furniture around and tossed pillows and cushions onto the floor until there was an imperfect circle. These Saturday evenings meant everything to him but tonight he had trouble keeping his mind off the screw-topped plastic tube chilling in the fridge beside a carton of eggs.

His place was tastefully furnished, nothing very expensive but each piece chosen with care. It wasn't a large house, about the size of his childhood home in Liverpool: living room, dining room, kitchen and master bedroom on the ground floor, two guest rooms up top. A small back yard had enough green space for an herb and vegetable garden and a barbecue.

There were a few admirable pieces scattered about the house, some objets d'art, wooden and brass statuary of Hindu gods, African masks, Chinese ceramics and, over the mantel in pride of place, a fine nineteenth-century copy of a drawing by Theodorus Pelecanos, from his fifteenth-century book of alchemy, of the pink and gold Uroboros. And books, of course: shelves and shelves of books on art, religion, the occult, mythology, philosophy, anthropology and the natural sciences. He aspired to nothing more materially. He was well-satisfied. Financially, he'd already achieved more than his father had during a life of heavy toil, and that was enough.

Jessie was in the kitchen making hummus. This, she held, was her main contribution to the salons. She had made it abundantly clear to

Alex that she felt intellectually outgunned by the high-octane minds who gravitated to Alex's orbit, so typically she remained silent through the proceedings, keeping the snacks coming, making sure the beer and white wine were well-chilled, and tending to accidents on their more avant-garde nights.

Alex sneaked up behind her, watching her for a few moments as she worked the food processor. He felt a powerful wave of love wash over him. Her red-orange hair, the color of leaping flames, fell over her black sweater. She was a foundling, a good ten years younger than he, plucked from a bookstore in Harvard Square where, three years earlier, he had been browsing on a Sunday. When he took his paper-backs to the register, he had looked across the counter into her milky oval face with jade eyes and cherry lips and those cascades and ringlets of Pre-Raphaelite fiery hair and had been utterly captivated.

She was a townie, a dropout, drifting on a quiet sea of menial jobs, enduring a succession of unreliable roommates. She'd never before had anyone like Alex in her life—a powerful spinning bowling ball, knocking a light pin into the air. She tumbled happily and landed squarely inside his sphere of influence. He was everything to her: father, brother, teacher, friend and lover. She idolized him and made few demands, grateful for every day with him; and he cherished and protected her like a delicate hothouse flower.

Now he surprised her by cupping her small breasts and using his nose to part her hair to find a patch of skin on the back of her neck to kiss.

She laughed. "What's that for?"

"Love."

"I like that. How many are coming?"

"I never really know. The weather's fine. Probably fifteen or so."

"I still miss Thomas."

"Me too." He let go of her.

"You worked all day," she scolded. "Lie down for an hour. I'll bring you some wine."

He kissed the top of her head. "I can't live without you."

"You don't have to."

Davis Fox arrived first, pecking both Jessie's cheeks, European style. Alex could tell straight off that he wished to talk. He took him into his bedroom and shut the door.

"Are you okay?" Alex asked.

"Just a bit pissed off."

"Why?"

"That FBI agent called me again."

"When?"

"This afternoon. He asked when we were having our next salon."

Alex blanched but tried to be nonchalant. "Really? What did you tell him?"

"I told him to ask *you* and then he asked *me* for your mobile number. When I said I was uncomfortable giving it out, he said he could get it anyway and asked why I was being unhelpful so I wound up giving it to him. I hope that was okay."

Alex reached for his cell phone on the bedside table. It was off and when he powered it back up, there was a message waiting from an unknown caller.

"Much ado about nothing," Alex murmured. "Let's hope they catch the murderer rather than wasting their bloody time on us."

He sent Davis to the kitchen for a glass of wine and sat on the bed to listen to the voice message. The nerve! O'Malley wanted to attend one of the salons, talk to the group about Thomas.

Alex felt a pitting nausea. O'Malley wasn't going away. He could hear the persistence in his voice. He angrily imagined calling him back, telling him to leave him the hell alone ... for the sake of his daughter. The threat would make O'Malley disappear. A fantasy.

Everything would have to move faster now. He was on the threshold. He would not and could not be denied. Every hour and every day standing between him and the answer was precious, every minute wasted, a tragedy. He wished he could have canceled the salon to get on with things, but that was out of the question.

The others arrived in ones and twos.

Frank Sacco, his young pimply technician, came and sat by himself. He never interacted much, a fish out of water, and Alex had long regretted ever having invited him. It wasn't a good idea to mix lab business with his other interests—especially now—but what was done was done; he couldn't disinvite Frank, not without raising a red flag.

Larry Gelb, a cherubic philosophy professor from Brandeis, arrived with his much younger Korean girlfriend, a former student of his, and tossed his Che-style beret onto one of the cushions. Arthur Spangler, a curly-haired biochemist from Tufts Medical School with nineteenth-century mutton-chop sideburns, headed straight for the hummus and began making the rounds, curious if anyone had any spliffs. The room filled with old friends and academic colleagues from the elite colleges and universities in Boston, warmed by one another's company and Alex's patented bear hugs, which he meted out in a distracted way.

Spangler sidled up to Alex and asked through a mouthful of chips and dip, "Any recreational pharmaceuticals tonight, Weller?"

"Unless someone surprises us, afraid not, Art. Going to have to make do with fermentation products. Jessie's got plenty of that in the kitchen."

"Pity. Who's going to be speaking?"

"Larry's got an interesting paper on something or another."

"Seems disorganized, Weller. Need to put our dues to better purpose."

"What dues are those?" Alex asked.

"Point taken." Spangler trundled off, continuing his quest for marijuana.

Erica Parris, a grad student at the Harvard Divinity School, unwrapped her scarf and made a beeline for Alex, literally tugging a young man by the sleeve. She was ruddy-cheeked from the long walk along the Charles and exuded her usual earthy sexuality. Alex once told Gelb that Erica reminded him of an archetypal fertility talisman. Brimming with enthusiasm, she chimed, "Alex, I brought a newbie! Meet Sam Rodriguez."

Her charge was a lean, muscular Puerto Rican youth with proto-dreadlocks, the harbinger of some future grander tonsorial concoction. His features were stunningly chiseled and handsome, although he appeared dazed by unfamiliar surroundings.

"Hello, Sam, welcome to my house. I'm Alex Weller." Alex wasn't in any mood to meet new talent but Sam made sharp confident eye contact, which made an instant positive impression.

"I'm Sam. My friends call me S-Rod."

Alex clapped him on the shoulder. "If we become friends, I hope you'll allow me to call you Sam. You seem like a Sam to me, not an S-Rod."

"Okay, man. We'll see."

"Have you known Sam long, Erica?"

"About forty-five minutes. We met on the steps of Widener Library when I was heading here."

"Well then, help yourself to wine or beer in the other room and we'll have a toast to new relationships," he said politely. "I assume Erica has told you about our salon."

"Sort of. Sounds wild."

"What attracted you?"

He pointed to the woman's thigh-high boots. "Her legs, man. I gotta be honest with you, that's the main reason."

She playfully swatted him.

"I like your honesty, Sam." Alex snorted. "You're at Harvard?"

Sam nodded. "A junior."

"What are you studying?"

"Computational sciences."

"Well, let's see if you connect to the kinds of subjects that interest us, Sam. If so, maybe we'll see you back. If not, at least we shared a moment of commonality on the subject of Erica's legs."

When all the cushions were filled and the circle formed, Alex took his place next to Jessie on a flat red pillow. For atmospherics, there was low light, a Govinda album—raga-style, electronic, hypnotic, playing softly in the background—and a smoky haze from burning sticks of sandalwood incense.

"Welcome one, welcome all," Alex began. He wasn't feeling his usual expansive self but the show had to go on. "We have a new friend with us, Sam Rodriguez from Harvard, who has no idea what he's gotten himself into. Say hello, Sam."

A salty wave. "Hey," and others waved back.

"For Sam's benefit, welcome to the Uroboros Society, named for the mythical serpent—"

"Who eats his own tail, right?" Sam interrupted. "An ancient symbol of infinity."

"I swear I didn't prep him!" Erica squealed.

"Yes, you're right, Sam. Full marks. The Uroboros is a symbol of the infinite and the immortal, the serpent who destroys itself then brings itself back to life. And what this rather dog-eared group of individuals who congregate here like to contemplate is the idea that life is only a short segment of a longer, more interesting and far more complex journey. We like to talk about concepts of heaven and hell and other manifestations of the afterlife. We aren't denominational; some of us don't even have a religious bone in our bodies. We often return to the subject of near death experiences, or NDEs, as a laboratory for the study of postlife consciousness. A few of us have been blessed or cursed with our own NDEs and we perpetually bore the others with the details. Again, for Sam's sake, raise your hands if you're in *this* club."

Alex raised his own hand high. Virginia, a patent lawyer in severe black-framed glasses, raised hers too. Two other men joined in.

"We talk. We meditate. Sometimes, some of us use adult substances like grass, ketamine, salvia, DMT or LSD to facilitate meditation and out-of-body experiences."

Sam grinned. "I'm down with that part, man. What's on the menu?"

"Just talk, I'm afraid. The cupboard's bare. Then some group meditation. But first, Larry Gelb is going to share a paper on circular archetypes in near death experiences, which I know will be fascinating. So I'm going to shut my gob now and Larry is going to commence to dazzle us, as is his wont."

Gelb immediately launched into his talk, so enthusiastic and animated he was unable to remain seated. After a few moments he sprung up and stood at the center of the circle where he rotated his body slowly, like a lazy Susan, sharing himself evenly.

He soon was speaking of Plato and his account of the near death experience of a soldier named Er, who described seeing a cosmic axis of light holding together eight spheres that revolved around the earth. "Over and over again," Gelb told the group, "going back as far as Plato, the image of a sphere or circle or mandala pervades the near death experience."

While he talked, Alex's thoughts caromed like molecules in Brownian motion, pinging from the speaker to Davis to Jessie to the new kid, Sam, to Thomas Quinn to Cyrus O'Malley to the pumpkin girl and always back to the tube in his fridge; then, a violent startling daydream. O'Malley was in his kitchen blocking his way. Alex saw himself savagely throwing him down, kneeling on his neck and plunging the surgical drill deep into his skull.

He shook off the disturbing image and became aware that Gelb was wrapping things up, intoning portentously, "I return, my friends, like a broken record—you see, another circular image!—to the indisputable fact that the occurrence of the same symbols and archetypes appearing in all cultures across the sea of time is indisputable evidence of the existence of a collective human unconscious, and I further challenge you to disprove the following: that lurking behind that collective unconscious is the presence of God."

Later, when they were alone, lying on top of their bed, Alex was rigid and staring, out of synch with Jessie, who was folded against him, sleepy and dreamy.

"What did you think of Sam?" he asked.

"I liked him."

"Me too. I watched him while we meditated. He got into it, with an intensity. Everything about that kid is intense."

"Do you think he'll come back?"

"I hope so. Probably depends on whether Erica sleeps with him." She laughed and said, "Do you want to make love to me?"

He turned to face her and propped his head on his fist. "Jessie, I need to do something tonight."

She reacted to his suddenly serious expression and stayed quiet.

He didn't speak for a few moments and instead tenderly moved some strands of hair out of her eyes until he said, "I may have made a breakthrough in the lab. There's only one way to know. Will you help me?"

"Now?"

"Yes."

"What do you want me to do?"

"Be my guardian angel."

He left the bed and returned with the plastic tube and a pipette, sat back on the edge of the bed, and held the tube up for her inspection. It contained a small amount of clear liquid.

"What is it?"

"Maybe nothing; maybe something important—maybe what I've spent my life looking for."

She crabbed herself across the bed till she was sitting beside him and tried to rub the sleep from her eyes. "Is it dangerous?"

"I don't know what to expect. There could be no effect, there could be potent pharmacology. I need you to watch over me. Will you do that?"

She hesitated then nodded.

"If I pass out, check my breathing and my pulse—I've taught you how to do that. If my respiratory rate goes below eight or above thirty, that's bad. If my pulse goes below forty or above one fifty, that's bad too. Call nine one one and tell them I've had an overdose. Tell them it was salvia. For God's sake don't tell anybody what I really did. If I vomit, keep my airway clear. If I'm scared, comfort me. That's all."

"That's a lot."

"I'm sorry."

She touched his face. "I know you've got to do what you think is right, Alex. I'm the one who holds onto you when you're having nightmares. But ..."

He waited for her to finish.

"... please don't leave me."

He kissed her cheek. "I won't."

He didn't hesitate. With an expert hand he pipetted up a precise tenth of a milliliter of clear fluid, opened his mouth and let a cold drop of liquid slide under his tongue.

11

Alex called it the runway, the interval between taking a drug and starting the flight. When he talked to neophytes about mind-altering drugs, he told them the runway was the time to get physically and emotionally prepared, like a pilot waiting for takeoff.

Be ready.

Stay alert to your surroundings.

Go through your safety checklist, like a pilot.

Who was watching out for you? Were the windows closed? Was the door locked? Was a water bottle handy?

For some drugs the runway was predictable: you knew how long you'd be waiting for liftoff. For LSD it could be an hour; for DMT maybe only a couple of minutes.

For this one—his beautiful, pure 854.73—he had no idea of when or even *if*. It could be a false lead, nothing to do with near death experiences. Or it could be the genuine article but nevertheless a chemical that couldn't be absorbed by mouth. He thought he'd be giving it the best shot by dripping it under his tongue. That way, the molecule might be absorbed directly through capillary-rich membranes, and if not, he'd get a second chance when he swallowed and the liquid passed into his stomach. If the experiment fizzled, he might have to try again by snorting the clear liquid into his nose, or worst case, he could inject it with all the hazards that might entail.

He was past the point of guessing.

Alex was comfortable, barefoot, breathing smoothly, lying supine on his bed, his head nestled into a soft satin pillow. His T-shirt was loose-fitting, soft from a hundred washes. He unbuttoned his jeans to unbind his waist. He removed the elastic from his ponytail and let his hair fall onto his shoulders.

Jessie was lying on her side, facing him, her sleepiness quashed by the gravity of the task Alex had given her. The light was perfect: restful for him but bright enough should she need to spring to action, grab the phone, and drag him onto the floor for chest compressions, as he'd taught her.

He reached over and put his hand on the contour of her waist. He gave her a little squeeze for reassurance; for thanks—for love.

The street was quiet, no passing cars at this hour. The bedroom windows were half open, letting the crisp coldness of the night sanctify the room. He felt completely comfortable, at ease, pleasantly tingling.

I'm ready for whatever comes.

It crept up on him like a cat stalking an unsuspecting sparrow. Waiting, waiting ... then pouncing.

One moment he was lying beside Jessie thinking about pulling her over for a kiss, and the next, his perspective violently flipped, in a way that ought to have alarmed him but didn't.

He'd been in this topsy-turvy world before—floating, hovering, observing, when he was a child—on the motorway.

It was a perspective he'd often dreamed about. In his heart, he'd always held on to the belief that he'd experience it one more time, at the very least at the moment of death but preferably before.

And here it was! Heady and exhilarating: a weightless perch for self-contemplation. He was hovering low enough to make out the pattern of blue veins in his own hands, geographic, like swollen rivers. Yet he was high enough to take in the entire bed, the whole room, its edges blurring as if seen through a fish-eye lens.

He was drawn to himself. He knew *her* face, *her* body well enough; but seeing himself—not in a mirror or photo but rather the living, breathing man as others see him—was jarring. Unsettling. Fascinating.

His eyes were closed and Jessie was whispering to him, touching his forehead, watching him breathe. "Alex, are you asleep?" she was saying. "Are you okay?"

He wasn't answering.

I have a good face, he thought, hovering. *Not handsome, not ugly … kind. It's a kind face. I know what I've done. But I'm still a good man. And now it's been worth it. For me. For Thomas. For those girls.*

He steeled himself, and as Jessie awkwardly felt for his carotid pulse, it happened.

A black fog rolled in and obscured the bed. Amorphous at first, it coalesced into a perfect circle and darkened into the blackest black he'd ever seen.

He took a deep breath. He'd be traveling soon.

And precisely at the moment his lungs filled to capacity the black disc became three-dimensional, a tunnel—and he was hurtling through it at seemingly unimaginable speed, though it felt frictionless, effortless. It wasn't as if he were plunging head- or feetfirst; it felt more like skydiving, arms and legs outstretched, but without any physical forces playing upon his body. He was completely comfortable, stress-less, fearless, his ears filled with the soothing sound of rushing air, though he could feel no wind on his skin.

The walls of the tunnel came alive with sparkling flashes that pulsed with blinding intensity then vanished, like light from the bellies of supercharged fireflies. There was no sense of directionality. He couldn't tell if he was falling, rising, or moving laterally, and it occurred to him that he could even be stationary, the tunnel hurtling toward and around him. Time too was unfathomable. He blinked for what felt to be a second but was unsure if a moment had lapsed or an eternity.

Finally, he saw what he was hoping to see: a pinpoint of steady, unwavering light ahead, slowly growing larger. He couldn't tear his eyes away; it appeared so welcoming, a lighthouse beacon in an impossible fog, and when it grew man-sized he entered this pure disc of light and all movement stopped.

He stood in a sea of whiteness so impenetrable he couldn't make out his own appendages.

He took a sharp breath to try to feel the whiteness against his throat, but it was neutral—not frosty or steamy—but without taste, unevocative.

Then, as the whiteness became by increments paler and more translucent, he was able to see his legs and outstretched hands, and finally, a terrain.

The scape was green and expansive, flat and limitless, monochromatic, matching the hue of a blade of spring grass. Yet it wasn't grass, just color; and when he took a tentative first step, the terrain was neither firm nor soft. He felt nothing against his bare feet.

Rising on the horizon from the green expanse was a field of faint blue whiteness, reminiscent of a pale dawn sky but too lifeless and unchanging for that, another expanse of tint without substance.

He strained his ears.

There it was!

The sound he'd tried to relive in his mind a thousand times, the sweetest gurgling.

At first he strode across the greenness but as the gurgling got louder he broke into a run, a joyous romp, like a boy flying through a field on his way home, hungry and thirsty after a long day of play.

And when it came into view, that lovely shimmering river, he pulled up and stared. It was more than familiar, long imprinted in his mind's eye. Its black shiny stepping-stones beckoned. The turbulence they caused must have been the source of the splashing and gurgling noises but the substance of the river appeared as light, not water. Perhaps, he thought, the sounds existed solely to make the stepping-stones more inviting for anyone standing on such terra incognita.

Across the river, the featureless green plain stretched and merged at the horizon into a pale blue infinite stretch of nothingness.

Then, he spied *something*—a small dark shape, amazingly far away. Slowly, it grew larger, until with straining eyes he could just make out a figure walking toward him.

For the first time, utter calm was replaced by rising excitement.

Please, please, be him.

And when he saw it *was* him his chest began to shudder and tears welled up.

The man stopped on the opposite bank of the river. Dickie Weller still wore his silly Liverpool cap and his favorite suede car coat. The red woolen cap was perched atop his big head and though he was on the opposite side, Alex could make out the pride stamped on his fleshy, ruddy face.

Dickie waved his arms exuberantly and shouted above the flowing river. "Alex!"

It was hard to speak through the sobs. He could only manage a single word. *"Dad!"*

"You're all grown up!" Dickie shouted. "You were a lad. Now you're a man."

Alex nodded.

"Come over! Come to me, son!"

"I want to!"

Dickie gently waved one hand like a traffic cop signaling a driver to proceed through an intersection. "Then come!"

Though the tears continued to stream Alex, was able to stop the sobbing because an intense, pure happiness was growing into a physical rush, more powerful than any ever experienced in a natural or chemical high.

He tentatively stepped onto the first black stone and the pleasure only increased.

"There you go!" Dickie shouted. "That's it!"

He was surprised to feel the stones against his bare soles, the first tactile input of the experience. Though they looked cool and slick, they felt warm and dry and he was able to push off confidently to the next one.

Midway across, he glanced down at the river. The flow was fast, the color iridescent. The urge to dip a toe passed. The opposite bank beckoned.

Dickie called out to him in encouragement. "You're halfway there."

"I'm coming, Dad. I'm coming."

And then, just past the halfway mark, something happened.

Behind his father, though visually unchanged, the limitless expanse at once took on another dimension.

Something was out there!

A presence: more than the hint of something, more than a notion, something terrifyingly wonderful.

One more stepping-stone ...

... Then another.

With each step he got closer to his father, closer to the presence.

The pleasure was indescribable, a million orgasms ripping through every cell in his body, an insane fireworks display reaching its climactic finale.

He looked down. *Three stones to go.* Three steps and he'd be on the other side. Three steps and he'd be in his father's brawny arms again— and merging with the overwhelming presence over the horizon.

Dickie was beaming, his arms outstretched. "Alex!"

"Dad!"

He pushed off toward the penultimate stone but his foot was rooted, as if stuck in thick wet mud.

Dickie's smile vanished. "Come on, son. You can make it!"

Alex strained with all his might but he couldn't advance. "I can't!" he screamed.

"You can!"

In horror he felt himself being sucked off the stones, reeling backward. He cried out, *"No!"* but he was powerless to stop it. His father was getting smaller, the presence fading, the pleasure and joy seeping from his being.

The reversal took on a breathtaking speed. He found himself in the sparkling tunnel, hurtling back, helplessly falling, to his bedroom, to his bed, and now he was back in his recumbent body looking into Jessie's scared, staring eyes.

"Alex, thank goodness! I didn't know what to do. I was going to call for help."

He blinked and looked around, his face wet with tears. "I was there! Do you understand? I was there!"

"Where?"

"There! The other side!"

He started shaking. She lowered herself onto him and held him maternally. "It's okay, honey, I'm here."

"Jessie?"

"Yes?"

The same words from long ago came to him again, but they were in a man's voice, not a boy's.

"I want to go back."

12

It was discharge day. At the dawn of Tara's illness, discharge days were full of hope and promise. An operation followed by a new therapy. A life continued.

Yet the last few of these were like heavy sighs. The reality was clear enough: the hourglass was merely being tipped on end until the grains of sand ran out once again.

Cyrus waited outside her room while the IV was removed and the nurses helped her dress. Then his stomach soured—a Pavlovian curdle—at the sound of Marian's heels clicking down the corridor.

She was alone; her husband was stuffed behind a large office desk somewhere downtown. She scowled when she saw him and with the usual venom spat, "You *knew* I was going to pick her up."

"I was in the neighborhood."

"You're supposed to see her on Saturday. Since you're here now, maybe you should give up some of that time."

"Come on, Marian, don't do this." He was angry but he also had a pleading tone.

"We have a court-approved deal." Then, adding a generous ladle of sarcasm, "I know you're capable of understanding court orders. After all, you're still with the FBI, aren't you?"

Ah, the FBI again. Early in their courtship and marriage she'd liked his job well enough. Her fellow was a protector of the innocent, a pursuer of the guilty. She'd enjoyed the way he slid off his heavy holster when he returned from work—very manly, very sexy.

It didn't take long, though, for her to figure out that federal agents had a skimpy financial upside. Their house was too small, the furniture undistinguished, the vacations domestic, the jewelry light on carats. There were the months when her takings from real estate deals exceeded his salary. Her upbringing made it distasteful for the woman to be the dominant wage earner. Discontent bored into her like a skin-penetrating parasite. She pushed him toward the private sector. She knew a Boston-based Fortune 500 company looking for a head of corporate security and she was enraged he wouldn't even consider it. The seeds of discontent were sown in the moist soil of her mind.

The nurse called through the door. "Almost ready."

Marian frowned. "By the way," she suddenly said, "did you have anything to do with having Doctor Weller removed from Tara's care?"

"Indirectly," he answered. "It was his decision."

"Why?"

"I can't talk about it. It's got nothing to do with Tara."

"He was excellent. So it affects Tara. I want him back."

"That's not going to happen," Cyrus said firmly.

"Tell me why," she insisted.

"I can't. It involves a case I'm on."

She was going to persist but Tara appeared, waiflike, wobbly on her feet, jeans loose, a woolly cap covering her baldness. They never fought in front of her. Each put on a happy face and waited competitively to see who got the first smile, the grace of first touch.

"Daddy!"

Cyrus could see Marian's jaw tensing as he dropped to his haunches to give her a hug. She disappeared in his arms, too small, too small; but having won the victory, he wasn't one to twist the knife. He released her and gently spun her toward Marian, who kissed her forehead and fought to hold back tears.

"Let's go home, sweetheart," her mother said.

"Is Daddy coming too?"

"I've got to go to work, honey. I just came by to spring you from this joint."

She brought her teddy up to her chest and pouted.

"I'm coming over Saturday," he added.

"When is that?"

"Just two days. If you're up to it, we'll take a drive."

"I'm not sure she'll be able to leave the house," Marian warned.

"We'll see," Cyrus said with a tired smile. "We'll see."

As they made their way through the lobby, two parents pushing their discharged daughter in a little hospital wheelchair, a casual observer would have thought them a handsome married couple doting on their sick child. Yet Cyrus couldn't wait to see Marian's back and only relaxed when she left to pick up her car from the garage. He waited with Tara curbside. It was cool, but she was well-bundled and seemed to perk up in the fresh air.

"What do you want to do when you get home?" he asked.

"I want to see my new dollhouse."

"Really?"

"Mommy said Marty bought it for me. I hope it's big."

"Knowing Marty, it'll be huge," Cyrus said.

When Tara was securely buckled into the backseat of Marian's Mercedes, Cyrus gave her cheek a peck and waved her off. As he headed for the garage, he heard his name called. "Mister O'Malley!"

It was Emily Frost in a navy overcoat, her cheeks flushed. "Has Tara left?"

Cyrus was colder than the morning air. "Just now. Her mother took her."

It was apparent they were going in the same direction. They walked side by side in uncomfortable silence until Emily piped up, "When I saw her earlier she was really excited about going home."

He grunted. "Yes, she was."

She took a good breath and said professionally, "I know you and your wife aren't in agreement on all aspects of Tara's treatment plan, but I'm grateful you've allowed me to continue to see her."

They entered the parking lot. He had to pay to exit, she had a card. He pointed at the ticket machine as a sign that he was going his own way. "I haven't changed my mind. I'm completely against it but Tara likes you and I don't have the stomach to take it to court. My wife's got deeper pockets than I do."

"Well, I'm still grateful. She's a special little girl." With that, she gave a terse good-bye and hopped onto an elevator.

As he corkscrewed down from one of the top floors of the parking garage he checked his BlackBerry for office messages. There was an e-mail from Avakian confirming their appointment in Cambridge; he had just enough time to get there.

At the second parking level he hit a sudden backup of four or five cars. At first he tapped the steering wheel impatiently; then he scrolled through a few more messages. With the brake lights ahead still glowing red he searched for the source of the problem and noticed a car down the line half in and half out of a parking space. The vehicle behind it was awfully close, stopped at an angle blocking both ramps. It looked like a fender bender. He checked his watch and swore. Cars were behind him now. He was well and truly stuck.

He lowered his window and stuck his head out for a better look. A man was shouting angrily. He didn't like what he was hearing, not cool for a hospital zone, especially a children's hospital. His cop juices started to flow.

He got out, approached the accident and had to suppress a smile. Blue overcoat, blond head. Dr. Frost had backed into a guy.

The smile faded when he got a look at the man haranguing her, a fellow in his late twenties with slicked-back hair. His shiny BMW was injured, a headlight smashed, its cowling dented. The guy's eyes were wild and his jugulars were full and he was cursing Dr. Frost with all the decorum of a street thug.

"Hey buddy!" Cyrus called out. "Easy with the language, this is a children's hospital."

Emily had been holding her own, steering the man toward neutrality, encouraging a quick exchange of paperwork but seemed relieved to see Cyrus.

The fellow gave Cyrus the finger. "This is none of your fucking business, man."

Cyrus kept moving forward. "You see, that's what I'm talking about. This place is full of sick children and upset parents. They don't need this. Trade your numbers and move on."

"Go screw yourself. She backed into me."

"I'm sorry, but you were coming down the ramp awfully fast," Emily added in her defense.

"The bitch shouldn't be driving."

Cyrus strode forward until he stood toe to toe with the man but half a head taller. "You're talking to my daughter's doctor."

The fellow seemed momentarily confused by the amalgam of calmness and menace in Cyrus's tone. "Back off, man, I don't care who I'm talking to. She's cost me a grand on my deductible."

"Your medical bills are going to come in way higher, pal," Cyrus said evenly, watching the man's fist ball up. "Not to mention your legal bills if you take a swing at me."

"Mister O'Malley, please, I'll be all right," Emily protested. "Why don't I just call security?"

Cyrus pulled an old cop maneuver, unfitting perhaps for an FBI agent, but instinctively satisfying. He pulled his coat and jacket back to reveal the butt of his gun snug against his upper chest. "Security's already here, Doctor Frost."

"What are you, some kind of cop?" The man backed off a step.

"Yeah, I'm some kind of cop. And let me ask you something. This lot's for hospital visitors. Something tells me you're not here for that. What's your story, pal?"

"I'm a district manager for a liquor wholesaler," the man said obligingly, staring at the gun. "I've got clients in the neighborhood."

"Okay, liquor man," Cyrus growled, "take the doctor's insurance info and hit the bricks. Now."

Within a minute the BMW was gone and cars started snaking up the ramp again. Cyrus trotted back to his car to unclog the down ramp but not before Emily, staring at him in sweet amazement, said, "Thanks for your help."

He smiled back, gave her a casual salute and was off.

The headquarters of the Harvard University Information Services department was at Holyoke Center, a sixties piece of architecture that still seemed to work as a counterpoint to the ancient red bricks of Harvard Yard. Cyrus blew in, not tragically late, as everyone had just exchanged business cards, not yet past the chitchat.

Avakian had been cracking up the other men with one of his stories. The assistant provost for Information Technology, a lieutenant from the university police and an IT manager from Harvard's Soldier's Field Road facility were huddled with him in a conference room, a couple of black binders lying conspicuously on the table.

Cyrus apologized, went through the introductions and started the meeting with his thanks. He acknowledged that the university didn't have to cooperate with their request for information but because it was a private institution it had the prerogative to do so. Subpoenas, probable cause arguments, all the insurmountable hurdles for an investigation at this stage were conveniently mooted by their helpfulness.

The assistant provost was happy to make some remarks and move onto another meeting. "Look, Special Agent O'Malley, we're always interested in assisting outside law enforcement whenever possible. And we've got a mandate to protect all our employees and students to the maximum extent possible. If we've got a bad apple, we should know about it."

"Absolutely," the police lieutenant agreed, "especially in a homicide investigation."

Cyrus was quick to respond. "We're too early in this investigation to have any suspects. We'd just like to be able to rule out Doctor Weller as a person of interest and move on if we can, to more productive leads."

Cyrus and Avakian soon were left alone with the IT manager, a young man who looked like he'd borrowed someone else's shirt and tie for the meeting. He explained how their logs worked: after 6 P.M. and on weekends all medical school employees had to swipe their ID cards on entry and exit at the security desks located at each of the Longwood complex research buildings. And 24/7 all internal card swipes were recorded at sensitive areas such as biohazard labs and animal facilities. The printouts on the table were records, sorted by calendar day, of Dr. Weller's building for the past two months. And to make their task easier, he'd had Dr. Weller's personal data outputted in red. He appeared quite proud of this software feature and Cyrus heaped praise on him for the convenience, making the young man as happy as if he'd pinned an honorary FBI badge to his lapel.

Cyrus wanted to key on four dates: the presumptive nights on which Thomas Quinn and the three prostitutes were murdered. Avakian donned thick-rimmed reading glasses and tackled the first two. Cyrus took the more recent killings. They dug into the binders while the IT guy took out his laptop and did his own thing. Half an hour later, they were done.

"I got nothing," Avakian grunted. "Weller's a goddamn workaholic. He was in the lab both nights from 7 P.M. or so till 5 or 6 A.M. when he clocked out. He's in and out of the animal rooms a lot but there's probably nothing unusual about that."

"Same for my nights," Cyrus said, closing his binder. He turned to the IT manager. "Is there any way of doing a sort, say for the past six months, to see if pulling all-nighters is unusual for him?"

"Sure, I can do that. Give me a couple of days."

Cyrus had a thought. "Is it possible to sneak out of the building without going past the security desk?"

"I wouldn't know," the young man answered. "Never been over there. I hang out in a server room miles away."

"What about CCTV over in his building?" Avakian wondered.

"The quadrangle's covered pretty well, but inside the buildings, not so much. I think it's in next year's budget but I could be wrong."

That was it. They had no more on Weller than at the start. Cyrus pressed the elevator Down button.

"What next?" Avakian asked.

"I've got a real interest in attending a salon next weekend."

"A salon?" the big man asked, screwing up his face. "You want to go to a beauty parlor?"

"Nope. It's the kind of place where eggheads slap themselves on the back and drink white wine."

"You're on your own, partner," Avakian said, stepping heavily onto the elevator cab. "My weekends are for football."

13

There wasn't enough, not nearly enough.

Alex had thought there'd be plenty of pumpkin girl's fluid to do the necessary structural studies but he was wrong.

He was making progress—undeniably. The mystery peak at 854.73 m/z was slowly yielding to the brute force of his science. Structural analysis of unknown compounds wasn't his field but he couldn't very well blithely hand out samples from a murder victim to academic collaborators. So he taught himself the techniques and borrowed time on machines he didn't already possess within his own lab.

This much he had learned, and this much was certain: the fraction was a peptide, a shortish chain of amino acids—but which ones, and what was their sequence and configuration? He'd need more of the mystery peak, more precious liquid to carry on.

And beyond the incumbent needs for analytical chemistry he *wanted* more for other reasons that burned inside him like molten metal, unquenchable fiery ingots impossible to ignore.

So, as if captive to a restless dream, he found himself once again riding around the dark empty streets of the city during one of the first sustained flurries of the season.

The girl's hair and shoulders were sprinkled in snowflakes. They melted one by one when she climbed into his heated car. He didn't really get a good look at her until he'd driven a block. She was the prettiest yet and disconcertingly similar in appearance to his Jessie. If her hair had been red he probably would have been tempted to let her out at the next light with twenty bucks for her trouble. But her hair was brown. And she was young. No more than twenty, he thought.

She was a chatty one—a self-described motormouth—who kept up a stream of nervous banter until he'd parked inside his Cambridge garage, closed the door and sat back beside her. She made it clear she wasn't going to play along with his desire to talk first. She didn't like the setup and let him know she wanted to get on with it. As he sputtered, she took matters into her own hands, unzipped his fly, peeled down his shorts and started to go down on him.

He didn't want any of his DNA inside her mouth!

As her lips were about to encircle his soft cock he panicked and pushed her shoulders hard, ramming her against the passenger-side door.

"Hey!" she shouted in alarm and pain. "What's your goddamn problem?"

He couldn't think of anything to say.

Instead, his big hands shot out like projectiles but she was too far away for a surprise attack and he failed to get a good purchase on her neck. She wriggled free and unleashed a verbal and physical counterattack that bewildered him with its ferocity. Arms, hands and fingernails moved in eggbeater frenzy. High-pitched screams pierced his ears, an untidy torrent of profanities and animalistic noises.

"Quiet, quiet, quiet," he implored blindly, his eyes tightly closed to protect his corneas from her razor-sharp nails. He was leaning over the console, pushing off against the driver's side door for leverage until his hands found their mark again, this time firmly. He felt the flat planes of throat cartilage, hard and satisfying under his thumbs, and began to squeeze. This one would get no narrative to send her off. She was too feisty and determined. No lullabies for—

He didn't know her name.

Suddenly, the flailing stopped and so did the punches. He tasted warm blood, his own blood. It would be over soon. Then he'd check his watch for time zero and get about his business.

He finally opened his eyes to see what she looked like at the last moments of consciousness. That much he owed her.

She was staring back with hatred.

The burning!

All at once he was enveloped in a cloud of hissing, searing pain.

His eyes smoldered so caustically he had to let her go to rub his stinging eyes.

Through the lachrymose haze he caught something in her fist, an object like a black lipstick.

Mace!

The girl was scrambling for her freedom and before he could react she'd slid over the console onto the rear seat with the alacrity of a big cat slipping its cage.

Coughing and spluttering, he lunged for her. His left hand grabbed onto her bejeweled low-slung belt that had been part of her seductive gear and was now only a liability. The leather held fast over her hips and allowed him to tug her away from the door handle.

He held onto the belt for dear life and used it to pull himself into the backseat where he wiggled his way on top of her. In doing so, his jeans and undershorts curled down to his thighs and if someone had come upon them, the first impression would be of an overheated couple about to make love, doggy-style.

But this wasn't love.

Alex managed to push his right arm around her neck far enough to get the crook of his elbow into position, surrendering to some primitive part of his brain that instinctively knew how to kill.

He pulled her neck into hyperextension and her screams became guttural. The upward force drove his face into the soft fabric of her jacket and he took advantage of the cloth to blot his stinging eyes.

She began to buck like an angry mare trying to unseat him. It didn't feel like he was killing her. Too much vitality was coursing through her strong body.

He arched his back to give himself better anchorage. With his free hand he reached over the top of her head and inched his fingers over her forehead, her nose, her clenched mouth until he got to her chin, which was nestled on his elbow. Three of his fingers managed to hook onto the hollow beneath her mandible and pulling with all his might, the combined energy of both arms working in unison set her neck at an unsustainable angle.

There wasn't so much of a snap as a dull giving way of ligaments. Her body went into spasm. There was a gush of warm urine against his thighs.

He let go and she was still.

His coughing and gagging picked up steam as his arm and shoulder muscles relaxed. He rubbed his eyes again on her jacket then stopped, wondering whether tears carried DNA—and suddenly aghast at being bare-bottomed, he hurriedly pulled his pants up.

He rose to his knees and exhaled hard, wheezy breaths until at last he had the presence to look at his watch.

How many seconds had passed?

Thirty?

He was shaking violently.

There were only two and a half minutes to get his drill from the shelf and collect his samples.

He wanted to vomit, to throw himself into a cleansing shower. He wanted to be far, far away from the backseat of the car.

He closed his eyes for a moment.

Come on, Alex, gather yourself, man!

If you don't, this girl would have died for nothing.

14

It was hard to imagine a more beautiful morning.

The air was crisp, frosty and vitalizing. A frozen crust had formed overnight atop several inches of unblemished snow and sunlight made it shimmer as if thousands of gemstones had been carelessly scattered about. Down a slope, the still pond water perfectly reflected bare trees from the surrounding wood. A hawk soared forlornly overhead, resisting migration to warmer climes.

Cyrus was only half watching the forensics team from the New Hampshire State Lab. Mostly he moodily imagined what it would be like to follow a trail beyond them into the thicket, and to wander alone among defoliated stands of birch, maple and oak.

He thought of the Robert Frost poem, *Stopping by Woods on a Snowy Evening*, and he became sad.

Tara would never know the joy and sorrow of poetry.

She'd never be kissed by a boy, never ride a horse; never dip her toes in the warm green waters of the Caribbean.

The crime scene crew signaled they were done and started packing their equipment and unrolling a body bag. Cyrus removed his glove and extended a hand to help Ivan Himmel up the snowy grade. The old man started to slip anyway and Avakian jumped down into the ditch to push while Cyrus pulled.

"It's not age," Himmel offered when he was on level ground. "I was clumsy even when I was young. Can we go back to my car to talk? My feet are cold."

"So is she or isn't she?" Avakian demanded.

"She is. Nice little bore hole like the others."

"Strangulation?" Cyrus asked.

"This one looks like a broken neck. I'd say an extension avulsion at C2 but I'll let you know when she's on the table. She was a very attractive young lady, by the way."

"How long's she been out here?" Cyrus asked.

"She's good and frozen," Himmel answered, trudging toward the highway. "I'll need to thaw her out first before I can do any calculations—but she wasn't walking the streets last night, that's for damn sure. Oh, and her fake fingernails were clearly cut off, not artistically. She was probably a scratcher but we'll still look for his DNA."

They were about to step over the police tape and brush past the chattering fishermen who'd found the girl but a man called up from the ditch, summoning them back. "Hey, look at this!" When they lifted the prone body a sheet of snow and ice fell away from her waist-length jacket. A large square of cloth had been neatly excised.

"He contaminated her and cut away the evidence," Cyrus said, looking down, shielding his eyes from the glare. "That, the fingernails ... he's a careful bastard."

"We'll get him eventually," Avakian said soothingly.

His partner's benign remark irritated him. It smacked of impotence. He thought of Alex Weller smugly reclining with his feet up on his desk. He had no proof, nothing but his gut, but that was sufficient for now. He felt a terrible urgency to solve the case.

Why—to prevent another hooker from winding up discarded by the side of the road?

Tara's sweet little face replaced Weller's in his mind. It revolted him that this man had examined, had touched, his baby.

It dawned on him. He wanted to be able to tell her, "Daddy caught a very bad man today and put him in jail." He would never tell her it was her doctor, the one with a ponytail. She didn't need to know that;

but he wanted to see her face light up and hear her giggle with delight at her daddy's cleverness. He wanted to tell her before it was too late.

"No, we'll get him soon," Cyrus snapped back.

There was no need to linger. They had the victim's identity because the killer was good enough to dump her with her shoulder bag in place, complete with wallet and a spent canister of mace. The cutaway cloth, the clipped nails, the lack of attempt to conceal the body, spoke volumes about the killer's confidence. As was the case with the others, they weren't expecting the body to yield anything about him.

"This one fought back," Avakian noted as they crossed the state line into Massachusetts.

"I hope it hurt like hell," Cyrus replied. "I hope she got him in the eyes and scratched the shit out of him."

"You still think it's Weller?"

"You know I do. I want to see what his face looks like."

"Can you believe he dumped her back at Pinnacle Pond, what, a hundred feet from the last vic?"

Cyrus ran his tongue over chapped lips. "Killing this girl took him out of his comfort zone. She didn't go down easily. Maybe he was rushed. Maybe he was exhausted or hurt. Maybe he was scared. He knew the layout up here: path of least resistance, a comfortable place in an uncomfortable night."

Avakian grunted his acceptance of Cyrus's theory and turned on his sports station for the remainder of the southbound ride, leaving Cyrus to stare fitfully at the cold white landscape.

There was something therapeutic about the standard British ringtone: *beh beh, beh beh, beh beh.* It was expectant, not urgent, familiar and welcoming. It tasted of milky tea, smelled of battered cod, sounded like bleating goats on a grassy hill.

Alex heard the tone replaced by a husky voice saying, "This is Joe."

"Hey, Joe."

"Unfucking believable! Baby brother!"

"You're back, eh?"

"With all me fingers and toes and all the dangly bits as well."

"When'd you get home?"

"A week and a bit."

"I left you a message."

"Yeah. I'm not good about returning things. Still have a library book from when I was twelve."

"How long till they send you over again?"

"I'm out. I told them to shove it. Six bloody tours, man! I'm too old for this shit."

"I can't believe it."

"You'd better. No more third-world shit holes for me. Closest I'll get to one is Luton."

"Jesus, it's good to hear your voice," Alex said wistfully.

"You okay, Alex? You don't sound good."

"I'm fine."

"Still with what's her name?"

"Jessie. Yeah, she's hanging in there."

"She must be mentally deficient."

"Come to Boston," Alex said suddenly.

"Why?"

"Why not? Stay with us. You haven't been for a dog's age. You've never seen my house."

"Like I said, I'm just back. I've got a lot of sorting out to do."

"I miss you."

"Then you're going to have to come here, mate. I met a lady who's got loose girlfriends. We'll get you taken care of."

"I can't change your mind?"

"You sure you're all right?" Joe asked. "You're not trying to tell me you've got two months to live or some bollocks like that."

"No, I'm good. Really."

"Well, that's fine then. You're good, I'm good, the whole bloody world is good."

Alex learned the name of the girl from the papers. Bryce. He held the tube up to the light. Bryce's clear, pure 854.73 fluid, lots of it, thanks to her tender age and refinements he'd made in the purification process.

Every drop was hard fought.

The girl had struggled to hold on to life. And four days after the murder, Cyrus O'Malley wanted to meet again. Alex had listened to the early morning voice mail and rushed into the bathroom to inspect his face. The swelling had gone down but the scratch marks, though healing, were plainly visible. He'd told Jessie he'd slipped on the ice and done a face-plant. She always believed what he told her, cooed in sympathy and gently applied antibiotic ointment with the tip of her finger.

O'Malley wouldn't be so gullible. He was on his way to Alex's lab and would be waiting for him.

The bathroom vanity was crowded with Jessie's tubes and jars. He started working on a particularly long, angry streak on his cheek. First some foundation makeup smeared in, then a twirl of powder, then a few light wipes with a bit of toilet paper: Jessie's technique. The scar disappeared. The others followed.

The meeting with O'Malley had been brief by the clock, long by perception. He was sure the FBI agent was scrutinizing his face but he'd kept the fluorescent lights off; the natural light of his office and makeup seemed to do the trick. The discussion revolved around Alex's whereabouts the night Bryce Tomalin was killed. When Alex replied he'd spent all night tending to an experiment in his lab he thought he detected incipient eye rolling from O'Malley. Then came a second request to attend a salon, which he parried by explaining that there wouldn't be any more till next year. As O'Malley was leaving, Alex politely asked after Tara and received a curt reply: she was fine. And that was it.

It took a quarter of an hour sitting quietly at his desk before he was composed enough to get on with his day.

This time he was sure he had a sufficient quantity to finish his analytical studies—that is, if he restrained himself and didn't use too much for personal trips. A colleague in a lab across the quadrangle who specialized in protein and peptide chemistry gave him after-hours access to her Applied Bio Voyager system to do peptide fingerprinting.

Once he had good mass data, he plodded ahead toward identification of the elusive structure doing ion trap mass spectroscopy on her Agilent XCTplus machine. One night rolled into another. The data wasn't making sense, things weren't fitting together. He needed help but was scared to ask for it. He'd keep pressing forward on his own.

It got dark quickly this time of year. Even though he and Jessie were having an early dinner, it was already black outside. He wasn't talkative and she followed his lead. They ate in silence like a couple of Trappist monks. Afterward, he helped clear the table.

"Do you have to go back to the lab tonight?"

"Not tonight."

"What then?" she asked. "You're in a mood. I can tell."

"What kind of mood?"

"You've got something on your mind."

"I've always got something on my mind."

She put down the pot scrubber, dried her hands and laid them on his chest. "You've got another sample, don't you? You want to take it again."

He kissed her. "Does anyone in the world know me as well as you?"

That made her smile. "No, just me. When?"

"Now. The dishes can wait."

He readied himself on the bed and Jessie obediently lay beside him, her head propped on an elbow. He gently moved strands of hair and secured them behind her ear so he could see her face better. Sometimes, he'd study that face when she didn't know he was watching. There was a sorrow in her moist green eyes that disappeared whenever he allowed her to dote on him. He filled a deep void, a chasm. Without him, where would she be? How would she get along? It was an abstract question. He needed her as much as she needed him.

He had a pipette in his hand. "I shouldn't take this," he said softly.

"Why not?"

"*You* should."

"Me? Why?"

"Because I love you."

She liked hearing him say that but then admitted, "It scares me."

"Don't be scared. I want you to know the joy I felt."

She frowned like a little girl. "Will I be okay?"

"Yes."

She let out a sorrowful, dutiful sigh. "Okay."

He didn't give her time to change her mind. "Open your mouth for me." He let the drops slide under her tongue and kissed her when she swallowed. "Here, let me make you comfortable." He sat her up, unbuttoned her blouse, took it off then unsnapped her bra. After he kissed each breast, he fetched one of his clean T-shirts, the ones she liked to sleep in. She slipped it on. He helped her out of her jeans and laid her back down, her red tresses overflowing a red pillow.

In his most soothing, caring voice, he bade her to close her eyes and breathe slowly and deeply. Then he held her hand, watched, and waited until ten minutes passed and her tight grip relaxed and went slack.

"Jessie?" he whispered.

He gently prodded her, then a stronger shake.

Her breathing was faster, her heart rate accelerated but she looked peaceful. He lifted an eyelid and saw the tranquility of a green eye and normal pupillary reaction to light.

He felt compelled to look at the ceiling: if she was hovering and looking down on the bed, he wanted her to see how calm and happy he was. He said to the ceiling, "I love you," and returned to tending her physical needs and protecting her during her journey.

At once it dawned on him that he was a scientist and even though this was Jessie, this also was an experiment. He hurriedly checked his watch and began to make time-based entries on a notepad grabbed from the dresser: her runway time, her heart and respiratory rates, her skin color and temperature.

Her fingers were making small grasping movements, which he noted. Her calf muscles were twitching. Each small sound she uttered he captured phonetically, every *ahhh, uh, hmmm, phoo*.

After a further fifteen minutes of tranquility she became restless and the beatific look on her face replaced with a strong grimace. She thrashed, rather violently. He held and talked to her, telling her everything was all right and that he was there with her.

Where was she in her journey? Was she being sucked off the stepping-stones in reluctant return?

Then, she was back, staring at him through wide green eyes that flooded with tears the moment she recognized his face. "Alex."

"I'm here, Jessie."

"I never …" She choked on her sobs and began to cough.

He sat her up, gently thumped her back, and held her. "I know," he said. "At least I think I know. Tell me when you're able."

"I-I was there," she finally sputtered.

"How was it? Was it beautiful?"

"Yes."

"How did it make you feel?"

"Happier than I've ever been. More than happy … I don't have a word for it."

"Did you see anyone?"

She nodded and began to sob again. He waited for her to cry herself out. "Gran."

"Your Grandmother Martha?"

She nodded.

"I'm not surprised." *The only one who'd ever treated little Jessie with tenderness.* He knew the family history well.

She used some of the tissues he handed her. "She looked lovely. She was so happy to see me. She wanted me to cross over. I almost made it …" Her voice petered out.

Alex clenched his fist triumphantly behind his back. "I know," he said. "I know." Then he asked, "How close did you get to her?"

"I made it to the last stepping-stone."

His eyes narrowed. "That's closer than I got!" *Bryce was the youngest*, he thought.

The younger the better.

"And Alex," she said after a while.

"Yes?"

"I think God was there."

15

His face was cello-shaped, too young for jowls but ample and bottom-heavy. With age and prosperity the jowls surely would come. His beard, cropped and black, spread lavishly over fleshy tan cheeks. He rubbed at the dense growth in a deliberately pensive way, as if to counter youthfulness with the theatrical gesture of gravitas. A single sheet of paper lay before him.

"So ... what do you think?" Alex asked.

Miguel Cifuentes was a gregarious sort of fellow who gave off an air of familiarity even to those meeting him for the first time. Alex had made his acquaintance three years earlier in the cafeteria, when without invitation Cifuentes joined him and amiably introduced himself.

Alex learned Cifuentes was an organic chemist, newly arrived from Mexico City where he'd recently received his PhD from the Universidad Nacional Autónoma de México. He'd come to Harvard to work in the lab of the legendary molecular biologist Martin Longacre, and he made it abundantly clear to Alex that he was one of the best young chemists to come out of the best chemistry program at the best university in Mexico. And miraculously, he was able to make these declarations without coming across as boastful or arrogant. His jovial self-confidence, then as now, proved to be thoroughly disarming.

Cifuentes finally spoke. "This is an interesting molecule."

"Yes it is."

The chemical structure on the page was computer-generated, based on countless hours of hard labor. Alex had been staring at it for the past two days so intently that he felt it had burned itself onto his retinas. He saw it on the mirror when he shaved in the morning. He saw it on the windshield of his car. He saw it floating in front of him whenever he closed his eyes.

Five amino acids, the building blocks of life, linked to one another in a daisy chain, a circle. A circle, believe it or not! Like the Uroboros! How perfect!

"What is it?" Cifuentes asked.

Alex had a rehearsed answer, part truth, part artifice. "It's a novel neuropeptide—at least I think it's novel. I can't find it in any online databases. It's from the spinal fluid of mice and dogs."

"And it's important why?"

"It's not normally present in detectable quantities. But it's produced in abundance during the moments before death."

Cifuentes snorted. "What else would I expect from you, eh?"

Alex played along. "Yeah, what else?"

"What's its locus of activity? Any idea?"

"I've found a new receptor in the limbic areas of the brain. But it's early days. I haven't even filed patents. It looks like this peptide binds like crazy in the amygdala and hippocampus."

"Ah, the old parts of the brain, the seat of the soul," Cifuentes said brightly.

"Good for you," Alex replied. "I'm duly impressed."

Cifuentes responded well to the stroking. "And the purpose of these receptors is?"

Alex was evasive. "To be determined. But I'm pretty excited."

The chemist waved his hand at Alex's paper. "So, it's a cyclic pentapeptide, five different amino acids, molecular weight about six hundred fifty. I'll take your word that it's novel. I've certainly never seen it before."

Alex tapped the page with his forefinger. "Can you make it?"

"Which one?"

Alex shook his head in confusion and tapped the diagram again. "This one!"

"Okay, time for a lesson in chemistry," the Mexican said with his trademark benign pomposity. "The compound has five chiral centers, see?" He took out his pen and pointed in turn to five carbon atoms in the ring. "Each one of these carbons can be cis or trans, up or down, mirror images of one another. With five chiral centers you can have thirty-two possible forms. So if your question is, 'Can you make it, Miguel?' my question back to you is, 'Which one?'"

"Christ," Alex whispered, his frustration palpable.

"Well, it's not quite as bad as all that," Cifuentes added. "Not all the forms are going to be stable. I can take you through the conformational physics if you've got the stomach for it, but some of the hypothetical combinations can't exist in nature."

"How many?"

"I'd have to do some work on it but I can see at least a dozen that are physically impossible or improbable."

"What about the *most* probable ones?" Alex asked with a touch of renewed hope.

"Look, if I had the time, I could model it out and list them in a probabilistic ranking but I'm a short-timer."

Alex vaguely remembered the details from their last cafeteria conversation. "When are you going back?"

"Less than a month. And man, am I busy trying to finish up! Between Professor Longacre and my wife, my balls are in a vice."

"I need your help, Miguel," Alex pleaded. "You're the best peptide chemist I know."

"I'm certain of that," Cifuentes replied with a grin. "But I'm not going to be able to take this on now. Maybe when I get my own lab set up in Mexico City. Give me three, maybe six months, and I'll collaborate with you. Okay, my friend?"

Alex remembered with exquisite detail the way the chemist perennially complained about his finances. He and his wife scrimped to get by on a postdoc fellow's salary and she couldn't get a work permit—not that she had the time anyway with the young kids. Though Miguel came from a reasonably comfortable middle-class family—his father owned a marginally profitable shoe factory—it wasn't until he came to Boston that he realized how impoverished he was relative to his American friends.

Alex looked into the young man's chestnut-colored eyes and had a brainstorm. "Did you rent an apartment yet in Mexico City?"

"Yeah. The lease starts in January."

"Nice place?"

"Nicer than what we've got here in Jamaica Plain but still a dump."

"They're not going to be paying well?"

Cifuentes grimaced. "Junior faculty, man. What can I say? Maria's going to go back to work but we'll have to pay for a nanny so it won't be a big net positive. It'll take a while but I'll get there. Full professors live pretty well in Mexico, and who knows, maybe I'll jump ship and work for a drug company to make some serious coin."

Alex sprung the trap. "Would twenty thousand dollars help get you set up?" He couldn't access his grant funds for something like this but he had savings in the bank.

The chemist sat up a bit straighter. "And where would I get that?"

"From me."

"And you'd want me to do what?"

"Make this peptide for me—the most likely configuration."

"How much of it do you need?"

"Milligrams for sure. Grams if possible."

"When?"

"As soon as possible. Definitely before you leave for Mexico. I'll give you ten thousand today, ten thousand on delivery."

"You'd give me ten thousand dollars now?"

"Interested?"

Cifuentes fingered his beard again and whispered, "Jesus, I don't know if there are enough hours in the day to get everything done."

Alex had a spare check in his wallet. It had been tucked away for a while and it was a bit grimy. He unfolded it and began to write *Miguel Cifuentes* on the Pay to the Order line.

Cifuentes licked his lips as if he could taste the money. "Do you have a name for this molecule yet?"

"Only an informal one. I'm calling it the Uroboros compound."

The chemist shrugged and snatched the check dangled seductively in front of his face.

16

Cyrus cracked off a mock salute as Marian and Marty left. The garage door rumbled, the car engine came to life and they were gone. He had Tara to himself for three hours. He selfishly hoped she wouldn't sleep the whole time.

Up in her room she was swaddled in layers of flannel, goose down and chiffon. He stood at the foot of her oversized bed and watched her breathe through her dry lips. Her eyes were closed. She was wearing padded headphones. The bedroom was packed with toys and stuffed animals and resembled a showroom at FAO Schwarz, years of gift-giving achingly compressed into a too brief period, credit cards swiped over and over to assuage grief. Cyrus felt a brief wave of compassion for good old Marty: the man probably didn't know what else to do.

Tara's eyes fluttered open and she pulled off her headphones. "Hi Daddy!"

"I'm sorry I woke you."

"I wasn't sleeping."

"You weren't?"

"No."

"Sure looked like you were."

"I was doing an Emily exercise."

"What's that?"

"She made me something for my iPod. Want to hear it?"

Cyrus squinted suspiciously, donned the headphones and began to listen to Dr. Frost's voice speaking to Tara, invoking her name, seeking to soothe her with soft, mesmerizing suggestions.

"Tara, now I want you to take a deep breath way down into your belly. Let it go and hear the whoosh of the air coming out. And when you're ready take another breath. Let it out with the whooshing sound, like the wind. Each breath leaves you more and more calm. Now, let your breathing slow down. Each time you breathe out silently, say to yourself 'calm.' Let that be your special word. 'Calm.' Breathe in and out. Make the whooshing sound with your lips. Say 'calm' each time. Just let go. Any bad thoughts, let them go. Let them go. Good. Now, Tara, imagine a place where you feel safe, secure and calm. Whether it's indoors or outdoors or a place you've never even seen. You're going there now. As you get there, you can see the shapes and colors of your special place, like a picture. And now you begin to hear the sounds of your special place. And now you can feel your special place against your skin. Take a deep breath. And as you let the happiness of your special place spread through your body, enjoy it, let it nourish and calm you. Stay there a while, and remember, you can go back there anytime you like."

He stripped off the headphones. Nothing too subversive. "Is it all like this?"

"Yes."

"So what's your special place?"

"My old room."

"Which room?"

"You know, in our old house when Mommy and you were still married."

Tara's old bedroom in Sudbury was half the size, fairly dark, fewer toys, no TV, no Wii, no Playstation. Just a five year old's bedroom with her original parents in her life. That was her special place.

Cyrus turned away so she wouldn't see him tear up. He wiped his face with his palms, snorted back the secretions and asked her if she wanted to play a board game.

Midway through Chutes and Ladders, Avakian called. Cyrus let it ring through to voice mail but later, when he went to the kitchen to get juice for Tara and coffee for himself, he returned the call.

"I talked to the IT guy at Harvard," Avakian reported. "Weller was checked into his lab the entire night when Bryce Tomalin was killed."

"Shocking," Cyrus deadpanned. "What about the pattern search?"

"It's not too convincing one way or another. He's pulled about a dozen all-nighters in the past three months on days we've got no known homicides. You could argue the guy's a workaholic."

"He may be," Cyrus said, "but he's other things too. How's the other project?"

The kitchen phone started ringing.

"Slow. When are you coming in?" Avakian asked.

The voice message began to play through the speaker. "Oh, hi, Mister and Missus Taylor, this is Doctor Frost calling from Children's. I was just checking on Tara and wanted ..."

"Gotta go," Cyrus said, abruptly hanging up on his partner. He grabbed the kitchen phone and hit Talk. "Hi, Doctor Frost, this is Tara's dad, Cyrus O'Malley. How are you?"

She hesitated a moment, reacting to the surprise, he imagined. "Mister O'Malley! I was calling to see how Tara was doing."

"When I came to visit this morning she was listening to your tape."

"I see. Did you listen to it too?"

"I did."

"And?"

"Very relaxing. Almost put me to sleep."

She laughed. "Well, that's part of the idea."

"I didn't hear the word *death* once, which is good."

"We only talk about death and explore a child's feelings about it if she asks. Tara hasn't brought it up explicitly. She talks around it."

"Like how?"

"For instance, last week she asked me what Daddy will do when she's gone."

"Jesus," he whispered. "What did you say?"

"I told her that you'd be very sad for a while but you'd carry her in your heart forever."

The tears started running again. "I will."

"Of course you will." He heard her take a breath. "I never properly thanked you for intervening after my fender bender."

"It was nothing. The guy was a jerk. I'm good with them."

"Still, thank you. It was very gentlemanly."

The words slipped out without premeditated thought. "Maybe we could get a coffee sometime."

He waited for one of those tiny moments of time that seem to take ages. "I'd like that."

On his way up the stairs he asked himself, *Christ, Cyrus, did you just make a date?*

17

Christmas week was dry and brutally cold. There were no big fronts heading toward New England so Christmas day would not be white.

Alex's lab was quiet. His research fellows had left town to visit with their parents and Frankie Sacco didn't have enough work to justify his brooding presence. Alex had patted him on the back and sent him home with the assurance he would fiddle the time cards so he'd be paid.

Alex came in early with a full day of experiments scripted in his head. He'd made progress on his new limbic receptor; in his notebooks it went by the designation LR-1. More and more, the evidence showed that he was dealing with a newly described type-2 sigma receptor—an electrifying discovery. For years he'd held the opinion that this poorly understood class of brain receptors well might play a role in near death experiences. The Uroboros compound had subpicomolar activity at the LR-1 receptor: minute, almost immeasurable concentrations had tremendously powerful activity. He was zeroing in on something important; he could feel it.

With the lab to himself and freed of inhibitions, he drew from a sad old well and began to part sing, part hum a medley of Christmas carols. He'd been a caroler in Liverpool as a boy. He and Joe had belonged to a church group that raised alms for the poor and he remembered the pride in his father's face when the group serenaded the pub; but when he got to Dickie Weller's favorite, *Good King Wenceslas,* his mood, already brittle, clouded.

> *Sire, the night is darker now,*
> *And the wind blows stronger.*
> *Fails my heart, I know not how,*
> *I can go no longer.*

He closed his eyes and saw his father standing on the other side of the river of light. Yes, he looked happy, but he was so alone, a solitary figure in an incomprehensible vastness. He wanted to be with him so badly it hurt. He had no more of the 854.73 fluid. All had been exhausted in experiments. He'd heard nothing from Cifuentes beyond an e-mail that he was working through synthetic problems. There was no way to reach his father.

Or was there?

It wasn't the first time he'd had that thought. He'd beaten it out of his mind before, but the grayness of the day, the emptiness of the lab, the approaching Christmas—always a bleak holiday since the car crash—all these things conspired against him. There was a razor-sharp letter opener in his desk. He could sit down in his comfortable chair, cleanly slice the artery at his wrist, look at the sky one last time and in minutes he'd be there, in his father's arms. Forever.

It would be easy, fast. All the troubles, all the struggles, his guilt over the killings would be over. Jessie would be sad and Joe would be bereft of family. He'd be abandoning his science before he had his answers; but still.

He shuffled robotically toward his office, toward the blade. At the very least, he'd hold it in his hand and think some more. Maybe he'd put it back in the drawer. Maybe he wouldn't.

His body stiffened at the sound of urgent knocking against glass. He automatically shouted, "Come in!"

Cifuentes opened the laboratory door, smiled wearily, and when he saw no one else was there he held out a small box wrapped in glossy red wrapping paper adorned with a gold stick-on bow.

"Merry Christmas, Alex."

"Miguel! I wasn't expecting you."

"Well, my friend, it's the time of year when people traditionally exchange presents. Here."

Alex accepted the package and said, "You're embarrassing me. I've got nothing for you."

"Oh, I think you do. Ten thousand dollars."

Alex tore at the paper, muttering, "Christ, you're joking! I'd no idea you'd finished."

Nestled inside a cardboard box was a screw-capped bottle, three-quarters filled with fine, snowy-white crystals.

"Just over nine grams," Cifuentes said proudly.

"My God!" Alex said. "That's a huge amount!"

"I'm a very good chemist, Alex. And I've been working my butt off. I've got a method that produces excellent yields. I made the most stable of the possible isomeric forms, one with alternating cis and trans moieties. Here's the structure." He fished out a folded three-by-five card from his pocket.

Alex was overcome. "Unbelievable. This is really unbelievable. I can't thank you enough, Miguel." He blinked away some tears and added, "You're a lifesaver, know that, mate?"

"Sure I am." Cifuentes chuckled. "So listen, I've got to run. My wife's going to kill me. I was in the lab all night doing the last purification step."

Alex told him to wait for a second, hurried into his office and pulled open the desk drawer to retrieve his checkbook. The letter opener was there, shiny enough to reflect his dark eyes.

He gently touched the edge of the blade and asked his father to wait.

Less than a mile away, Cyrus was at a coffee shop on Brookline Avenue nervously checking his watch with the anticipation of a teenager. He had a nice warm table away from the entrance and was nursing a dark roast. Emily was only a few minutes late but he couldn't help wondering if he was being stood up.

When she arrived she was bundled against the cold, her face half hidden in a scarf. She unwrapped it on the way to his table, exposing frosted cheeks. Sliding into the booth, she said hello and told him she'd need to keep her coat on till she warmed up.

"It's brutal out there," Cyrus agreed.

"I'm always cold," she said. "It's my southern blood."

By the time her cappuccino arrived, she'd peeled off her gloves and removed her coat. They were done talking about the weather.

"I'm glad we could get together," Cyrus said.

"I'm sorry it took a while to arrange. One of the doctors on my service broke her leg. It's been hectic covering for her."

He watched her sip at her coffee and suppressed a smile when it made a foamy moustache. "So, listen," he began. "I want to apologize."

"For what?"

"For unloading on you the first time we met. It wasn't cool."

"You don't have to apologize, Mister O'Malley."

"No, I do. It was a knee-jerk reaction."

"But perfectly understandable."

"You think so?"

"There's nothing harder than having a sick child—nothing. The rules of civility can be legitimately suspended."

He smiled at that. "For how long?"

"Well, not indefinitely." She laughed. "But seriously, I'm sure it would have been better if both you and your ex-wife had participated in the decision to have me consult on Tara's case. You were blindsided."

"I was."

"How's she doing?" she asked.

He rubbed his hands together, a nervous habit he'd recently picked up, but he stopped doing it out of self-consciousness when she noticed the gesture. "Every day she fades a little, sort of like an old photograph left in the sun. We're losing her."

He didn't want to cry but his eyes began to sting. She responded by reaching out and touching his hand. It was a momentary gesture but feeling three cool fingertips against his skin was strangely calming.

Her blue eyes were damp too. "I'm so sorry," she said. "She's such a sweet child. It tears your heart out."

She's not putting it on, he thought. *She loves my little girl too.* "I don't want to let her go," he whispered.

"I know you don't."

He looked away, focusing on a bus passing outside. He filled his lungs with a stuttering inhalation and said, "This thou perceiv'st, which makes thy love more strong, To love that well, which thou must leave ere long."

She looked at him quizzically and said, "That's beautiful. What is it?"

"Shakespeare. Sonnet Seventy-three, if memory serves."

"An FBI agent who quotes Shakespeare?"

"I was a literature major in college—well, before I dropped out of college."

"You're an interesting man, Mister O'Malley."

"Is if okay if you call me Cyrus?"

"Yes, if you call me Emily."

"Deal." He waited for several moments before asking, "Can I see you again?"

She smiled but shook her head. "I don't think so, Cyrus."

"Are you seeing someone?"

"I'm seeing your daughter! She's my patient."

"I'm not up on the rules of engagement here," he confessed. "Would a date violate some kind of ethical canon?"

"Yes," she said softly.

"Well, I wouldn't want to do that. What if you just agreed to have another coffee with me in the new year? Would that be okay?"

Her eyes sparkled when she said, "That would be delightful."

He called for the check. "Do you know a neurologist named Alex Weller?" he asked suddenly.

She nodded. "Sure I do. He's on staff at Children's. I've seen his name in Tara's chart. He saw her for her seizures. Why do you ask?"

"Just curious. What do you know about him as a person?"

"Not very much. We're not close. He seems very professional. I've only seen him a single time in a social setting."

"When was that?"

"He invited me to his house a couple of years ago after he heard me give a talk on modern perspectives on Kübler-Ross's *On Death and Dying*. Apparently, he's had a long-running salon."

"The Uroboros Society."

She furrowed her brow. "You've heard of it."

"What was your take on it?"

"I didn't completely love it, to be honest. I found it a little creepy, a little too fringe for my taste; kind of a hippie-ish approach to the subject of death. They didn't do anything when I was there, but I think they've used drugs to get into group altered states. Not for me!"

"Do you think a guy like that should be seeing kids?"

She got up and put on her coat. "I wouldn't begin to judge him by one glimpse of his extracurricular activities. He's got a sterling reputation around the hospital. Why the interest?"

"Just asking," Cyrus said. "He's kind of on my radar screen."

"What is it?" Jessie asked.

"Guess," Alex replied.

He'd surprised her by coming home early. She'd been vacuuming the rugs when he snuck up and pulled the plug from the wall, countering her fright with a bear hug that turned her screams into squeals.

He led her to the kitchen table, unfolded a small square of the red wrapping paper and revealed a tiny mound of white crystals. One sneeze and the crystals would be gone.

"Is it your Uroboros chemical?"

"It is."

"Oh my God, Alex," she said with wonderment. "Have you tried it yet?"

"No yet."

"When?"

"Now, if you'll be my guardian angel."

"Of course I will. How much are you going to take?"

"It's a bit of a shot in the dark, so many damned variables; but my best calculation is that half a milligram ought to be equivalent to the liquid dose."

"Is there enough for me when you're done?" she asked expectantly.

He took another red square from his breast pocket. "Would I leave my sweetheart out in the cold?"

She kissed him and with the taste of her lip gloss on his tongue he licked the mound of crystals off of the paper and led her by the hand to the bedroom.

18

His heart leaped. Everything was the same: the floating, the tunnel, the light, the pale green terrain, the gurgling sound of the river of light.

Then, there he was—Dickie Weller with his red cap waving him on as before, every bit as beckoning.

Alex's joy was overwhelming as he took his first step onto the smooth river stone. Over the sounds of turbulent flow, he heard his father egging him on in that boisterous voice of his. At the midway point, Alex looked beyond Dickie, searching for the presence on the horizon. There was a hint of the otherness, not as powerful as he'd remembered, but *something* definitely was out there—something amazing, something divine. He'd have to get closer.

Yet, despite his father's plaintive exhortations and his own irresistible urge to reach the other bank, his feet became rooted at the halfway point. There was nothing he could do. No amount of physical or mental strain would allow him to lift his leg off the stepping-stone onto another.

Then all at once, he had the sickening, helpless feeling of being peeled backward, away from the river, away from the greenness, back into the tunnel and back onto his bed—where he awoke, his chest heaving.

"Alex!" Jessie exclaimed. "It's over. You're back!" She was holding him. He felt her hot breath against his face.

He started to cry, succumbing to a perfect blend of joy and sorrow. "Everything was the same," he sputtered. "My father was there ... the river ... but ..."

"But what?"

"It was amazing, Jessie, I won't say it wasn't ... but I couldn't get as close to the other side. I didn't feel the intensity of that presence beyond the horizon. It was all the same but dialed down a few notches. Christ, though, don't get me wrong, it was great, insanely great."

He downed a mug of cold water in a series of violent gulps and let the spillage drip down his chin onto his chest.

"Are you hungry?" she asked.

He shook his head.

"Is it okay if I take mine now?"

He kissed her forehead. "You want to see your grandmother, don't you?"

"Desperately."

He pushed himself off the bed. "Give me a minute to get myself together. Then it's your turn."

He was stroking her arm when her eyes fluttered closed and he maintained tactile contact during her entire trip. Her face was a window. Through it, he could glean what she was experiencing: the exhilaration of hurtling through the tunnel, the pleasure of emerging into the other realm, the ecstasy of the river, the comfort of seeing her grandmother and, finally, the shock of being pulled all the way back to their bed. She was out for just under thirty minutes. While he was under the influence, his own perception of time had been hopelessly confused. He wouldn't have been surprised if his trip had lasted a second or a week.

He could see her eyelids start to lift and wanted to make sure his face was there for her to see. He smiled at her first recognition and lightly kissed her lips. "Hey, you," he said.

"Hey."

"You okay?"

She nodded. "The same thing happened to me, Alex. I couldn't get as close. She wanted me to come but I couldn't get there."

"I know."

"It was unbelievable but not like the last time. The last time was better but it was still great."

She began to weep. He held her tightly, giving her comfort and said, "Don't worry, baby, you're home now."

She closed her eyes and regretfully replied, "But I'm not, Alex. This isn't my home. That was."

The first solid break in the case came from grunt work. Cyrus's idea was simple enough: they knew the probable dates on which the murders took place. Though he wasn't a suspect—the evidence was far too thin—Alex Weller was nevertheless a person of interest. He'd been conveniently logged into the security desk of his lab on each of these nights. Yet what if he'd been able to sneak out of the complex, pick up hookers in the South End, kill them and dump them? He didn't do these things on foot. He had to be using a car.

Inside Avakian's office was a tripod with a map of Boston. Likely routes from the Longwood medical area to the South End were lined in red and the location of public or private closed-circuit TV cameras were marked with black pins. An assistant U.S. attorney in Boston obtained subpoenas from each CCTV operator covering the relevant nights and the result was a Mount Everest of digital data.

There weren't any shortcuts. He checked with DMV about the possible vehicle: human eyes had to scan hundreds of hours of CCTV output looking for a white Honda sedan, Alex Weller's car. And if they found any likely matches, there needed to be a screen grab that captured Weller's license plate.

Cyrus got Minot to sign off on a requisition to bring in a couple of retired special agents for contract work. So, for a modest per diem, two former Boston bureau agents, Harriet Hillman and Timothy Bell, sat in a darkened room drinking coffee and watching mind-numbing black-and-white footage of nocturnal streets.

Two days after Christmas, Hillman was staring at a feed from a camera atop one of the parking garages at the Beth Israel Deaconess Hospital. She pushed the Pause button to put a few drops of Visine into her dry eyes. When she blotted away the excess with a Kleenex she noticed half of a white car in the frame. She punched the Slow-Motion button and hit Pause again when the rear end of the car came into view.

"Tim!" she screamed. Her video partner almost detached himself from his chair but soon he was agreeing with her that it was a Honda Accord and that three of the license plate numbers were clearly visible. This was Weller's car. The date was 23 October. The time was 1:18 A.M. Carla Goslinga had been murdered that night.

The next day, Cyrus and Avakian showed up without warning at Alex's lab. If he wasn't there, they'd try his home address in Cambridge. Cyrus wanted an element of surprise to catch him off guard.

Frank Sacco had been washing glassware at one of the sinks and had a towel in his hand when he answered the door. He audibly grunted at their presence and told them to wait. His boss, he told them, was in the back.

Three men filled up Weller's stuffy office and seemed to suck the oxygen out of it. Cyrus and his partner stood while Alex remained behind his desk, staring at them with wary suspiciousness. Avakian moved to shut the door but Alex told him he didn't mind it open. With Sacco nearby, Avakian shrugged and left the door ajar.

"We want to talk about the night of October twenty-third," Cyrus began.

"What about it?"

"You told us you were working all night in this lab."

"If that's what I told you. I'd have to check my calendar again. I don't have a photographic memory of these things."

"Go ahead and check," Avakian urged.

Alex sighed and opened the calendar on his desktop computer. A few clicks and he said impassively, "Yes, I worked that night."

"All night?" Cyrus asked. "Without leaving the lab once?"

"All night. I had an experiment running."

"Then how do you explain this?" Cyrus produced a time-stamped photo of Weller's car at the corner of Brookline Ave and Francis Street.

Alex studied it and as he did, Cyrus observed the man's face. Aside from a furrowed brow, he gave nothing away.

Finally, Alex said, "I'm afraid I don't have an explanation."

"Is that your car?" Avakian demanded.

"It appears to be, yes."

"And you park it in the faculty lot on Longwood Ave?"

Alex nodded.

"Was the car there the next day when you clocked out?" Avakian continued to press.

"I suppose it was," Alex answered somewhat wearily. "I have no recollection of it being otherwise."

Cyrus leaned over the desk and took the sheet from Weller's hand. "Then let me ask you again, how do you explain this?" He was beginning to feel triumphant. He was one step away from having probable cause to seize the car for a full forensic romp.

Alex took a deep breath and seemed as though he were about to repeat his befuddlement when Sacco poked his head in. "I'm sorry for listening," he said in his heavy townie accent. "I couldn't help hearing what you were saying. Don't you remember, Alex? That was the night I picked your car up and took it back to Revere to do the brakes for you."

Alex brightened. "Yes! I remember now. Thank you for eavesdropping—ordinarily, not a virtue, but under the circumstances, quite useful."

"What are you, a mechanic or a lab tech?" Avakian sounded fed up.

"I know my way around cars," Frank replied with a toothy smile. "I make a few bucks on the side."

"And you can verify this?" Cyrus asked.

Frank shrugged. "I think I've got the Honda's original calipers and rotors in my garage. Want them?"

"Yeah, we want them," Cyrus said bitterly.

When the FBI agents were gone Alex summoned Frank back into his office. "Thank you," he said.

"No problem."

"Why did you do that for me? You fixed my brakes in September."

"You've done a lot for me, Alex. Forget about it."

"These guys have been up my butt over something."

Frank waved him off. "You don't have to tell me anything."

"I owe you for this," Alex said. "I owe you big time, mate."

Frank half smiled. "I'm sure you'll find a way to pay me back."

19

New Year's Eve was harshly cold. It started to snow in the evening, a few fat flakes progressing to flurries, the thin outer bands of a proper nor'easter. As the wind picked up into the night, so did the snowfall until there was a good accumulation with much more to come. Throughout the city, nocturnal plans were being scuttled. There was a general hunkering down to see in the New Year at home.

Avakian pulled off the quintessential suburban swap that evening. He sent his fourteen-year-old daughter to baby-sit at his neighbor's house and had the couple over to drink martinis and watch a DVD.

Emily Frost had volunteered to be on call for the Children's psychiatry service. She didn't consider it much of a sacrifice. She was a nondrinker, had few friends in Boston, and wasn't exactly turning down exciting plans for the evening. Her roommate, a pediatric surgeon, was visiting her parents in New York City and Emily had the flat to herself. So she kept her beeper on her hip and settled into an easy chair with a book. She'd taken a recent interest in Shakespearean sonnets and lightly skipped from one to another as the snow fell.

Marian and Marty canceled plans to go out to a restaurant owing to the blizzard; and besides, Tara had developed a smidgen of a fever. Marian was hovering, checking the girl's temperature every hour but Tara looked fine and Marty was discouraging his wife from subjecting everyone to a harrowing drive to the emergency room if it wasn't absolutely necessary.

Cyrus was in his garden apartment steadily working through a six-pack of beer. As usual, Brazilian music was leeching through his thin walls and he was employing Bach as a countermeasure. The TV was black, the way he liked it most of the time. His book for the night was *King Lear*, his favorite of the tragedies, so miserable in its conceit that he thought it might take the edge off his own misery. He came to a familiar passage.

> *As flies to wanton boys, are we to the gods;*
> *They kill us for their sport.*

He let the book close and rubbed his eyes with the heel of his palm.

Is that all we are, he thought, *flies to wanton boys? Is there no bigger rhyme or reason? What about God? What about His purpose? And if* He *had a grand plan, what possible reason could there be for Tara's sickness?*

It flew against his core beliefs but maybe the truth was darkly simple: fate was nothing more than randomness. God was an artifact of man, built to give false hope. There was no grand architect after all. His little Tara was only a fly swatted by wanton boys, furiously buzzing on the windowsill with a crushed wing, trying to keep alive.

Alex and Jessie were comfortably lying on top of their bedcovers, each eager with anticipation. Alex would go first, then Jessie, willing subjects in a grand experiment to find the right dose of the Uroboros compound. If half a milligram only got them halfway across the river, then perhaps a full milligram would get them further; but that wasn't happening. Doubling the dose got them no farther than midstream.

So, they tried increasing the dosage again, and again, until two and a half milligrams landed Alex in an unresponsive state for hours. Jessie had spent a frantic night checking his vital signs, wondering if she should call an ambulance, but she held off for fear they'd be found out, that she'd never be able to take the drug again.

When he finally did come to he had this to report: despite its longevity, his experience was the same—certainly marvelous and wonderful, but no better than lower doses and still less ecstatic than the pure liquid they'd first taken.

So they'd settled into a pattern of taking only a miniscule mound of crystals, half a milligram at a time, each trip a marvel. They never tired of them. Once they returned, all they could talk about, all they could think about was the next time, and the next time, and the next time.

Yet, that didn't stop Alex's mind from grinding away.

The natural compound was better than the synthetic one—and the younger the "donor" the more profound the experience.

There was more work to be done. He needed more samples, younger victims. He'd foolishly believed the killings could stop, that the man-made chemical was enough. He'd been wrong. He had to follow the science.

And on New Year's Eve, he had the darkest thought of all.

I'm a pediatrician.

I see hopeless cases every day … children who are going to die …

I can help them get to a better place.

One child in particular came to him; a pretty little girl beyond help—a little girl with a father who was persecuting him, trying to derail one of the most important scientific inquiries of all time.

Tara O'Malley.

Jessie called his name and brought him back. He opened his mouth and let her lovingly drop the crystals onto his tongue. He would start the New Year with a joyous journey to the other side—for more time—more achingly wonderful time with Dickie Weller.

20

There was a pile of boots and shoes in the hall amidst a spreading puddle of melted snow. Alex flitted nervously around his living room spending a moment or two with everyone. All the regulars were there: Davis Fox, Arthur Spangler, Larry Gelb with his young girlfriend Lilly, Frank Sacco, and Erica Parris.

Spangler leaned in close enough for Alex to smell the mints and pipe tobacco on his breath. "Surely you've got something for us tonight, Alex. I mean, start of the year and all that. Don't really have the stomach for another lecture about archetypes."

"We'll see, Art," Alex replied. "I'd hate to disappoint you."

Spangler told him not to be so damned enigmatic but Alex had spotted someone entering and left the professor wondering.

To his delight, Sam Rodriguez was back. He clapped the young man between the shoulder blades. "Good to see you, mate."

"Yeah, I thought I'd give it one more shot." As he said this, he was looking at Erica's round backside.

"Uroboros or Erica?" Alex asked.

"Whatever, man." Sam chuckled.

"Well, I'm glad you're here. Jessie's in the kitchen. She'll get you something to drink."

At eight o'clock Alex asked them all to take their places on cushions in their traditional circle. Fourteen were present. He stood astride his cushion and winked at Jessie, the two sharing the secret.

"Happy New Year, one and all!" he boomed. "Hope you had a good holiday and all that blather. I think this is going to be an interesting year for our little group, a breakthrough year. Starting tonight." He paused for effect and scanned the candlelit room for reaction, pleased that everyone appeared keenly attentive. "We all share a common interest in trying to figure out how our lives fit into the bigger picture. Is this, our interval, our time on earth between birth and death, is this all there is? Well, you know where I've stood on this. And everyone here who's had a near death experience stands at the same place. We believe there's more. Call it afterlife, call it heaven, call it anything you please, but we come to this belief not through religious doctrine or indoctrination. We come to it because some of us have, and all of us have read about and talked about, vivid life-altering experiences that lead us to a profound conclusion. And you know that here in our salon, we've shared these experiences, we've studied the Jungian collective unconscious, sacred texts, myths, the scientific literature, anything that might bring us closer to answers. And we've been engaged in active exploration, taking substances to try to bring us closer to that line between life and death, to try to get a glimpse of what might lie beyond. Now these chemicals have been crude, even primitive, I'd say: LSD, salvia, DMT, ketamine. Okay, we've had a bit of fun but the experiences we've had are so varied, so heterogeneous, that I'm afraid they're false approximations of NDEs. Well, tonight, my friends, all of that changes."

Arthur Spangler couldn't contain himself any longer. He was hyperkinetic, almost bouncing on his cushion. "Christ, Alex, this is so goddamn overwrought. Spit it out, will you? What do you have?"

Alex laughed and briefly disappeared into his bedroom. When he returned he had a juice goblet in his hand filled with thin tubes of multicolored wrapping paper, each one sealed with twisted ends. The packaging was Jessie's idea and he loved it. Elegant thin straws filled with his crystals. "This. This is what I have."

"Okay, what is it?" Gelb asked.

"I call it the Uroboros compound. Most of you know that in my research I've been searching for the biological basis for shared and common near death experiences. I think I've found it. It's a naturally occurring brain chemical produced in abundance at the moment of death. It seems to be common to several mammalian species."

Frank Sacco looked surprised and almost hurt. Alex could read the disappointment on his face that he'd been kept in the dark about experiments going on in his own lab.

Sam Rodriguez politely raised his hand as if he were in class. "What about humans?"

Alex kept a poker face and thought, *yes, man too*, but said, "That would be a tough experiment to do, Sam, unless you'd care to volunteer. To isolate the chemical one would need to severely oxygen-deprive the human brain, as I've done with animals. It would be rather difficult to get that by an ethical review board! Having said that, you're looking at two people who've taken this drug and are here today to talk about it." He told Jessie to stand up. He put his arm around her. "The two of us have been using it for several weeks. We can honestly say it's the ultimate experience. There is nothing like it. Nothing."

Jessie nodded. "I can't even describe how beautiful it is."

Spangler continued his display of impatience. "Well, what's it like, Weller? Give us some details!"

"Here's why I'm not going to do that," Alex replied. "I've got enough here for everyone. If you want to try it, Jessie and I will stay sober and look out for you. When you're done tripping, we'll compare notes. I don't want you to be influenced by the power of suggestion."

"How long's the trip?" Erica asked.

"For Jessie and me, with the dose I'm offering tonight it's been lasting less than hour. It comes on pretty fast, though."

There were questions about safety, side effects and the like.

Alex patiently listened to the concerns and said he wasn't going to lie to them. He candidly admitted that two people wasn't much of a sample size. Still, he and Jessie had no ill effects even in higher doses but he couldn't offer any guarantees. It was risky. Everyone needed to accept that—but trust him, he said, it was going to be worth the risk. Anyone who was worried or scared should sit it out and help as monitors. Whatever happened, he demanded that everyone swear to secrecy as they'd done each time when they'd collectively taken recreational drugs.

He went around the circle polling each member to see whether they were in or out. Spangler was in immediately, showing almost a childlike glee. Through a pinched-faced skepticism, Gelb said yes, and his girlfriend Lilly obediently followed suit. Erica and Sam were quickly on board. Virginia Tinley, the patent lawyer with owlish glasses and severely pulled-back hair, openly debated the pros and cons with herself for all to hear. She was scared of any and all drugs—including aspirin—but was one among them who'd had a bona fide near death experience. It happened in her doctor's office after an injection, whereupon she'd had a severe anaphylactic reaction and cardiac arrest. She remembered floating, entering a tunnel, seeing light ahead, feeling free and happy for the first time in her life but that's as far as it went. She was successfully resuscitated and came back convinced there was profound meaning in what happened. Now she surprised the others when she stopped debating herself, looked into Alex's eyes and said "Yes."

Davis Fox also said yes enthusiastically. When Alex got to Frank, the young man nodded but threw in a zinger. "I can't believe you held out on me, Alex. I mean, I *work* with you."

Alex kept a smile as he thought, *no, Frank, you work for me, and it was a mistake to ever involve you with Uroboros.* Instead, he said, "Sorry, mate. It was one of these need-to-know projects. You're going to like it though."

All told, three people declined: an ever-quiet MIT student from Korea, an architect whose wife was expecting a baby within a week and was constantly checking his iPhone for reports of the first signs of labor, and an anatomy instructor at Tufts Medical School who just couldn't get around his fear of taking an unknown drug.

Alex cheerfully recruited the nonparticipants into the ranks of caretakers and assigned them each two or three people to monitor.

Alex turned down the music while Jessie went around making sure all the candles were safely out of the way. Then, like a high priest delivering a sacred offering, he moved around the circle, letting people choose a thin straw of paper from the goblet.

"What do you do with it, Weller?" Spangler demanded, sniffing at the paper tube.

For everyone's benefit, Alex explained. "Untwist one end and let it out on your tongue. Be careful. There's only a tiny amount of crystals in each one. It's a little sour but not too bad. It'll mostly dissolve but swallow when the urge comes and the rest will go down."

No one wanted to go first. In the low light of flickering candles, all of them fiddled with their straws and watched what the others were doing.

Sam Rodriguez, fed up with the group indecision, piped up. "Screw it." He bit the end off of his blue straw and poured the crystals into his mouth. After he swallowed, he announced, "Tastes like a bad sour ball. Everyone who doesn't go now's a pussy." He crossed his arms and looked around the circle with attitude.

One by one the participants followed his lead, emptying their straws and swallowing. Jessie made the rounds with paper cups of cold water to wash away the sourness and the caretakers took their positions behind their charges. Alex whispered tenderly to Jessie that their turn would come later.

Alex would remember the next hour for the rest of his life.

Ever the scientist, he recorded as many details as he could but the task soon became overwhelming. With nine subjects there were too many time points, too many observations to jot down. Time to first eye-fluttering, to recumbency, pulse rates, respiratory rates, pupillary reactions, facial expressions, twitches; stray words, moans, and sighs. He also had to keep reassuring the three new caretakers that everything was okay, that the unresponsive people lying on the floor were doing fine, that everything was going well. The Korean caretaker started to cry and Jessie wound up spending more time reassuring her than watching her three charges—Gelb, his girlfriend Lilly, and Virginia, whose thick glasses miraculously stayed in place the entire time.

Alex was particularly interested in their faces, assiduously trying to read the shape of a mouth, lines on a brow, moistness of the eyes, what was happening inside their heads. Sam was smiling impishly most of the time. Erica looked peaceful but twitched with small, constant movements, like a puppy sleeping. Gelb wore a quizzical expression not terribly different from his usual demeanor. Lilly, nestled next to him, had tears streaming down her smooth cheeks. Virginia concerned him more than anyone else. Her pulse was racing at 140 and she was breathing fast and moaning loudly, not in pain but apparent pleasure. "Jesus," he whispered to Jessie half in jest, "I think Ginny's going to come!" Her visceral responses didn't fade in a climax, however; they remained intensely plateaued, and Alex nervously kept up with her vital signs. Forty minutes into the trip, he openly fretted about her persistent tachycardia. "I wish I could pull the plug on her, Jessie," he whispered. "This is too much for her. I'm getting worried."

Then, in just under an hour, one by one, they started coming out of it, blinking their way back to Alex's living room. He furiously tried to record their ending times and their reactions at the moment of awareness, all the while kneeling by Virginia and continuing to fuss over her. She was still far away but her pulse, though fast, wasn't thready; it remained strong and regular and her color was good.

Sam, first in, was first out. He awoke with a surprised look and tried to stand but his legs were rubbery and he planted himself back on the pillow. His wandering eyes searched out Alex, who would later tease him that the first words out of his mouth were wholly prosaic.

"Holy ... shit ... man. *Holy shit.*" Then the young man buried his face in his hands and his chest began to heave.

Jessie rushed to his side and rubbed his shoulders with the flat of her palm, softly saying, "I know, I know, I know."

Gelb was next. The man had a perpetually mischievous quality, like the cat who's just eaten the canary. He awoke with a shock and instinctively reached for Lilly, who was still asleep. "Lilly!" he cried. "Wake up! I was with my mother! Did you hear me, Lilly? My *mother* was there."

Alex went to him and took his hand. "Lilly will be back soon, Larry. Give her a few minutes."

"Christ, Alex, I've never, ever, in my whole life, experienced anything like this."

"I know, Larry. Here, have some water. We'll talk about it soon. Wait for Lilly. Be there for her when she wakes up."

Erica was next, sobbing joyously; then Spangler, looking dazed; then Frank, visibly trying to hold himself together and avoid a public show of emotion. Then Melissa Cornish, a young professor from Northeastern; Vik Pai, a grad student from Harvard Divinity School; and Steve Mahady, a science teacher from Boston. All except Virginia were conscious and the room was filled with these words: *Oh my God! Christ! My mother! My father! My brother! Did you see it? There was a river! It was amazing! I had no idea! Jesus, Alex!*

Virginia was the last one. As Jessie and the caretakers saw to the needs of the awakeners, Alex returned to her side and silently prayed she'd come back. And then, an hour and a quarter after her exposure, she roared back, thrashing and shouting like a Holy Roller about the glory of it all, the glory of God! Alex tightly wrapped her up in his arms, not because he felt close to her, but because he was scared she might flail about and hurt herself.

She was screaming, "Patty was there! Patty was there! She was with God, I'm sure of it! Oh my God! Oh my God!"

"I'm happy for you Ginny," Alex said. "Believe me, I am. Who's Patty? Tell me who she is, sweetheart."

"My sister! She's my twin sister! She's been gone for twenty-five years. Oh my God, she was calling me! Please let me go back there, Alex! You've got to help me!"

The woman was near hysteria and her shouts and physicality were disorienting everyone else in the room trying to come to grips with their own experiences. Alex had Jessie grab hold of her and frantically went hunting for his bottle of Christmas brandy, which he hadn't put back in its usual cupboard. When he found it he poured out several fingers and forced Virginia to drink it down in one go. She coughed and sprayed, protesting she didn't drink, but she held it in and measurably calmed.

The living room grew quieter. Some were mute, others spoke in small knots; and then Alex stood and spoke to them, hands deep in his pockets, his head slightly bowed. He suddenly felt tired. "Hi. Wow. This is something else, isn't it? I know you've just gone through some profound stuff and you may want to be on your own to reflect on it, but I think it's important for us to stay together for a while to compare notes, to talk about it. That's how we'll learn. That's how we'll become enlightened."

The stories began and as they circled the room, speaking in hushed tones and shedding tears, the weightiness of the night kept tipping the scales.

It was all the same.

Each and every one of them described the same journey down to the smallest details.

The only divergence was the man, woman, or child on the other side of the river of light. For Spangler, it was his brother, Phil, who'd died in Vietnam. For Sam, it was his father, killed in a mugging when Sam was a boy. For Gelb, it was his elderly mother, who'd died of a stroke fifteen years earlier. For Lilly, it was her grandmother, passed ten years now, in Taiwan. For Erica, it was her favorite aunt, who'd doted on her until her recent cancer death. For Davis, it was his granddad, Clark, the kindest man he'd ever known; and Virginia tearfully told everyone about her twin's long-ago plunge through an icy pond and the hurt she still felt every day of her life. All of them too talked about the same sensation: of something else out there beyond the limitless plain; something wonderful, something important.

Only Frank Sacco refused to speak, his lips as tight as an unshucked oyster, his posture cramped and uncomfortable. Alex passed over him gently, but he kept sneaking glances Frank's way for the rest of the evening, wondering what was going on behind the young man's diffident mask.

When the last of them had spoken Erica raised her head. "You know what that was? It was bliss ... pure bliss."

Amid murmurs of assent, Spangler stood up, his stiff knees audibly crackling. "For Christ's sake, Weller, I've pretty much been an atheist my entire adult life but do you know what I think?"

Alex shook his head and waited for Spangler to go on.

The man gruffly wiped the tears from the corners of his eyes. "I'm the last person on earth to say this, but I think tonight, right here, in this place, we've just proven that there's an afterlife."

21

Virginia Tinley had trouble getting her house keys from her pocketbook, her hands were shaking so. Once she negotiated the double locks she turned on the lights and went straight to her bedroom. She was a meticulous bed-maker: perfectly aligned peach bedspread, three rows of frilly pillows, and a stuffed moose that had been her twin's dearest childhood toy.

She had no concern what a man would think of a thirty-five year old with a stuffed animal on her bed because she'd never had one over. Not that she lacked desire—there were two partners in her law firm whom she quite fancied—rather, men didn't appear to be attracted to her. She'd long since stopped worrying about that though, instead filling her life with things that made her happy: books, films, her annual holiday to St. Barts, and this weirdly wonderful Uroboros Society that gave her a pathway to explore her spiritual side.

She'd surprised herself by agreeing to take Alex's drug. Every time he'd offer up a chemical substance for the group she'd taken a pass, even on marijuana. She didn't like the feeling of being high and would become paranoid about getting into trouble, losing her bar license and her job. Yet something about the wild look of excitement in Alex's eyes made her throw caution to the wind that night. She had a deep feeling about these crystals of his, and though it was definitely un-Ginnylike, she had, in the end, opened her mouth and sprinkled them in.

Now she kicked off her shoes, slid across the bed and nestled among the pillows, drawing the plush moose to her chest. It smelled of age and childhood, the smells she remembered of her sister. Her glasses were still on. She removed them and carelessly tossed them toward the foot of the bed. They bounced off but she didn't care.

When she closed her eyes she was back, emerging from the tunnel onto the green plain and walking expectantly toward the sounds of the river. The joy of it! The rapture! Her body shuddered; and when she replayed the vision of her perfect little sister, close across the river, the feelings of pleasure became so intense they began to hurt.

Patty!

There she was! A happy ten year old, jumping up and down on the riverbank as though it were Christmas morning, exuberantly waving at Ginny with both arms. She looked as fresh and pretty as the day she fell through the ice, never to return.

Virginia opened her eyes and was back in her bedroom. She thought she was going to cry again but she didn't. Instead she sat up and started to undress and when she was naked she started to run a bath. She added bubbles and watched them froth.

She never walked naked around her flat even when alone, but she did this time and made herself an herbal tea while the bathtub filled.

She carefully stepped into the water and slowly submerged herself to the neck before lifting her arm above the bubbles for the teacup she'd placed on the side of the tub.

She smiled. Perfect pleasure: the hot soapy water, the zesty orange tea, the visions of her beaming sister. For the first time in her life she felt completely happy.

A kitchen paring knife was beside the teacup. She grasped it and without a moment's hesitation made a deep cut through her wrist until blood came out under pressure. She let her wrist sink and the bubbles quickly turned pink.

It didn't hurt.

It felt wonderful.

"I'm coming, Patty," she said. "I'm coming."

22

"She doesn't want any more chemo. I don't want her to go through another course," Marian said stubbornly.

Cyrus squeezed the telephone as if it were Marian's neck. He tried to modulate his voice. If he blew up, she'd blow up and the conversation would be over. "But you said her MRI looked worse."

The astrocytoma was growing again, resistant to the drugs.

"We've gone through this before, Cyrus. They've got nothing else for her."

"There's new things every day. You're the Internet expert. Aren't your goddamn brain cancer blogs talking about new things?"

"There's nothing left," she said. She started crying with the intensity of a burst dam. "Why can't you understand that ... There's nothing left!"

With that she hung up, beating him to the punch.

He stared at the phone and returned it to the cradle. Severe sunlight was pouring through his office windows; he had zero interest in seeing the cold blue sky so he louvered all the shades closed.

The files on the head drillings sat untouched on his desk. The case wasn't cold, but it was cooling. He had nothing on Alex Weller beyond deep suspicion. A string of bank robberies on the South Shore had risen to the top of his pile. Unfortunately, he and Avakian had to interview a bank manager in an hour. He'd have to try to tuck Tara away into a place in his mind that allowed him to keep functioning.

He didn't feel good about it but what else was he supposed to do? Shut down, take a medical leave, sit in his rotten apartment and get drunk at noon with a book in his lap?

Alex had spent the day after the Uroboros salon in a state of giddiness bordering on agitation. The Sunday paper was left in its plastic wrapper. He and Jessie hardly ate. When they tired of rehashing the events of the previous night Jessie had begged Alex to let her take one of the remaining straws. As he watched over her, he furiously jotted more notes into one of his bound lab notebooks. There needed to be a record, a scientific record of what had happened the previous night.

Someday, he thought, looking at Jessie's flickering eyelids, people will look back on that Saturday night in Cambridge, Massachusetts, as one of the great days in human history. He'd caught himself at that notion and snorted at its pomposity; but then again, was it really that grandiose?

Mankind had been obsessed with concepts of life after death since the dawn of history and probably earlier. Despite the greatest Western philosophers—Aquinas, Descartes, Leibniz, Kant, Hegel—the only "proof" of the existence of God rested upon clever arguments printed on paper. If you were a believer, that belief welled up from cultural and religious springs, certainly not from empiricism.

Saturday night changed all that, hadn't it? How else could a rational mind reconcile that a group of dissimilar men and women with such vastly differing belief systems all shared a common—no, a nearly *identical*—experience under the influence of a drug derived from the human brain at the moment of death?

Yet, amid the heady excitement, he'd been troubled by something and now, on Monday morning, he was still troubled. As his lab buzzed with activity, he sequestered himself in his office, hunched over, sorting through online science journals, copiously writing notes, jotting down references, ideas.

Why was the afterlife experience more intense with the natural chemical? No one who took the synthetic compound had gotten beyond the midpoint of the river. Why? And why was his and Jessie's perception of a Godly presence so much more vivid with the natural substance? And the bliss, to use Erica's word—why had the bliss they'd felt been even greater?

He kept coming back to Miguel Cifuentes' comments about isomers. The answer, he thought, had to lie there. Cifuentes had taken his best guess about the most likely of a dozen or more isomers of the peptide based on nothing more than physical chemistry and probability. He could have chosen the wrong one. Or perhaps it was even more complicated. What if the brain in the throes of death produced a mixture of isomers?

The telephone interrupted his train of thought. He looked at it with irritation, was going to let it ring through to voice mail, then noticed the caller ID and responded, "Davis, how are you?"

Davis Fox sounded upset. "Alex, have you heard?"

"Heard what?"

"Ginny's dead!"

Alex sucked in hard. "What happened?"

"Erica called me. She found out from Liam. She slit her wrists. A friend of hers, not one of us, found her last night when she couldn't get through. Christ, Alex, are you thinking what I'm thinking?"

"That it was the drug?"

"Yeah."

Alex's mind raced. He couldn't shake the déjà vu. In retrospect, he'd expected it; it was almost as if he knew it had already occurred. He avoided Davis's question. "Who else knows? In Uroboros?"

"I'm not sure. I'll call around if you want me to."

"Do it. Then phone me back."

Davis didn't hang up right away. He clearly wanted to say something else. "Alex, I haven't been able to stop thinking about Saturday night. Maybe Ginny did the right thing."

Alex grunted a nonresponse, hung up, and grabbed his coat. It was too stuffy. He had to take a walk, do some thinking in the cold air. His Chinese postdocs smiled at him as he strode through the lab. Frank Sacco furtively looked up then buried his head back in his work. He'd avoided Alex all morning just as he'd done on Saturday night, when he'd slinked off without a word.

Alex did a few circuits of the quad, his hiking boots grinding into the granular ice melt. Before Saturday, he hadn't given Ginny two thoughts. She was bright enough, he supposed, but boring, a milquetoast. She wasn't well-read in the fields that interested him and rarely added anything meaningful to the group's conversations. Her only compelling attribute was that she was a card-carrying member of the near death society. Her NDE was a "good one." It gave her credibility.

Ginny. *A suicide!*

He'd been riveted by her exaggerated reaction to the drug. She was an outlier, and in science one learned from outliers. She'd been out longer than the others, was wilder when she returned, half crazed. She desperately wanted to go back to her twin. She'd begged him.

Now she's gone and done it, he thought, *she's bloody well gone and done it.* He sighed and thought back to the moments he'd spent holding a sharp letter opener, contemplating doing precisely what she had done.

He kept walking until the rims of his ears were numb from wind chill. Back in his cramped office he sat down, his body heavy and wooden. There was so much to do: so many questions, so many experiments. He'd get busy in the evening when the lab cleared out—away from prying eyes. He'd come to enjoy night work.

His knuckles skimmed the spine of his lab notebook, which he'd carelessly left out in the open. There was an old coffee mug in his credenza filled with rubber bands. He tipped it out and retrieved the little brass key hidden among them. The key opened the lower locking drawer of his desk. When he deposited the notebook he saw it was missing.

The bottle of peptide—gone!

In a frenzy, he searched the drawer, then his desk, then his office. He felt his throat tighten. It *had* to be here! No one else knew about it. No one had a key. That bottle had been there Saturday morning when he'd come in to weigh out individual doses for the salon later that evening. He was absolutely certain he'd returned it and locked the drawer. He'd been more than careful. He'd been paranoid about it, as he had been about everything since he'd drifted to murder. He tried to control his breathing while he searched the office again.

Then it slammed him. *Frank.*

Who else but Frank?

He had access. Since Saturday he knew about the drug. Moreover, he'd been acting strangely all morning. Alex opened the door and called the young man in, trying to sound as matter-of-fact as his dry voice would allow.

"What's up, Alex?" Frank asked, looking down at his shoes.

"Something's missing from my office. Know anything about it?"

"Missing? What?" Frank asked defensively.

"Never mind what. Have you been in my office?"

"No."

"Have you been in my desk?"

"No!"

"Were you in the lab yesterday?"

"No! What are you accusing me of, Alex?"

"If you're lying, Frank, so help me God …"

"I'm not lying. Can I go now?"

Alex stared at the man even though he was refusing eye contact. "Let me ask you something, Frank. On Saturday night, everyone spoke except you. What was your experience like?"

"It was good."

"Good?"

"Yeah, same as everyone else. Pretty much like the others."

"Ginny Tinley's dead. She killed herself."

Frank finally looked at Alex square on. "No shit."

"Yeah, Frank. No shit."

"Can I go? It's lunchtime."

Alex made two phone calls. The first was to the security desk in the lobby. He asked the guard on duty if she could check the log to see if one of his employees had come in on Sunday. The guard replied that she didn't have logon access to the weekend data. She'd call her supervisor if Dr. Weller wanted to see if he could help. Alex recoiled at the suggestion. He had no interest in drawing attention. No, he replied, she could drop it. It wasn't important.

The second call was long distance.

The resonant voice of Miguel Cifuentes was on the line. "Alex Weller! Happy New Year!"

"You too, Miguel, how's life back home, mate?"

They chatted for a couple of minutes, Alex struggling through the banalities. Finally, he asked how close he was to having his lab set up in Mexico City.

"I'm already up and running. Why?"

"You know the pentapeptide you made me?"

"Sure."

"I'm going to need more of it. Right away."

"How much more, my friend?"

Alex pursed his lips then said, "All you can make."

23

The next one was the easiest.

This time Alex had no internal debate about right and wrong, good and evil. He was on a mission. He had the validation he needed to wash away sticky moral qualms. He awoke every morning with a mounting sense that he was at the center of greatness. Standing like Faustus in his magic circle, he felt that another world was being revealed to him, a confluence of science, faith, religion and philosophy. Grand ideas, giant visions dwarfed a small, single life. And besides, there was no doubt, none whatsoever, that his victim would thank him if she knew what lay in store for her a mere four minutes after her heart stopped beating.

The girl was sleepy from drugs and kept nodding off in the car. He asked her how old she was. She said eighteen but she looked younger. He hoped she was. In his garage, when he got back in the car after closing the door, her eyes were closed, her chin on her chest. He didn't wake her. As soon as he put on his gloves he strangled her. His technique had improved and maybe his hand strength too. She had the most spindly neck of any of them. Her struggles were light and she went down fast. He laid her down beside the car, got his samples then put her in his polythene-lined trunk and drove off.

When he backed out of the driveway he looked up at their bedroom window. The lights were off. Jessie was there, dreaming. He was tired. He wished he was curled against her. She was a lovely sleeper.

This time he paid more attention to the disposal. He didn't want to deal with Cyrus O'Malley again. There were more important things to do. This girl would have to stay hidden longer.

He drove south into Rhode Island. His plan drew on his memory of a beach walk he and Jessie had taken two Novembers earlier. Isolated seasonal cottages in Narragansett, dolefully shuttered for the winter. In the dark, he found a cottage cluster, chose one and forced a door. With plastic bags rubber-banded around his feet to avoid footprints, he dragged the girl's body into a bedroom and shoved it under a stripped bed where it would freeze. No odors till the spring. Spring was a long way off.

When he pushed himself off the cold floorboards some loose change in his pants spilled out. He swore repeatedly and went groping for the coins in the dark. After a minute of feeling around and under the bed, he was well enough satisfied he'd recovered them all. He shut the door behind him. He had to get back to his lab and process her fluid. Numerous experiments were planned to test for isomers of the Uroboros compound—and if any was left over, he wanted it for himself.

Days later, his purifications and analyses were done. He had his answer.

The sleepy girl's Uroboros compound was a mixture of no fewer than six isomers! Only one of them was Miguel's; nature was proving to be complex. The dying brain was producing an array of pentapeptides, similar to one another but subtly different. Perhaps more than one key fit into the lock of his LR-1 receptor—or maybe there were multiple variants of the LR-1 receptor, each unlocked by a specific key. He wearily came to the conclusion that it might take years to fully understand the biology.

Foremost on his mind, though, was to sample this girl's pure, natural compound. The sleepy girl was the youngest yet. After the experiments were done, enough was left over for a single dose, and one night he eagerly took it under Jessie's watchful eye.

This time he got to the *last* stepping-stone!

Dickie was only an arm's length away when Alex was snatched back into the tunnel. He'd been close enough to see the pink flush of his cheeks, the stubble of his beard. He was agonizingly close to physical contact! And despite the heartbreak of the final denial, he felt utter joy when he returned. It was, he told Jessie, the most profound euphoria he'd ever felt. Something powerful and pure was out there, waiting for him.

When he'd talked himself out and was thoroughly spent he happily fell asleep in Jessie's arms.

The following evening he was at Children's Hospital, stealing through the semidark corridors of the neuro ward at midnight. He went there directly from his lab, fast-walking the few blocks in the frigid air. He was careful and deliberative. To be safe, he slipped out the rear of his building at the loading dock exit and planned to return the same way. If all went well, he'd be back at his bench processing a precious sample within the hour.

This time there'd be no body to dispose.

He didn't have to go past the nurse's station to reach Paulo's room. The corridor was deserted. He quietly pushed open the door.

Paulo Couto was a four year old with a large inoperable brain tumor. He was Brazilian, born to undocumented parents who waited too long to get the kid attention. At this point, all the doctors could do was to throw on some radiation, high-dose steroids for brain swelling, and antiseizure meds. The neurosurgeons were running the show. Alex was the neurology consult. The epilepsy drugs he prescribed were working as well as could be expected but it was window dressing. The child didn't have much time.

The latest maneuver was to plant a VP shunt to drain the buildup of fluid from his brain into his abdomen to prevent coma and death. The shunt would buy days, maybe weeks.

Alex gently palpated the rigid plastic tube that lay just under the skin. It ran from his neck along the chest wall. Below the diaphragm it plunged into the peritoneum. When he felt the soft belly, the boy woke up and blinked in confusion.

"Hey, Paulo. How're you doing?"

The boy smiled and pointed at Alex's ponytail. Kids liked his long hair and funny accent. Obligingly, he shook his head, making his ponytail sway like a horse's tail.

"Just checking on you, buddy. Go back to sleep."

The child fidgeted a little and drifted off again.

The door was closed.

None of the night nurses had seen Alex come onto the floor.

He had a syringe in his pocket.

Three minutes.

He studied the boy's steroid-bloated face.

It would be so easy to press his large hand against his mouth, pinching his nose.

At three minutes he would stick a thin needle into the shunt tubing, taking a few cc's of clear cerebrospinal fluid. It would leave a pinprick mark on the skin, unnoticeable.

The boy wasn't on a monitor.

He'd be found at the next vital signs check.

There was a Do Not Resuscitate order in his chart.

Phone calls would be made; it would be a peaceful end, a good end. His parents would pray and say he was in a better place.

They'd be right.

Jessie was at a girlfriend's house and Alex was alone.

He washed up the dinner plates and tidied the kitchen before opening the fridge and retrieving the plastic tube he'd brought home from the lab.

In the bedroom, he kicked off his shoes and reclined. The tube was cold in his palm.

Everything had gone smoothly. Alex received a courtesy call from the hospital the following morning informing him that Paulo Couto had died during the night. An expected death.

He was done. This would be his last experiment before moving on to the next phase. Tonight he'd answer the last great question.

What would the experience be like with the natural pentapeptide from a child?

He'd taken the Uroboros compound so many times he had no trepidation about being alone, but in case something went wrong he penned a short tender note to Jessie that he left on the dresser.

He emptied the tube into his mouth and waited. He'd have his answer …

… And soon he was standing on the bank of the river of light watching his father, Dickie, waving at him, and noticed too how smoothly confident were his strides across the stepping-stones. With every step the pleasure mounted.

Four stones to go. Three. Two. He stood squarely on the last stone, an arm's length from his father. "Come on boy!" Dickie urged. "Only one to go, then you're here. You can do it!"

His heart exploded with joy when he felt himself pushing off with his right foot.

His left foot touched the opposite bank!

Then both feet!

He was there!

And then his arms were around his father's neck. It was warm, full of blood. He heard his father say, "Hello, boy."

There was someone behind Dickie.

He couldn't see who it was, but he *felt* a presence, an overwhelming power.

His father was about to encircle him with his arms when—

He was wrenched away, literally snatched from his father's loving grasp and hurtled back, back into the tunnel, back into his bedroom.

It happened so fast, this passage from one world to the next. The cruelty of the return stung his eyes.

Tears started to spring from the deepest well of his soul. And when Jessie came home an hour later he was still holding onto himself, rocking himself, crying.

24

A party was getting under way in a residential loft off Kenmore Square a short distance from Fenway Park. The hosts were an Australian couple, commercial artists celebrating a contract their small company had landed to do ad work for a software company. Throngs of friends and business associates milled around their cavernous space on the fifth floor of what once had been a paint factory.

Loud music bounced off the walls and throbbing subwoofers sent impact tremors through the old floorboards. By 11 P.M., the loft was packed. Scores of urbanites pressed up against the banqueting table sampling platters of food and bowls labeled SHEEP DIP. They filled their glasses with an inexhaustible supply of Fosters and Australian whites. The room undulated with disinhibited dancing bodies.

The hostess stretched on her toes and shouted into her husband's ear that she didn't recognize a lot of the people. He shouted something back but she made a sign she couldn't hear him. He cupped his hands and boomed again, "I don't care!"

A slim young woman in a minidress was dancing by herself in front of a large industrial window flanked by two potted palms. She had commandeered her own bottle of wine and interrupted her steps every so often to take a swig directly from it. When she threw her head back her long black hair touched her waist.

A young man spent several minutes watching her. The beat of the music and the foliage surrounding her made it look like he was stalking prey in the jungle. Unnoticed, he edged himself within striking distance then made his move by extending his empty glass. She looked at him in a soft unfocused sort of way, wiped the top of the bottle with her thumb then poured until the glass overflowed. Laughing, he pulled it away and took three large gulps. He reextended his arm and she poured again. Soon they were dancing in and out of the palm trees and he was trying to plant a kiss through the fronds.

"What's your name?" he shouted to her.

"Jennifer. What's yours?"

"William—let's find someplace quieter!" he yelled.

He took her by the hand and pulled her through the crowd. They explored the perimeter of the loft, trying doors until they found a bedroom. The bed was stacked with coats. He locked the door behind them and because he was muscular he was able to lift her up in the air as if she were a small child and toss her onto the coat mountain. Over the muffled music he heard her dissolve into giggles. He dove on top of her, stripped her bare from the waist down and the two of them burrowed into the coats like gophers.

Minutes later, an arm popped out then a leg. "That was fun!" she said giddily.

"Want to have more fun?" he asked.

"Sure. How?"

"A friend of mine gave me something new to try."

"A drug?"

"Yeah."

"What's it called?"

"Bliss, I think."

That set her off laughing again. "Who doesn't like a little bliss? What's it do?"

"It's supposed to give you some kind of spiritual high. Like a very mellow acid. He told me it was the best trip he ever had. I've been waiting for the right occasion. How 'bout it?"

A saucy head whip sent her hair flying. "Yeah, sure. Anything once."

He still had his suit jacket on and pulled out two thin red straws of red paper. After finding his half-full wineglass on the floor by the bed, he spilled the contents of both straws into the glass and swirled it around. "Let's share," he said.

They each drank half and settled back into the coats.

"How long does it take?" she asked.

"I forgot to ask."

"Are you friends with the Gibbons?" she asked.

"Who're they?"

"The people throwing the party!"

"No. I came with a guy who knows them. What about you?"

"I did a summer internship with their company last year, in between my first and second year at RISD."

"What's RISD?"

"Rhode Island School of Design."

"You're an artist?"

"I want to be one."

"Cool," he said. "That's really cool."

"What's your name?" she asked.

"William. William Treblehorn."

"Not Bill or Billy or Will or Willy?" she asked playfully, poking his chest.

"Nope. William."

"Then you're not allowed to call me Jenny. It's Jennifer to you."

They talked and played with each other awhile longer until both of them nodded off.

Outside the bedroom door a knot of people congregated in animated discussion. A man kept jiggling the doorknob and banging on the door with the heel of his hand.

Finally, he said, "Someone's probably passed out drunk in there."

"Well, I need my coat."

"It's after one-thirty. I've got to go."

"I'll see if Bernie has the key."

The host was dragged to the door and tried it himself. "I don't know where the bloody key is. We never lock it," he said, swooning with drink. "I'll see if Nan knows where the heck we keep it."

A minute later he returned with Nan, who was swaying herself and proudly displaying a key.

"She's the best damn wife a bloke could have," her husband declared. He fumbled with the lock and flung open the door.

A blast of cold air hit him full on. The industrial-sized window beside the bed had been pulled open. The wind was howling through. The icy blast momentarily forced him to shut his eyes.

He blinked a few times then cried out, "Bloody hell!"

A young man was standing by the window completely naked. He was staring out with a wild look in his eyes, his blond hair blowing straight back. He turned at Bernie's voice and faced the people who were poking their heads into the room.

"What the hell is going on in here?" Bernard demanded.

William sank to his knees sobbing. "I saw my grandfather! I saw him!"

"Course you did, me old fruit. Let's find your clothes then get you the hell out of my house. Will someone help me find this bloke's clothes?"

"She saw someone too!" he cried.

"Who did?"

"Her name was Jennifer. She said God was there!"

"Okay, steady on. Where's Jennifer?"

"She said she wanted to be there forever."

"Fine, fine." The fellow looking for his clothes signaled he couldn't find them. "If you can't find his things then just chuck over a coat, will you, mate?" Bernie said. "I can't have a naked man about. Now where did you say Jennifer is?"

"Down there."

"What do ya mean, down there?"

The young man pointed.

The host began sobering up as he crept to the window. He reluctantly stuck his head out and beneath him, clearly illuminated by a streetlight was the naked body of a woman with long black hair surrounded by a spreading pool of blood.

25

Frank Sacco was a regular at the Seagull Lounge on Revere Beach Boulevard. In the summer it was a cheerful kind of place where locals mixed with sandy day trippers, a joint where you could score a decent bowl of chowder with your beer. In the winter, though, it was a dark, depressing dive for hard-drinking townies who weren't much interested in soup.

Frank's cousin, Stevie, worked there and when he was behind the bar Frank got plugged into a buy-one-get-one-free mode. As the evening progressed, Frank got happier and expansive, flashing a fat roll of cash, buying rounds for the entire place.

"What's with you?" his cousin asked, pushing another shot of Canadian Frank's way.

"Just feeling good, Stevie," Frank replied, slurring his words. "It's all good."

Stevie pointed at the roll in Frank's fist. "Yeah? You come into money?"

"I got a little business on the side."

The bartender looked over at one of the occupied booths. "That's cool, but stash the cash. Don't be looking for trouble."

Frank peeled off a few twenties, dropped them on the bar and said, "This is for you, man. You're a fucking good guy."

His cousin tried to give the money back but the bills slid back and forth on the beer-splashed wood until Frank won and Stevie reluctantly took them and said, "I'll put this in my pocket if you put yours away too."

Frank agreed and called for another round.

The scene was playing out in front of two regulars. John Abruzzi and Mario Fortunelli had spotted Frank's kielbasa-sized bill roll. Abruzzi, a brawny guy in a cashmere pullover, had been to the barber and in between sips of beer moodily plucked bits of hair from the inside of his collar. With mounting curiosity he approached Frank and clapped him on back. "Hey, Frankie, what's going on?"

Frank grinned back. "Not much, man."

"Last time someone bought a round in this bar, there was a wake."

"No one's dead this time," Frank replied.

Over Stevie's suspicious glances Abruzzi invited Frank back to his booth and told the pimply Fortunelli to slide over. Even though they were young guys, not much more than a few steps removed from their days as street punks, there was a pecking order between them that Fortunelli understood. Abruzzi's uncle was a ranking member of the local Colombo crew. Fortunelli had no such connections.

"How're you doing, Frankie?" Fortunelli asked. He'd gone to high school with Frank but they hadn't exactly been friends. In fact, Frank had been scared of the kid's reputation as a crazy-ass.

"I'm good, man. How're you?"

"Can't complain," Fortunelli answered.

"Hell you can't!" Abruzzi laughed. "Alls he does is bitch and moan like a whiny little bitch."

Fortunelli came back with a weak "Yeah, right!" then clammed up.

Abruzzi leaned across the table and lowered his voice. "So Frankie, you look like you've been doing all right. You still working in a lab or something?"

"Yeah, still a tech over at Harvard Med."

"Don't you love the sound of that, Mario?" Abruzzi said, picking another hair off his neck. "Frankie's at Harvard. So how come a guy busting ass as a nine to fiver's got enough cash to sink a fuckin' battleship?"

Frank was too drunk to notice the iciness that had crept into Abruzzi's voice. Abruzzi was only a few years older than Frank but thanks to cockiness and size it seemed as though they were separated by a generation. "I've got a side business," Frank whispered.

"Oh yeah? What kind of business?" Abruzzi asked.

Frank looked across the table blearily and slurred, "B'lieve it or not, I was thinking about talking to you guys because, t' be honest, I've taken this about as far as I can. Maybe you can help me."

Fortunelli began to snigger but a dirty look from Abruzzi shut him up. "Yeah, maybe we can. What's this involve?"

"Drugs," Frank whispered again.

"We're familiar with drugs," Abruzzi quipped. "Which ones in particular?"

"None you've heard of," Frank said.

Fortunelli couldn't contain himself. "C'mon, Frankie. John's like the motherfucking Physician's Desk Reference. He's got it covered."

"Yeah," Abruzzi agreed. "I've got an advanced degree in that shit."

"It's called Bliss," Frank said. "Heard of that?" At their shrugs he added smugly, "Didn't think so."

"So, what is it?" Abruzzi said.

"It's a designer drug. My boss invented it. He's wicked smart."

"What's it do?"

Frank smiled. "It takes you to God, man."

"God?" Abruzzi asked. "As in Jesus Frickin' Christ?"

Frank nodded.

"You're such a bullshitter," Fortunelli jeered.

"Okay," Frank said, getting steamed. "Whatever you say I am, I am. See you around, Mario."

Abruzzi settled Frank down by telling Mario he'd bust his mouth if he opened it again. "Seriously," he asked Frank. "What's the high like?"

"It's like nothing in this world, man," Frank said, suddenly drifting to another place. "I've seen stuff … All I can say is, it's the best thing ever happened t' me and I'm not the only one. Everyone who takes it freaks out but in a good way, in a very good way, man."

Abruzzi looked interested. "So what are the economics?"

Frank glanced around the bar. "Izzit okay if we don't talk about it here?"

"Yeah sure," Abruzzi agreed. "Where? When?"

"I gotta meet a guy," Frank said. "How 'bout you guys come over t' my place, like midnight."

"Midnight it is," Abruzzi replied, slapping a few bills down on the table. "Save a couple of hits for your buddies. We may want to try this shit."

A solitary man gingerly walked up Huntington Avenue in the Jamaica Plain section of Boston. A wintry mix of sleet and snow earlier in the evening had turned the inclined sidewalk into a bobsled course. One of the last Arborway trolleys of the night squealed past him, headed inbound to Park Street. It started to sleet again and the man raised the hood on his sweatshirt over his head.

He crossed the road stepping over the trolley tracks and looked behind him to make sure he wasn't being followed. Then he made a beeline to one of the darkened doorways of one of the squat brick apartment buildings and slipped inside. He pushed a buzzer and almost immediately was buzzed in. The interior door unlocked and he sprang up two flights of stairs and knocked on one of the doors.

"Is that you, Jimmy?" a muffled voice called out.

"Yeah, it's me."

Both men were jittery. Jimmy, a hatchet-faced young man with the small edgy movements of a greyhound looked around the dimly lit flat. It was decorated retro sixties with batik on the walls, paper lanterns, and tatami mats.

"This place reminds me of a museum. Did I ever tell you that?"

"Every time you're here. What do you have for me?" The other man was heavyset, with an untucked shirt and an unruly beard.

"My usual supplier let me down this week, know what I mean?"

"C'mon. You don't have any grass?"

"Nada. I'll be restocked next week."

"Acid?"

"I haven't seen the guy who gets it for me. He must've moved away. But don't worry, man, I got something for you."

"I don't want other stuff."

"What I've got is brand new."

"What does it do?"

"It's supposed to give you some kind of amazing trip. My guy told me it's totally insane."

"What's it called?"

"Man, it's so new it doesn't even have a name. No, I'm wrong. This guy Frankie said it's called Bliss."

"Have you tried it?"

"I told you before. Drugs don't agree with me. I just sell them."

"How much is it?"

"Seventy-five bucks a hit."

"No effin' way, Jimmy! I'm not giving you seventy-five bucks for something I never heard of. Take off."

Jimmy grinned. "Yeah, you're right. It's expensive shit. I'm going to give you a deal since it's new. I'll give you the first hit free if you buy the second for my ask. And if you think you got ripped off, I'll take twenty off your next grass buy. How's that?"

"You're a businessman, Jimmy."

Jimmy took two red paper sticks out of his sweatshirt pocket and dangled them in front of his customer, who reluctantly reached for his wallet.

"I hope you like it, man. If you do, tell your friends."

Frank Sacco lived on the top floor of a Revere triple-decker in an apartment that had been his grandfather's. He'd purged it of most of the old-man stuff, replacing the lumpy sofa and armchairs with smooth black leather gear and dumping the old cathode-ray TV for a skinny LCD. He'd kept the heavy bedroom furniture, though, and every time he pulled open one of the dresser drawers he got a whiff of Grandpa Sal.

The sock drawer was where he kept Alex's bottle of Bliss. Under his t-shirts were stacks of cash. He retrieved the bottle and returned to the living room where Abruzzi and Fortunelli were sprawled on the sofa, wet shoes on the coffee table.

"Here it is," Frank said proudly.

Abruzzi took the bottle, opened it, and sniffed at the white crystals. "So how'd you get this?" he asked.

Frank threw back some beer. "I know where my boss keeps his keys. He's pissed off but he'll make more."

"He doesn't suspect you?"

"Maybe he does, maybe he doesn't. I don't give a shit. He's got no proof."

Abruzzi rescrewed the top and passed it to Fortunelli, who repeated the sniff maneuver and shrugged his shoulders at the lack of odor.

"So, take me through the economics," Abruzzi asked.

Frank put down his beer and took the bottle back. "There's eight grams of Bliss in here," he said. "That's eight thousand milligrams and the dose is half a milligram, like a really tiny amount. So, in this bottle I've got sixteen thousand hits." He reached into his shirt pocket and pulled out four red straws. "This is how I package them, in Christmas paper with some sugar to sweeten the sour taste. That was my idea. It's like a brand. People like that. I've been selling it through some guy I know but he's nothing, a punk. That's why I'm talking to you."

Abruzzi took one of the straws. "How much per unit?"

"I'm selling them for fifty bucks. I hear they're getting marked up to seventy-five, maybe a hundred on the street."

Fortunelli whistled but his partner dismissed him with a wave. "Okay, Mario, you fuckin' Einstein, how much is this bottle of shit worth wholesale, at fifty bucks a pop?"

Fortunelli furrowed his brow then smiled. "Eighty grand."

"You're such a dumb shit, Mario. It's eight *hundred* grand! This bottle of Frankie's is worth the better part of a million bucks! And if it's so great, you could double the price, right? So, Frankie, tell me what makes this shit so great?"

Frank took a deep breath and began describing his Bliss trips. He didn't seem to care that Fortunelli was making faces the way he'd done in the back row of English class whenever they had to read literature. Abruzzi was paying attention, hanging on his words.

Yet when Frank began to talk about seeing a solitary figure waiting for him on the other side of a shimmering river he had to stop abruptly. His lip quivered and he fought off tears, clearly ashamed to be weeping in front of a couple of tough guys from the neighborhood.

"So who was it?" Abruzzi pressed. "Did you recognize the guy?"

"Yeah, I knew him."

"Spit it out!"

"It was Kenny Longo."

"What the fuck!" Fortunelli exclaimed, suddenly interested in the story. "The kid you killed?"

"It was an accident!" Frank shouted. "He was my best friend!"

Two thirteen year olds in a basement, shooting with air pistols at a cardboard box. Horseplay. Waving of arms. A *thwock* as a puff of compressed gas was released; then a *snap*, like the sound of a pellet hitting a piece of wood. Only it wasn't wood. It was Kenny's skull bone. The kid dropped to his knees and wordlessly died.

It was Kenny on the other side waving at Frank, looking as young and fresh as the day he bled out on the basement floor. To Frank's relief, Kenny wasn't the least bit mad at him, in fact he seemed ecstatic to see his old chum and called out in a high-pitched boyish voice. "Frankie! Hey, Frankie, come on! You can make it!"

And when Frank finally recounted the experience to the two men on the sofa—something he'd been unwilling to do in front of Alex or the high-minded farts in the salon—he lost it and began to bawl as he'd done years earlier, standing at the curb while paramedics took Kenny's lifeless body away.

Fortunelli, disgusted at the emotional display, got up from the sofa to fetch another beer from the fridge. Abruzzi urged Frank to calm down. There was no empathy in his voice, just an urgency to extract more info.

"So I hear you, Frankie, but tell me this. You seem all broken up. I thought you said that people like this shit."

"They do. I do. I'm crying, right, but I'm not hurting, if you know what I mean. It's the opposite. It's the greatest thing that's ever happened to me. Kenny's there. I always thought he'd be angry at me but he wasn't. There's a heaven, man. I've seen it."

Abruzzi nodded. "I'm glad to hear you're so passionate about this shit, Frankie. It's a terrific testimonial but I'm like a few moves on the chessboard ahead of you. I'm thinking about the business angles. The economics of what's in this bottle's making me weep too. Tears of joy, like you. But then what? How do we get more of it?"

"Almost no one knows about it yet. My boss had a chemist make it. From what I know I don't think it's going to be that hard to make more. There's probably lots of chemists who can pull it off."

"Do you know what goes in it?"

"You mean the formula?" Frank asked.

"Yeah, the formula."

"No, my boss won't show anyone but any good peptide chemist can figure it out from the powder."

Abruzzi looked around for a pen, tore off a corner of a magazine page and asked Frank to spell peptide chemist for him. When he was done he asked, "So you want to do business with us, Frankie?"

"Yeah. There's a lot of potential. To be honest, I'd rather take the drug than sell it."

"What do you think a fair split would be?"

Frank wiped his eyes dry with his sleeve. "I don't know, fifty-fifty?"

"You think that's fair?"

"I don't know. Sixty for you, forty for me?"

Abruzzi laughed. "Frankie, you're negotiating against yourself. You're crap at business."

"I know I am."

"So I'm going to give you a quick lesson in how I negotiate. You ready? I'm going to take a hundred points and give you zero points."

Frank looked confused. "But ..."

"Shhh," Abruzzi said, putting his finger against his lip. He winked at Fortunelli, who was still standing, slurping from a can of beer. "You don't like that deal?"

Frankie began to smile as if poised to absorb a practical lesson being delivered with humor.

Abruzzi smiled too. "Good. I'm glad to see you're happy."

Fortunelli was gliding behind Frank's chair. A second later there was a *crack* and the room misted with blood and smelled of gunpowder.

Frank lurched forward, glanced off the coffee table and hit the floor hard.

Rising to his feet, Abruzzi shoved the bottle of Bliss into his coat pocket and smirked. "Say hello to Kenny Longo for us, okay?"

26

Cyrus was on the Mass Pike driving to work, his mind dulled in commuter mode. WBZ Radio was airing more stories about the William Treblehorn case. Even though the event was still fresh, Cyrus was already tired of it. Rich kids behaving badly ... drugs ... a death. Suicide? Accident? Murder? He was glad it wasn't his problem.

William Treblehorn had been arrested, held overnight then released. Treblehorn's father was a big-time corporate lawyer. The family was *uber* connected and papa assembled a dream team to represent the kid before the sun rose. The investigating detectives immediately disliked the preppy blonde and harbored suspicions but could find no hard evidence to refute Treblehorn's assertion that Jennifer Sheridan had taken her own life during some sort of bad trip.

Treblehorn was dazed yet freely admitted he gave her a dose of something called Bliss. The assistant district attorney assigned to the case had a problem. She'd never heard of the drug and could find nothing in any online databases or unofficial drug sites to help her out. If it wasn't a controlled substance, it wasn't illegal. She considered filing reckless endangerment charges but tucked the notion away for another day pending further investigation.

Treblehorn, led by a phalanx of lawyers, walked out the front door of the police station the next morning shielding his face from the crush of media surging toward him. He ignored their shouted questions and concentrated on the only thing that really mattered to him.

How can I get more Bliss?

The *Globe*, the *Herald*, and all the local TV stations committed major resources to covering the case and its sensational angles: prominent family; pretty, talented dead girl; sex, drugs, and death. Yet this was no run-of-the-mill drug. The story would have been scorching enough had the kids been taking something conventional like meth or acid—but what the hell was Bliss?

When the arresting officer's report was released, written in the pinched language of police documents, the public read about Treblehorn's description of a profound spiritual experience, meeting his grandfather on "the other side," reluctantly returning to the "real world."

It all sounded loony, almost jokeworthy, until a local substance abuse specialist, a psychologist at Tufts Medical School, came forward with descriptions of Bliss highs he'd begun to see in a few of his patients.

Cyrus turned up the volume on Vincent Desjardines' interview. He spoke haltingly, like a man unaccustomed to a microphone in his face.

"You mean to tell us, Doctor," the interviewer asked, "that all of the people you've seen who've taken this drug, Bliss, claim to have the same vision or hallucination or what have you?"

"That's correct."

"Can you describe this hallucination for us?"

"Users describe a feeling of floating over their own body then traveling through a tunnel toward a bright light and coming upon a river with stepping-stones. They always see someone on the other side of the river and they go on to describe a vivid encounter with a deceased friend or loved one. There's also a sense of a Godlike presence across the river."

"Godlike?"

"Yes, but nothing specific. And every one of the eight patients I've interviewed describes an overwhelming desire to reuse the drug and repeat the experience."

"And you get the same descriptions from every one of them?"

"Yes. Remarkably similar from one user to the next."

"Have you ever dealt with a drug that causes the same hallucination in different people?"

"Occasionally, drugs like LSD or mescaline or psilocybin will cause stereotypical or similar types of patterns among users but this seems to be quite unique."

"Explanations?"

"I don't have one. There needs to be more work in the area."

"We'd like to come back to you in the near future and to talk some more about this drug, Doctor."

"I'd be delighted."

Cyrus was about to switch to a music station when the rest of the news began to roll out but a name he heard snapped him to attention.

Frank Sacco.

Frank Sacco, twenty-six, found shot to death execution-style in the early hours of the morning in his apartment in Revere. Police investigating, details to follow.

Cyrus speed-dialed Avakian's mobile. "You in the office yet?"

"Just got here. What's up?"

"Check our notes on the head drillings. The guy who works for Alex Weller, Frank Sacco. Tell me his age and address."

"Why?"

"Just check, okay?"

In a minute, Avakian was back. "He's twenty-six, lives on Dehon Street in Revere."

Cyrus pulled into the fast lane and stepped on the gas. "Okay, Pete, you've got to meet me there right away. He's been murdered."

Cyrus and Avakian arrived at Sacco's apartment at the tail end of the crime scene investigation. The Revere detectives were waiting for the medical examiner and his team to finish up and roll the body onto a stretcher so they could get out.

The lead detective's name was Lombardy, a veteran with a hair weave and a gut draped with an extralong necktie. He wanted to know why the FBI was interested in his case and grudgingly had to make do with Cyrus's vague response that there could be a linkage to another matter under the bureau's investigation. Lombardy compliantly passed on what he knew.

The elderly woman who lived on the second floor of the house woke up to the sound of loud footsteps beating down the stairs at about 1 A.M. She looked out her bedroom window and saw two men get into a car and speed off. She went back to sleep but woke again at 4 A.M. worried that perhaps she should have called the police. She put on her robe, went up the stairs to see if everything was okay, saw Frank Sacco's door wide open and retreated to her apartment to call 911.

Sacco was dead, face down, with a single bullet wound to the back of his head. The skin, easily visible through his short hair, was split with a star-shaped wound, the edges of which were blackened: a contact wound, the gun having been pressed against his skull like a Chinese state-sponsored execution. The bullet exited through his mouth, clipping a couple of teeth on the way out. It was lodged in the floor near the coffee table, a fully jacketed .380.

There was no sign of forced entry. A bottle of Windex and a couple of rags were on the coffee table. Lombardy guessed the killers had the presence of mind to wipe away any prints. They weren't idiots: even the Windex bottle was clean. Robbery didn't appear to be a motive. The man's wallet was in his bedroom. The place wasn't ransacked. Something interesting, very, was in the dresser—a stack of cash, almost $8,000.

"That's a lot of money for a lab tech," Cyrus said.

Lombardy looked up from his pad. "So you know the guy."

"Yeah, we know him," Cyrus answered. "He works at Harvard."

"This looks like a drug deal gone bad. That's what I think," Lombardy said. "You following a drug angle here?"

Avakian shrugged. "Not that we know of."

"Well, that's my working theory," the detective said. "We'll see if it holds up."

The medical examiner announced he was ready to turn the body and his assistants did the honors.

Everyone in the room saw the same thing at once.

"What the hell's that?" Lombardy asked.

Three thin tubes of red paper were poking out of Sacco's shirt pocket.

"Check it out, would you, Doc?" Lombardy asked the ME.

The pathologist used a forceps to remove one of the tubes. He shook it lightly. "There's something in it," he said.

"Open it," Lombardy urged.

With fresh gloves, the ME unwrapped the tube on top of an evidence bag. A tiny amount of snow-white crystals spilled out.

"I told you it was drugs!" Lombardy triumphantly exclaimed.

"What do you think it is?" Avakian asked.

The ME fetched a magnifying loupe from his tray and squinted through it. "I doubt it's coke or speed, the quantity's too small. I don't think it's LSD. Frankly, I don't have a clue. I'll send it over to the drug unit in Sudbury and you'll know when I know."

Cyrus had a request. "Before you take him away, do me a favor and check his head for another wound."

"What kind of wound?" the ME asked, bagging the powder.

"An eighth-of-an-inch drill hole in one of the temples."

The pathologist looked at Cyrus as though he were mental but knelt over the body to take a closer look at Sacco's skull. "No. Nothing else."

Out on the sidewalk, Cyrus and Avakian pushed through a growing throng of reporters and bystanders. When they were out of earshot, Avakian asked, "You don't think Weller was involved, do you?"

"It's completely different from the others. I can't see it."

"Want to talk to Weller again?"

"Yeah," Cyrus told him, "but not right away. Let's see what the police come up with on Sacco first. I can't see asserting jurisdiction from what we've got so far."

Avakian agreed. He got to his car first. "The kid was probably into dealing and got whacked for it."

"Yeah," Cyrus agreed, "but what *kind* of drugs?"

Alex rarely watched television but that evening he sat with Jessie, cemented to the local news because so much of it touched home.

The instant he heard about the Treblehorn case, Alex began to fret. An ecstatic drug experience leading to an alleged suicide—so soon after his bottle went missing? Then, as details began to emerge, he knew it in his heart. It had to be his pentapeptide.

On the streets.

He'd been preoccupied with his research and working to exhaustion but this couldn't be ignored. The previous night he'd rehearsed how he'd confront Frank: how he wouldn't let him off the hook until he confessed to what he'd done.

Frank, though, never made it to work. Then the nonstop phone calls began pouring in from people who'd heard about the murder—including members of the Uroboros Society, each of whom added the exact same coda to the conversation: When are we going to get more drug?

Frank's elderly neighbor now was being interviewed on TV. He was a good kid, she told the reporter. She'd known his grandfather. Who would do such a thing?

"Yeah, who?" Alex asked grimly.

Jessie touched his shoulder. "We shouldn't be sad. We should be happy for him."

"He's in a better place, for sure," Alex said. "But who put him there?"

"Do you think he stole your drug?"

"Yes I do."

The TV news turned to the Treblehorn case. Jennifer Sheridan's high school yearbook photo filled the screen. Tomorrow would be the funeral in her hometown in Connecticut. Treblehorn's lawyer was onscreen again, reasserting his client's innocence.

A reporter now stood on Harrison Avenue outside Tufts New England Medical Center. Earlier she'd spoken to drug abuse specialist Dr. Vincent Desjardines about the mysterious drug that had led to Sheridan's death.

The ferretlike weak-chinned man in his fifties looked stiffly from behind his desk into the camera. "I'm seeing more cases every day," he explained, holding up a red paper straw. "I got this from one of my patients. This is the drug they're calling Bliss."

"What is it, Doctor?" the reporter asked.

"We don't know yet. We're having it analyzed."

Jessie gasped and pointed. "Alex! It's yours!"

Alex nervously got off the couch, smoothed back his long hair and started pacing. "Jesus, Frank … what did you do?"

At that moment, Cyrus too was pacing in his apartment, on a frustrating call with his ex-wife. He wanted to speak to Tara but Marian claimed she was sleeping. Tara's naps were getting longer, she told him, and her energy was fading. He asked her to check; she huffed loudly and unhappily obliged. He was feeling rotten about not calling during the day but he'd been too busy. The TV was droning in the background, Vincent Desjardines behind his desk—holding up a red paper stick identical to the one found in Frank Sacco's pocket that morning.

"Jesus," Cyrus whispered.

When Marian came back on the phone to confirm that Tara was asleep, the line was dead.

27

Vincent Desjardines looked even smaller in person than on TV. Cyrus dwarfed the man, and whether it was his bulk or his badge, he seemed to intimidate him as well. That the wall behind Desjardines' desk was covered in diplomas and association memberships, including a PhD in psychology from the University of Illinois, did little to instill self-confidence.

Desjardines began with an edgy preamble that he was unaccustomed to media attention and public scrutiny and that he was finding it disruptive to his normal routines: he was neglecting his practice at one of the largest drug abuse clinics in the city. Yes, Bliss was a fascinating new drug that had appeared out of nowhere, but he had a legion of heroin and meth addicts who required his attention too.

"I need more staff," he lamented, as if Cyrus could authorize hiring requisitions.

"I won't take too much of your time, but I need to know more about Bliss. We're in the middle of an active investigation."

"On the drug?"

"Not specifically, but the drug may be related. We're working on a homicide case—multiple homicides, actually."

Desjardines arched his brows in alarm. "Oh!"

"So what can you tell me?"

The psychologist had a tabbed three-ring binder filled with meticulous notes. He opened it, put on glasses then said quickly, "I hope you're not expecting any patient-specific information. You'd need a court order to even begin talking to me on that level."

Cyrus assured the doctor he wanted to know about Bliss, not his patients.

Desjardines nodded, looking to his notes. His first indication of something new, he explained, came from a multiple-drug user, a young Puerto Rican man he referred to as DF, with a long history of marijuana, Oxycontin, and heroin abuse. During the interview, Desjardines thought what he was hearing so extraordinary that he asked permission to record it. "Do you want to hear the tape?" he asked Cyrus.

"Of course."

Desjardines fast-forwarded past the patient's name and clinic number and hit Play.

VD: How have you been since your last appointment?
DF: I've been good. Really good.
VD: I'm glad to hear that. Tell me about your level of drug use?
DF: I've been clean.
VD: That's excellent, but I guess that surprises me.
DF: Well, almost clean. I don't know if you count Bliss.
VD: What is Bliss?
DF: It's new. At least I never heard of it before now. I'm not interested in the other stuff anymore.
VD: I'm afraid I'm at a loss. Is it ecstasy? LSD?
DF: No. It's way different.
VD: How so?
DF: It connects you to something. It takes you to the other side. You're like floating over your own body, then you go zooming off toward a light.
VD: I see. Is this is a tablet, a capsule, an injectable?
DF: It's a powder. You put it on your tongue.
VD: I'm sorry for interrupting. You said you see a light. Is that it?
DF: Only the beginning. After the light, you're there—on the other side. There's a beautiful river. You want to go to it. You feel good about being there ... very good.

VD: All right ...

DF: There's these stones leading across. High out of the water, *if* it's water. I'm not sure. I mean it sounds like water. Then I see my old man.

VD: Your father?

DF: Yeah. But he died when I was a kid. The crazy thing is, he's there the way I remember him, right down to the shirt he always wore. He's waving at me. He's happy as shit.

VD: Then what happens?

DF: I get all excited, like a kid on Christmas, you know. And I start to cross over on the stones. The closer I get to him, the better I feel. It's a huge rush. A total body rush. Like nothing else. Like the best shit times a million.

VD: Okay, and then?

DF: The closer I get, the better it feels. It's hard to believe but it keeps building. My dad's yelling his ass off, he's jumping up and down, then I get the feeling that someone's behind him, way off in the distance. I can't see anything there but I feel it. It feels like ...

VD: Like what?

DF: It sounds stupid, but it feels like ... like God is there. But before I can get any closer I'm heading back the way I came, really fast, like you're riding the wind. Then it's over. You can't believe it's over. You don't want it to be over.

VD: And that's it. That's the end of the trip?

DF: That's it. It's always the same.

VD: You've taken it more than once?

DF: Three times. It's amazing each time but always the same.

VD: Well, that's interesting, isn't it? Tell me, how long does each trip last?

DF: Maybe thirty minutes, maybe longer.

VD: Are you awake during this experience?

DF: I don't know what you mean. I feel awake.

VD: Has anyone seen you while you're under the influence?

DF: I've always been alone.

VD: And the trip is universally positive?

DF: *Positive?* It's so fucking fantastic it hurts. Does that make sense? As soon as it's over I want to do it again: to see my dad and to see if God's there.

VD: Are you a religious person?

DF: Me? I'm a Catholic. But I don't go to church.

VD: Okay. Where did you get the drug?

DF: You know. On the streets. I know a guy who turned me on to it.

VD: Do you know where it comes from?

DF: No.

VD: Is there a lot of it going around?

DF: A lot? I don't know. I few people I know have taken it.

VD: What does a hit cost you?

DF: It's expensive, seventy-five a hit.

VD: The other people you know who've taken it: How do they describe their trips?

DF: That's the weird thing. They all had the same experience as me. Except that the person over the river is always someone they know. Or knew. It's always someone who's dead.

Desjardines clicked off the recorder.

"What did you make of it when you heard that?" Cyrus asked.

"I didn't know what to think. I was intrigued, of course. I did what scientists are supposed to do when they have more questions than answers. I tried to get more data."

He began, he said, to look for other cases; it didn't take long. One by one, patients trickled into his clinic. By the time William Treblehorn was arrested, Desjardines was the first and only medical expert on the street use of Bliss.

When he sat down to ponder his initial collection of eight cases—most involving heavy substance abusers—he was struck by something: despite the similarity of the experiences described, consequences varied.

"Eight cases?" Cyrus repeated.

"Until yesterday," Desjardines replied, pointing to a stack of e-mails he'd printed out. "Colleagues from all over New England have been contacting me about similar cases. I've lost count. I think more than twenty, but they're lacking the details of my cases," he said, tapping his notes. "If I had help, I'd be returning these e-mails and getting more info."

"I want to come back to what you said about differing consequences in your eight cases," Cyrus said.

Desjardines started flipping through the binder, spouting off details.

Subject 1. DF: Twenty-four-year-old Hispanic male, the recorded interview. The man had taken Bliss several more times, though he could scarcely afford it. He said he'd rather have the drug than put food on his table.

Subject 2. JE: Seventeen-year-old white male. History of heavy marijuana and alcohol abuse. Used Bliss six times. Sees his deceased grandmother. Refuses to return to high school. Withdrawn. Placed on antidepressants.

Subject 3. BN: Twenty-two-year-old black male. Crack addict. Has taken Bliss several times. Sees a friend of his from high school who was shot and killed five years ago. Has stopped smoking crack and now devoutly attends his mother's church in Mattapan. Says he is "full of joy."

Subject 4. EW: Forty-five-year-old white male, stockbroker. Alcoholic, history of methamphetamine abuse. Used Bliss over ten times. Saw his mother. Had euphoric reaction. Immediately quit his job. Stopped drinking. Sits around the house in meditative state. Wife is pleased about the drinking but worries about loss of financial support.

Subject 5. RG: Thirty-one-year-old black female. Took drug twice. Became hysterical after each trip. One day after second exposure, died of heroin overdose. Police report lists it as accidental but sister thinks it was intentional.

Subject 6. FC: Twenty-four-year-old white male. LSD, ecstasy user. Nightclub sound man. Sees his mother, who died in a house fire. Is relieved she doesn't appear burned. Wants to keep going back to see her and plans on taking more drug if he can find/afford it. Thinking about quitting his job as it now seems "trivial."

Subject 7. JL: Thirty-year-old Hispanic male. Heroin addict. Used Bliss half a dozen times. Won't divulge whom he saw across river. Says "it's personal." Has used heroin a few times since taking Bliss but thinks he can quit now.

Subject 8. TY: Sixty-four-year-old white male. Methadone addict for over twenty years. Chronic poor health, heart failure. Took drug three times. Sees his deceased wife. Seems more relaxed and tranquil than VD ever recalls. Missed his last appointment. No response to phone calls. Urgent need to follow up on patient's status.

Cyrus's hand cramped from rapid note-taking. Stretching it out, he asked, "Is that it?"

"Essentially. When I read about the woman who jumped out the window after taking Bliss I called the police to tell them what I knew."

"On the news last night you showed one of the red tubes. Where'd you get it?"

"I had my first patient buy me a couple. On the street they're called *sticks*." He fished one out of his desk.

Cyrus inspected it. The stick was identical to those in Sacco's pocket. "What did you do with the other one?" Cyrus asked.

"I sent it to the hospital toxicology laboratory for analysis. They had to refer it out to some place in Kansas City. I'm waiting for the report. For all I know, it's in my inbox. As I said, I've been swamped."

"Could you please check?"

The small man sighed and swung his chair around to access his e-mail account. "Christ!" he exclaimed. "They sent it to me yesterday. That's what happens when you're understaffed." He clicked on the attachment. "I'll print it out."

Desjardines inspected the two-page report. "Well, this is interesting! I've never seen this compound before and apparently the lab in Missouri hasn't either. It's a circular peptide: five amino acids in a ring structure." He looked up and sniffed, "Where the hell did it come from?"

The doctor made a copy and handed it over. To Cyrus, it was gobbledygook. He folded it and put it away.

"So, give me a bottom line," Cyrus said. "What are we looking at here?"

"My bottom line?" Desjardines frowned. "My bottom line is that I've got a very bad feeling about this drug."

28

The Chinese grad student in Alex's lab who picked up the phone finally told an insistent Cyrus she thought her boss might be working out at the Harvard indoor track. He liked the idea of catching Weller off guard so he jumped in his car and headed to Cambridge. Avakian was at a parent-teacher meeting at his daughter's school so Cyrus went alone, trying hard not to think about all the future parent-teacher meetings he'd be missing.

He parked near the Harvard football stadium and showed his badge to get into the Gordon Indoor Track. This late in the morning there weren't many runners. He spotted Weller immediately, tall and lanky, ponytail bobbing against the back of his t-shirt as he circled the banked brick-red oval. Cyrus climbed onto the bleachers and watched him for half a circuit. He was fluid, a natural runner, and Cyrus felt a pang of jealousy at Weller's long, seemingly carefree lopes. He'd been a good runner himself years ago. He tried to imagine the fine feeling of cruise speed but it was difficult to remember. Perhaps one day he'd start again. Maybe in the spring.

Weller came out of the turn and promptly locked onto Cyrus. He didn't slow down or stop, didn't register surprise or alarm—only a thin-lipped smile and a jabbing finger to his wristwatch, a sign that Cyrus would just have to cool his jets.

I'll wait for you, Cyrus thought. *You're running in circles.*

Weller eventually stopped in front of the bleachers and stood, hands on hips, while Cyrus climbed down. In between breaths he said, "Sorry to keep you waiting ... but you lose the benefit when your heart slows down ... at least that's the theory."

"Do a lot of running?" Cyrus asked.

"Just enough to counteract the beer."

Cyrus refused to respond in kind. "Do you know why I'm here?"

"Frank Sacco?" Alex asked. "Is the FBI involved with Frank's murder?"

"We're aware of it. I'm interested in what you know." He studied Weller's eyes for an evasive glance, a twitch, but there was nothing.

"I know what I've seen on the news, read online. It's horrible. I've known the lad for three years. He was a good worker, a pleasant fellow; never had issues with him. I was shocked he was involved with anything like this."

"Anything like what?"

"Whatever it was that would have led to someone killing him!" Alex had a water bottle and towel on the lowest bleacher step. He reached for them.

"Do you know where he lived?"

"Of course. Revere."

"Ever been to his house?"

"We didn't have that kind of relationship."

"Did he ever go to your house?"

"Yes, several times."

"I thought you didn't have that kind of relationship."

"He attended my salon."

"The Uroboros thing."

"That's right."

"Active participant?"

"He wasn't much of a talker."

"When was the last time he attended?"

"A couple of weeks ago. Early January sometime."

"I thought you said you'd invite me to the next one you had."

A sip from the water bottle. "Must've slipped my mind."

"When was the last time you saw him?"

"At work the day he died. He seemed perfectly normal."

"Nothing at all to indicate he was nervous, stressed out, in any kind of trouble?"

"Nothing."

"Where were you two nights ago? In your lab again?"

"No, actually. I was home with my girlfriend the entire night."

"I might want to talk to her."

"She'd be delighted, I'm sure."

"Any past issues with Sacco's performance, his behavior, any signs of drug use?"

Alex toweled his arms dry. "He was a bit rough around the edges but he came to work without fail, did his job adequately and that's that. So, look, I've really got to get back to the lab. Is there anything else I can help you with?"

Cyrus watched closely as he told him, "Yeah, there's one more thing." He produced Desjardines' report and showed it to him. "Ever seen this chemical?"

Cyrus almost wished he had the guy hooked up to a polygraph because from the outside he looked cool and nonchalant when he answered, "I certainly have. I discovered it. Where did you get this?"

"You discovered it?"

"That's what I said. No one else has seen this so I'm surprised, to say the least."

"You don't look surprised."

"I'm British. Maybe you're not used to our demeanor."

"Maybe. Are you aware that a new drug called Bliss is on the streets?"

"I've read a little about it. I don't follow the news religiously."

"Well, it looks like your chemical *is* Bliss. This was analyzed from a sample bought on the street."

"I see," Alex said evenly. "Mind if we sit? Bit much to take in."

They sat on the lowest step. Cyrus let Alex read through the lab report more thoroughly.

"Do you want to know why I may not have seemed as surprised as I might have been?" Alex asked.

"Try me."

"This compound, this pentapeptide: I had a small supply of it locked away in my desk. It went missing."

"When?"

"About a month ago."

"Did you report it to the police?"

"No."

"Why not?"

Alex paused. It occurred to Cyrus he was rehearsing the answer in his mind. "It's a thorny matter of intellectual property. I haven't filed patents yet. I'm not ready scientifically. If I filed a complaint with the police, I would have had to prematurely disclose details, such as the structure."

"Uh huh," Cyrus said skeptically. "What's your reaction to it being used as a street drug?"

"I'm horrified by the notion. It's not intended for human use. There's been no testing whatsoever."

Horrified? You don't look horrified, Cyrus thought. "What's the source of the chemical? How'd you discover it?"

"You recall I'm interested in the biology of the dying brain. My compound was isolated from the brains of animals suffering from severe oxygen deprivation, close to time of death."

"What kind of animals?"

"Mice, rats, dogs."

"You used the word *isolated*. How do you isolate it?"

"You mean my techniques?"

"Yeah. How do you get the chemical out of the brain?"

"Well, you put a needle into the brain and extract a sample. Why do you need to know that?"

Cyrus didn't answer. He felt his heart pound and tried to sound as controlled as Weller was. "What about humans?"

"I wouldn't know that, would I?"

"That'd be a hell of an experiment," Cyrus said. "What would you have to do, drill a person's brain?"

"It's a ridiculous idea! I can't imagine anyone volunteering for that!" Alex collected his things and stood.

"Yeah, you definitely wouldn't raise your hand for that kind of maneuver," Cyrus said. He stood too. "What's the purpose of the chemical?"

"I'm sorry, its purpose?"

"Yeah. What does it do?"

"It activates a receptor in a part of the brain called the limbic system. Beyond that, I don't know. It's early days in the research program."

Cyrus said suddenly, "Did it occur to you that Frank Sacco might have taken your chemical?"

"Until now, no. Based on what I've just learned, I'd have to consider it. He didn't have a key to my desk but maybe he knew where I kept it. I'm very troubled, to say the least. I've got to go. Sorry."

Cyrus walked with him toward the locker room. "So what do you make of the wild trips people are describing, the ones who've taken your drug?"

Alex stopped at the locker room door. "I hadn't been paying much attention. Obviously, now that I know it's mine, I plan on paying quite a bit. I'm very troubled, but I'm a scientist so I'll process whatever data comes my way." He swung the door open then recollected himself. "I've been remiss. I've neglected to ask after your daughter."

Cyrus winced. "She's fine."

"Seizure-free?"

Cyrus wouldn't let him take back control. "I said she's fine. I'll be back to you soon with more questions."

"I'm sure you will."

Then Cyrus he lowered his voice and said, "I know what you did."

Alex looked at him quizzically. "What did you say?"

At the question, Cyrus turned his back to him and left.

29

"Don't take it so hard."

Stanley Minot was doing his best to be supportive but Cyrus was in a foul mood. The U.S. attorney for the District of Massachusetts had shot down their request for a search warrant on Alex Weller's workplace, home, and automobile. Despite a loosely cohesive story, there was no credible evidence, in her opinion, to link Weller to the murders of Thomas Quinn, any of the prostitutes, or Frank Sacco. "Keep digging," she'd said before escorting him and Avakian to the elevators at the Moakley Federal Courthouse.

"Weller's our man," Cyrus told Minot glumly. "I know it, you know it."

Minot dug his hands into his sweater pockets, stretching them out, as he often did when he was about to be philosophical. "Look, I think you're building a case. The circumstantial evidence is getting compelling but you've got to convince the U.S. attorney, not me."

"I think Weller's a twisted fuck," Avakian volunteered.

"Well, that'll put us over the evidentiary hurdle, Pete." Minot laughed.

Minot's mobile rang. He stepped out of Cyrus's office to answer it.

"What now?" Avakian asked O'Malley.

"We need to interview Weller's girlfriend again. She vouched for him the night Sacco was killed but she was shaky. Maybe we can get her to slip up. And we need to get the names and addresses of everyone who's in this Uroboros deal."

"Bunch of wackos," Avakian observed.

"Maybe. But we need to talk to them."

Minot came back with a grave face. "When it rains it pours. We've got to drop everything."

"What is it?" Avakian asked.

"Kidnapping. And I was going to catch up on paperwork today."

"Why's it ours?" Cyrus asked sourly.

"It's probably interstate," Minot said. "A guy's wife and baby were taken from Nashua. The kidnapper's plates were from Mass. Grab your stuff. We're going to Woburn."

"Why Woburn?" Avakian groused.

"The husband works there at a biotech company."

"What's he do?" Cyrus wondered.

Minot checked his notes. "Says he's some kind of a chemist. A peptide chemist."

Paul Martell was in his midthirties, a man with a pasty complexion and a doughy body. Love handles bulged around his polo shirt and spilled over his khakis. His eyes were red; it looked to Cyrus that he'd been bawling his eyes out.

They interviewed him in the company's boardroom. Chemotherapeutics, Inc. was a start-up operation, only a few years old. Cyrus heard something about cancer and made a mental note to check if they had anything new going for brain tumors. The company's CEO was pacing the hall outside the boardroom incessantly yapping on his mobile. He was the one who found Martell in the lab burning the midnight oil over the weekend. Martell broke down and told him what was happening. The CEO called the police.

On Friday night, Martell told O'Malley and his team, he and his wife, Marcie, were watching TV. Their six-month-old baby was asleep in her crib. Marcie, as usual, had one ear on the TV, one on the baby monitor. The doorbell rang, probably a neighbor, she thought, but it wasn't.

Two men barged in. Martell didn't know them—and still doesn't. They brandished guns, made no effort to conceal their faces. They told him they knew he was a peptide chemist. They had a bottle of powder. They wanted him to make them more of it, right away: and to keep him motivated, they were taking his wife. Then they heard the baby crying on the monitor—the kid too. Martell needed to get cranking. They wanted half of the goods Saturday night. They'd check it out. If it was good, they wanted the other half Monday. Then they'd let his family go. If the stuff he made was crap, God help him.

"How'd they know you were a peptide chemist?" Cyrus asked.

"They said they needed one, asked around, knew someone who knew me from somewhere and Googled me. That's all I know."

Martell told the kidnappers he had no idea what the crystals were or how long it would take him to do a synthesis. His problem, not theirs, he was told. They made his wife bundle up the baby and get in a waiting car. As it drove off, Martell saw a Mass plate and glimpsed only one number, a three. It was a black Maxima, he thought.

The other one climbed into Martell's passenger seat and made him drive to the research facility. He told him he'd be calling to check on him and warned him not to call the police or he'd crush the baby's head and make his wife watch.

Martell threw himself into the task, running around various labs, utilizing the company's sophisticated hardware. By 4 A.M., he'd analyzed the compound and knew its structure.

"What is it?" Cyrus asked.

"It's a circular peptide," Martell answered. "A new one on me."

Cyrus wasn't surprised. He sighed and showed Martell the Desjardines structure. "This it?"

"Yeah!" Martell exclaimed. "That's it. That's the exact isomer!"

"Were you able to make it?" Minot asked.

"Yes. I've made circular peptides before. I ran it through our peptide synthesizer and did the linker chemistry. No problem."

"How much did they want? Cyrus asked.

"They said they wanted a minimum of one hundred thousand doses, about fifty grams of compound."

Avakian whistled. "At the current street price, that's ten million bucks worth."

"Street price of what?" Martell asked, dazed.

"Bliss," Cyrus answered. "Ever hear of it?"

"I've been making Bliss?" Martell moaned. "I had no idea."

"How much have you made so far?" Minot asked.

"About twenty-five grams. The guy who drove me here picked it up Saturday night. I'm just purifying the second batch now."

"So another fifty thousand hits are on the streets?" Avakian howled. "Man alive!"

"Look, I don't care about that!" Martell cried. "I want my wife and son back!"

Minot was soothing, something he was good at. "We'll get them back, Mister Martell. Believe me, we will."

"She's so scared." He started sobbing.

"How do you know she's scared?" Cyrus asked.

Before the chemist could respond, Minot said helpfully, "Of course she's scared."

Martell, though, looked at Cyrus. "Because I talked to her," he replied.

When? they all wanted to know.

"Last night?"

How?

"On her cell phone. She had it in her bag when she left. They called me on it and let her speak to me."

Minot jumped up muttering, "Can they be that stupid?" He got her number from Martell and sprinted into the hall.

Martell looked alarmed.

"No, it's good. In this case stupidity is very good," Cyrus reassured him. "If we have her phone, we have her."

By the time it was dark, a coordinated plan was in place involving the FBI, the Mass State Police, and the Boston Police Department. Minot handled interdepartmental issues and left the tactical plan to Cyrus and Avakian, who mapped out a minute-by-minute scenario.

Marcie Martell's cell phone signal was tracked to Clark Street off of Hanover in Boston's North End. Multiple drive-bys gave them a high probability the source was a five-story narrow brick apartment building with only ten units.

At four in the afternoon, Comcast agreed to cut off cable service to the building. Within five minutes, the cable company received calls from three of the apartments reporting the problem. Cyrus chuckled at the speed as he and Avakian, dressed in Comcast gear, responded to the service call.

For an hour they had nearly free rein of the building, sketching the layout and planting listening devices. They were most suspicious about one of the units on the top floor where a woman angrily refused them access. On the roof, they scoped out access points from adjacent buildings and took photos to help them finalize the takedown plan.

Then they left and had the cable turned back on.

Two hours later, they instructed Martell to call his wife to confirm her safety. She was tired but fine—but most importantly, the FBI listening team picked up her ringtone in the hall outside Apt. 9, top floor, rear.

At 11 P.M. a car pulled into the vacant parking lot of Chemotherapeutics. It was Martell's Kia, driven by John Abruzzi. He was on his own. When Abruzzi knocked on the glass door Martell came out and handed him a large plastic jar of powder. A sniper from the state police had Abruzzi in his sights with instructions to fire if he made a move to attack the chemist but the exchange was benign.

"Your first bottle was good, at least that's what the junkies reported," Abruzzi joked into the microphone Martell was wearing.

"Will you let my wife and son go now?" Martell pleaded.

"Soon. Go back home and wait. And keep your mouth shut about this. We know how to get you. Be smart. When we need more, next time, maybe we'll pay you. Bring you over the wall. Don't be a jerkoff and you'll do good."

Another car pulled into the lot.

Abruzzi tossed Martell the keys to his car, climbed into the other sedan and drove away.

Cyrus was inside the company building, peering through the blinds of a darkened window. "Okay, he's rolling," he announced into his radio. "Keep four vehicles on him at all times and don't move on him till you get the word."

A quarter of a mile away, a state police helicopter was waiting in a parking lot to fly Cyrus to Boston. Within fifteen minutes he was disembarking onto the helipad roof of Mass General Hospital and was then whisked off to Boston Police District A-1 on New Sudbury Street where the operation was being staged.

Minot sat quietly, watching Cyrus lay out the tactical plan to the Mass police SWAT commander and Boston police support teams. When O'Malley was done, Minot patted him on the back in his fatherly way, filled his pipe bowl with fruity tobacco and wished him luck.

At midnight, the state police SWAT team was in place on the roof of the Clark Street building. Eight armed men in flak jackets, night vision goggles and assault rifles anchored their rappel lines.

Cyrus was in an unmarked communications van up the block near North Street. Before giving` the go ahead he called Avakian, who was in one of the cars trailing Abruzzi.

"Where's your guy?" Cyrus asked.

"He's still in the Seagull Lounge in Revere. We've got front and back covered. He's not going to be showing up at your party."

The lights were black in Apartment 9.

Cyrus gave the green light.

On the count, the SWAT commander initiated.

There were two windows at the side and two at the rear. With a looping rappel the first four went through the windows boots first. Then a second wave crashed in.   Cyrus sat forward, eyes closed, straining into his headset. The sound of crashing glass had barely stopped when he heard the first cracks of gunfire.

Pop. Pop.

The voices were eerily businesslike.

"One male down in bedroom two!"

A woman cried out, "Mario!"

Pop.

"One female down bedroom two."

"I'm in bedroom one. I've got the baby. Cover the door. I think the mother's okay. Are you Marcie Martell?"

"Yes!"

"How many of them are in here?"

"Two men! One woman!"

"Where's the other guy? Who's got the other guy?"

"Watch out. I think he's behind the sofa."

Pop. Pop. Pop.

"Second male down!"

"We're clear! Get the paramedics in!"

Moments later, the street was alive. A burly cop walked out of the building with the baby in his arms, his mother supported between two other officers.

Cyrus watched Marcie Martell emerge. She looked like a woman who'd been through hell. He called Avakian.

"It's over on Clark Street. Pick up your guys."

Avakian and four special agents calmly walked in and took down John Abruzzi and his driver without a struggle. The large plastic bottle was in Abruzzi's coat pocket.

"It's sugar, asshole," Avakian said. "Where's the first bottle?"

Abruzzi thrust out his chin. "I don't know what you're talking about but if I did I'd bet it's long gone. I'd bet it's all over the fucking streets already."

30

Cyrus was too busy to leave the office but he refused to cancel the appointment. Days after the North End raid he was still grinding away on his after-action reports but that morning he kept thinking about his date, if that's what it was. Emily Frost was getting under his skin, creeping up on him, invading his thoughts at odd times—while reading; shaving; eating cereal.

He was determined to be on time. In fact, he blew into the coffee shop a few minutes early. She was there already in a booth, on her cell phone. She waved and kept talking as he sat and stripped off his overcoat. He could tell from her tone she was in doctor mode talking to a family. He tried not to eavesdrop on the content but listened to the sound and cadence of her voice. She was able to blend gravitas with warmth. It was soothing. He could use some of that.

She finished up. "I'm sorry. How are you, Cyrus?"

He was pleased she'd remembered their deal on first names.

"Fine, Emily. Busy but fine."

"Still reading Shakespeare?"

He laughed. "That's like asking me if I'm still breathing air."

"You've got me doing it too. The sonnets are really lovely." They ordered their coffees. "How's Tara?"

"Not bad, not good," he said heavily. "Every time I see her she seems to be getting a little farther away. Does that make sense?"

She smiled sadly. "Yes it does. Like a star getting dimmer."

He swallowed hard and nodded.

"How're *you* doing?" she asked.

"Ordinarily, I'd be bitching about being out-of-control swamped with work but I think the distraction's probably a good thing."

"I'm sure you're right. Can you talk about any part of your work? Or is it confidential?"

The coffees arrived and he watched to see if she was going to get cappuccino foam on her upper lip again. She did and he liked it.

"Have you heard about the drug, Bliss?"

Her eyes widened. "You're working on that!"

"I've gotten drawn into it through a related investigation."

"I'm fascinated by it, absolutely fascinated," she enthused. "I've been reading everything I can. I even saw my first patient last week, a fifteen-year-old girl who attempted suicide after taking it. We've got her as an inpatient."

"It's spreading like crazy," he said. "The world's gotten more dangerous in the past few weeks."

"More dangerous and more comforting at the same time, don't you think?"

"How do you mean?"

"Many people find the notion of an afterlife comforting. It's the foundation for great religions. People want to believe there's more."

"Your patient tried killing herself. There've been plenty of successful ones. But not everyone opts for that. What do you make of it?"

"I don't think the drug's effects are monolithic. Maybe the underlying psyche of the user predicts the response. If a person has a marginal, unfulfilled life full of sorrow, then maybe suicide and the promise of something better proves irresistible."

"Choosing death over life," Cyrus mused.

"From what I've read and heard from colleagues who've seen more patients than I, users describe experiencing feelings of incomparable joy and peace, the purest pleasure they've ever had."

"And those who don't want to off themselves?"

She paused. "My guess is that healthy, self-actualized people may find the experience gives them an added dimension. For them, heaven can wait, though it might change some of their lifestyle decisions."

Cyrus took on a mocking tone. "They zoom through a tunnel toward the light! They see a beautiful river! There's a loved one waiting for them! They feel the presence of God! What's your explanation for these identical hallucinations?"

Emily chuckled. "Your skepticism comes through loud and clear but there really are only two explanations, aren't there? Either it's a drug-induced hallucination with mass suggestibility … or it's real."

He allowed the waitress to refill his cup before exclaiming, "Real?!"

"Who am I to say the afterlife doesn't exist? Most people think it does, you know. Ninety-two percent of Americans believe in God, eighty percent believe in an afterlife. Heck, one in three believes that the bible is the actual word of God!"

"What do you believe?" Cyrus asked. As soon as he said it, he realized it wasn't an appropriate question but before he could retract it, she answered.

"I'm a card-carrying agnostic," she replied. "Since you asked me, I guess for me to ask you the same thing is fair game."

He shook his head and looked out the window for a few seconds. "I'm a practicing Catholic," he answered. "I have faith. But for me, these kinds of things have to be necessarily abstract. To solidify concepts of God and afterlife in specific imagery … I don't like it. It goes against my grain."

"I understand completely." She bunched her lips in curiosity. "So what's the FBI's role in Bliss?"

"Like I said, I'm coming at it from another angle, which I can't go into."

"I'm sorry," she apologized. "I'm too nosy. Does anyone know where it came from?"

"Yeah, that's another thing I can't talk about."

"There I go again." She laughed.

He changed the subject. "The crazy thing is, the drug's not illegal! Using it *or* selling it. There's nothing the authorities can do."

"Is something being done about that?"

"The DEA's looking at it. Drugs don't get scheduled overnight but if it were me, I'd be working overtime."

"I think your concern is well placed. I don't know if the drug is addictive in a classical sense, but it surely is seductive."

"Remember I asked you once about Alex Weller?"

She nodded.

"You said you went to one of his salons. Do you remember a nurse named Thomas Quinn? Or a lab tech named Frank Sacco?"

"There were so many new people there and it was a couple of years ago. Sorry."

"Have you seen Weller lately?"

"No, why?"

"No reason." Her cup was empty. "You want another one?" he asked. "Something to eat?"

"I've got to get back for clinic," she said.

He called for the check. "Can I ask why you chose to work with sick kids?" He couldn't bring himself to say the word *dying*.

"I had kind of a rough childhood myself," she admitted soberly. "I empathize with kids in crisis. I don't only see cancer patients. I do all sorts of trauma work. If I go home at night feeling I've helped a child, then I've had a pretty good day."

He left some money on the table and at once had a thought that pleased him.

"Can I see you again?" he asked.

"Another coffee would be great," she replied.

"Actually, I had another idea."

"I'm still your daughter's doctor," she gently reminded.

"No, a professional idea." He laughed. He told her what he had in mind and asked if she'd join him day after tomorrow.

"I'd love to," she said, checking her calendar. "I'd really love to."

Jessie took off Alex's shirt and began to knead his shoulder muscles. He was tense and a back rub usually helped. He hadn't been sleeping well, he'd become withdrawn, spending hours alone in a darkened room. In retrospect, his life had been so simple. His quest to understand his childhood NDE had driven the choices he'd made in a singular way. It drove him to study brain sciences; it drove him to study philosophy and religion. Yet, now that he'd made his break-through, complexities flooded in as if a dam had been breached. He felt as though he were holding onto a sapling that was bending in torrential floodwaters, in mortal danger of being swept away by the powerful forces he'd unleashed.

For a man who always strived to be in control, the sudden lack of control was eating at him. He couldn't control Cyrus O'Malley, who was pursuing him with a bulldog's tenacity. He couldn't control the Uroboros compound anymore. Even its name had been taken away from him. Bliss. On the street it was becoming some kind of vast uncontrolled experiment that would eventually lead back to his door. And when that happened, O'Malley would be there, smugly wielding handcuffs, taking him away to prison for life. He'd rather die.

Death had become an overwhelmingly appealing option. He knew with the certainty of a replicated scientific experiment what awaited him and it was so much more alluring than life, particularly the anxiety-filled existence he now was experiencing. With the stroke of a blade or ten minutes in a running car in his closed garage he'd be with his father forever. He'd learn, once and for all, what lay on the other side of that river.

I should do it, he thought. *With Jessie. It's not a matter of if but when.*

At first he'd shunned the media coverage of Bliss because it con-jured up images of O'Malley knocking on his door; but the scientist in him eventually was drawn to it. It was *his* discovery, *his* creation, and people were eagerly reporting their experiences everywhere. Vid-eos, blogs, postings, and tweets were popping up all over the net and TV and newspaper coverage was becoming ubiquitous.

One particular piece haunted him. A pretty girl posted a YouTube video of her coming out of a Bliss trip. She was crying and laughing at the same time, saying, "I can't understand why everyone isn't taking this. Everyone needs to know. Everyone needs to understand. Fuck every-thing else. This is the only thing that matters. Come on people, join me."

Come on people, join me.

He watched the video over and over until it came to him. He knew what he needed to do.

"Feel better?" Jessie asked, her hands moving down his spine.

"Yes. How about you?"

She was simple, innocent. When something bothered her she didn't bottle it up, she came out with it. "I'm still worried about the FBI agent who came to see me about Thomas and Frank."

He couldn't shield her from the FBI's harassment. O'Malley had shown up at his house while he was at the lab and had grilled Jessie for an hour. She was bewildered by the visit. Why did he want to know where Alex was the night Frank was murdered? Why was he interested in the Uroboros salon? Why did he want to talk about Thomas Quinn's death? She was careful, of course; Alex had prepped her never to talk about drug use at the salon or Bliss. Even so, she'd been rattled by the encounter.

"Don't worry about it," was all he could say. "You did well."

"I still don't know why he asked all those questions. It's almost like he thought you had something to do with Thomas and Frank's deaths."

"He's misguided. He's got a warped idea of the truth."

"I miss Thomas," she said. "I've been thinking about him."

"I miss Thomas too but I don't miss Frank. He stole from me. He wasn't a good person. He got what he deserved."

She tenderly kissed his thick burn scars. "Frank's in a better place. They're both in a better place."

Alex turned around and pulled her into his chest. "You're a wise soul," he said. "But don't go joining him, okay? I need you here with me. We've got work to do."

"What kind of work?"

"Jessie, this is something I've been thinking about. Actually, it's *all* I've been thinking about. Frank let the cat out of the bag prematurely, but look what's happening: hundreds of people, maybe thousands, have taken Bliss. It's triggered a new kind of joy and understanding. Why stop here? Isn't it our responsibility to do more for more people?"

"Our responsibility to do what?"

"Bliss is mine. I'm its father. A father has a responsibility for what he creates. I've got some ideas, Jessie—important ones. But I can't do it alone. I'll need help. I want to talk to a few of the Uroboros people, the ones we can really trust. Erica, Davis, maybe Sam, the new bloke, a couple of others. We may need to go somewhere else, someplace where we can work quietly, without O'Malley or anyone else interfering. You'll come with me, won't you?"

She didn't ask questions. "Of course I will. I'll go wherever you go."

He kissed her passionately and nuzzled her. "I have two more doses of the liquid—the last two." *Paulo Couto's precious last drops.* "Shall we take them now?"

She nodded happily.

"You first," he said.

After he pipetted the drops onto her tongue, she lay on the bed and asked, "Alex, why are the drops better than the powder?"

The question caught him off guard. He answered cautiously. "The crystals are synthetic. The liquid contains the natural chemical. There are small differences between the two but critical ones. I'm working to get a better understanding."

"Where does the liquid come from?" she asked, closing her eyes, waiting for its effects.

"Animals," he said quickly. "I don't want to be grisly, but it comes from animals and it isn't easy to prepare. Don't worry about these things. Just relax and have a beautiful time. I'll be right here when you come back."

The next day, Alex found a FedEx box waiting for him at the lab. It was from Mexico. He hurried into his office, closed the door and ripped the box open. Inside were two large plastic bottles. The only markings on the labels were the weight of the contents: one read 35 GRAMS; the other, 46 GRAMS. He pumped his fist in triumph. Eighty-one grams! Almost 200,000 doses! "I love you!" he said out loud and immediately hit his speed dial.

In seconds, Cifuentes was on the line.

"Alex! I'm guessing you got my package!"

"Oh, man. You're the best. Eighty-one grams! You're too much!"

"That's what my wife was telling me last night." Cifuentes chortled. "I'm glad to help my old friend."

"Tell me how much I owe you. I may not be able to pay you all at once, but give me a target."

"Actually, Alex, I don't think I want money from you. With respect, I'd like something else."

"Tell me. Anything I can do for you."

"I want to know if this peptide is the drug that's being called Bliss in America."

Alex breathed hard into the handset. "I'll be honest with you, Miguel. One of my lab techs stole your original supply and started selling it. I was horrified."

"I read in the papers that it's going for a hundred bucks for half a milligram."

"That's what I've heard too."

"Okay," Cifuentes said. "That's all I needed to know. We're square, my friend."

Alex tried to read between the lines but decided to keep his conclusions to himself. "Miguel, look, there's one more thing. I've got reasons to believe that other isomer combinations might be even more interesting. Is there any chance you could do some more explorational chemistry for me?"

There was a long pause on the line. "That's kind of you to think of me for that, Alex, but frankly, I think I'm going to be extremely busy in the near future. So, stay warm up there and take care of yourself. Okay?"

31

Frieda Meyer's house was a lovely old colonial shoehorned into a small tree-filled lot in Chestnut Hill, a five-minute walk from the heart of the Boston College campus. Cyrus had rarely returned to the college: after all, he wasn't an alumnus, he was a dropout. So there was no small pleasure revisiting the campus in a semiofficial capacity.

He'd rehearsed what he would say when he placed the call. A secretary told him to hold the line and a minute later, a familiar voice with an authoritative German accent cut in.

"Hello, this is Professor Meyer."

Cyrus cleared his throat. "Professor, my name is Cyrus O'Malley. I'm sure you don't remember me but I was one of your students twenty years ago."

"It's an interesting name, Mister O'Malley, but you're right, I don't recall you. Undergraduate or graduate student?"

"Undergrad."

"How may I help you?"

"Have you heard about the drug known as Bliss?"

"Bliss? Is that the one that's said to produce divine hallucinations?"

"That's right. I'm with the FBI now, in the Boston office. Bliss is something of a problem, as you've probably seen."

"What's this to do with me, Mister O'Malley?"

"When I was a sophomore I took one of your courses, Two Thousand Years of Faith."

"I still teach it. It's very popular because it's a gut. You have to work hard to get below a B minus."

"That's why I took it. I recall the *Underground Course Guide* said, 'God forgives and so does Prof. Meyer.'"

She laughed heartily. "Well, I'm glad something stuck with you."

"I was wondering if I could come over to talk about it with you. I'm trying to understand the phenomenon better, on a religious and mass psychology level."

"I must say, what I've heard about this drug intrigues me. There are interesting implications of induced collective spiritual visions. I'd be pleased to visit with you. It might be fun. I rarely get involved in anything topical."

"I appreciate it. When's a good time?"

"How about my house on Wednesday? Four o'clock. Proper tea-time."

"That'll be fine."

"Do you mind if I invite a couple of my colleagues?" she asked. "It might make the discussion livelier."

"Are you sure it's okay, my being here?" Emily asked as he stopped at the curb.

"Absolutely. She's bringing some people too. You know more about this stuff than I do anyway. I need an interpreter."

"Hardly! But I've been looking forward to this."

While Cyrus rang the doorbell, Emily admired the canary yellow clapboard house with black shutters and black door. "Such a pretty place," she whispered.

When Frieda Meyer opened the door Cyrus was momentarily taken aback. In his mind's eye she was an attractive middle-aged woman whose long hair flowed as she strode around campus at an athletic pace. The woman at the doorway had left middle age behind and was borderline frail in appearance, her hair piled into a silver bun, albeit her voice had lost none of its vigor and youth.

"Hello there!" she called out. "Come inside. You found us all right?"

"Yes, thank you. No problems. Professor, this is a friend of mine, Doctor Emily Frost. She's a psychiatrist who's also interested in the drug."

"Welcome to the both of you." She studied his face. "Now I've seen you I'm quite sure I don't remember you," she said bluntly. "But never mind. There've been so many."

They hung their coats and followed her into the sitting room, a space miniaturized by a concert grand squeezed into the corner. The rest of the furniture was forcibly arranged to accommodate the piano, pressing the sofa and chairs into a small conversation area around a rug.

Three men rose and Meyer took Cyrus and Emily by the arms like children to introduce them in turn. They were fellow faculty members in the Theology Department: Rabbi Paul Levin, roughly Cyrus's age, a smooth-shaven man with a small yarmulke held in place with a bobby pin; Prof. Walid Sharif, a plump olive-skinned Egyptian in his fifties with a perpetual smile; and Father Andrew Clegg, a tall Jesuit in his sixties with a shock of white hair, who radiated an aura of good health.

They sat and exchanged small talk until Meyer poured the tea. Then she sat lightly in one of the chairs and pointed at Cyrus with a cookie. "You know, your namesake, Cyrus, King of Persia, was an interesting fellow. He was one of history's most tolerant and visionary rulers. When he conquered the Babylonian empire in 539 B.C. he didn't impose the Persian gods on his new subjects. He encouraged the restoration of ancient temples. He even invited the Jews back to Judah to rebuild their own temple. Maybe you were destined to spread religious tolerance yourself."

"I don't know about that," Cyrus replied shyly.

"Why don't you tell us about this Bliss drug so we're all singing off the same hymnal?"

He told them what he knew. It was a circular peptide, he said, recently discovered by a Harvard neuroscientist from the brains of animals at the brink of death. It targeted receptors in the limbic part of the brain.

"I'm a little fuzzy on anatomy," Meyer said. "What is that?"

Emily helped out. "It's a group of structures deep in the brain controlling emotion, behavior, long-term memory. It's very ancient from an evolutionary sense. The earliest mammals had limbic brains. Sometimes you hear it called the seat of the soul."

Father Clegg eagerly jumped in. "If I recall an old *Scientific American* article, drugs work on receptors like keys in a lock. I can fancifully imagine this circular drug fitting precisely into a circular keyhole in the seat of the soul. I'm reminded of the God-shaped hole."

The professors murmured while Cyrus looked puzzled.

Clegg continued. "The God-shaped hole is an expression of the emptiness that exists in the consciousness of nonbelievers or those who've lost faith. It's almost as if this drug fits this God-shaped hole in a metaphorical way."

Levin leaned forward. "I find this very disturbing, even frightening. This is a drug-induced image of godliness. It's not arising from faith. It's coming from pharmacology."

"I agree it is disturbing," Sharif said. "And that makes it fascinating. I hardly know where to start."

"How about *In the beginning*?" Meyer asked, provoking some merriment.

"You've all probably read about the striking similarity of the hallucinogenic experience from person to person. The only significant difference is the identity of the greeter, usually a deceased relative or friend. This is the part that's incomprehensible to me," Cyrus said. "That's what I want to understand."

"Why does it have to be an hallucination?" Meyer asked.

"As opposed to real?" Levin scoffed.

"Frieda is being deliberately provocative, I think," Sharif said.

"Am I?" she challenged. "Isn't this the proof philosophers have been searching for? Isn't this proof that an afterlife is real, that God exists within each and every one of us? Humor me with your thoughts, oh esteemed colleagues."

Levin chuckled. "Okay, Frieda, I'm game. The rabbis of the first century pointed out that God was utterly incomprehensible. Moses failed to penetrate the mysteries of God. King David threw in the towel, admitting that it was a futile task since God was too much for the human mind. Jews were even forbidden to pronounce his name as a reminder that any attempt to understand him was pointless. His divine name was written YHWH and *Yahweh* wasn't pronounced in any reading of the scripture. One of the favorite synonyms of God used by the Hebrews was *Shekinah*, derived from the word *shakan*, to pitch one's tent. Wherever the Israelites wandered, God was there with them, in their own tent, in their own soul. Also, the Torah teaches Jews not to think of God watching over them from above. Instead we are encouraged to cultivate a sense of God within so that our dealings with one another become sacred encounters. So the concept of God inside of us is very old."

"Saint Augustine dwelled on this subject," Clegg observed. "He too believed that God was to be found not on high but deep within, in the mind. He wrote about something he called *memoria*, or memory, which really wasn't memory in the way we regard it but something closer to what the psychologists would call the unconscious. It was through this unfathomable world of images, plains, caverns and caves that Augustine descended to find his God. He could only be discovered in the world of his mind. He wrote in his *Confessions* a passage I committed to memory some years ago because of its power: 'Late have I loved you, beauty so old and so new; late have I loved you. And see, you were within and I was in the external world and sought you there, and in my unlovely state I plunged into those lovely things which you made. You were with me, and I was not with you. The lovely things kept me far from you, though if they did not have their existence in you, they had no existence at all.'"

"That's so beautiful," Emily murmured.

Sharif slurped the last of his tea. "To be sure, there is a dichotomy of revelation within all our religions. The God of the Jews may dwell within; yet, undeniably, one of the most powerful parts of the Old Testament is where Moses came down from Mount Sinai, having shielded himself from the revelation of his divine presence, which made the skin of his face shine with such an unbearable light that the Israelites could not bear to look at him. That's an *external* revelation. In my religion, the prophet Mohammed also was on a mountain, Mount Hira, on the seventeenth night of Ramadan in the year 610. He was awoken from his sleep and found himself enveloped by a devastating divine presence, which commanded him: *'Iqra!'* Recite! And though he protested that he was not a reciter, or holy soothsayer, he was enveloped again by this presence until the breath was squeezed out of his body. After the third command to recite, the words of a new scripture, the Koran, began to pour from his lips. That too is an external revelation. However, in Islam, one can also find writings that suggest that God is within us, indeed within everything. The eleventh-century theologian Al-Baqillani developed a theory known as atomism to give a metaphysical basis for Moslem faith. Simply put, there was no reality but al-Lah, the God. The entire universe was reduced to innumerable individual atoms and nothing had a specific identity of its own. Only God had reality. Only God could save man from nothingness. It was a metaphysical attempt to explain the presence of God in every detail of our lives and a reminder that faith did not depend on rational logic."

Levin got up and made fidgety circles around the piano while talking next. "This notion of an inner path to God reminds me very much of the early Jewish mystics, particularly the Throne Mystics of the fifth and sixth centuries, and the Kabbalists of the twelfth and thirteenth centuries, who sought the personal God from within. Mystics through the ages have used various techniques—fasting, vigils, chanting—to attain a state of alternative consciousness to reach the spirituality inside of them."

Sharif interrupted him. "Yes, Paul, this is true for the mystical Sufi Moslems as well. They used to chant themselves into bizarre unrestrained behaviors."

"The common denominator among the mystics," Levin continued, "was their reaction to an increasingly cerebral faith. You know, believe because you are meant to believe. The mystics felt the need to connect more directly to God's presence, which was constantly with them. They embarked on inner journeys to find him. Rabbi Akiva described his ascent through the heavens to the Throne of God, encountering on his way stones of pure marble. This was a metaphor for a journey to the depths of the mind, involving great personal risk because one may not be able to endure what is found there."

"Will you permit me to quote Augustine again?" Clegg asked.

"You can quote him all evening if you wish, Andrew," Meyer said approvingly.

"All right then. Augustine experienced a personal ascent to God at Ostia, which he wrote about. 'Our minds were lifted up by an ardent affection toward eternal being itself. Step by step we climbed beyond all corporate objects and the heaven itself, where sun, moon and stars shed light on the earth. We ascended even further by internal reflection and dialogue and wonder at your works and entered into our own minds.'"

"Mohammed too had a similar experience when he made his Night Journey from Arabia to the Temple Mount in Jerusalem. He was transported in sleep by Gabriel on a celestial horse and in heaven he was greeted by Moses, Abraham, Jesus, and a crowd of other prophets. Then Gabriel and Mohammed made their way on a perilous journey up a ladder through the seven heavens until finally they reached the divine sphere."

"Those who've taken Bliss also describe a very specific journey," Emily said.

"Until they snap out of it and return to reality," Cyrus added.

"Or another manifestation of reality," Meyer said with a twinkle in her eye. "How can we be so sure that these inner journeys aren't real too? There's a collective reality I'd like to talk about."

"Here comes Carl Jung!" Clegg warned.

"It's an inside joke," Levin explained to Cyrus. "Frieda is a Jung junkie. We've never had a theological discussion without her bringing up Jung."

"Guilty as charged!" Meyer exclaimed. "You see, Mister O'Malley, my grandfather was a psychiatrist who was friends not only with Sigmund Freud but also with Carl Jung. When Jung and Freud had their famous rift my grandfather acted as go-between to try and patch things up but their differences were more than academic. The bitterness couldn't be healed. I've been a Jungian my whole life."

"Don't forget what Jung once said," Sharif added, ready to laugh at his own words. "Thank God I am Jung and not a Jungian."

"I admit that there have been Jungians who haven't covered themselves with glory, but I'm not one of them," Meyer replied, wagging her finger. "Look here. There are inescapable Jungian elements in the Bliss story. Do you recall the terms *archetypes* and *collective unconscious* Mister O'Malley?"

"From your course, professor, a long time ago."

"Well, Doctor Frost, as a psychiatrist, I'm sure this will bore you to tears, but Jung didn't coin the term *archetype*. He borrowed it from the Platonic philosophers and applied it to psychology. He described them as 'typical modes of apprehension' or patterns of psychic perception and understanding common to all human beings as members of the human race. Jung was a student of anthropology, myth, religion, and art. His broad knowledge of these disciplines allowed him to see that the symbols and figures that continually appeared in his patients' dreams were identical to the symbols and figures that had appeared and reappeared over thousands of years in myths and religions all over the world. Jung found it particularly significant that he was often at a loss to trace the appearance of such symbols in his patients' dreams to the patients' individual lives. You see, Jung bought into Freud's theory of the unconscious part of the way. He agreed with Freud that there was a layer of the unconscious he called the *personal unconscious* that was identical to Freud's concept of the unconscious—that is, a repository of repressed personal memories or forgotten experiences. In the Freudian unconscious lay the memories of everything the individual had experienced, thought, felt, or known that was no longer held in active awareness. Jung, however, felt there was more. He conceived of a second layer of the unconscious—the *collective unconscious*—to account for similarities in psychic functioning and imagery throughout the ages in highly diverse cultures. The collective unconscious was the realm of archetypal experience. Jung believed that becoming aware of the figures and movements of the collective unconscious would bring an individual directly into contact with essential human experiences. He felt the collective unconscious to be the ultimate psychic source of power, wholeness, and inner transformation. Based on his research, he felt he was on strong scientific ground for his assertions."

"So Frieda, you're suggesting that this drug is providing a channel into the collective unconscious?" Clegg asked with an amused tone.

"Why not?" she posited. "The dream state takes us there. So does meditation. Why not a drug? Do any of you have a better explanation to account for these phenomena? Look at the archetypes here: to start with, emerging from darkness into the light. Throughout recorded history—in myth, in legend, in the bible, in the Koran—light represents the energy and radiance of the spiritual being. 'Let there be light!'

"Then there's the river. The River Jordan? The River Styx? One must always cross a river to get to the other side. And lastly, the gatekeepers: those who wait to escort the person to heaven or the underworld or the afterworld or whatever you wish to call it. Myths and religions are riddled with these images."

Levin leaned forward. "What about the image of the gatekeeper as a loved one? That sounds more like some of these near death experiences we've all read about. Someone almost dies in a hospital emergency room, feels himself hovering over his own body watching the proceedings, enters a tunnel, sees Christ or an angel or some spiritual being, and then encounters a deceased loved one who's presumably there to ease him down the road. Then the doctors bring that person back and he lives to tell about it."

"Maybe Bliss is stimulating the same receptors in the brain that are activated in near death experiences," Emily suggested.

"Or maybe this whole thing is mass hysteria," Levin said caustically.

"I agree," Sharif said. "People, especially young people, are eminently suggestible. There's a spiritual void in our society. People are looking for something to give meaning to their lives, and organized religion, I'm sorry to say, doesn't provide the answers to satisfy many of them."

Meyer lightly pounded the arm of her chair. "Don't be too dismissive of the phenomenon that's being described. Perhaps we are witnessing biological proof of the existence of the collective unconscious. Maybe we are witnessing proof of the existence of God! Please gentleman, keep your minds open. As theologians, it's our responsibility to study this phenomenon with our biological colleagues and offer spiritual interpretation."

Cyrus saw a youthful exuberance and vitality in Meyer's face that brought her closer to the way he remembered her. She was enjoying herself, playfully feeding off her colleagues' skepticism.

Clegg stretched out his long legs and extended his neck to relieve the tension in his shoulders. "This has been an interesting discussion, Frieda. Thank you for inviting me. My bottom line is that I believe in God. I don't believe in Jung, I don't believe in molecules and receptors. I do believe God is in each one of us, but in a metaphorical, not a literal sense. I must agree with Paul and Walid that this drug Bliss is causing mass hysteria. We do have a responsibility here but it's a responsibility to make sure that religious belief isn't corrupted and trivialized by a drug experience." He looked at his watch and vigorously sprang to his feet. "My goodness, where's the time gone?" The other men followed suit.

Meyer saw the professors out and came back with Cyrus and Emily's coats.

"Was this useful?" she asked Cyrus.

"Very much so. Thank you."

Meyer warmly clasped Emily's hand then took his and vigorously shook it. "This has been one of the most stimulating afternoons I can remember. For an old woman it doesn't get much better than this! Tell me, Mister O'Malley, what grade did you get in my course?"

"I got an A."

"Good lad. Well done."

32

Two days later, Alex was in London, bleary from a sleepless night on the Boston to Heathrow flight. He was traveling light, a backpack only, with enough clothes for a couple of days.

He stood before a door badly in need of paint. He buzzed several times then hammered it with his fist for good measure. The flat was small and even if Joe was asleep, the racket would have woken him. Disappointed, he tried his mobile.

"Yeah?" the voice was thick and sleepy.

"Joe, open the bloody door!"

"Alex?"

"Yeah."

"What do you mean, open the door?"

"I'm standing in your hall, man!"

"Where?"

"Hackney, where do you think?"

"What the fuck are you doing in Hackney?"

"Visiting you, you idiot. Open the door."

"Won't be a big help to you, mate. I'm at my girlfriend's in Wapping. Joke's on you."

An hour later, Alex was standing in front of the proper door. Joe was unshaven and woozy, bare-chested, his sweatpants low on his hips. He hastily put down his coffee mug to hug his brother and ushered him inside.

"Michelle's not here, mate. She's got a real job."

Alex blinked into the bright light flooding in through two huge windows. "Christ, Joe, what does she do?"

The flat was starkly modern with blond wood everywhere and enormous picture windows that took in an expanse of the Thames and the Tower Bridge.

Joe scratched his hairy chest and laughed. "She's a lawyer. Can you imagine me, with a bloody lawyer?"

"Does she know you're a psycho?" Alex asked.

"Yeah, she's onto me. I'll be back in my shithole in Hackney before long, I expect. Why the hell are you really here?"

"I told you. To see you."

"Something's fishy but I'll get the truth out of you. Have a coffee. Enjoy the view."

They talked about Joe mostly, about the army. Three tours in Iraq, three in Afghanistan with the 11 DOD Regiment. He'd used up most of his nine lives as a staff sergeant in ordinance disposal. He'd seen it all, done it all, had mates killed by snipers and booby traps. He had photos on his mobile of Helmand, where everything—the roads, the buildings, the men—were sand-colored.

"That's me, on the floor, passed out drunk on my last night there. I'm done, Alex. Paid my fucking dues."

"What now?" his brother asked.

"Mooching off of a rich lady's a good start, don't you think?"

London was warmer than Boston and Alex was keen to walk. Joe agreed, as long as the ultimate goal was to wind up in a pub.

They followed a route along the river, the waters slate-colored and whipped by a stiff wind. Joe knew the area better than Alex, if only because his new woman was outdoorsy with some appreciation for local history. They made their way down St Katherine's Way toward St Paul's, Joe talking and pointing, a regular tour guide. "See that?" he waved over at the smart three-master tied up in St Katherine's dock. "That's the Great Turk, a man o' war. Nice, eh?" Joe cooed at some of the private yachts moored in the marina and chattered on about the virtues of water over desert.

They turned onto Wapping High Street, which gently followed the course of the river. "This bit here," Joe pointed at all the modernity. "In the sixteenth century it was all sailors and whores. Filthy place. I probably would've been right at home." A bit further west, in front of the headquarters of News International, he said, "Did you know, that's where the *Sun's* published? Dickie would've worshipped here. Sacred ground."

"I think they do the *Times* too," Alex said.

"No titties in that one," Joe said, dismissively.

They arrived at their destination near the narrow alleyway leading to Wapping Old Stairs and the rocky riverbank. The pub, Town of Ramsgate, had been the scene of more dramatic events in history than two brothers catching up. The capture of the bloodthirsty "Hanging Judge" Jeffreys during the Bloodless Revolution in 1688; convicts bound to Australia, chained in the basement, awaiting their pitiless passage. It was filled with nautical bric-a-brac, pleasantly deserted in a lull before the lunch rush. They took their pints to a corner table.

"You ever see Aunt Peggy?" Alex asked. She was the cold woman, Dickie's sister, who reluctantly raised the two boys.

"Not likely. You?"

"Christmas cards," Alex said. "That's about it."

At last Joe said, "Don't you think you ought to tell me why you're here?"

"I want you to come with me back to the States."

"I told you *no* before. Why wasn't that good enough?"

"I'll tell you the reason."

"Go on."

"I've discovered something important."

Joe drank several gulps. "Not surprised. You're a clever monkey, Alex. If it makes you filthy rich, I'll take care of your security."

"I'm not interested in money."

"No, course not. Spill the fucking beans, will you?" Joe said impatiently.

In a low voice, Alex told him everything, everything except the murders. He described Bliss trips in exquisite detail, talked about their profound effects on people, the effect it had on him. Joe was drinking faster than his brother and stopped him to get another pint. He returned to the table rolling his eyes. "Go on. You were saying?"

"I was about to tell you who I saw."

"Okay, who?"

"Dad."

"How's old Dickie then?"

"You're not taking me seriously."

"I am serious—seriously drinking, mate."

Alex drank some more of his first pint to humor him. "I want you to try Bliss."

Joe laughed. "No fucking way."

"You won't believe it, Joe. It'll change your life."

"I don't want to change it. It's good enough the way it is."

Alex took a red paper tube out of his pocket. "Please."

"You carried drugs on the fucking plane, Alex? Are you crazy?"

"It doesn't look like anything. Will you?"

"No! I'm a beer man. I'll smoke a little, but that's it. No wacky stuff for me. Look, I hope you had some other reasons for coming over here because it's an expensive way for me to tell you to go fuck off."

They hung out all day, with Alex taking a nap on the fancy sofa. Before Michelle came home Alex tried to bring up Bliss again but his brother shot him down. Later, the three of them went out for a bistro meal, compliments of the lawyer. She was a nice enough lady, Alex thought, but there wasn't an abundance of chemistry between her and Joe. They were from different orbits. Joe was right. He'd be back in Hackney soon enough.

"How long are you going to be staying, Alex?" Michelle asked.

"Not long. A day or two."

"You're welcome to stay with us," she offered. "If you're happy to kip on the sofa."

"You know, I'll stay at Joe's place if that's okay. It's closer to where I've got some business to do."

"I'll give you a ride," Joe said. "Least I can do for you."

It was late when Joe turned the key in the door of his Hackney flat. The place was a mess with dirty clothes and the detritus of a long army career strewn about.

"There's clean sheets in the closet if you want to do up the bed," Joe said.

"Any beer?" Alex asked.

"I've always got beer." He pulled two cans from the cupboard. "Last drink of the night. I've got a lady in waiting."

When Joe went to use the loo, Alex calmly emptied a straw of Bliss into Joe's lager and gave the can a shake.

They talked some more and finished their drinks. Joe was ready to go, still alert, and Alex stalled him, keeping the conversation going, reminiscing about the bad old days after they were orphaned, when Joe used to bash any kid who messed with his skinny brother.

"Fuck me," Joe said suddenly. "I can't be that pissed."

"You all right?" Alex asked, studying him like a specimen.

"I'm knackered as hell," he said sleepily.

"Lie down for a minute. It'll pass."

Alex helped him to his bed and took his shoes off just as he slipped into unconsciousness.

He pulled up a chair and sat beside Joe, watching his face, checking his pulse, waiting for his brother to return.

Joe's mobile rang a couple of times, leaving missed calls from Michelle. On the third try, Alex picked up and apologetically told her that Joe was passed out from drink. He'd put him to bed. She laughed it off and said it wasn't every day he got to see his brother. She forgave him.

Before an hour had passed, Joe was back, blinking and smiling.

Some people came out of a Bliss trip talking a mile a minute, uncontrollably voluble. Joe was the laconic sort, a man of few words, and even Bliss didn't change that.

"Jesus, Alex, you gave it to me, didn't you?"

"Are you mad at me?"

"I'm not mad at you. I saw Ma. She was so fucking happy."

Alex smiled. "I'm sure she was. Will you come with me, Joe?"

He shakily propped himself to a sitting position. "Yeah, I'll come."

33

Alex was cautious, bordering on paranoid. All the way across the Atlantic he worried that Cyrus O'Malley might have him picked up in the customs hall ... or in the terminal ... or at his home. So he had Jessie meet them at Terminal E at Logan with a bag full of clothes in the trunk. As he was collecting his things to deplane, he realized wistfully that he'd probably never see his house again. It didn't matter.

Jessie was waiting at the arrivals hall with a large purple scarf wrapped around her neck and an electric smile. Alex hugged her so hard she couldn't breathe. She emerged from the clinch laughing and put out her arms to welcome Joe.

"So this is your lass," Joe said, kissing her on the cheek. "What are you doing with a wanker like him?" he asked playfully.

"I don't know what a *wanker* is," she said sweetly. "But I love him."

"Never mind," said Joe, hoisting his duffel bag. "To each his own. Show me America then."

"I need to show you my lab first," Alex began to explain.

"I need to give you something," Jessie interrupted Alex as they were getting into the car. She handed him an envelope. "It's from Arthur Spangler."

"Is he okay?"

"He's dead," she said. "His brother found this letter to you in his pocket."

Alex unfolded the handwritten note.

Weller. Thought I should take the precaution of penning this in case I go too far. As a scientist, you need to know this info. I've gotten a good supply of Bliss on the streets and have been experimenting with higher doses to achieve greater effects. 3 mg put me out for a long time but didn't improve the performance. One way or the other I'm determined to cross that goddamn river! Tonight I'm taking 10x the usual dose = 5 mg. If I don't wake up, then you've got yourself some data on the lethal dose. Cheers!
Art.

Alex folded the letter into his breast pocket. "I'm going to miss him," he said. "But I'm happy for him."

Alex drove from the airport to the medical school, pulled his car into the alley behind his building and stopped at the loading dock. It was 9 p.m. and the alley was deserted. He let himself in with his pass key and led Jessie and Joe up the rear stairs to his floor. Thankfully, all the labs up and down the corridor were dark so they could work in isolation. He commandeered some trolleys in a common equipment room and they wheeled them into his lab.

Alex went around the lab pointing at this computer, those HPLC columns, that rack of tubes and beakers, and Joe and Jessie dutifully unplugged and stacked and carried until all the carts were full of gear. Alex cleaned out his desk, retrieved his notebooks and secured the new bottles of pentapeptide from Mexico. They were finished in ten minutes.

Soon they were in the clear, driving away from Boston, heading toward the highway, Joe sharing the backseat with the equipment.

Past midnight, the car left Route 95 at Bangor, Maine, for a smaller artery. Joe was snoring in the back. Jessie kept stroking Alex's arm and shoulders to keep him alert.

After a while, he caught sight of a sign for Lucerine-in-Maine, a happily whimsical name that told them they were on track. In half an hour they spotted the turnoff to Ellsworth and began heading toward the rocky coast.

Jessie was reading from the directions she'd gotten from Erica and had Alex turn at a mailbox with Parris clumsily printed on its side in white paint. They drove for a good quarter mile along a winding gravel road until an imposing shingled house came into view. At the front door, Alex killed the engine and declared, "We're here."

He was first out and immediately bombarded with wonderful sounds and smells. Seagulls cried overhead and nearby waves rolled and crashed against rocks. The air was cold, clean, and salty. He tried to pick out things in the pitch dark. A light went on in a second-floor window. Erica opened it and called out.

Joe woke with a start, declared he had to take a piss and proceeded to splash the gravel by the rear tire.

"You'll grow to love him," Alex told Jessie, his arm wrapped around her waist.

The house belonged to Erica's parents, long-term summer residents of Bar Harbor. It had been in the family for generations. Over the gabled entrance was a carved wooden sign, Welcome to High Cliffs.

Erica flung open the door in her pajamas. She hugged Alex and Jessie and ushered everyone in to the most beautiful house Alex had ever seen. He instantly felt comfortable. *A good place to start something important*, he thought.

It was eighty years old, two dozen rooms, built at a time where grace and beauty came from the understated quality of the joinery, the gull-winged sweep of a staircase, the warm succulence of wood grain. The entry hall and adjoining rooms were oversized and filled with furniture from a bygone era of casual seaside elegance. Straight ahead was a great room that ran the entire length of the back of the house with multiple clusters of overstuffed sofas and chairs and a vintage Steinway at one end. At the other end was a stone fireplace, large enough for three people to stand upright in the firebox. Most of the floor was covered by the largest Persian rug he'd ever seen.

"It's a beautiful house, Erica. Thank you," Alex said.

"Think there's any drink about?" Joe whispered to him.

"We'll get you sorted out, don't worry," Alex said.

"We've got everything!" Erica exclaimed, overhearing him. "The kitchen and pantry are through there. Help yourself."

Joe winked at Erica and said, "I think I'm going to like it here."

Erica announced she was going upstairs to rouse everyone and Alex didn't stop her. The moment, he felt, was weighty. It should be marked with words. It would be a pity to wait till the morning.

It took ten minutes for everyone to get down to the great room for a sleepy but happy assembly. The core of the Uroboros salon was present: all those whom Alex truly had wanted to join him.

Davis Fox was there, cozy in a terry cloth robe. Sam Rodriguez had been sharing a bed with Erica. He'd pulled on jeans and a sweatshirt and was grinning from ear to ear. Melissa Cornish, a six-footer, had her old basketball sweats on; in her youth she'd been a top player at U Mass. Alex had met her long ago at a jogging track. She taught criminal justice at Northeastern and was one of his original Uroboros members. Vik Pai had managed not only to shave but get dressed in khakis and a white oxford shirt. He was small but sturdy with a dazzling flash of Bollywood looks. Vik was another original, a long-term grad student at Harvard's Divinity School with an interest in cross-cultural views of death and dying. The last two were Steve Mahady and his girlfriend. Steve was a science teacher from Boston Latin School, a heavily bearded bear of a man who'd been with Uroboros for four years. Since joining he'd never missed a meeting and was probably Alex's fiercest loyalist. His girlfriend, Leslie, was a quiet systems analyst who worked for Verizon, a woman absolutely devoted to Steve and rarely more than inches away from him at all times.

Alex proudly introduced Joe to the group and the man endeared himself by placing bottles of beer into willing hands.

"I know it's late," Alex began. "But I wanted to say something tonight. I called out to each one of you and you all said *yes*. You were the ones I wanted for this journey. And you gave me your answer. You dropped your everyday lives and came here without even knowing why I wanted you. That devotion means a lot to me. Now I know it's not devotion to Alex Weller. It's devotion to our shared experience. Each one of us has taken Bliss—thank you, Erica, for naming it! Each one of us has been touched by it, changed by it. And we understand that our collective experience is meaningful not only to our own lives but to our fellow man. We have a responsibility. You know it, I know it. It's a responsibility to share our knowledge for the benefit of others. There *is* an afterlife. Millennia of arguments and speculation and blind beliefs are over. We have proof. And that means there *is* a God, a God of some sort. The comfort that brings, the overwhelming joy of not being alone and adrift in the universe, that knowledge is something we have an obligation—no, a *duty*—to share. So tonight, my friends, I formally declare that this small band of truth-seekers and truth-tellers assembled here in this magnificent house, we will form the nucleus of a new movement: a movement that will rock the world and forever change it. Humanity doesn't have to be governed by fears, worries, jealousies—small, petty things—any longer. We have the ability to move people onto a new plane where higher issues reign. So tonight, our little Uroboros Society becomes something larger, grander ... *global*. Tonight the Inner Peace Crusade is born and you, my friends, are its founding members. So, let's drink a toast to us, to the Inner Peace Crusade! I hope you like the name. It's the best I could come up with!"

They drank and chatted excitedly for a few minutes until Sam piped up and asked, "So, Alex. I've got one question: You got any Bliss?"

Alex laughed and replied, "Actually, Sam, I've got a shitload of it!"

Most of them took Bliss that night and the household didn't become active until late morning as people began filtering down from the upper floors.

Alex awoke with Jessie in the large corner master bedroom. There was a sound of seagulls and waves and the room was flooded with light. He got out of bed, careful not to wake her, and went straight for the windows. The scene beneath him was breathtaking, a strip of snow-covered lawn giving way to a sheer cliff face. Large waves pounded and sprayed against smooth dark boulders on a stony beach. The ocean was heaving and swelling all the way to the horizon where it seemed to merge with a hazy sky. Seagulls swooped past the window, fixing him with one-eyed stares.

From another window he tried to get a look up the coastline but found the view obscured by thick pine woods that surrounded the property.

He got dressed and descended the grand stairway, sliding his palm over its smooth walnut banister polished by generations of children's backsides.

The house was coming alive. In the dining room, Sam and Leslie were on their laptops. In the kitchen, Erica, Davis, and Melissa were cooking eggs. In the great room, Joe was making a fire, regaling Sam and Vik on the fine points of disarming roadside IEDs.

Alex greeted each one, exchanged hugs and cheek kisses, eventually making his way to the coffeepot. He helped himself to a giant mug and pulled Erica aside. "The house is brilliant. Thanks."

"I'm glad you like it."

"You're sure it's safe? Your parents won't be showing up unexpectedly?"

"They're in Spain for the winter. It's all ours."

He sought out Sam and Joe, had them get their coats and led them through the French doors of the great room onto the wrap-around porch at the rear. The sun was poking through a gap in the clouds and the air felt mild. If the Adirondack chairs and rockers hadn't been encased in a hard crust of snow, they might have sat to take in the view. Instead they stood at the railing and marveled, raising their voices to hear one another over the waves.

"It's fabulous, isn't it?" Alex said.

"Amazing," Joe replied.

"Look, over there." Sam pointed to a cluster of islands covered in evergreens out in Frenchman's Bay. "Erica said those are called the Bald Porcupine Islands. And out that way is Egg Rock. You gotta love these names. Nothing like that in the Bronx."

"When'd you get here?" Joe asked.

"Just a couple of days ago. We've kept to the house. Laying low." He pointed at Alex's chest. "Waiting for orders from the big guy."

Alex chuckled. "I've never been called big guy before."

"Get used to it, man," Sam said. "I've got a feeling a lot of people are going to know you pretty soon."

"I think you already see where I'm going with this, Sam. That's why I wanted to talk to you and Joe alone. I do have big plans. If things play out as I hope they will, this movement's going to get big, fast. So even though we're going to try to keep our group small, we'll need some organization, some hierarchy. That's where you two come in. I want you to be my go-to blokes: my right arm, my left arm."

Joe shrugged. "Whatever you want, Alex."

Sam, though, anxiously asked, "Why me? I'm new. Why trust me?"

"Instinct. I liked you and trusted you from the day we met. You're smart and you've got personality. I want you to help me with information. We need a web presence. We need to communicate. I need you to spearhead that for me."

"Sure, Alex," Sam agreed. "I can do that."

"And you, brother of mine, warrior. I need you to head up security. We're going to be wanted men soon enough. We're going to be hunted. You've got to see to it we survive long enough to get our job done. Will you take that on?"

"Headbanger in chief? Yeah, no problem. Born to the job."

Alex relaxed and allowed himself a satisfied smile. "Now we can get serious," he told them over the crashing surf. "God, I love the ocean." Then he put his arms around both men. "Let's go inside and see if anyone wants to take more Bliss."

34

The basement seemed to go on forever, a rabbit warren of finished and unfinished spaces. The house had a stone foundation with an unheated basement so Alex had to work with the fingers cut off a pair of gloves. He set up in a chilly room that once had been a woodworking shop, though all that remained were the wooden workbenches now, which well suited his purposes. After stringing extension cords and power strips, he plugged in one computer and analytical machine after another, waiting for the blown fuse that never came. Satisfied he had the power he needed, he moved on to setting up tubes and racks and beakers in the way he was accustomed.

Sam came down and watched him work. "It's creepy down here, man," he said.

"Well, it's got atmosphere, doesn't it? It'll do."

"Do for what? What's the plan?"

"Who knows how long we'll be here? I can't be idle. There's still work to be done on figuring out how Bliss works, what it's doing in the brain. I can't do all of it with these instruments but I can do some of it."

"You're a workaholic," Sam observed. "For me, I'm happy to ditch school and do something different."

"You won't be idle either, Sam. I've got a lot planned for you."

"Yeah, I've already been scoping out servers around the world where we can burrow in and hide. When they shut us down in one place, we'll be up and running in another. We'll always be a few steps ahead."

"That's why I wanted you, mate."

"When are you going to tell me—*us*—what it is you want to do, Alex?"

Alex sighed. The time had come to let the thoughts crowding his mind spill out. He was a scientist, not an evangelist, and the newness of the role felt like a suit of ill-fitting clothes.

"Do you like the world we live in, Sam? Does it make you proud to see all this cruelty, greed, selfishness, and violence around you? Does it make you feel good that children grow up having their goals defined for them by advertising men? Western society has hollow values. It's amoral. We're a rudderless ship. And if someone's going to tell me that it's not so bad, that I'm exaggerating, then what about the rest of the world? Without the veneer of decadence, in places where there is real poverty, you can see even more clearly how base and futile most people's lives are. Mankind desperately needs spiritual guidance."

"That's what religion's for, no?"

"Well, yes! But religions accomplish almost nothing. It's like putting a Band-Aid on a deep cut. Religions give rules of conduct, simple, easy-to-understand guidelines. *Thou shalt do this, thou shalt not do that.* And they hold out some abstract concept of God and heaven to induce people to toe the line. It's not enough! Very few, maybe only handfuls of mystics through the ages could truly comprehend on a visceral and intellectual level the enormity of two absolute truths. Number one: God exists. Number two: there is an afterlife. Bliss is like truth serum. Everyone who takes it experiences the holiest of holies. It cuts through all the crap and delivers the truth, plain and unvarnished."

"I don't disagree with what you're saying but what do you want us to do about it? Do you want the whole world to take Bliss?"

"That would be wonderful, but not very practical! But you're on the right track."

"What then?"

"I think we can help mankind achieve spiritual reorientation if just—I don't know—just a few percent of adults take Bliss. Maybe that would be sufficient to permanently change the status quo."

"Where's all that drug going to come from?" Sam asked incredulously.

"I don't know for sure. My friend in Mexico is probably cranking away. And others will follow. Profits will speed the way for prophets."

"Okay, so we sprinkle the drug around and get a good chunk of the population to use it. What do you think happens then?"

"This is theory, of course, hypothetical, but I think we'd achieve a critical mass of spirituality, enough to destroy our degenerative foundations, the worst trappings of civilization. They'd crumble. We'd have a simpler, purer way of living."

Sam laughed nervously. "What about all the chaos, man? Destruction? Death? A crumbling civilization means farmers not farming, factories not making shit, power stations not making power. We'd have some kind of postindustrial toilet bowl, a twenty-first-century Dark Ages."

"I agree there'll be some chaos and death. But you're making the incorrect assumption that death is a bad thing. You see, that's wrong. Our life on earth is not permanent. Everyone can agree on that. The act of dying is a transition state, merely a bridge from the physical world to the spiritual world. There's nothing bad about death. There's nothing to be feared. I think Bliss teaches that."

Sam looked uncomfortable. "I don't know, man. This seems pretty radical."

"Before Bliss I would have agreed; but one's perspective changes fairly dramatically, doesn't it? It's hard for me to even remember what the old state of mind feels like. You might hear the word *Death*, I hear *Deliverance*. You might say *Dark Ages*, I hear *Enlightened Ages*. A world saturated with Bliss would certainly be more primitive from the standpoint of technology but it would not be Dark. Perhaps people would choose to live simpler, moral lives, forsaking petty disputes and war, and preparing themselves for the inevitability of an eternal afterlife in God's grace."

Alex saw the look of skepticism in Sam's young face. "Come on, Sam, let's go outside."

They got their coats and went out back, crunching through the thin snow to the edge of the cliff. Below them, it was low tide and thirty yards of rocky beach was exposed. Cut into the cliff was a narrow but even stone stairway with rails leading down to the beach. Gingerly, they made their way down the icy stairs to sea level where they found a flat dry boulder, sat, and watched the rolling breakers. Alex chose this moment to remain silent and let the power of nature speak. The two men stayed there, side by side, watching the tide come in. Then finally, unable to contain himself any longer, Alex announced to Sam, "I'm throwing down the gauntlet. Thirty days. A month is going to be long enough to change the world forever. I want to start a countdown."

In the evening, after supper, Alex assembled his followers in the great room. With a glass of wine in hand he looked relaxed, confident. Jessie sat nearest to him, lovingly looking up.

Before he'd spoken to Sam that morning, his ideas had been cloistered; now, after hearing them strung into fully formed notions, he felt emboldened. They didn't sound like the ravings of a lunatic, did they? He sounded reasonable, rational, measured. He could do this! He could step up onto the stage his science had created.

Or was it a pulpit? He smiled to himself. *They're not so different, are they?*

"Okay, my friends," he began. "It's time for me to fill you in on some of the ideas I've been having. They're big ones—maybe even courageous. But they're ideas that can't be transformed into action without your help. You are the vanguard of the Inner Peace Crusade." He laughed. "God, the name does sound a little much, doesn't it? But I think we'll grow into it."

He rehashed the message he'd delivered earlier to Sam. While he did, he studied the expressions around the room, the stray comments and sharp inhalations, looking for signs of understanding, approval, resistance—and concluded it was, at best, a mixed bag. These were good people who wanted to do good things. The prospect of being agents of disruption and despair wasn't sitting well. Before he laid out his actual plan, his full agenda, he needed to convince them, really convince them, like a salesman who needed to close the deal.

"Before I go on," Alex announced gravely, "I have a confession to make. It's about Thomas Quinn. You all read about it, you all talked about it. His murder. I hope you won't think differently about me when I tell you this, but I was there when it happened." He waited for the gasps, which came. "It wasn't murder," he said. "It was suicide."

He told them that Thomas had been confiding in him that he was distraught about a failed relationship. He'd been struggling mightily with depression. After a tearful telephone call, Alex said he'd become so concerned that he left work and drove up to Thomas's house in New Hampshire where he found him on the floor of his bedroom unresponsive, a needle stuck in his arm and a vial of potassium chloride on the dresser. Quinn was without a pulse but still warm. Alex administered CPR but realized he was beyond resuscitation. As a neurologist, he knew. There were no doubts.

"So, don't hate me for what I'm about to tell you," Alex cautioned his audience, "but I made a split-second decision to make something positive from Thomas's own decision to end his life. You know that the Uroboros compound, Bliss, came from my work studying the brains of oxygen-deprived animals. Here was an opportunity to see if it also was made by humans at the point of death. I didn't call nine one one. There was no point. I took Thomas's needle and syringe out of his arm, I flushed it of chemicals in the bathroom sink, and I used it to extract a sample of his cerebrospinal fluid. There, I've said it."

Jessie was crying and Erica too.

"But he was dead … right?" Davis asked, trembling.

"Irretrievably at the point of death, yes," Alex answered.

"Then I don't see that you did anything wrong," Steve Mahady said emphatically. "If he was dead, he was dead. You're a doctor, you should know."

"Thank you, Steve. I appreciate that. Obviously, I couldn't leave him there after the procedure I'd done on him, so I put Thomas in my car and left him in a place where he'd be found. And then I processed his precious fluid. I found the Uroboros compound. Without Thomas we wouldn't have Bliss."

Alex looked down guiltily and started to weep. Then Jessie rose and stood by his side. She kissed him and asked if he was okay. Then others rose, one by one, and told Alex they still loved and supported him. Joe just shrugged and muttered that he didn't know the chap but it didn't seem that big a deal, blokes kicked it all the time.

Alex thanked them and motioned for them to sit. "Please ... there's more to the story. You need to know that I personally sampled compound isolated directly from Thomas's fluid. Jessie, you tried it too, though I spared you knowledge of its source. It was different from the Bliss you've all taken."

"How?" Sam asked.

"It was much more potent. The experience was more intense, more significant. The chemical Bliss you've taken is amazing, but the natural compound is beyond it. It leaves you with no doubt, none whatsoever, that God is there, waiting for us with our loved ones. I call it Ultimate Bliss. I'd like to find a way for you to try it. Only then will you fully appreciate the mission we're on and only then will you fully appreciate that the end will completely justify our means."

Sam understood what Alex was saying before it registered with the others. "Jesus, Alex," he said softly. "That's what your lab in the basement is for."

Melissa Cornish raised her hand then stood up, stretching out her tall frame. Her lips were trembling and she spoke haltingly. "Ginny Tinley was my friend. I've thought ... a lot ... about what she did after she took Bliss ... I've thought that way too. Whenever I take Bliss I see my mother. I was fifteen when cancer took her. I've missed her every day. I'm happiest when I see her on the other side of the river ... My only question, Alex, is ... will it hurt?"

"I'll make it like falling asleep," he promised her. "And when you wake up you'll be on the other side in your mother's arms forever."

35

30 DAYS

A vakian was trying to rub a spot of red sauce off his tie when Cyrus barged into his office. "Want half?" He pointed to his meatball sandwich.

"Weller's disappeared," Cyrus said.

"I didn't know you were looking for him."

"I'm trying to keep the heat on, keep the questions coming, get him to slip up. But no one's seen him in his lab. He told the Neuro department at Children's not to book any new consults. The mail's piling up at his house in Cambridge, his girlfriend's not around. He's flown the coop."

"Christ, Cy; aren't we busy enough? There haven't been any more drill bit murders, we've got nothing hard on the guy, and if you haven't noticed, we're up to our asses in alligators." He pointed at the copy of *The Herald* on his desk.

The headline blared, BLISS-KRIEG: It's All Over New England, Spreading Around the Country.

Cyrus was well aware. Bliss was becoming a mini-epidemic. The drug was plentiful and getting cheaper. No one knew where it was coming from but it was everywhere. New England was the epicenter, with growing pockets in New York City, Newark, Miami, Phoenix, San Diego, and Los Angeles—and everywhere the drug went there were consequences: kids dropping out of college, people not showing up to work, sporadic suicides. Bliss rapidly had become one of those cultural memes that appears out of nowhere, hits the Internet and spreads like a brush fire. Talk shows were all over it, dinner tables, church groups, Sunday sermons.

"If you don't think Weller is masterminding this whole thing, you were born yesterday, Pete," Cyrus said.

Avakian took a huge bite of his sandwich and Cyrus had to wait for him to chew. "It's not what I think … it's what Stanley and the U.S. attorney think. First of all, we still have nothing beyond circumstantial pieces of evidence linking Weller to the Quinn murder and the other head drillings. And beyond the fact that Weller admitted to discovering the drug, what do we have there? We pretty much know Frank Sacco ripped him off. We know Frank got hit by Abruzzi, we know the Abruzzi crew got the chemist in Woburn to make more of it, and if this guy could make it, others can too, I imagine. How's this lead to Weller?"

Cyrus poked his own chest twice. "In my heart I know it does."

"That's generally not persuasive in the courts," Avakian told him, chomping away.

Cyrus's mobile rang. The caller ID startled him. Emily Frost. She'd never called him before. He sat down numbly at Avakian's conference table.

"Emily, hi … how are you?"

"I'm fine Cyrus. You?"

"Okay …" Fear bubbled up. "Are you calling about Tara?"

"Oh, no! I'm not. How is she?"

He was able to breathe. "She's okay. Nothing new."

"Cyrus, I was calling about the website. Have you seen it?"

"What website?"

"The one that popped up this morning; everyone's talking about it around the hospital. Alex Weller's on it."

As he listened to her, he got up and shooed Avakian out of his seat to access his computer. The URL was innerpeacecrusade.net and clicking on it launched a video with a smiling Alex Weller standing in front of a purple curtain.

"Okay, got it," Cyrus said. "Let me take a look at this and call you back."

"What's this?" Avakian asked.

"In my heart, Pete, remember?" He poked his chest again for effect and turned up the volume.

"My name is Alex Weller. I'm a doctor and a scientist. I discovered a drug that's become known as Bliss. I want to talk to you about it. And I want to talk to you about what I think it means for you, your friends, your family, for all your loved ones, alive and departed. We're at the dawn of an amazing new era. Have you ever driven through a bank of fog, struggling to see where the road is taking you, and then the fog clears and you can see your path with great clarity? That's what Bliss is doing. It lifts the fog of our ordinary life on earth and reveals a bright, amazing path to something much more important. A joyous life after death, a certain wonderful afterlife populated with dear ones who have made the passage and something more. God!"

Avakian was stooping over Cyrus, literally breathing on his neck. "Holy shit, Cy. You were right about this guy."

In the video, Alex continued to speak for five more minutes, laying out his grand vision for a post-Bliss world, the treatise he'd presented to his followers. He then concluded with the following. "So I'm asking you to join me in a new movement, the Inner Peace Crusade, to nudge mankind toward a happier, more meaningful and yes, *blissful* path, where we will stop forever the usual practice of making ourselves and our fellow man miserable: where we will stop conflict; stop war; stop suffering. Stop worrying and start living in the absolute knowledge that this life of ours is only a transition to something truly magical, truly wonderful—truly blissful. And today, the Inner Peace Crusade is beginning a countdown to a day I call Ultimate Bliss Day. My friends, let the countdown begin!"

The video went dark and a red-numbered digital display appeared below it: 29 DAYS, 22 HOURS, 18 MINUTES, 44 SECONDS …

They watched the seconds tick off then heard Stanley Minot running down the hall, calling their names.

36

28 DAYS

The first recorded episode of someone receiving Bliss against his or her will occurred in Homestead, Florida. Two female factory workers at the Homestead Lamp and Shade Company were on lunch break at a picnic table behind the factory. It was a sunny day, the temperatures hovering around 80. Phyllis Stevenson smoothed suntan lotion on her neck and shoulders while her friend, Meg Street, sat across from her and opened a Tupperware box.

Meg pointed over Phyllis's shoulder and grunted. "The Fred man is coming."

Phyllis rolled her eyes.

Their foreman, Fred Farquar, waddled toward them, his fleshy pink arms poking out of a short-sleeved shirt.

"This ain't the beach, girls," he called out. He drew up behind Phyllis, stood over her and stared down her cleavage. "You missed a bit. Want me to help?"

"Get lost, Fred," Meg said.

"I could get lost in between those," he replied with a leer.

Phyllis stood up and almost hit him on the chin with her head. "Leave me alone! For once and for all, just leave me alone!"

"I'll leave you alone for twenty minutes, honey," he shot back, startled by her vehemence. "Then get your butt back inside. Don't forget to enjoy your lunch, now." He ambled back to the factory, chuckling.

Phyllis sat back down again and pounded the table with her fist. "I hate that man. If it weren't for this damn job I'd hit him with a sexual harassment claim. But you know how those things go: you make 'em from the outside looking in."

"How 'bout we get even with him?" Meg said. "How 'bout we give that sonuvabitch an attitude adjustment?"

"You mean cut off his ding-dong?" Phyllis giggled.

"No, I'm serious. My brother-in-law's been taking this new drug, Bliss. You heard about it, right? It's had an amazing effect on him. He used to be a lying cheating scumbag, sort of like my Ronnie but worse, and he's completely turned around since he begun taking it. He don't curse no more, he don't drink no more, and I even seen him at church. I say we slip some to the Fred man."

"That's got to be against the law," Phyllis said.

"Maybe, but who'd know? We'd be careful."

"What if it killed him?"

"It won't kill him … at least I don't think so. You sleep on it."

The next morning, Meg brought in a stick of Bliss. With a nod from Phyllis, she sneaked into Fred's office off the main shop floor and poured the contents into an open can of Pepsi on his desk, gave the can a little shake then casually walked out.

Throughout the morning the two women laughed nervously among themselves while they soldered lamp bases. An hour before lunch they heard shouting coming from Fred's office and hurried over with other workers.

Fred's boss, the general manager, was standing over him yelling for someone to call an ambulance. Fred was cross-legged on the floor yammering about his mother, Ruth.

"I think he's having a stroke," the boss declared.

Fred was carted off to the hospital for a battery of tests. Everything checked out and he returned to work the following Monday. Phyllis and Meg spent an anxious weekend more worried about being caught than anything else. First thing Monday morning, they knocked on his office door to see how he was doing. He looked up, happy to see them.

"Come in, ladies. Have a seat."

They eyed each other. He'd never offered the slightest civility in the past.

"How you doin', Fred? You gave us a scare," Meg said.

"I've never been better. I feel terrific. I honestly do."

"You do?" Phyllis wondered.

"I do. Something happened to me last week, I don't have a clue what, but I believe I had a visitation by God Almighty. I feel cleansed and purified."

"You do?" Phyllis remarked again.

"I do. I'm not a religious man—at least I wasn't one—but I had quite a session." He dabbed at his eyes with his handkerchief. "Maybe I'll be comfortable enough to share it with you one day. I only hope it happens to me again."

"That's good, Fred," Meg said, easing toward the door. "We're glad you're feeling good."

"Phyllis ..." Fred called out. "I want to say something to you ..." he dropped his chin to his chest. "I want to apologize for being a jerk. It'll never happen again. Will you accept my apology?"

"Sure, Fred. Sure I will."

The two women walked themselves to the ladies' room, shut the door, and when they made sure they were alone, burst into hysterical laughter.

"That's the best shit in the world, Meg!" Phyllis roared, propping herself on a sink.

"Honey, my Ronnie is getting a dose in his Bud Light tonight, I can promise you that."

Ted's Automotive in Worcester, Massachusetts, was a three-bay shop with a gas pump and a tiny convenience store. Ted Sperling, a gruff, unshaven man, finished filling a customer's tank with regular and returned to the warm garage. He employed three mechanics, Ramon and Hector Manzilla, brothers from Panama who'd worked for him for a decade, and a newer fellow, Bobby Lemaitre, a long-haired kid, something of a free spirit. Ted had his doubts about Bobby's personality but the kid was such a slick mechanic he overlooked the intangibles.

The guys were sitting on stools, drinking coffee in between a couple of cars on lifts.

"I ain't touching that shit." Ramon was adamant. "Put it away."

Hector chimed in, "Me neither. You're a young guy. You're making a mistake."

Bobby held his ground. "No, no, it's totally cool, man. When I was a kid, my cousin Greg, a crazy little dude, got wiped out by a car on his skateboard. I swear to God, I've seen him twice. He looks like the happiest son of a bitch on the planet, except he ain't on the planet, if you know what I'm saying. I love this shit. I'd take it every fuckin' day if Ted paid us better."

Ted limped through the bays and sidled up to them. "What the hell you talkin' about?"

Hector and Ramon clammed up but Bobby said, "I ain't ashamed about it. It ain't illegal."

"What ain't illegal?"

Bobby held up three sticks of Bliss.

"I know what that is," Ted said bitterly. "Keep that out of my shop."

"It ain't illegal," Bobby insisted, "and I don't take it at work, for fuck's sake. It puts you out like a light. Makes it hard to turn a wrench."

"I still don't like it," Ted repeated. "Put it away."

Bobby shrugged, went to the rear bays and put the paper sticks in the socket drawer of his toolbox, with Ted watching him every step of the way.

At quitting time, Bobby was fuming. He came storming over to the brothers and demanded, "What the fuck, man! Who took it? One's missing. I had three."

Ramon and Hector looked at each other. Hector said, "I swear it wasn't us, man. I saw Ted go in there when you were in the john. He took one out."

"You're shitting me! That asshole!" Bobby shouted.

Ramon took out his wallet. "How much was it?"

"Forty bucks."

"Here." He gave Bobby a couple of twenties.

"Why're you covering for him, other than he's the boss?" Bobby asked.

"Give him a break, man," Hector said. "You know what happened to him. You know, the crash and all."

Two weeks later, Ramon and Hector pulled into the service station with a couple of empty pickup trucks. The garage was dark, the pumps were off. A FOR SALE sign was hammered into the hard flowerbed.

Ramon honked and Ted came out of the bare store.

"We're here to pick up our boxes," Ramon said.

Ted opened the bay doors and let the brothers back their trucks in.

He watched silently as they wheeled the heavy toolboxes up ramps onto the beds of their trucks and tied them down.

Finally, he said, "I'm sorry. You've been with me a long time."

"We understand," Ramon said. "Hopefully, we'll find something else."

Ted seemed inclined to say more. "It's just that I don't see the point of it anymore. Since I took Bliss. You know what happened. I killed my Denise. I killed my girls."

"It wasn't your fault," Hector told him. "Black ice's a bitch. What could you do?"

"No, I was going too fast ..." He shook his head. "Here's the deal. I thought Denise'd be mad at me for what I did. But for the past two weeks, I've been taking Bliss two, three times a day, and every time she's so damn happy to see me and I'm so damn happy to see her. I'm not into the shop anymore. I don't see the point. I'm sorry for pulling the plug and I hope you land on your feet, but I don't see the point anymore."

He waited for them to drive off and closed the doors behind them.

Rachel Mahoney reported to work at the Tall Pines nursing home in Austin, Texas, to start her regular eight-hour evening shift as a nurse's aide. She and a second aide and their supervisor, a registered nurse, covered two wards: twenty men and twenty women. It was an established facility with relatively well-off patients and a solid reputation.

At nine in the evening she made rounds, pushing a juice cart from room to room, checking on her patients, tucking them in and offering a bedtime drink. She had a spring to her step, different from her usual plod. At each stop she said cheerfully, "Orange, grape, cranberry, or apple?" Every time she poured a juice she dissolved a dose of Bliss in each Dixie cup.

Half an hour later, she snuck out of Tall Pines without telling her supervisor, got in her car and drove off, whistling and humming.

She never came back.

The next day, all the Austin TV stations led off the morning news with the Tall Pines story. In the middle of the night, the nurse and the remaining aide on duty became alarmed by their elderly patients awakening with manifestations of hysteria. Some were laughing, some crying, some were shouting uncontrollably. The nurses rushed from room to room but quickly became overwhelmed. Fearing some kind of environmental contamination, they put out the call to emergency services. As the patients were being wheeled out on gurneys to waiting ambulances, they chattered excitedly and called out to long-lost husbands, wives, brothers, or sisters. There was talk of God.

Investigators had their early suspicions. Rachel Mahoney was missing. The intoxications had the hallmarks of Bliss ingestion. But before the lab results were back a posting appeared on the voluminous message board on the Inner Peace Crusade website.

I gave these dear old people in Austin doses of Bliss. I can't think of any greater gift. Now they know that God is within each and every one of them. They know he's within their reach, waiting for them. They know they'll be met by people who loved them. I hope they'll be able to face their last days with dignity and hope, maybe joy. I know not everyone will agree with what I did but it makes me feel wonderful. It's the best thing I ever did. Love, Rachel.

25 DAYS

"The director personally wants *you*." Stanley Minot was doing his best to balance pride for the office and concern for his man.

"Look, Stanley ..." Cyrus started to say.

"Cy, don't even think about telling me no. This is too big and it's too specific a request."

Before Tara's illness, he'd been as ambitious as the next agent. Now, he felt numb on the subject of striving.

"Why me?"

"The task force is a big deal. Top priority. You know Weller better than anyone in law enforcement. You know the drug. The North End raid put you on the radar screen in Washington. I'll reassign most of your other work and Pete'll have to pick up some slack. Bob Cuccio, the assistant director for criminal investigation, is the other FBI member on the task force."

"There's a lot of space on the org chart between me and Bob Cuccio."

Minot smiled. "That's why this is good for you. Next Thursday. The White House."

Cyrus looked puzzled.

"You know, big building on Pennsylvania Ave with pillars?"

"Funny. Why there?"

"Neutral territory. When you've got Homeland Security, NSA, FBI, DEA, FDA, NDIC, NIH all in one room you better go for neutral turf. And by the time you have your first meeting, hopefully FDA and DEA will hand you a big stick."

On a cool morning, a steady stream of men and women filed into the largest meeting room at FDA's Parklawn Building in Rockville. At 9 A.M. sharp, Marvin Wolff, the chairman of the Drug Abuse Advisory Committee, called the proceedings to order. The DAAC had been convened in record time, at the insistence of the Drug Enforcement Administration, to take up the narcotic scheduling of Bliss.

Over the next several hours the committee heard testimony from FDA, DEA, and National Institute on Drug Abuse staffers on the abuse potential of the drug, geographic data on usage patterns, suicide and morbidity statistics. Vincent Desjardines, who still had more Bliss patients than anyone else in the country, was brought in to testify and he nervously walked through a PowerPoint presentation. In the open public hearing, the mother of Jennifer Sheridan and other relatives who'd lost loved ones to suicide gave tearful testimony. To be sure, there were Bliss proponents there too. They were given a half dozen slots to speak about how the drug was a tool for enlightenment and self-discovery and that restricting its use would be a blow to spiritual freedom, an anathema. While they talked, surly DEA agents sitting in the audience scowled and whispered among one another conspiratorially.

Shortly before noon, the chairman called for open debate among the committee members. There was little dissent. All members strongly supported imposing severe restrictions on Bliss. When they were done, Wolff called for a vote. It was unanimous. Bliss would be immediately classified as a Schedule I drug, placing it in the same category as heroin, cocaine, and LSD. It was now illegal to make, use, sell, or possess the drug.

Law enforcement had its big stick.

The morning after the first Bliss task force meeting, Cyrus was at Reagan National Airport waiting to board the shuttle back to Boston. He called Marian to check on Tara. The girl came on the line sounding cheerful, which improved his mood no end. Then he called Emily

Frost to confirm they were still on for coffee later that afternoon. She sounded cheerful too and with that he stepped lightly onto the jetway.

Back at the office, Cyrus briefed Minot, did some paperwork then dashed off to the Longwood medical area. Emily was already at the coffee shop, smiling at him when he pushed through the door.

"How was Washington?" she asked.

"I've never seen so many puffed-up pompous pricks in one room."

She laughed. "Sounds like a faculty meeting."

Cyrus told her what he could. She was becoming his sounding board on matters related to Bliss and they'd been speaking on the phone almost daily. He wished he could go all in and tell her details about the investigation but he was careful about confidentiality. She was a good listener, a "professional listener," he joked, but she also was smart and insightful and helped him connect dots.

The task force had the formal name JTF-B, for Joint Task Force–Bliss. It was the brainchild of the attorney general to bring coordination to what was becoming a national issue now that the drug had appeared in all fifty states. Other countries already were reaching out to the United States for information and assistance, as the drug was showing up in clusters in Central America, South America, and Europe. It appeared that most of the Bliss was coming into the States through the porous Mexican border but beyond that the sources were unknown.

Cyrus confessed to Emily that he had far less interest in interdiction and enforcement strategies, which had dominated the proceedings, than in Alex Weller. In fact, his role at the White House meeting had been limited to delivering a brief profile on Weller, heavy on facts, with a dollop of his suspicions about the murders.

"I know you don't like him," Emily said, "but is there anything he's done that's criminal? From what I've seen, he's evangelical about Bliss the way Timothy Leary was about LSD. I know it may be distasteful to some, but why is it a crime, even with the drug being scheduled?"

Cyrus sighed. "I wish I could tell you everything, but you're right. He's not officially a criminal—yet. Have you seen the message board on his website?"

"It's as addictive as the drug," she joked.

"There's another layer to the website, a link to an encrypted area. Believe it or not, we've got guys at the NSA and Defense Department who can't break it. Weller's got someone working for him who knows his beans. He's got the ability to send and receive encrypted messages."

"To what end?"

"I wish we knew. I wish we knew what his countdown clock was all about. I wish I could tell you more about why I want to nail him."

"Me too," she said.

He looked up from his coffee. "I talk in my sleep."

"Hey, Cyrus," she said gently but emphatically. "I'm still Tara's doctor."

He smiled a you-can't-blame-a-guy-for-trying kind of a smile. "Let me walk you back to the hospital."

The cadence of their steps made their shoulders touch from time to time. Neither made an attempt to separate the few inches it would have taken to prevent contact.

"Can I ask you something?"

"Sure," she said.

"You told me you had a rough childhood. You know more about me than I know about you."

"Why do you want to know about me?"

"You're my daughter's doctor," he said, laughing. "I'm being diligent."

"Now you're mocking me."

"I'm not. I want to know because I'm interested in Emily Frost, the person."

She sighed. "I was eleven. We lived in a small town in Virginia. My mom got divorced when I was one. I don't remember my daddy, never saw him again, don't know what happened to him. I do remember my momma's boyfriend, though. He moved in when I was six. They fought a lot and they drank a lot. He was rough with her but she was rough with him. She split his lip, broke his hand with a pot."

"Tough gal," Cyrus said.

"Yeah, she was tough. He came at her in the kitchen one night with his fists. She picked up a steak knife and cut him. He took it away from her and put it through her chest. She died later, in the ambulance. Meanwhile, he ran into the bedroom, got his gun, came back into the kitchen and blew his brains out against the refrigerator door."

Cyrus stopped walking. "Where were you?"

"With my aunt, a schoolteacher; I used to stay there a lot. It was sane there and she liked to read to me. She wound up taking me in, raising me."

"Jesus," he whispered. "I'm so sorry."

"No, I'm glad I told you."

They started walking again in silence, all the way to the hospital entrance where she let him touch her hand when they parted.

38

22 DAYS

Communal life in Bar Harbor was taking on a rhythm like the tides as winter began to lose its grip and the snow cover began to recede.

In the mornings, they'd cook as a group and clear up. Sam would assemble the website team in the dining room for daily tasks and log onto the High Cliffs wireless network. Vik and Davis's job was to scour the site's message board, dozens of other Bliss sites that had sprung up around the world, and a host of news and social media links. Alex enjoyed receiving a summary of Bliss-related news over his lunch.

Leslie became Sam's technical lieutenant and the two would decode private messages sent to Alex by ever-forming Inner Peace Crusade satellite groups and encrypt messages Alex wanted to send out. Also, throughout the day they'd rotate the website through a succession of proxy IP addresses to hide their tracks and prevent authorities from shutting them down.

Twice a week, Jessie and Erica would make a run to Ellsworth to the big-box stores, careful not to draw attention by shopping locally in Bar Harbor or frequenting any one place.

Big Steve Mahady gravitated to Joe. Steve was a hunter and had an easy rapport with him. Erica knew where her father hid the key to the gun safe that was stocked with pistols, hunting rifles, and a good supply of ammo. The two men would hang out on the grounds, guns shoved into their coat pockets, keeping an eye on the driveway and surrounding woods, Joe happily drawing on a cigarette.

Alex liked sitting in the library, writing on a pad and watching the waves form in the distance. Jessie spent most of her time near him, filling his coffee cup, being there when he wanted to stroke her hair. He was making an effort to keep his head from swelling in conceit, but it was getting harder by the day. His website had gotten hundreds of millions of hits, *Bliss* and *Alex Weller* were the most Googled items on the web and the news was dominated every day by the growing "epidemic," a term Alex had come to despise.

Despite efforts of the DEA and Immigration and Customs Enforcement to police the border crossings and clamp down on smuggling, there seemed to be a sufficient supply of Bliss to feed the growing demand. Every time Alex read of a seizure at the Mexican border, he thought of Miguel Cifuentes, grinned, and wondered; but on Sam's advice, he and everyone else switched off their cell phones for good. He doubted he'd ever speak to Miguel again.

In any event, his mind was onto bigger topics: just over three weeks to go. There was so much to do, his head spun. *Direct action. Action by proxy.* The world had to be ripe for his plan; otherwise the countdown might come and go with a thud. He wished he hadn't been so aggressive. Thirty days! He couldn't very well reset his clock ... how would that look?

That evening, like all other evenings, they had a group dinner then retreated to their bedrooms to take Bliss. It was a paler experience than the Ultimate Bliss they'd all taken but it was still marvelous, as always. They were grateful to Melissa for her sacrifice, for letting them unpeel the next layer of the onion. Later that night, when they gathered around the fire in the great room to talk about the future of the movement, Alex looked around the circle and wondered who would be next to sacrifice him- or herself for the greater good.

In Rhode Island, Dan Mueller was making his way from cottage to cottage, doing his first property check since New Year's Day. He was paid by the local beach association in Narragansett to do monthly inspections of the seasonal units but in January he tore ligaments in his ankle and he was damned if he was going to make the rounds on crutches. The cottages could wait for him to heal.

He swore out loud at the sight of Unit 6. The back door jamb was missing a splinter the size of a chair leg and small pieces of wood littered the deck. "For Christ sakes," he grumbled. "Goddamned kids."

The broken door didn't need a key. He swung it open and looked into the unit, expecting to see a royal mess, but everything in the living room looked fine. The kitchen and bathroom were okay too. He went into the bedroom prepared to find piles of beer cans or some sign of mischief but everything was neat and tidy. He turned to leave but something under the bed caught his attention. Flexing his good ankle he lowered himself onto one knee to get a better look.

His other leg buckled and in an instant he was down on both knees, as though in prayer.

"Oh my good Lord!"

The Rhode Island medical examiner remembered the memo he'd received a few months earlier from the Boston FBI office: Be on the lookout for unusual skull piercings, particularly in young female homicides. The frozen girl had a telltale wound in her temporal bone. Alarm bells went off.

Cyrus and Avakian were on the scene within hours of the discovery.

"How long's she been here?" Avakian asked, his hands in his pockets for warmth.

"There's no telling," the ME said. "I've had a striped bass in my freezer since last summer. It's softer than she is."

"Any other evidence?" Cyrus asked. He tried not to look at the girl too closely. She was very young.

The Narragansett chief of police was there personally. He didn't get many murders in his town. "Just this," he said, retrieving a plastic evidence bag from a larger brown paper sack. "There was a coin under her body, a quarter."

"Do me a favor," Cyrus said. "If you find fingerprints, e-mail them to me right away."

The following evening, Alex finished the last of his chicken curry and sat quietly at the head of the kitchen table listening to the happy banter of his people. The kitchen TV was on low but no one was paying any attention. The days were getting a little longer and there was a lovely glow to the evening sky. In an hour or so, they'd take Bliss—but several had told him privately that they desperately wanted Ultimate Bliss again. The last time the topic came up as a group, no one had stepped forward. Alex had an idea. He'd spent the day thinking about it and now was the time to put it into play.

"I have an announcement," he said.

The table went quiet.

"I think it's time for us to take Ultimate Bliss again." He got up and went to a cupboard where he'd left a glass bowl earlier. "I think we should do a lottery. I think that's the best way to go. Does anyone disagree?"

Everyone had thin-lipped looks of surprise but no one objected. They all agreed it was a good idea. They'd abide by it if that's the way Alex wanted to go.

"I've got your names written on slips of paper," he said, holding up the bowl. "I'll pick one. I'll do it tonight and I'll process the fluid. We'll be able to take it tomorrow."

Jessie was looking down at her shoes, her lip quivering.

You don't have to worry, Alex thought. He'd folded her slip smaller than the others; Joe and Sam's too. They were too important to him. He put his hand into the bowl, felt around, and fished out one of the bigger ones.

He was about to unfold it when he saw a face on the TV. "Turn up the sound," he ordered.

Erica got up and pushed the Volume button.

Cyrus O'Malley was at a podium adorned with the FBI seal speaking into a bank of microphones.

"Today, the FBI is announcing the arrest warrant for Doctor Alex Weller. Doctor Weller, who is well known for his Internet postings regarding the illegal drug, Bliss, is wanted for the murder of Amber Fay Hodge, seventeen years of age, a resident of Roslindale, Massachusetts, found murdered earlier this week in Narragansett, Rhode Island." A picture of Alex appeared on a screen behind him. "This is Doctor Weller. His fingerprints were found at the murder scene. Currently, his whereabouts are unknown. If you have information about his location, I urge you to come forward to your local police or the FBI."

Alex got up and turned off the TV. Then he returned to his chair. The room was silent. Every eye was on him. "I'm not surprised," he said. "I thought it would come to something like this. This man, Cyrus O'Malley, has had it in for me. Jessie and Davis know it. Now that Bliss is a phenomenon, they're trying to stop our movement by stopping me. It's not going to work. I don't know this woman. It's trumped up. Sam, we need to put out a statement on our website tonight. I'll write it now."

"What about the lottery?" Jessie asked.

Alex tossed the chosen slip back into the bowl without looking at it. He stared hard at the TV screen and watched Cyrus's muted lips move.

"Forget the lottery," he said. "I've got a better idea."

39

19 DAYS

Tara's babysitter that afternoon wasn't really a babysitter. She was one of her mother's best friends, a woman named Jane who lived in the same subdivision, three houses down. A couple of times a week she'd come over to give Marian a break, letting her have a chance to get her hair done or take a class at the health club.

While Tara napped, Jane sat on a padded rocker by Tara's bed reading a magazine. The doorbell rang.

It wasn't the kind of neighborhood where people were suspicious about opening doors in the middle of the day. At first glance, the men looked pleasant and friendly: a large man with twinkly eyes and a full brown beard, and a more athletic-looking fellow with darting eyes.

"Hi," the large man said. "Are you Marian?"

"No, I'm her friend, Jane. Can I help you?"

"Is Marian home? Or her husband?"

"I'm sorry. Are they expecting you?"

The smaller man took a handgun from his pocket, pointed it at her head and shoved her inside. When she screamed he threatened in a foreign accent, "Shut up right now or I'll make you shut up. Where's the girl?"

Jane tried to contain her hysteria and could hardly make it up the staircase without her legs giving out. When her sobs got too loud for the rough man's liking she felt the gun stick into her ribs.

At the door to Tara's room, she managed to stammer, "Wh-What do you want?"

She was told to sit on the rocking chair. As the girl slept on, the rough man kept the gun pointed at her while the bearded one took gauze and duct tape from his pocket. He covered Jane's mouth with cloth, made some quick tape loops around her head and when she was silenced, made bigger loops to cocoon her to the chair. The other man relaxed and put his gun away.

Jane stared with wild eyes as the rough man leaned over and plucked Tara from her bed, bedclothes and all. She woke up, confused. "Who are you?"

"I'm a friend of your daddy's and a friend of your doctor's. Doctor Alex, remember him? The one with a ponytail."

She nodded.

"They want to see you, sweetheart."

"Why aren't they here?"

"They want you to come to them."

"Why did you put tape around Jane?"

"Too many questions, love. Time to go." He looked at Jane and said to her, "You tell Cyrus O'Malley that Alex Weller's got his daughter. You've heard of him, right?"

She nodded in terror.

"You tell him to lay off—to leave Alex alone. You tell him the alternative's not pretty." He spied a cluster of medicine bottles on the dresser. "These hers?"

Jane nodded and the bearded man scooped them up.

At the door, Tara screamed and pointed to her bed. "Freddy! Give me Freddy!"

Joe Weller pointed with his chin, "Christ, Steve, get her bloody bear, will you?"

40

18 DAYS

Cyrus couldn't find a way to shut down the panic. No body position, no thought process—nothing could squelch the white-hot fear that stabbed at him unabated from the moment he heard Marian screaming into the phone.

Stanley Minot pulled every available agent in the Boston office onto the hunt for Tara's abductors and put in an SOS to Washington to send more. Avakian tried to get Cyrus to go home or at least to his own house so Pete's wife could look after him. O'Malley refused to leave the office, though, and Minot didn't have the heart to force him away. He sat at his desk, staring out the window in shell shock, until Avakian came in and said, "There's someone in the lobby for you, an Emily Frost. Do you want to see her?"

Cyrus had phoned her, a short woeful call. She dropped all her appointments and came as quickly as she could.

"My God, Cyrus," she said when Avakian left her at his door.

"Emily."

He was ashen. She pulled a chair over and sat beside him. "Has there been any news?"

He shook his head. "There's a team at Marian's house. They're interviewing her friend. They're doing forensics. I swear to God, I'm going to kill him."

"I know," she said gently. "It's hard to comprehend his cruelty. I'm not going to ask you how you're doing but how's Marian?"

"Marty told me they had to be put on tranquilizers. As much as I want to kill Weller, she wants to see me dead."

"It's not your fault."

"She thinks it is. For Christ sake, Emily, maybe she's right."

"That's not true! You were doing your job." After the news conference on Weller's arrest warrant, Cyrus and Emily had talked on the phone long into the night. He'd finally been able to unburden himself, to tell her what kind of a monster Weller was. "Even with everything I know about him now, to use an innocent child to get to you … it's horrible," she said, touching his sleeve. "Your friend Pete asked if I could get you to leave for a couple of hours. Can I take you for a drink? Please?"

Minot took personal charge of Tara's case. In his day, he'd been a good field agent and years as an administrator hadn't much dulled his edge. When he learned that one of the abductors was probably British, he had one of his agents play the neighbor, Jane, audio clips of a variety of English accents. She picked the one from Liverpool.

Following the lead, Scotland Yard was contacted to check on relatives of Alex Weller. They e-mailed back that he had a brother, Joseph, recently honorably discharged from the British army. Following that lead, a check of flights from British airports showed that a Joseph Weller had entered Boston on a tourist visa seventeen days earlier.

Agents showed his passport file photo to Jane. They had an ID.

In short order, Joe Weller's photo was disseminated to news channels and Internet sites everywhere, right next to his brother's. The two came to share the top two spots on the FBI Ten Most Wanted List.

Alex was in the kitchen having a cup of tea with Joe when the breaking news flashed onto the TV. Joe's photo lit up the screen.

"You're finally famous," Alex said.

"'Bout time. Wonder how they found me that fast?"

"O'Malley's not stupid. Looks like you can't go home now."

He snorted. "Don't want to. I like hanging with you."

There was a scream from the hall stairs. It was Erica. "Alex! Come!"

Erica and Jessie were at Tara's bedside. The girl was thrashing, contorted.

"She's having a seizure," Alex said calmly. "Joe, you got your wallet on you?" Joe handed it to him and watched Alex work the leather in between her clenched teeth until her tongue was protected. Then he sat beside her, rubbing her cheek, soothing her. "You're okay, love. You're okay. You'll be out of it in a bit. Don't worry. Doctor Alex is here." In a minute her body was slack, her breathing normalizing. Alex looked up. "When she's with it, I'm going to up her dose of meds. She's precious cargo."

Jessie looked at him with amazement. She'd never seen him with a patient, never known him to be as tender with anyone other. "You're wonderful," she whispered to him.

"Don't be too impressed," Joe said, "he's still a wanker."

Sam rushed in. "Alex, there's something on the website. You've got to see it."

Joe punched his brother's shoulder as he passed. "A cult leader's work is never done, is it?"

In the dining room, Sam pointed to the computer. "This got logged on to the message board a minute ago."

Alex sat in Sam's chair to read it. It was from Cyrus O'Malley, with an embedded photo of Tara.

Everyone who reads this message board needs to know that Alex Weller, the head of the so-called Inner Peace Crusade, is a common and vicious criminal. He's wanted for murder of a young woman named Amber Hodge and he and his brother are wanted for the kidnapping of my eight-year-old daughter, Tara. He thinks he can make the authorities stop looking for him by holding my little girl. He's wrong. Don't buy into his hype about Bliss. It's a dangerous drug that kills people and ruins lives. And help me find him and get my daughter back. If you've seen her, please call the number below anonymously. There's a $100,000 reward from the FBI and it's the right thing to do. Please help me find my daughter.

"What do you want me to do?" Sam asked.

"Take it down. Let's not confuse people about us. Later tonight, when the girl looks better, send O'Malley a proof-of-life photo, something with a time- and date-stamped website in the frame but nothing identifiable in the background. Send it to his FBI e-mail address. Tell him if he reposts the message we'll kill her."

"Will do, Alex."

"And get some sleep tonight. Tomorrow we're going on our first direct action mission. It should be a blast."

41

17 DAYS

They packed themselves into Erica's Dodge van at dawn for the five-hour drive toward Merrimack, New Hampshire. Sam drove with Steve beside him. Alex and Jessie kept low in the back since Alex's face was increasingly recognizable. Joe stayed at the house on patrol as usual, and Erica, who had bonded the most with Tara, looked after the girl. She tried to make it fun for her, like camping, and to some extent it was working. Tara seemed happy to be getting all the attention and enjoyed her trips down to the rocky shore.

They arrived in Merrimack at lunchtime and immediately drove around the industrial park that was home to Meecham's Brewery. It was one of Meecham's six regional breweries, an old red-brick factory that produced millions of cans and bottles of Meecham's Premium Beer every month. There was a high brick wall around the brewery and an iron gate across the main service road into the complex. A huge billboard across the street from the factory showed a man's fist around a frosty amber bottle with the slogan, *When you really want a cold one ...*

As they drove past the gate, they spotted the curly-haired guard in the security hut, who gave them a thumbs-up.

"That's our guy," Sam said.

"You're sure?" Alex asked.

"Let me park and talk to him."

Sam got out and approached the security hut. After a minute he returned with a large shopping bag.

"It's cool," he said. "Kevin's a huge supporter. I've talked to him on the secure portal a dozen times. He and his wife've sold their house and emptied out their bank account. Look."

The bag contained a couple of dozen ziplock bags filled with white crystals.

Alex whistled. "I've never seen so much."

"What about access?" Steve asked.

"He's going to unplug the security cameras at the gate and in that building over there for thirty minutes. That's how much time we've got."

On the signal of the guard, the gate rolled open and Sam drove through. The only condition was that the guard wanted to personally meet Alex. He poked his curly head through the rear window, held both of Alex's hands and thanked him from the bottom of his heart for changing his life for the better.

"No, thank you," Alex told him. "And thanks to you the world's going to take even more notice of our little movement."

The guard told Sam where to park and assured him the side door of Building 7 was unlocked.

The heavy wooden doors opened inwards. The four intruders felt dwarfed by the cavernous factory, a maze of piping, catwalks, and two-story stainless steel fermentation vessels. They spent several minutes walking around the brewery floor, trying to make sense of the complicated-looking machinery.

"How do we get inside these tanks?" Alex cried.

"Let me get up on that walkway above the tanks," Sam offered. "Maybe I can find hatches up there. Kevin said we were on our own to figure it out."

He and Sam climbed up and inspected the pipes leading into one of the vessels. "There aren't hatches or portholes. It's nothing like we thought," Sam called down. "It looks like the tanks are filled through these pipes and emptied through those over there. It's a hands-off process."

Steve called Sam over to inspect something on top of the tank. "I think we've got a possibility here. Give me your monkey wrench."

Steve loosened a huge nut around a pressure valve. When he got it off, he was able to pull the pressure valve and its hose out of the tank, leaving a two-inch opening. He shined a penlight inside and called down. "It's full of beer! We can use these openings!"

Sam climbed down to the brewery floor where Alex and Jessie were unpacking plastic bags. "How much drug do we put into each tank?" Sam asked.

Alex pulled out a notebook and pen, glanced at the tanks and shrugged. "Give me a minute. They're bigger than I thought. It's not going to be easy getting exactly half a milligram into each bottle." He scribbled some calculations then looked up and said, "Hell, I don't know. Let's put three bags in each vat."

Sam and Steve sprang into action, scurrying to the top of each fermenting tank, unscrewing the pressure valves, funneling in Bliss and carefully screwing the valves back in place. Within half an hour they were finished. Before they left the factory floor they checked to make sure their presence there would remain undetected. The loading dock was piled with cases of Meecham's Premium. Sam and Steve winked at each other and soon were loading their booty into the back of the van.

Back at the guardhouse, Kevin asked how they got on.

"We did well," Alex told him. "How long till this batch hits the stores?"

"I don't know for sure," the guard said. "Far as I know, we sell it as fast as we make it."

Alex laughed. "Let's hope everyone really wants a cold one soon. Inner Peace, my friend."

On the return trip, Jessie snuggled against Alex. An hour into the journey she whispered to him something that seemed to have been on her mind. "You're not going to hurt the girl, are you?"

He patted her on the head. "What do you think I am, a murderer? Of course not. She's a sick little girl, Jessie. Her tumor's growing. But when nature calls, if I'm there, I'll be ready to harvest her. She'll be in a better place and we'll have the gift of the finest experience you can imagine: Ultimate Bliss, from a child. It'll be amazing, I promise. In the meantime, Cyrus O'Malley's going to have to back off and let us finish our work."

Satisfied, she fell asleep on his shoulder.

Sam's cell phone rang. It was one of the prepaid, untraceable units he'd picked up at the Wal-Mart in Ellsworth. "Yeah? Hey Leslie, what's up?" He listened for a minute then said, "I'll tell Alex. He's going to be stoked. And let Joe know we've got a lot of beer for him."

"What's going on?" Alex asked from the backseat.

"We got an encrypted message from Japan. This thing is about to go to a whole 'nother level."

42

16 DAYS

The annual G8 summit was a careful blend of working sessions and photo-ops. On this afternoon, the pendulum had swung toward style over substance as the leaders of the United States, Britain, France, Italy, Japan, Canada, Russia, and Germany convened at the Imperial Palace in Kyoto for a traditional tea ceremony served by the country's most accomplished geishas.

The Imperial Tea Room was a fourteenth-century pagoda now used exclusively for ceremonial purposes. Once the small house had been swept by security and deemed threat-sterile, representatives of the National Police Agency Imperial Guard joined with U.S. secret service agents and protective services agents of the other world leaders to form concentrically secure perimeters around the royal grounds.

The presidents and prime ministers were in business attire. The geisha who greeted them at the teahouse door asked them to remove their shoes and began a pleasant running commentary of the history and art of the tea service.

The tea ceremony, she told them, was considered very spiritual and relaxing, tea thought to be a link to nature, to which the Italian prime minister joked, "Give our Russian friend a double dose to calm him down."

She told them that the Japanese word for tea ceremony was *chado*, meaning "way of tea." The tearoom had fragrant tatami mats and she cheerfully chided them that Chado practitioners and guests are not permitted to step on the cracks between the straw mats.

The president of the United States, John Redland, was jet-lagged and irritable and was almost tempted to step on a crack to see if there'd be an international incident but he controlled himself. Instead, the Canadian prime minister, who must have had size 14 feet, kept accidentally landing on them with no ensuing calamity.

The room was decorated with beautiful flower arrangements and Zen calligraphy wall hangings. Through a large window they had a postcard view of a traditional water garden. The guests were seated on decorated cushions on the tatami with their legs folded under so that they were sitting on their feet. The geisha demonstrated the proper style but the only man who took to it naturally was, of course, the Japanese prime minister, who coached his colleagues, particularly the tall American, on how to shift their feet without offending etiquette or disturbing the ceremony.

Before them, a woman in a red kimono stood behind a black-lacquered table and presented each implement for inspection and explained in English their role in the ceremony. The type of tea, she explained, was called *matcha*, a bright green variety with a bitter flavor but pleasant aroma.

She demonstrated that the chado required specialized tools, a bamboo whisk called the *chasen*, hemp tea cloths known as *chakin*, a small bamboo scoop or ladle called a *chashaku*, and the tea container called the *chaki*. Then she proudly held up an ancient black ceramic bowl, the *chawan*, in which the tea was to be served. It was sixteenth-century pottery, done in the Raku ware style, a true museum piece, she said, used only for the most esteemed guests.

In a small room off the main chamber, a butler tended the charcoal fire that was heating the water. The heavy iron pot was simmering. He was careful not to let it get too hot since a boiling temperature was not optimal for the tea. He was alone in his task, listening through a curtain to the geisha's lecture.

He looked around to make sure none of the police were watching and removed a small appointment book from his inside pocket which had made it past the security screen. Inside was a folded square of paper. It contained a small mound of white crystals that he quickly stirred into the steaming water.

When the geisha lightly summoned him the butler brought out the iron pot and placed it on the table on an iron grate. They bowed to each other and the butler left, his job here done. He managed a sidelong glance at the dignitaries seated before him but his face was stony, betraying nothing.

The butler walked quickly back to the main palace kitchen where he entered a utility closet, found the *tantō* knife that he'd stashed and proceeded to disembowel himself in an efficient act of seppuku.

As he was bleeding to death, the geisha was adding hot water to the chawan and stirring the matcha into the water with a bamboo whisk to ensure a smooth consistency.

When the tea had properly steeped she poured it into fine ceramic teacups and bowed to each man who, in turn, was instructed by the Japanese prime minister how to bow back.

President Redland sipped at the tea and suppressed a grimace. He didn't like tea. What wouldn't he give right now for a Starbucks dark roast?

After tea, each guest was served a small confection, *wagashi*, delivered on a ceramic dish and eaten with a wooden pick. Redland didn't like that either and resisted the urge to check his watch. He knew he'd have to endure twenty minutes or so of small talk before getting limoed back to his hotel for a shower and a catnap. With the exception of the Japanese prime minister and the French president, who was extremely interested in the geisha, none of the men seemed to be having a rip-roaring good time.

The head of President Redland's secret service detail, Andy Bostick, was only a few feet from the teahouse door when he heard the first shout. When he and a bevy of officers rushed in he saw that the Japanese and French head of states had pitched forward unconscious. The German chancellor looked woozy, like he was about to pass out. Bostick drew his machine pistol and scanned the room for assailants but there were none. He holstered his weapon and he and another agent grabbed Redland and rushed him toward the door, screaming into his cuff microphone, "This is a Code Nine! We've got Rushmore on route to the Stagecoach. Let Pivot know we'll be at Nighthawk in two minutes. I want wheels up to Kansai the second we roll up. Tell Angel we'll be heading back to the Ranch as soon as the chopper touches down!"

As the president was being thrown into his limo in a daze, ambulances started screaming onto the palace grounds. Each head of state was being handled and evacuated by his or her own people. The limo sped off toward the Kenshun-mon Gate at one corner of the palace grounds and by the time it screeched to a stop at the side of Marine One, Redland was unconscious. Agents carried him up the stairs where a naval surgeon, a nurse, and his personal physician, Martin Meriwether, grabbed him and laid him out in the aisle. They quickly checked his vitals and hooked up a cardiac monitor. "What happened?" the surgeon shouted.

"All of them," Bostick answered, "they're all dropping like flies."

"Poison," the surgeon grunted, pulling a blood sample from an arm vein. "We may have to intubate him."

"Not so fast," Meriwether said, as the chopper lifted off. "His vitals are okay, his color's good. He's got tachycardia but his EKG looks fine. Let's hang on. How long till we get to Air Force One?"

"Seven minutes," Bostick said.

"I say let's watch him. There's nothing we can't handle once we get there. This isn't cyanide or something immediately lethal. Let's stay cool."

Air Force One was fully fueled and waiting on the taxiway at Kansai International Airport. Redland was stretchered onto the big plane and they were airborne in two minutes flat.

In the medical bay, the doctors nervously stood over him, ready to intervene in any way necessary; but thirty minutes into the flight, he was waking up spontaneously, pulling at his chest leads, his eyelids fluttering in confusion.

"Are you okay, Mister President?" Meriwether asked.

"Jesus Christ, Martin!" Redland said, trying to sit up. "I don't know what to say! I just saw my father. He was waiting for me in the most amazing place." Redland's eyes were wild and searching. "I don't know how to tell you this so I'll just say it. God was waiting for me too. I don't know what the hell's going on but it was the greatest thing that ever happened to me."

Meriwether looked at the doctors and agents crowded around the president's bed. He said only one word. "Bliss."

43

1 5 DAYS

"Are you all right?" she asked. He could hear her kettle whistling in the background.

Emily had been calling Cyrus at the end of every night and the beginning of every morning.

"Still nothing," he said. "No leads."

"I'm sorry. Any more photos?"

"Just the one. As of two days ago she was okay."

"I'm sure she's still okay. Did you get any sleep?"

"A couple of hours."

"Can you rest today?"

"I'm in my car on the way to the airport," he said. "There's an emergency meeting of the task force."

"About the G Eight?"

"How'd you guess?"

"Not much of a guess," she admitted. "Will you call me later?"

"You know I will."

The fallout from the G8 was seismic. The Bliss epidemic and the Inner Peace Crusade's countdown clock were already big news. Now there was nothing else, as if every other molecule had been sucked out of the news cycle and all that remained was Bliss—and every news channel had the Inner Peace Crusade countdown clock on a screen crawl.

When Cyrus arrived at the Roosevelt Room at the White House the other task force members shook his hand and whispered private words of concern for his daughter but he was determined to keep his travails private and said as little as possible.

Bob Cuccio delivered the briefing on the G8 fiasco. A member of the Imperial household, a senior butler named Shunji Murakami, had spiked the water kettle with Bliss and then committed suicide. According to his wife, he'd been using Bliss since it first appeared in Japan and had become obsessed with it. A search of his computer found he'd been sending messages to the Inner Peace Crusade website and had offered his services for a "great deed."

Despite what the public had been told President Redland was not back to his normal self. After leaving the Bethesda Naval Hospital, he was taken to Camp David where he remained in relative seclusion, functional, but in a state of agitated anxiety. The attorney general and the chief justice of the Supreme Court had been in consultations with the vice president and the cabinet but no one was inclined at the moment to invoke the Twenty-fifth Amendment. Redland was still compos mentis, at least legally, and the prevailing sentiment was that a transition of power would be seen as too disruptive in the midst of a crisis.

The same couldn't be said for two other G8 attendees. The Canadian prime minister resigned from office citing psychological stress, and the French prime minister had attempted suicide when he returned to Paris, though news on that had been suppressed. The other world leaders seemed less affected, which, according to the government's mental health experts, pretty well reflected the diversity of the Bliss experience among the general population.

The task force reiterated the urgency of tracking down Alex Weller and the group formally expressed their outrage at the kidnapping of Cyrus's daughter. Cyrus bowed his head during the brief pronouncement then stood to give his report: The Inner Peace Crusade's website was shuttling so fast from one proxy server to another that tracking down a physical location of Weller's computer was impossible; the FBI's hotline was inundated with purported Weller sightings but none had panned out. He concluded by saying, "It's hard to imagine that anyone in the country hasn't seen pictures of Alex Weller or Joseph Weller." He lowered his voice, "Or my daughter."

The group went on to discuss contingency plans to protect against the poisoning of other government officials and the need for the urgent development of a Bliss rapid-detection assay to efficiently screen water and food channels. The CDC and FDA were investigating an outbreak of putative nonintentional Bliss intoxications in New England, and the breaking news as of that morning was that beer from Meecham's brewery well may be involved. A team of inspectors was en route to the brewery in Merrimack, New Hampshire, with the intention of a precautionary shutdown and emergency recall. The DEA was devoting its full resources to identifying the major suppliers of Bliss and decapitating the epidemic. At the end of the meeting, an assistant secretary of the Treasury made a brief presentation on a new ominous issue: the growing economic impact of Bliss usage. Some leading indicators of industrial productivity and consumer confidence were showing slippage and the markets were reacting badly. The Treasury and the Federal Reserve were following the situation closely and the assistant secretary promised to provide the task force with more data when available. On that note, the meeting was over.

Alex poked his head into Tara's bedroom.

"How's my girl?" he asked.

She was clutching Freddy the Teddy, watching a video on a portable DVD player. The room was littered with new toys that Erica and Jessie had bought her on their shopping trips to Ellsworth. Erica was sitting on an armchair, reading a book.

"Fine," Tara said listlessly.

"That's good; let me have a closer look." He felt her pulse, checked her pupils and eye movements.

"When can I go home?" she asked.

"Soon," Alex said. "Very soon."

"Can I talk to Mommy?"

Erica's lower lip trembled. "Not today, maybe tomorrow," Alex said.

"Daddy?"

"Doctor Alex has to go now. You give our patient anything she wants, okay, Erica?"

Erica swallowed and nodded.

It was a long drive to New Haven, but Alex was happy to leave the house again. The brewery raid had been exciting and he'd been looking forward to more "direct action." He assembled the same travel team as before: Sam and Steve up front, he and Jessie in the backseat. They arrived after dark at the warehouse of the Beaver Brook Water Company, a company that provided coolers and five-gallon bottles of spring water to homes and businesses in Connecticut and New York.

The parking lot was nearly empty. Steve got out of the van, stretched and slowly started walking toward a single car. A man got out of the sedan. "You Jason?" Steve called out.

"Yeah," the man said nervously. "You with them?"

Steve nodded. "Everything cool?"

"Yeah. Pull into the garage behind me. I've got my truck in there. Will I meet him? Alex?"

"Definitely. He wants to shake your hand, man."

Jason Harris, the Beaver Brook driver, closed the garage door after Sam pulled in. Steve got out first and checked the place out, his hand on the gun in his jacket. When he was satisfied they were alone he signaled it was okay for the rest of them to get out. When Alex emerged, Jason was rock star dumbstruck until Alex warmly greeted him and gave him a strong hug.

"Thank you," Alex said. "This is going to help us a lot."

"Whatever you need to do," Jason said to them, "let's get going with it—I've got to roll out of here at five A.M."

"We're ready to work."

"I gave my crew the day off. You'll be able to help me with the deliveries?"

"I'm a little recognizable," Alex said, "so I'll stay in the van with Jessie, but Sam and Steve are your guys. They're trainable."

Jason smiled. "They only need to push a dolly."

They got down to the task. There were pallets of several hundred five-gallon water bottles laid out before them. They used syringes to draw up a concentrated solution of Bliss from a plastic canteen then injected a precise volume through the top of each plastic water bottle with large-bore needles. A spot of superglue was applied to seal the holes and each bottle was given a good shake.

They finished loading the delivery truck after midnight and crawled back into the van for a sleep. Jason napped in the cab of his truck. A little before 5 A.M., Jason woke them with a large sack of fast-food breakfast and a tray of coffees, and in the thin light of dawn he drove out of the garage with Sam following closely behind.

Beaver Brook serviced a number of New York investment banks and hedge funds. Jason made his first stop at 6:30 in midtown at the service entrance to Sproutt and Company, a large bond-trading operation. While Alex and Jessie waited in the van, Steve and Sam donned Beaver Brook baseball caps and helped Jason unload and stack the rectangular bottles on dollies.

On each floor of Sproutt they sought out the Beaver Brook watercoolers in the break rooms and kitchens, and systematically replaced the bottles in use with new ones. By the time they'd finished, the offices and trading floors were packed. At their last stop, a break room on the thirty-eighth floor, Sam nudged Steve to make sure he noticed a young man filling a jug with new water and pouring it into a coffeemaker.

Outside, they gave each other fist bumps and drove away to their next stop, a hedge fund on Sixth Avenue.

The management of Sproutt knew they had a problem on their hands by midmorning. Throughout the building, dozens of people who used water for coffee and cold drinks dozed unresponsively at their desks and computer terminals then awoke in varied states of agitation, confusion, and reverie.

A flood of 911 calls hit the system, ambulances started to arrive and by lunchtime all trading operations shut down. Emergency personnel on the scene and doctors in the crowded emergency rooms quickly made the diagnosis of mass Bliss intoxication. An army of police and public health officials descended on the quarantined building but by the time the bottled water was identified as the likely source, over 200 employees had been affected, many of them never to return to work.

Just when the authorities thought the situation was under control, the next wave hit at Paddington Ventures on Sixth Ave.; then another at Briggs Asset Management downtown on Broad Street; and a last at the Cantwell Bank on Wall Street.

Alex gleefully listened to news radio stations on their way back to New Haven. Mass warnings were broadcast cautioning against drinking from commercial watercoolers. At least a thousand people had been hospitalized and panic was sweeping the city.

With every breathless report Alex excitedly tousled the hair of Sam and Steve in the front seat and squeezed Jessie's thigh. He couldn't wait for the moment Sam could pull out his laptop and post an announcement on their website.

"This is a great day!" Alex exclaimed. "And it's just the beginning."

Earlier that morning, Jim Bailey drove his oil truck up the long driveway and brought the heavy vehicle to a stop at High Cliffs. The old man eased himself down from the cab and ambled over to the front door. The ocean breeze carried a sweet hint of spring but Bailey, a lifelong native of Bar Harbor, hardly noticed. It was just the beginning of another long workday. He pushed the buzzer with a thick finger.

When he heard the doorbell Joe Weller wondered if Davis Fox had locked himself out after his morning jog. He put his coffee cup down. He was alone on the ground floor. Everyone else was still in bed. He opened the door, expecting to see Davis, but there was the oil man instead. "Oh yeah, hi there," the old man said. "Bailey's Oil. You part of the Parris family?"

"No," Joe said, hesitating. "I'm a friend."

"Any family about?"

"Erica's upstairs, I think."

"We got an automatic low oil alert back at the office. You weren't due for a refill till later in the month. Thermostat must've been set higher than usual for the off season. I expect you want a delivery today, right?"

Joe was getting uneasy. "Let me get Erica. She can probably help you."

He shut the door and silently cursed himself for being sloppy, roused Erica from her bed next to Tara's and told her to take care of the situation. She shushed him not to wake up the girl, pulled on a robe, and hurried down where she chatted with the oil man and authorized a delivery. When the truck finally lumbered off, Joe relaxed and went for a walk and a smoke. When Davis Fox came jogging back up the drive Joe told him about the small drama.

Instead of making his next fuel stop, Bailey went back to his office, sat at his desk and rang the Bar Harbor Police Department. "Yeah, this is Jim Bailey over at Bailey's Oil. I think I just seen one of the Bliss fellows everyone's been looking for. Over at High Cliffs. Recognized his face from the news. Maybe I'm crazy but I'm pretty sure it's him."

44

14 DAYS

They were preparing a celebratory feast. Erica was roasting a leg of lamb and everyone was helping out with the fixings, even Joe Weller, who usually begged off kitchen duty. Alex was due back in a couple of hours and they wanted to welcome him with a great meal and good wine. The kitchen TV was just loud enough for them to be able to follow the breathless news flow from New York City, where the mass Bliss intoxication was wreaking havoc.

Joe had talked with Alex after lunch on their prepaid mobiles. The mission had gone flawlessly and Alex was ebullient. They were taking their time heading back to Maine, staying comfortably below the speed limit.

"Are you ready for the endgame?" Alex had asked Joe.

"You know I am."

"Two weeks to go. We'll be leaving Maine soon."

"Do you know where we're going?"

"Sam's got a half a dozen offers on the net. We'll sort through them and make a decision. How's the girl?"

"According to Erica, sleepy but pouty," Joe had answered.

"Tonight's her night," Alex had said softly so as not to wake Jessie. "I'll do it after dinner then process her sample."

"Looking forward to it," Joe said.

"You won't believe it. It's amazing."

It had been sunny most of the day but by five o'clock a sheet of clouds moved in and the sky whitened. In the kitchen, boiling pots were steaming the windows.

"I'll get Erica to check on the meat," Leslie said.

"You're incapable of opening the oven door and checking yourself?" Davis joked.

"I have math genes, not cooking genes," she replied.

The doorbell rang.

Joe put down his beer and unpocketed his gun. "Shit, what now? Vik, have a peek out the dining room."

Vik scrambled off and was back in several seconds. "It's the oil man again."

"Christ. Go see what he wants."

"Should we do anything?" Davis asked.

"It's probably nothing," Joe answered, but he clicked off the safety.

Vik opened the door. The Bailey oil truck was in the driveway. Jim Bailey looked at him for a moment like a scared rabbit and without saying anything bolted to his left.

In an instant, Pete Avakian was filling the doorway in full protective gear. The Hostage Rescue Team, hastily flown in from Quantico that morning, streamed in left and right from behind the truck.

Avakian pulled Vik outside by his sweater. Another agent immediately Tasered him to the ground before he could utter a word and three men dragged his slight body away. Two columns of agents entered the front door and Avakian radioed, "We're inside."

From the kitchen, Joe heard a noise and called, "Vik, everything all right?" He moved cautiously toward the front hall.

There was a crashing sound in the great room followed by a *BOOM* as a flashbang grenade broke through the glass and exploded. A second FBI team that had motored to shore on a Zodiac and scaled the cliffs burst in.

Through the kitchen window Joe caught sight of a flak-jacketed agent in the back yard and loudly swore. He ran up the rear kitchen staircase seconds before agents entered pointing weapons and shouting at Leslie and Davis, "FBI! Get your hands up and don't move!"

In terror, both were thrown to the floor and handcuffed. "Where's Tara O'Malley?" Avakian screamed at them.

"Don't say anything," Davis said defiantly, but Leslie began to cry and said, "Upstairs."

Avakian shouted into his radio, "She's upstairs. We're going up the rear stairway."

Cyrus was standing on the gravel drive next to Minot. Neither was wearing protective gear. When he heard Avakian's transmission he rushed ahead, Minot shouting at his back, "For Christ's sake, Cy! You agreed to hold off till they got her!"—but he was through the front door.

Joe ran into Tara's bedroom. The girl had just awoken and looked dazed. Erica was standing helplessly in the middle of the room. "Joe, what's happening?"

"Move that chest in front of the door!" She was frozen. "Do it!" he screamed, waving his gun wildly and pulling the cell phone out of his pocket with his free hand. When Alex answered he shouted, "The FBI's here! Turn around!"

"Bloody O'Malley!" Alex said. "Where are you?"

"In the girl's room."

"Do what you have to do, like we discussed. And Joe, I'll see you on the other side, mate."

"I'll be there with fucking bells on."

"I love you," Alex said.

"You too." Joe threw the phone down.

Erica still hadn't moved. She stood between Joe and Tara, her jaw trembling.

"Move out the way," Joe told her.

"Don't, Joe. Leave her alone."

"I said *move!*"

"No!"

Joe squeezed off a round. It passed cleanly through Erica's heart and lodged in the wall behind her. She seemed to sigh as she dropped to her knees; Joe now had a clear line of sight to Tara. The girl cried out for Erica and began to climb out of bed.

Joe aimed for her forehead.

Avakian booted the door open and he and a second agent were in the room. They didn't shout a warning. That instant they opened fire and put six bullets into Joe's upper back, and when he pitched over, Avakian planted two in the side of his head to be sure the job was done.

Cyrus was at the doorway. Tara was screaming and spattered in blood. He rushed in, swept her into his arms and out the door. "Daddy's here, baby! Daddy's here."

"We've got two suspects down in a front bedroom!" Avakian shouted into his radio. "The girl is safe. Repeat, Tara is safe."

From the hall Cyrus called out to Avakian, "Is that Alex Weller?"

Avakian flipped the body on its back with his foot. "I think it's his brother."

From downstairs an agent came on the air. "There's a guy in the kitchen who says Alex Weller's not here, that we'll never get him."

No, we'll get the bastard, Cyrus thought, squeezing Tara to his chest. *I'll get him.*

45

14 DAYS

"Where are we going to go?" Jessie asked wearily, staring at the leafless trees along the highway.

"I've got a place we'll be safe," Sam said, and after batting it around for a while, Alex made the decision. They turned at the next exit and reversed direction, heading south, toward New York.

An hour north of the city, news of the Bar Harbor raid reached the radio. Joe Weller and Erica Parris were dead. Three others were captured. Tara O'Malley was rescued. Alex Weller was still at large. Cyrus O'Malley released a statement through the FBI thanking his colleagues for their courageous help in recovering his daughter.

No one in the van spoke for a long while. Sam and Jessie silently wiped away their tears while Steve clenched and unclenched his fist. He whispered he'd never see Leslie again. He was sure of that.

Alex finally said, "I'm not sad for Joe and Erica and you shouldn't be either. We all know they've made it all the way over. Imagine how happy they are, how lucky they are to be done with all the bullshit. We'll be with them soon enough, but we've still got work to do to. Leslie, Davis, and Vik will be okay. Don't worry about her, Steve. Leslie's strong. And you will see her again. If not here, then there." He patted the big man on the back and sighed. "I think it's time for Cyrus O'Malley to stop trying to stop us. It's funny, I hate the man's guts but I think I know a way to make his life better."

It was late when they crossed the Bronx River and exited onto city streets. Sam found a parking space in front of a shuttered bodega, killed the engine and said, "Welcome to Walton Avenue."

It was chilly and not many people were out. Sam had them stay in the van and hustled to the building entrance: scuffed black doors in a soot-white-brick apartment block. He pressed a buzzer and when he heard a crackling "Hola," he said, "Hi Ma, it's me."

Asuncion Rodriguez was thin with severely pulled-back hair streaked with gray. She cried when she saw her son at the door of her sixth-floor apartment and shifted back and forth between relief and anger. Where had he been? Why hadn't he called? Was he okay? Was he in trouble? Why had he dropped out of school? What would his father have said?

Everything was all right, he told her. He was with good people, doing important things. He was sure his father would approve. Then he said, "Ma, I've got friends with me. Can we stay a few days?"

When Alex, Jessie, and Steve marched through her door, Mrs. Rodriguez stared at Alex and kept firing angry looks at her son. Before Sam could make introductions, she muttered an apology, pulled Sam into her bedroom and scolded, "You think I don't know who that is? You think I don't know? What have you gotten yourself into?"

"He's a good man, Ma. A great man. I want you to keep an open mind. Please do that for me. If you turn us away, we'll have big problems."

Her mind turned to practical matters. "Where will everyone sleep?"

He laughed and kissed her cheek. "The girl can have my bed. The guys can sleep on the sofa and the floor in the living room. We'll be fine."

She frowned. "You take the sofa," she insisted, waggling her finger.

Marian ran down the hospital corridor as fast as her high heels permitted, with her husband fast-walking behind her.

Cyrus and Emily were outside Tara's room, close together, quietly talking.

"How is she?" Marian called out.

"She's weak but okay," Cyrus said. "She's asleep but you can wake her up."

She drew within inches of his face. "I hate you for this," she spat. "If it wasn't for you, she wouldn't have been involved."

Cyrus stayed mute; Emily couldn't. "I'm not sure that's fair or helpful," she said.

"Why are *you* here, Doctor Frost?" she hissed.

"Cyrus called me. I was concerned about Tara."

Marian looked at her icily then brushed past to see her daughter.

"You all right, Cyrus?" Marty said.

"Thanks for asking, Marty, I'm fine. We got lucky today."

When they were alone again Cyrus said, "I'm going to hang around here tonight, in case Tara wants to see me."

"I'll stay with you," Emily said. She grasped his hand and held it for several seconds before a nurse appeared from a nearby room and she had to let go.

FBI interrogators questioned Davis, Leslie, and Vik intensively for two days until they were satisfied they had no idea where Alex Weller was. They all refused to reveal with whom Weller was traveling and nothing could change their steadfast resolve to protect their compadres.

Cyrus immediately went back to working leads. All the killed and captured in Bar Harbor were members of Weller's Uroboros salon, so it stood to reason that those still with him too were members. If the FBI could discover their identities, they might get a lead on the whereabouts. Weller's girlfriend, Jessie Regan, was missing and Cyrus was confident she was one of them. Another man had been positively ID'd: a delivery driver for the Beaver Brook Water Company. He was found dead in the cab of his truck, a carbon monoxide suicide.

That left two other men, seen on CCTV footage making water deliveries in New York: one small, one large with a beard, both in bulky jackets and pulled-up hoodies, neither seen full face. From their physiques, neither could be identified as Alex Weller and their identities remained unknown.

Cyrus and Avakian took a break and got lunch at the Kinsale Pub near their office. They sat at one of the barrel-topped tables eating sandwiches. Avakian looked wistfully at the bar while sipping soda through a straw.

"We'll come back after work to get you a real drink," Cyrus promised.

"When's that going to be?" Avakian wondered. "We've been going nonstop."

Cyrus produced the list of known Uroboros members. Emily had been helpful. She recalled the names of a couple of them from her single meeting. Interviews led to more names, two of whom were now deceased, Virginia Tinley and Arthur Spangler, apparent Bliss suicides.

Cyrus unfolded the paper and took out his pen. "We know the list isn't complete, but let's do what we've always done, divide and conquer. You take half and I'll take half and let's meet back here around seven."

"Yeah, okay," Avakian grunted. He sniffed the beer fumes in the air and tossed his striped tie over his shoulder to avoid staining it with fallout from his pastrami sandwich.

A chubby middle-aged man entered the pub with a young Asian woman and the two were seated at a table near the bar. Larry Gelb kept his beret and coat on and nervously fingered a menu while his girlfriend, Lilly, walked quickly past Cyrus's table on her way to the bathroom.

At once, Gelb rose from the stool looking ashen, grabbed his chest and sank to his knees, groaning. One of the waitresses saw him fall and screamed for someone to call an ambulance.

Cyrus sprang up and hustled to the man's side. Avakian sighed and reluctantly left his pastrami to help his partner.

"You okay?" Cyrus asked Gelb, feeling for his neck pulse.

"My heart," Gelb managed through clenched teeth.

"Do you have any medicine with you?"

"Maybe my pocket."

Avakian started rifling through the man's pockets, coming up empty. The manager came over and told them the paramedics were on the way.

Lilly came out of the ladies' room and went straight for Cyrus's table. When she was certain all eyes were on the commotion, she emptied a stick of Bliss into Cyrus's Diet Coke and one into Avakian's Dr Pepper and stirred with their straws. Then she ran to Gelb and sank to the floor in hysterics. "What happened? What happened?!" she screamed.

Cyrus was relieved to hear the siren approaching from the direction of Mass General close by. "The ambulance is on the way," he told the young woman.

"Do CPR!"

Avakian got up off his knees. "Lady, he's conscious. He doesn't need CPR."

Within half a minute the ambulance arrived and Gelb was stretchered out with Lilly in tow. Cyrus and Avakian returned to their table and Avakian poked his sandwich, which had cooled.

The manager came right over. "Thanks, guys. Really appreciate it. Lunch is on us."

"Jimmy, I'd love to take a freebie but you know our rules," Avakian told him. "You can, though, put my sandwich back under the heat." He sucked thirstily through his straw.

Cyrus was about to do the same when his mobile rang. "Marian," he explained. He answered, listening; then he snapped the phone shut. "It's Tara. I've got to go."

O'Malley's eyes told the story. "I'm sorry, Cy," Pete said. "Give me the list; I'll take care of everything. Call me later and let me know how she is."

Cyrus picked his coat off the hook and ran out to Cambridge Street to hail a cab, leaving Avakian to finish his meal alone.

After he was done eating, Pete groggily asked for the check. When the waitress returned she found him slumped forward, his bald head balanced precariously on the table. "Jimmy!" she yelled. "Call the ambulance again!"

The manager ran over, took one look and cried out, "What *the hell* is going on today?"

46

13 DAYS

The ICU sounded like a mechanical rain forest with its chirping monitors and windlike whooshing of ventilators. Tara was in and out of consciousness but breathing on her own. The neurosurgeons told Cyrus she'd bled into her brain from scar tissue near the tumor. She'd had a sustained seizure in the ward before being transferred to the unit but she was relatively stable—for now. Surgery was not an option. It would kill her.

Marian had gone downstairs for a coffee and he was grateful to be alone with Tara, free from his ex-wife's venomous stares. He whispered to her that he was there and lightly stroked her cool cheek. It was late afternoon. His cell phone was off per ICU protocol and he hadn't given work a thought until one of the nurses came in and told him they were holding a call for him from a Stanley Minot.

At the nurse's station, Cyrus picked up one of the flashing lines.

"Cy, Stanley."

"Thanks for calling. Tara's had a setback; I should've let you know I wasn't coming—"

"It's Pete," Minot interrupted. "Someone probably slipped him Bliss while you were at lunch. They took him over to Mass General. When he woke up, by all accounts he was calm. He was smiling, talking about seeing his dad, couldn't have been happier. Then he got a hold of his service weapon and shot himself. I'm sorry, Cy ..."

Cyrus's cop brain overrode his emotions for a few moments and he said mechanically, "There was a fat guy at the restaurant. He must've faked a heart attack while a girl, Asian, spiked our drinks. The ambulance took him to MGH."

"Cy," Minot said gently, "we're all over it. He checked out of the hospital against medical advice. We know who he is and we've gone looking for him. Tell me what I can do for you."

Cyrus began to sob. "Has someone called Jeanne?"

"I talked to her. She's on the way to Boston."

"I … I want to see her," Cyrus said, trying to speak, "… b-but I can't leave Tara."

"I'll tell Jeanne. You stay with your daughter."

Tara died that night.

An hour before she passed she gave her parents one last gift, a couple of minutes of lucidity. Her eyes opened and she felt for her stuffed bear and smiled when her hand clenched its ragged plush. She looked to her left and saw her mother, who was fighting back tears. Then she looked to her right at Cyrus. "Hi Daddy."

"Hey, baby."

"Can I have some juice?"

Marian rushed out to get some and Cyrus said with a catch in his throat, "You know I love you, sweetheart."

"I love you too, Daddy."

"Do you hurt anywhere, are you comfy?"

"I'm okay."

Marian brought in a cold juice box and put the straw in her mouth.

"How's my baby?" Marian asked.

"I'm okay." She drank some more and said, "Can Freddy come with me?"

Marian didn't understand but Cyrus did.

"Yeah, he can come with you."

"I'm not scared."

"I know you're not. You're the bravest girl in the world," Cyrus said, close.

"I'm sleepy."

"Then shut your eyes, sweetheart. Mommy and I will be right here when you wake up."

The chief resident in neurosurgery was called when Tara's breathing took on a crescendo-decrescendo pattern. The doctor knew her patient well and was visibly sad when she told Cyrus and Marian that she thought Tara was having a second bleed, a bad one.

Marian held one of her hands. Cyrus tucked the bear under her arm and held the other one and the doctor stood at the foot of the bed watching the monitor instead of the girl. An ICU nurse closed the door to her room, pulled the curtain and joined the vigil.

When she took her last, long breath and her monitor showed zeros, Marian began to wail and ran out of the room, the nurse following her to help.

Cyrus stayed with Tara for the next hour while the nurses disconnected her lines and prepared her to be taken away. He didn't want her to be alone.

It was too much to bear.

Two funerals in two days.

Cyrus was like a sleepwalker at Pete Avakian's requiem service. He sat with Stanley Minot in a pew crammed with colleagues from the Boston bureau. The Armenian priest was a young man with a heavy black beard, resplendent in a blue and gold silk robe. Cyrus was somewhere else, his mind in a thick fog until the beauty of the priest's words penetrated and briefly brought him back to the moment.

"In the Heavenly Jerusalem, in the abode of angels, where Enoch and Elijah live dovelike in old age, being worthily resplendent in the Garden of Eden; O merciful Lord, have mercy upon the soul of our departed Peter."

Tara's funeral mass was harder, nightmarish. Cyrus was in the front pew with Marty, sandwiched between him and Marian. Nothing seemed real. It was as if he didn't recognize the familiar confines of St. Anselm's Church or the melodious voice of Father Bonner. Family and friends seemed strangers. The crying sounded like discordant music. Tara's little coffin looked incongruous. What was it doing there? Where was she? Then he had an overwhelming urge to check that Freddy the Teddy indeed was inside with her. Perhaps Marty sensed Cyrus was about to stand because he put an arm around his shoulders until the impulse passed.

Outside the church, Emily was waiting for him. He hadn't seen her since Tara passed. She was wearing a black dress under her blue overcoat. Cyrus thought it looked new. There was a hint of warmth in the air and he noticed the first birdsong since the start of long winter. "Will you come to the cemetery with me?" he asked her. She nodded and an usher guided them to one of the limos.

Cyrus steered clear of the gathering at the home of one of Marian's friends. In fact, when he walked past Marian at the end of the Rite of Committal at the graveside at St. Patrick's Cemetery and suffered one more hateful glare he wondered if he'd ever have to see her again.

Instead, numb and tired, he allowed Emily to take charge and bring him to a diner not far from his apartment. He hadn't eaten in two days and though still not hungry, he ate to eradicate the dull pounding in his head. She didn't require conversation and he was grateful for that. They dined largely in silence and when they were done she said, "Let me take you home."

Ordinarily, he might have had more pride about letting her come into his untidy place but he didn't care just now. She followed him in. Though bright outside, the apartment was dark and when he opened the blinds in the living room his prosaic view of the parking lot was revealed in all its glory. What she focused on instead were stacks of books, growing out of the floor like stalagmites. She touched one of the piles, waist-high.

"Oh my … so many books."

"I need bookcases," he said, taking her coat.

"I like them this way."

"It's hard getting at the bottom ones."

He had a bottle of vodka in the freezer and he went to fetch it while she wandered through his vertical library. Shakespeare. Marlowe. Keats. Burns. Hawthorne. Eliot. Proust. Fitzgerald. Steinbeck. Faulkner.

He uncapped the bottle, sat down hard on his reading chair and poured two measures. She took one.

"You're an unusual man," she said.

"Just because I like to read?"

"You don't fit into a neat category, as do most people."

They drank without toasting.

"What's your category?" he asked.

She took the drink over to the sofa, swallowed the icy, viscous fluid and scrunched her face in its aftermath. "I'm going to let you come to your own conclusion about that."

He noticed her looking at one small colorful stack by the window, children's books. "Those are Tara's. When she came over she liked to read with me."

"She was such a lovely girl."

He poured a second drink for himself and downed it. He didn't want to cry anymore if he could help it.

Her iPhone chimed in her handbag. She glanced at it.

"Do you need to get that?" he asked.

"I'm not on duty. It's just a news alert."

"What?"

She looked closer. "President Redland's just stepped down. The vice president's going to be sworn in."

"I suppose we ought to watch this," he mumbled, then searched for the remote until he found it under the sofa.

The TV screen had the ubiquitous crawl of the Inner Peace Crusade's countdown clock, which now stood at 11 days. A reporter was standing on the White House lawn in front of the curved driveway and portico.

"Beyond the terse announcement from the White House that President Redland is voluntarily resigning from office for health reasons effective five P.M. today, there have been no official statements. We have learned from high-level sources, however, that the president has never fully recovered from his Bliss poisoning at the G Eight summit in Japan and that administration officials and the vice president have been anticipating this development as increasingly inevitable."

Cyrus changed the channel.

Beneath the anchor desk was yet another countdown clock. The male and female anchors stared into the camera, grim-faced.

"While we await the swearing-in ceremony and Vice President—or should I say soon to be President—Killen's first press conference, we're going to take you out around the country to examine the current crisis. It's an economic crisis, a social crisis, and now, increasingly, a political crisis. The cause, as everyone knows, is the worldwide Bliss epidemic and the evangelical and some would say *sinister* Inner Peace Crusade, which has resorted to worldwide acts of sabotage to promote its ends, whatever those may be."

"That's right, Sally. As bad as this epidemic was a few weeks ago, it has gotten much, much worse. The National Institute of Drug Abuse, which has been tracking usage patterns, estimates that fifteen to eighteen million Americans now have taken the drug at least one time, yet even that number, the agency admits, could be low. Whether you believe, as millions clearly do, that Bliss proves the existence of a divine afterlife or that contrary to that belief it's a psychedelic fool's gold, one thing is certain. The effects of Bliss in cities, towns, and neighborhoods throughout the country have been devastating."

"Larry, places like Willow Run, Michigan, have been hit hardest by the crisis as our reporter, Bob Tucker, found out earlier at Carlson's Coffee Shop, a local gathering place for the shell-shocked residents of this town."

The reporter leaned forward across a booth in a diner and posed a question to two burly men. "Can you tell me what life has been like in this town?"

One of the men looked him in the eye and said, "It's been hell, worse than the last recession. We've got two big employers in town and both are in a tailspin. When you've got so many folks who just flat-out stop going to work after taking this Bliss, you can't keep these production lines going. We're not getting parts from other factories too. Before this started, we were running three shifts; now we're down to one. A lot of people have lost their jobs. I don't know any business in town that's hiring. Most of my friends are living off of unemployment and draining their savings. We're worried about our houses."

The other man banged his coffee cup down on the saucer. "You add to that the personal problem that some folks have had with Bliss. My family's been spared, thank God, but I've got friends and neighbors who've lost loved ones."

"Lost to suicide?" the reporter asked.

"Doesn't matter if they kill themselves—once someone's taken that stuff, they're good as gone," he answered.

Out front of Gracie Mansion in New York City, another reporter stood under an umbrella. "This is Martin Flores. New York, like other major cities in America, has been particularly hard hit by the Bliss crisis. Adding to the woes of unemployment is a feeling that social decay and unrest are right around the corner. In the best of times, New York can be a tough place to live if you're poor and disadvantaged. In times like these, no one was particularly surprised when the streets of Mott Haven erupted in violent riots last week after police attempted a mass arrest of members of a local gang who were allegedly supplying Bliss to their neighborhood. We asked Mayor Alex Strauss about the big mess in the Big Apple."

The mayor gesticulated behind his office desk. "The problems we had last week in the Bronx could turn into something positive if it makes people realize we've got to come together and fight this drug problem with community unity. The alternative is divisiveness and disorder. For me, as mayor, that alternative is not acceptable."

"People in that neighborhood were angry because the police were cutting off the flow of Bliss. What does that tell you?"

The mayor hammered his fist into his palm. "It tells me that this is a dangerous, addictive drug. I'd like to see a lot more done on treatment and detoxification. I'm committed to education and treatment. That's got to be the way forward."

The next shot was the floor of the New York Stock Exchange. A reporter stood rooted on one spot while a maelstrom of activity circled around her. "This is Wilma Fiorentino. Today was a day like many recent days on the New York Stock Exchange: frantic high-volume trading and sharp declines in the Dow and other indices. I asked Chief Market Analyst David Mann from JP Morgan how low the Dow could go."

"Well, we can't predict where the floor will be. We don't have any historical precedents for what's been going on in the markets the past few weeks. We're not in complete free fall but the parachute is very small and it has holes in it. Wall Street is looking to Washington to do something drastic on the political front and we're not alone on this. Every country's markets have taken a huge hit. The economy needs shock therapy and that means very decisive action from the White House and Congress to stop Bliss, stop the Inner Peace Crusade, and restore public confidence."

Cyrus switched the TV off. "I don't want to see anymore."

"Alex Weller makes me so angry," she said. "He's a flaming narcissist. He got some megalomaniacal view of the world, of his own vision of things, which makes him blind to the pain and heartache he's causing. And the people who're following him as a messiah or guru either have no idea or choose not to believe that he's a murderer. I mean, God, Cyrus, he brought his lab equipment to Bar Harbor, like a Frankenstein."

"He would have used Tara, I'm sure of it." Cyrus stared at the black TV screen. "I'm going to kill him."

She sighed. "So, what do you want to do now?"

He filled their glasses. "This."

By the time it was dark, Cyrus was very drunk and low-slung in his chair. Emily had been more moderate in her consumption but she was in no shape to drive.

While he dozed, Emily went into his bedroom, stripped the unmade bed and looked in closets until she found clean sheets. She made a crisp, fresh bed and pulled him out of the chair. Once between the sheets, like a little boy, he automatically pulled his trousers and shirt off and dropped them on the floor where she retrieved and hung them up.

"Give me that book," he said drunkenly, pointing to his night-stand. It was a thin volume of poems. "I want to read a poem."

She sat on the bed. "Which one? I'll read it to you."

The room was moving and the book was moving. He found it with difficulty and stabbed a stanza with his finger. "This."

When his head fell back onto his pillow she read from Philip Larkin's *Aubade*. It was sad, very sad. It was about the inevitability of death.

He snorted his drunken approval, closed his eyes and was asleep within seconds.

It was too early for her to sleep but she slipped off her shoes and lay on the bedspread beside him and when the morning came, she was still there.

47

10 DAYS

Over Stanley Minot's perfunctory objections, Cyrus threw himself back into work. There was an urgent Bliss Task Force meeting in Washington and he was determined to attend, rising early to catch the first shuttle, shaking off his hangover as best he could, seeing Emily off. He channeled his despondency into a rage as hot as a smithy's forge and refused to grieve any more until Alex Weller was stopped.

Entering the conference room, Cyrus was greeted with grim handshakes and downward gazes as other task force members awkwardly tried to acknowledge his ordeal; but he stoically refused to let the façade he'd constructed crack. He sat and opened his briefing book.

The session was called by the DEA. There was a major new lead that required urgent action. Chris Webber, chief of intelligence from DEA, went to the podium and remotely started the projector.

"As you know, multiple Bliss manufacturing sites have sprung up around the Americas and around the world in the past few months—but we've always thought there's been one principal source, based on some chemical fingerprinting we've been able to do. We now have good evidence that a factory in Zapopan, Mexico, in the State of Jalisco, is that principal source. Two weeks ago, a Texas state trooper stopped an eight-ton Mercedes Benz truck with Louisiana license plates outside of Beaumont, Texas, for a minor traffic violation. The trooper wrote out a ticket and was about to let the driver and his passenger go when he noticed the barrel of a shotgun under the driver's seat. He made an arrest and a subsequent search of the truck revealed one hundred kilos of Bliss, packaged into paper sticks, hidden inside fertilizer bags inside welded compartments. The street value of the bust was somewhere in the neighborhood of two hundred million dollars."

There were murmurs around the table when he showed photos of a dozen large bags.

"We resisted compromising sources of information so the bust was kept quiet. The driver and passenger were both Americans. The driver was uninteresting, an unemployed dishwasher from New Orleans who didn't know much about anything. The passenger was the one we focused on. His name is Doug Greene: this guy." He showed his picture. "Around New Orleans he's a well-known drug runner. We pushed hard, broke him down, and he talked. Apparently, this was their fourth or fifth Bliss run. The gang Greene worked for was a heavy money operation that in essence has the Bliss franchise for southeastern United States. Greene's job was to drive the truck down to the Mexican border at Laredo and pull into a remote farm north of town right on the border line. Here's an aerial shot. He'd meet a Mexican national there named Romo and give him a few suitcases full of cash—about ten million for the last transaction. The DEA immediately began a stakeout of the farm, including wiretaps and listening devices. The farmer is a Mexican-American who we now know is a cousin of this fellow, Romo.

"About a week ago, we observed Romo on the property but couldn't figure out how he got there. Then we picked up conversations about a tunnel. We raided the farm while Romo was still there and found a tunnel coming out under the dirt floor of the barn. It led a half mile due west under the interdiction fence and terminated under a storage shed on a farm on the Mexican side. We also found another ten kilos of Bliss Romo had just brought over. During questioning, Romo proved to be pretty full of himself: he came on like a big shot and hinted that he had a lot to say if we'd cut a deal. We told him we'd play as long as the information was valuable. It didn't take long before he told us about the Guadalajara Chemical Company located in Zapopan. We immediately contacted the Agencia Federal de Investigación. I'd like to introduce Deputy Director Luis Rocha of the AFI to brief you on our planned and joint operation. If all goes according to plan, we will have dealt a major blow to Bliss trafficking."

Luis Rocha took Webber's place at the podium.

"The AFI and the Policía Federal immediately began to investigate the Guadalajara Chemical Company. It's a small privately owned company that for the past thirty years manufactured bulk chemicals for the agricultural and pharmaceutical industries. Here it is, on the outskirts of the city in an industrial park. Lately, it's not a very successful company. The sons of the founder weren't so interested in the business and it's gone downhill. We discovered the sons recently leased the business to a young chemist from Mexico City who made them an offer they couldn't refuse, a share in profits from Bliss manufacture. The chemist's name is Miguel Cifuentes. This is his passport photo."

Bob Cuccio from the FBI looked at Cyrus "You ever heard of this guy?"

Cyrus shook his head.

"Until just before Christmas he worked as a chemist at Harvard Medical School," Cuccio explained. "What are the odds he and Weller knew each other?"

"I'd say high," Cyrus answered. "I'll get on it."

Rochas continued. "Cifuentes has begun to spend money like a drug lord. He's got a hacienda, cars, boats, even a private plane. He's also got a private army guarding the factory. We've been doing surveillance the past week so we think we know the weak spots. We're ready to go. We're hitting the factory tomorrow afternoon."

After the meeting, Cyrus pulled Cuccio aside. "This is a joint raid, right?"

"You heard Rochas. The DEA's going to be there."

"Don't you think the FBI ought to have a seat at the table?"

"Who are you suggesting" Cuccio asked.

"Me."

"Do you think that's a good idea? You've just been through a lot."

"Let's just say I've got skin in the game."

Cyrus disembarked from an unmarked DEA Learjet that had powered down in a remote corner of the airport in Guadalajara. He slipped on sunglasses to shield himself from the early morning glare. A customs agent checked his passport on the tarmac and asked him if he was armed. He replied that he wasn't and was waved into a black Escalade with tinted windows that had drawn up to the nose of the plane.

He slipped into the rear seat next. Inside was a compact, muscular man in casual, plain clothes, who extended his hand. "I'm Colonel Ramon Vazquez, deputy commanding officer of the Guadalajara division of the Policía Federal. I'm very sorry about your loss, Mister O'Malley. Let's see if we can do something about it."

Cyrus was driven into a congested downtown district of Guadalajara where he and Vasquez were dropped off on a narrow back street near a tobacconist. Cyrus spotted lookouts on both sides.

"Our men," Vasquez said.

Vasquez led him into an alley that ran perpendicular to the street and down a flight of concrete steps into the basement entrance of a nondescript office building. They rode an elevator up to the fifth floor into an office suite where numerous clerks, secretaries, and men with holstered pistols were working alongside a handful of American DEA agents.

Vasquez took him into his private office and opened his desk drawer. "If you're going with us, you shouldn't be naked." He handed him a Glock 25 and three loaded clips. "It's what the Secretaria de la Defensa Nacional issues," he said proudly. "Look on the slide." It was engraved S.D.N. Mexico DF, C. O'Malley. "I had your name added last night. It's a gift. Use it in good health."

In the most crowded conference room Cyrus had ever seen, Vasquez did a run-through of the operation. There were a good thirty men in and around the table and half of them were smoking. The room was hot and Cyrus's eyes stung from the smoke; he felt queasy too by the sickening mélange of colognes. The plan, though, was simple enough: attack with overwhelming, brutal force. There was something satisfying in its lack of nuance.

At three in the afternoon, the Guadalajara Chemical Company was operating at capacity. The factory had a sprawling one-story footprint, a corrugated iron roof, and was situated in a light-industry area of Zapopan just north of Guadalajara. A newly installed electrified fence surrounded the compound. Outside the rear entrance, a new Sikorsky sat on a yellow bull's-eye helipad.

About sixty production workers were on site manning the plant's manufacturing lines. The only product they made was Bliss. The raw materials needed to make Bliss, the reagents and amino acids, were received and processed at one end of the factory, and at the other end, unskilled workers weighed out finished product and hand-rolled tubes of colored wrapping paper around each dose. Outside, guards paced the perimeter fence with automatic weapons concealed by loose jackets.

At the front of the factory were small offices for the managers. Inside one, Miguel Cifuentes sat at his desk talking on the telephone, placing his usual afternoon call to his wife in Mexico City to check on her and the children.

Wealth was more of a burden than he'd anticipated. Although he no longer worried about how to satisfy his wife's material desires on a professor's salary, there were new concerns. Bliss had generated so much revenue that he was literally drowning in cash. He'd stopped trying to keep a tally and became reliant on accountants whom he suspected of stealing from him. His conspicuous consumption was drawing attention from authorities in Guadalajara and Mexico City, and he'd begun to pay out hefty bribes to keep local police and tax officials at bay. Fear of theft and kidnapping prompted him to spend lavishly on private security for himself and his entire family. Forced to spend long spells in Zapopan away from his family, he'd developed a nervous tic and had put on weight.

Miguel told his wife he loved her then hung up and massaged his throbbing temples. His assistant saw he was off the line and brought in a folder of faxed invoices from amino acid suppliers in Greece and Switzerland. When he leafed through them he became incensed. "These guys are thieves," he sniffed. "They've doubled their prices again. They don't even bother to offer an explanation anymore."

All at once he heard the thumping sound of a helicopter approaching low. It confused him since he was sure his helicopter was already on the pad.

He felt the percussion a moment before hearing the blast. Then a series of higher pitched explosions, each like an exclamation point, coming from all sides. His office windows blew in, splattering him with shards of glass. Bursts of automatic gunfire punctuated the air.

Bleeding from superficial cuts to his arms, neck, and face, he staggered to the hallway where his employees were frantically fleeing.

"What's happening?" he cried.

One of the security guards ran into the building, breathing hard. He stopped in front of Cifuentes and ejected a spent clip from his machine pistol. "We're being attacked!" he screamed. "It's the federal police—they're all around us!"

"What should I do?" Miguel implored.

"Do? Take this. Do what you have to do." The guard pulled a revolver from his belt, slid it across the tiles to the wide-eyed chemist, and ran down the hall.

Cyrus and Vasquez monitored the raid from their hovering chopper and listened to the battle chatter. Cyrus was frustrated at his inability to follow the rapid-fire Spanish over his headset but every few seconds, one of the DEA agents on the ground broke into English.

Cyrus watched Vasquez's men storm through gaping holes in the compound fence in their light-armored half-tracks. The initial wave killed a number of security guards. Others took up defensive positions behind a refrigeration unit and the rest retreated inside the cinderblock factory building. From these positions they sprayed the advancing police with automatic fire.

Vasquez loudly groused to Cyrus that he didn't like the way things were progressing. "I'm not interested in a long affair," he grumbled and instructed the pilot to land in a field near the factory.

Vasquez ordered his men to hold fire and, megaphone in hand, boomed out from behind one of the half-tracks, "This is Colonel Vasquez of the Federal Police! You are completely surrounded. Throw your weapons through the windows and start coming out with your hands above your heads. Otherwise you'll be killed. You have one minute."

One of the security guards pulled a female employee over to a blown-out office window and held a gun to her head. "Get out of here!" he screamed. "We'll kill everyone, starting with the women!"

"Don't be crazy!" Vasquez replied through his megaphone. "Give up and it'll go better for you."

The gunman disappeared.

"How are you going to play it?" Cyrus asked the sweating Vasquez.

"If they don't surrender in one minute, we'll use tear gas and we'll take the place. I don't want to get into a standoff."

In the lull, Miguel slumped onto the floor behind the desk of his bombed-out office and absently picked pieces of glass from his hand. No one could hear it but he was saying over and over, "Why did I start this? Why did I do it?"

Vasquez followed the sweeping second hand of his watch and with fifteen seconds to go said to Cyrus, "This is not a legitimate hostage situation. All the people in there are voluntary employees. Let's end this."

"This is your turf, Colonel," Cyrus said.

In response to the tear gas fusillade, a handful of people ran out of the building and were captured. Vasquez ordered a full assault. His men donned gas masks and stormed the building. In the battle that followed, almost forty civilians and three policemen were killed before the operation was declared successful by Vasquez's squadron lieutenant.

"Come on," Vasquez, told Cyrus. "Let's have a look."

They went in through the rear. Inside, Cyrus blinked at the sight and caustic smells of carnage. Shot-down and blown-up bodies littered the factory floor. Medics ran among the survivors doing triage. Ruptured reactor vessels released slurry onto the floor and shoes and clothing were stained with a pasty mix of chemicals and blood.

One of the DEA agents came over, lowered his assault rifle and clapped Cyrus on the back.

"Do we have Cifuentes?" Cyrus asked him.

"I don't know. There's a shitload of bodies."

Cyrus and Vasquez made their way to the front of the building, their guns held straight out before them, tactically. Outside one of the offices they heard a low voice, a man softly praying. Vasquez put his finger to his lips and tip-toed inside.

Cyrus came in behind.

A young man with a fleshy face and neat beard was cowering against the back wall behind a desk. He was pointing a gun at them, his hands violently shaking.

"Miguel Cifuentes," Vasquez said in English. "Put the weapon down. You're under arrest."

"No!" Cifuentes exclaimed like a petulant child. "I don't want to be arrested."

"It's not a choice. Put the gun down!"

Cifuentes instead raised the pistol higher. "No!" he shouted hysterically.

Vasquez kept his finger firmly on the trigger and his eyes on Cifuentes as he said to Cyrus, "It's okay. For your daughter."

Cyrus firmed his lips and without hesitation fired a single shot through the chemist's forehead.

48

9 DAYS

With one bathroom and five people, the small apartment was crowded and uncomfortable and Mrs. Rodriguez wasn't making things any easier. She rebuffed Jessie's attempts at bonding and wouldn't allow her into the kitchen—and she refused to speak to any of her guests except for her son, whom she continually berated in Spanish.

"Sammy, when are these people going to go?"

"We're making plans. We'll be leaving soon."

"I don't want you to go with them."

"I have to, Ma. I want to. Every time I take Bliss I talk to Dad—like he's in the room. It's the greatest thing. We're trying to bring this to everyone, the whole world."

"Every day, I talk to him too—but in my heart. That's the right way to talk to the dead."

"But I see him for real."

"Faith comes from here," she said, pounding her thin chest. "Your father's in here. God is in here. That's what faith is about. You can't find it in a drug."

"You don't understand."

"No, *you* don't understand. I want them to go and I want you to go back to school!" she cried, slamming her bedroom door.

Sam retreated to the living room where Alex and the others were watching the news, monitoring the latest Bliss developments.

They were dumbstruck by the breaking news from Mexico that Miguel Cifuentes was dead and that arguably the largest worldwide supplier of Bliss was out of action. Yet Alex remained unperturbed. "Don't worry," he told them. "My guess is that half the peptide synthesizers on the planet are being used to crank out Bliss. It's too lucrative. It can't be stopped. We can't be stopped."

They were also hoping for word on Cyrus O'Malley. As usual, Steve furiously worked the remote control, skipping all over the dial before finally settling on one channel again. "Do you think Art and Lilly were able to get to him?" he asked.

Alex nodded. "Art's resourceful. Maybe it's done and O'Malley's seen the light." He said that mischievously. "Maybe we've seen the last of him."

Sam sat on the carpet, cross-legged, opened his laptop and waited for a cellular signal.

"Your mom sounded pretty upset," Jessie said. "I feel bad."

"She'll be okay," he answered tersely.

"We need to get out of here," Alex said. "We've only got nine days to go. We need to settle on our destination."

Steve stood and irritably paced like a tiger in a tiny cage. "Alex, we've been through a lot and I trust you completely, you know I do, but isn't it time you told us what's going to happen when the countdown's over? Don't you trust us enough for that?"

Alex resisted an autocratic urge to silence Steve with a sharp rebuke. Wasn't it obvious? If he'd been loose with his intentions, the authorities would've already sweated the info out of the survivors in Bar Harbor. Sam and Jessie understood that. Why couldn't Steve?

"In good time, Steve. I'll tell the three of you soon. Let's get to where we're going first. So Sam, where are we going?"

Sam worked his track pad. "I'm just seeing if we got a follow-up message from that guy, Erik."

"If everything's cool, that's still my first choice," Alex said.

Sam looked up. "It's here. From Erik. It's cool. He says it's a go."

Alex clapped his hands once, producing a happy, staccato sound. "Sam, go meet your friend tonight and we'll hit the road in the morning. I'm excited. The name says it all, almost like it was fated. My friends, we're going to Rising City."

"How dangerous is this?" Steve asked, locking the van.

"On a scale of one to ten?" Sam paused. "I'd say eleven."

Steve swore. "I'm sure as hell not scared of dying but I'd rather not get tortured first."

"Just let me do all the talking. Keep quiet and look badass."

"I'm a schoolteacher," Steve groaned. "What am I gonna do, threaten to send these guys to the principal's office?"

It was near midnight on a dark moonless night and East One Hundred-seventieth Street in the South Bronx had scant foot traffic. Two young men in puffy jackets appeared in the doorway of a brick housing project.

"Who're you?" one of them called out.

"I'm Sam. I'm here for Jorge."

The men scanned the street and motioned for them to come inside.

"Turn 'round," one of them said, pointing to the bank of mailboxes.

They were frisked. They found the bottle in Steve's jacket but left it alone when Sam told them it was for Jorge. They were led up two flights of stairs to a long bare hall where sounds of TVs and bursts of laughter spilled from behind closed doors.

The puffy jackets knocked on one of the doors, the peephole went dark and the locks unbolted. Sam and Steve followed them inside.

A young man with bronzed skin and deep acne scars was sprawled on a leather sofa, alone. He raised his hands like he was welcoming royalty. "Oh my god, Scholar Sam! What the fuck, man!"

"Hey, Jorge, what up?"

"You still look wicked smart. I couldn't believe it when I heard you wanted to talk to me. Who's that, your muscle?" he laughed, pointing at Steve. "That big guy's scared shitless. Don't worry, dude, I ain't gonna fuck you up 'less Sammy tells me to."

They'd been two kids in elementary school, Sammy the brain, Jorge the dunce, a screwup. Sam instinctively looked out for him, defending him verbally, and Jorge repaid the favor by punching the daylights out of anyone who messed with Sam's glasses or his book-filled backpack. Sam went on to become one of the bright stars of the South Bronx while Jorge thrived on the streets, rising to head up a chapter of the violent Latin Kings gang. There was no contact between the two since childhood but much in the way that Androcles and the Lion remembered each other, they now shared a slice of childhood memories.

"How's life, man?" Sam said, looking at the expensive electronics lining the walls of the modest apartment and the long-legged women flitting in and out of the bedrooms. "You look prosperous."

"I can't complain. So, what the fuck are you doing back in the hood?"

"Just some business."

"Business." Jorge laughed. "I thought your business was gonna be running Microsoft or some shit."

"I had a change of plans. You heard of Bliss?"

"Yeah, course I have. You into that?"

"Big-time."

"On what level?"

"All levels."

Jorge sat forward, interested. "Yeah? I wouldn't mind getting a piece of that shit."

Sam asked Steve for the bottle. "This is Bliss, a lot of it. It's got a street value of a quarter million bucks."

"No shit. Let me see." Jorge unscrewed the bottle and sniffed at the mouth. "So what do you want me to do?"

"I want to give it to you," Sam said.

"For how much?"

"For nothing."

"Why, because when I was eight I kicked butt for you?"

"I need a couple of things in return."

"What?" Jorge asked suspiciously.

"I want you to spread it around the streets, 'cause that would be cool. And I need guns and ammo. Everything you can put your hands on tonight."

Jorge laughed again. "You going to war, Sammy?"

"Yeah, something like that."

Sam and Steve were back at Walton Ave by 2 A.M. toting two extremely heavy nylon carry bags. As soon as Sam unlocked his door he saw that something was wrong.

His mother was up when she should've been long asleep. She was in the living room, sitting beside Jessie on the sofa, her cheeks streaked with tears.

"Ma, what's wrong?"

She sprang up, ran to him and flung her arms around his neck. "Sammy, I was with Papa. He looked so good. He was happy, like you said. Sammy, I can't believe it, I can't believe it."

He extricated himself from her grasp and turned to Alex, who was coming out of the kitchen with a cup of tea. "Alex, how could you do that? Give my mother Bliss without her permission, without my permission?"

"Look how happy she is, Sam. It's for her own good—and I need to know she'll be our friend when we leave tomorrow. We can't risk getting caught when we're so close."

Sam bitterly shook his head but held his tongue.

"You're right, I should have talked with you first," Alex said. "But the end justifies the means, Sam. You should know that by now."

49

8 DAYS

Thirteen hundred miles. At the speed limit, driving straight through, with Sam and Steve alternating shifts at the wheel, they figured they could make it in about twenty-two hours.

They were on the flats, Cleveland in the rearview mirror, Chicago ahead, then Illinois, Iowa. If all went well, they'd be there before dawn.

In the backseat, Alex propped his feet on one of the gun bags. If things didn't go well, if they got stopped along the way, then they'd litter I-80 with spent casings, that's for sure.

Next stop, Nebraska. Nothing is going to prevent that.

Jessie awoke from a nap. "Hungry?" Alex offered a bag of sandwiches and fruit.

"A little." She picked a banana.

"Are you excited?" he asked her.

She nodded but then admitted, "I'm a little scared."

"All adventures are a little scary."

"Just don't leave me. I don't want to be alone."

"I'll never leave you."

Rising City, Nebraska. Population: pushing 400. It was still a couple of hours before sunrise when they skirted south of the tiny town without even knowing it. The blackness on both sides of the state road was cornfields that wouldn't be planted for a good month.

Steve was navigating. "I think we're almost there," he guessed. "About three miles."

They'd had the road to themselves for the past hour but Sam began to squint, dry-eyed, at a bothersome pair of headlights in his mirrors. "Just pass me, okay?" he complained, slowing a bit.

The trailing car slowed too.

Sam looked over his shoulder. "I don't like it," he told Alex. There were half a dozen cars behind that one.

Alex unzipped the carry bag and started passing out guns, keeping the battered TEC-9 machine pistol for himself. "We're so close," he said wearily. "It's a pity."

"If he's police or FBI, he's unmarked," Sam said. "There's no light rack on its hood."

"I think that's our turn ahead," Steve said. "Do you want us to take it or drive by?"

"Take it," Alex said. "If they're following us, we'll know what we're dealing with."

Sam signaled and made a slow right turn at a mailbox stenciled with the name Bolz. The drive was pitted dirt. There was a yellow house ahead, its lights on, then a cluster of unlit barns and beyond the buildings, the nothingness of farmland.

"Shit … the car's turning."

Alex snapped back the bolt handle. "I've never fired a gun before," he said grimly. "I wish Joe were here."

A circular drive in front of the farmhouse was packed with cars and people were milling around the porch wearing heavy coats in the early morning chill. A middle-aged man started waving at the van and running toward them.

"I bet that's him! I bet that's Alex! Hey, Alex, I'm Erik. I'm Erik Bolz!"

Sam braked and Steve jumped out the passenger side, a semiautomatic pistol in hand.

"We're being followed!" he shouted at Erik.

"No, you're not!" Erik called back. "That's a friend of mine in that Jeep. That's Ken Donovan. And behind him is Gus French. They're here to meet you."

"How'd they know we were coming?" Steve asked.

"I may have told a couple of folks," Erik said. "But don't worry. They're all Bliss people. They're all with you. Tell Alex Weller he can come on out. He's safe here. You're all safe."

50

7 DAYS

The sun rose splendidly over the featureless horizon and slowly began to warm the clumped sandy soil.

The Bolz corn farm was four hundred acres, a typical size for these parts. In the morning light, Alex walked the land with Erik. A thirty-acre field north of the house, neatly laid out in furrows, was already strip-tilled and spiky with the stubble from the previous harvest.

"I tilled this field out of habit," Erik said. He was a clean-shaven, earnest Lutheran who worshipped in town, a pillar of the community. "Not going to be planting it, though," he explained. He waved his hand to the north and the west. "Not going to plant any of it. Don't really see the point. All my needs, all my wife's needs, are being satisfied by Bliss." He kicked at a furrow. "Down here it's godless and barren. Up there, it's a different kettle of fish. You changed our lives, Alex. Our only son died by drowning. We visit with him once or twice a day now."

"I'm happy for you, Erik, and I'm grateful to you for letting us come here. Our time is short but with your help, we'll be able to do great things."

"Your clock's at seven days," Erik remarked. "We're excited to see what happens on Day Zero."

Alex wasn't sure if he was being probed for information; still, he replied, "I'm excited too. Day Zero will be beyond description."

Erik insisted that Alex and his people take the farmhouse while he and his wife move into their RV out back. They wouldn't be alone. Friends of theirs were setting up camp beside them, a dozen vehicles, campers and tents. Alex accepted the house with a certain noblesse oblige, aware of his unique position as head of this ersatz community. In the master bedroom, behind lace curtains that billowed in the wind, he patted the newly made bed and sank into its softness, pulling Jessie on top of him. "These people think I'm special," he said.

She kissed him. "You are."

Downstairs in the living room, Sam slouched on a lumpy floral couch with his shoes on the coffee table inches from the Bolz family photos. With his laptop propped on a cushion he typed away, dutifully following Alex's instructions to the letter, attaching his message and the GPS coordinates of the farm. When he was finished he climbed the stairs, found his assigned room and collapsed on the bed. The sound of Steve's snoring coming through the wall didn't stop him from falling right to sleep.

Alex slept the daylight away and awoke in a dark bedroom, disoriented, until he felt Jessie beside him and remembered where he was.

Noises were coming through the open bedroom windows: the sounds of motors, people talking, laughing, radios; he got out of bed naked and padded across the floorboards to see.

The front windows provided a view up the drive to the state road. From both east and west, there was an endless stream of headlights converging on the farm.

"Jesus," Alex whispered. "Prove it and they will come."

The Butler County sheriff was in meltdown mode. He didn't know the governor, didn't much like him, and sure as hell hadn't voted for him, but now the man was calling him every hour. The sheriff took the call on his mobile, his car parked in the middle of the state road a mile to the east of the Bolz farm. A row of deputy sheriffs' cars completely blocked both lanes. He had a second roadblock in place a mile or so west of the farm. He'd caused a traffic jam, the likes of which he'd never seen.

"Yes, sir, I understand the importance of controlling the situation, but there's not a lot we can do about folks just pulling off the road and driving through the damn fields to get to Bolz's farm."

He massaged the back of his aching neck with one hand while listening to the governor yell at him.

"Yes, sir, I understand that people can't drive across private property but I've only got so many deputies down here."

There was more yelling as he watched hundreds of red taillights moving at speed through the dry cornfield.

"Hell yes, Governor. Send the state patrol in. Send everyone you've got. This is way over my pay grade."

Alex woke Jessie, Sam, and Steve. Erik was waiting for them on the porch. The night air carried sweet hints of spring. His wife, LuAnn, offered food and drink but Alex had something else he wanted to do. Erik led him and the others out back where the small camp from the morning had morphed into something altogether different.

It was no longer possible to see where back yard ended and tilled field began because hundreds of stationary headlights and taillights were there, fanning out into the darkness, merging into one huge glowing dome.

Steve tried to persuade him to hold back but Alex insisted. "They want to see me and I want to see them."

He waded into this makeshift campground where he was recognized immediately.

Men and women poured out of their cars, trucks, campers, and RVs to see him, talk to him, touch his sleeve, tell him about the way Bliss had changed everything. People waved sticks of Bliss at him, laughing, crying. Surrounded by the adoring masses, Alex turned to Jessie with tears in his eyes. "I called them … and they came."

Alex sat around the farmhouse kitchen table with Sam, Jessie, and Steve. They were giddy about the explosion of people around them and after a hearty supper they were in high spirits.

"It's time," Alex said suddenly, leaning his chair back on two legs.

"Time for what?" Jessie asked.

"The clock stands at seven days. I want to tape two messages: one to be played tonight, the other to be played on Day Zero, just in case I'm not here to do it myself."

"What are you going to say?" Steve asked.

"Ah." Alex sighed. "What am I going to say? It's time I told you, my loyal kitchen cabinet." He smiled, waving at the pots and pans. "You've earned the right to know my intentions."

The others put their silverware down, kept themselves still.

He stood. It seemed appropriate to be proudly upright.

"Today, I'm going to tell people we have seven days left to contemplate the world with all its flaws, its warts, its meanness and cruelty. I'll tell them that Bliss has shown us a new path to inner peace and enlightenment: that this world of ours is transitory and base; that the afterlife is permanent and glorious. I will tell them that in six days a new era will begin, the Inner Peace Era, and that this era will change everything we know—for the better."

He gazed out the window. In the evening light rose a cloud of dust from the continuous cascade of cars busting the blockades and coming in over dried-out fields.

He turned back to the kitchen table. "The bible says that God created the world in seven days. It's laughably primitive, but it's evocative, isn't it? Let's turn it on its head. We started the clock twenty-three days ago. Since then Bliss has literally exploded. Who knows how many people have used it! Millions? Tens of millions? Its impact has been enormous: spiritually, socially, economically ... the pump is well-primed. Today, let's reverse that biblical seven days. Let's begin the last phase of the countdown. In seven days, we're going to start again and return to God."

"What's going to happen, Alex?" Jessie asked in a dry, hushed voice.

"In seven days, I'm going to tell people that their day has come: that their wait is over. That it's time for them to cross over forever and join their fathers, mothers, sisters, brothers, children, friends—all the dearly departed ones waiting for them. I'll tell them how much Bliss they need to take. I'll tell them to fly off buildings, use gas, open veins, string a rope, use any means of their choice to leave this world and enter the next. For good." His eyes danced. His voice rose. "And think of it! If ten million people or more act, if it's only a fraction of that, the world will never be the same again. It'll be a post-Bliss society where those who choose to stay won't live for a single hour without thinking about those who chose to leave. Many will turn to Bliss, perhaps trying it for the first time, and more will choose to cross over. The tide will have turned. Mankind will be focused on its spiritual future rather than its mired past. The world won't look the same or be the same. It will be a new golden age. It will be glorious."

No one spoke.

The evening wind carried the sounds of children playing in the nearby field.

Finally, Jessie asked, "Will we leave too?"

"It'll be your choice, everyone's choice; but I'll be going. My father's waiting."

Jessie's voice sounded like the chirping of a little bird. "If I go too, will you be there?"

"I'm sure of it," Alex promised. "I'll be there for you."

Cyrus's phone rang, muffled. He felt for it and just before it went to voice mail he found it on the floor near the bed, under Emily's dress. It was a Saturday afternoon and he'd been sleeping.

Stanley Minot was on the line.

Cyrus listened then hit the switch on his bedside lamp. Emily emerged from under the covers with a squint and heard his end of the conversation. When he was done he tossed the phone back onto her clothes pile.

"What's the matter?" she asked.

"We've found Alex Weller."

"That's good, no?"

"Not exactly," Cyrus said, slipping into his boxers. He got up, opened his blinds and went back to bed to slide his palm over her bare back. "Thank God you're in my life."

51

6 DAYS

Who will stop the rain, who will stem the tide?

In the morning sun, Alex walked through the community he'd begun to call New Rising City, thinking about the forces of nature.

I can't be stopped either.

There were thousands of people.

Thousands.

Erik's tilled field was full and more were coming, spreading out into adjoining fields, forming neighborhoods and villages within the larger city. Responding to Alex's message, they'd brought provisions, food, water, propane: enough to sustain themselves for a good week.

"I'm Alex," he said to a young family cooking eggs and bacon on a propane grill beside their tent and pickup.

"We know who you are," the woman said, holding her baby up. She wanted Alex to touch her head and he obliged, stroking the girl's silky hair.

"I'm glad you came," Alex said.

"Can't think of anywhere else we'd rather be," the man avowed. "Will you eat with us?"

"Thank you. I've got to visit with others. There're so many."

"I understand," he said.

"Will you continue to follow me?"

"Yes, we will," the woman affirmed, giving her breast to her baby. "We seen your new message. Six days now. We're with you. God bless you, Alex."

Alex puffed out his chest and proceeded to the next encamped vehicle.

Erik Bolz used his authority as landowner to attend to organization and he was good at it. He didn't much care about his precious land anymore but he was concerned for all these souls, and as their host of sorts, he felt some responsibility for their well-being. Big Steve Mahady fell easily into place as his right-hand man. Early in the morning, the two rode a tractor into the mass of humanity in the direction of a curiously loud voice. Outside a camper covered in Bliss bumper stickers they found a fellow with a bullhorn and confiscated it for the greater good.

People were willing to help. There was no shortage of men with pistols and rifles and a militia was formed in quick order to patrol the perimeter and prevent the media and law enforcement from coming onto private property. Steve assembled the ragtag squad of farmers, tradesmen, students, salesmen, even an accountant and a lawyer, and addressed them proudly. They were the movement's minutemen, citizen-soldiers willing to fight and die to protect Alex Weller's mission to bring a new age of spirituality to the world. Alex, he told them, was fearless. He knew the authorities were after him and that they'd do anything, including fabricating charges, to suppress the movement— but he was comfortable in revealing his presence at Rising City; surrounded by so many like-minded people, he felt safe and secure. So exchange mobile numbers, Steve told them. Keep in touch, keep vigilant, stay strong.

When the men dispersed to take on the perimeter of New Rising City, Erik remarked, "Impressive, Steve. You ever been in the military?"

"Close," he replied. "I was a public school teacher."

Erik threw himself into more prosaic tasks. He took his backhoe and chose the location for latrine pits and garbage tips. Then he and a crew of men strung hoses from the barns to make outdoor showers and watering spots.

"I don't know if this is enough," he declared to his wife at the end of the day, "but it's better than nothing. Never seen anything like this."

"It's like Woodstock," LuAnn said, shading her eyes to the setting sun.

"This ain't a rock and roll crowd," he pointed out. "Looks more like the infield at the Indy Five hundred."

Then there was the delicate problem of suicides. People brought Bliss with them—a lot of it—and though there was a whiff of cannabis here and there and plenty of beer cans about, the predominant drug at the farm was Bliss; and with it, the inevitable few were overwhelmed by rapture and decided to overdose or take their lives in other ways, some messy, some clean.

When the first body was found that afternoon, Erik used his bullhorn to ride through the fields asking if there were any morticians or funeral directors in their midst. There was one. An older man named Jennings came forward and was proud to take responsibility for laying out the dead and burying them in a remote corner.

Alarm bells went off in Washington as soon as Alex's call for assembly went out. The news media with their bird's-eye view helicopters buzzing the Bolz farm was a better source of real-time information than the static views at the law enforcement roadblocks. Every bureaucrat glued him- or herself to a cable channel of choice to follow along.

The Bliss Task Force met telephonically in emergency session. It was decided that there was nothing inherently illegal about a mass gathering on private property and the vigorous enforcement of narcotics laws was not a winning strategy. The target of law enforcement efforts had to be Alex Weller. He was a known fugitive with a federal arrest warrant and therefore the operation to capture him was placed in the jurisdiction of the FBI with support from the

U.S. Marshals. Bob Cuccio would be in charge of the exercise and manage it locally. The White House chief of staff was on the call and warned, "Do what you have to do, but for God's sake, we don't want another Waco."

Cyrus rang Cuccio after the conference call was over. "Bob, I want in."

"Don't you think it's too soon?"

"I'm already back at work. When Weller's in custody, I'll do my mourning."

"Okay, Cy. You're on the team. See you in Nebraska."

5 DAYS

Cyrus rested his head against the cold plastic window of the Learjet. Below him the land looked like a brown-toned patchwork quilt.

"The Earth is flat," he said.

Emily craned to see out his side. "No, Nebraska's flat."

They were alone in the cabin. The pilot came over the intercom. "We'll be landing in Lincoln in fifteen minutes."

Cyrus didn't give a damn about conflicts of interest. He was beyond that. He approached Stanley Minot and told him he needed a consultant psychiatrist at his side in Rising City to help him chart the best course with Alex Weller. He recommended Emily Frost for her expertise in the psychology of death and her direct knowledge of Weller's personality. He neglected to mention that he and Emily were sleeping together and he didn't much care if that lack of disclosure ever came back to bite him. Besides, they'd save the U.S. government the cost of a hotel room.

It was a magnificent sunny day and Alex was in a splendid mood, spending a rare few minutes on his own. That morning he'd toured New Rising City and was treated like a king visiting his subjects. The settlement had spread onto one of Erik's western fields and now a full eighty acres was filled with acolytes. No one had a good count but it didn't matter; Alex knew there were thousands and they were still coming.

More armed men were recruited to patrol the perimeter and they held their ground, keenly watched through high-powered binoculars by FBI agents who'd obtained permission from neighboring farmers to set up their own perimeter. Between the two groups was a no-man's-land of untilled fields.

Helicopters crisscrossed overhead. Their constant droning was irritating at first but now was part of the permanent soundscape and Alex hardly noticed them. Some were news choppers; others were FBI and state patrol. When Alex walked among his flock he held an open umbrella over his head to protect himself from being a target. Everyone with an umbrella opened theirs too. From the air, umbrellas appeared to be sprouting around the farm like flowers opening in the morning sun.

After lunch, Alex took Bliss and when his trip was over and Jessie left for the kitchen, he lay propped on the pillow utterly peaceful and mellow. He opened his laptop set on his belly. Sam told him he'd posted a new magazine article on the IPC website and thought Alex would want to read it.

Alex found the piece from *BusinessWeek.* "Is Bliss a Threat to the Global Economy?" A photo of an executive carrying an attaché case and opening a glass office door was captioned, *Are your employees members of the Inner Peace Crusade?*

Scott Truro, vice president of human resources at Manhattan-based French-Casper Publishing, is a worried man. Three times in the past month, he's had to tell his boss, CEO Charlotte Giddings, that staffing problems were acutely affecting the company's ability to produce product and compete for business. The problem isn't labor unions or workplace illness. The problem is Bliss, the mind-altering drug that produces a spiritual high. Twice in two weeks Truro had to face critical manpower shortages at the company's Newark production facility, literally shutting down the presses. It doesn't stop there: In the company's tony midtown offices, the no-show rate in the ranks of designers, writers, and editors has been astronomical.

Across the country and the rest of the industrialized world, similar scenes have been playing out in shop floors and office. Fanning the flames of this disturbing trend is the elusive and murky organization known as the Inner Peace Crusade, founded by a Harvard doctor, Alex Weller—now wanted by the FBI for murder—which seeks to turn as many people as possible to their version of the path of righteousness. Using the Internet as its trumpet, the IPC has recruited unknown hundreds of thousands of followers into this virtually structureless organization. Like a latter-day Timothy Leary, the turn-on, tune-in, drop-out LSD guru of the sixties, Weller has galvanized the movement with his erudite and personalized accounts of glimpsing the afterlife and has promulgated an enigmatic Internet countdown clock, now standing at five days, which has rattled the nerves of authorities around the world as to its intent. Weller now claims to be inside a spontaneously growing tent and camper community on a farm in Rising City, Nebraska, which has swelled to thousands of occupants. Surrounded by federal officers, there are mounting fears of a Waco-style standoff.

As the country heads back toward certain and deep recession, the ripple effects are being felt throughout the global economy. Bliss abuse in Europe and Asia hasn't quite caught up with America but it's gaining steam. Throughout Europe's economic centers—Frankfurt, Paris, Milan, Geneva, London, and Madrid—output is down and all indices of economic productivity point to a distracted and disaffected workforce. Even Japan, a bastion of workplace loyalty and stability, is experiencing a wave of Bliss-induced production delays and plant closings.

One person whose business has been thriving is Dr. Vincent Desjardines, one of the country's leading experts on the behavioral effects of Bliss. Spotting a need, the psychologist left his practice and set up Desjardines Associates, a consulting company that works with corporate clients to prevent Bliss abuse in the workplace and attempt to deprogram the hooked. Desjardines admits that prevention is easier than converting a user. "You have to understand," he says, "this is a very powerful drug. For many people, their day-to-day existence becomes intolerably ordinary and inconsequential. Waking up in the morning and going to work seems pointless. If they don't opt for suicide, which is fortunately not terribly common, they tend to hang around their homes, taking repeated doses of the drug and spending down their savings. We've not had much success in winning these people back, even with immersion therapy techniques. The real hope, like many things in medicine, is prevention rather than cure."

What kind of preventative measures work? So far, Desjardines claims that intensive mandatory companywide seminars to educate employees of the dangers of Bliss, complete with vignettes of suicides and family breakups, slow the rate of spread through an organization. But the most important maneuver, he claims, is to root out and expel any employees who seem to be followers or members of the Inner Peace Crusade. Desjardines gets animated when he talks about the IPC. "Some people who take Bliss don't drop out and withdraw into a shell. Instead they become obsessed with spreading the word like missionaries looking for converts. They tend to be extroverts, people with strong convictions and beliefs to start with. Make no mistake about it: once they formally or informally ally themselves with this movement, they become a dangerous and destructive fifth column within a company. Through persuasion or actual sabotage they will get converts."

Meanwhile, at retailing giant Four Seasons Apparel in Atlanta, Georgia, Ann Rosenberg, the newly appointed human resources chief, has been getting an earful from the company's chief financial officer on the deteriorating economic picture at the company. At the Four Seasons warehouse and distribution center in suburban Atlanta, a few employees started a chapter of the Inner Peace Crusade and wreaked havoc through the organization. And if that wasn't enough, consumer demand throughout the retail sector is as weak as people can remember. Still, Rosenberg is pleased about her promotion even though she hasn't had time to hang her pictures. "I've wanted this kind of job my whole career. I only wish the previous head of HR hadn't quit after taking Bliss."

Editor's note: Last Wednesday, BusinessWeek *experienced the ravages of Bliss firsthand. Writer Stephanie Vogt, 26, a contributor to this article and a four-year employee of the magazine, took her own life following a single dose of Bliss.*

Alex smiled and decided to add a post to a long comment thread attached to the article—but his train of thought was interrupted by loud percussive *whumps* from fast-approaching helicopter blades.

There were shouts outside and someone downstairs called his name.

He put on his shoes, ran down the staircase and headed for the back yard where Erik emerged from his RV. He and Steve were pointing toward the east.

"They're coming!" Steve shouted at him. "It's an attack!"

Four AH-64 Apache helicopters with U.S. Air Force insignia were coming in low and fast.

Alex was dumbfounded. The FBI had called the Bolz farm to try to set up a line of communication but he hadn't allowed it. The previous day, there had been a leaflet drop over the fields asking people to leave the site and urging Alex Weller to turn himself in to the authorities and avoid confrontation. Would they ratchet things up so quickly? Risk mass casualties with a full assault?

Steve raised an elk rifle one of the militiamen had given him as a present.

"Don't shoot!" Alex shouted. "Let's see what they do."

"Please Alex, go inside!" Steve insisted.

Alex ignored him, fascinated by the spectacle.

One chopper took the lead and three held back. The lead craft slowed to a hover less than thirty feet over the back yard, creating a deafening prop wash. A side door slid open and a helmeted soldier leaned out, a megaphone in one hand.

"Hold your fire!" he boomed. "We are not hostile!"

"Who are you?" Steve shouted at the top of his lungs.

"Major Ben Thomas, U.S. Air Force, Fifty-fifth Wing, Air Combat Command, Offutt Air Force Base, Nebraska."

Alex decided to speak. "What do you want?" he shouted.

"We want to join you and we want to help protect you!" the major thundered. "Me and my men don't report to the United States government anymore. We report to God!"

53

3 DAYS

As Moreno Stasi was wrapping up his RAINEWS 24 broadcast segment outside the Duomo in Milan, reporters in every major city on all continents were working on some variant of the same assignment.

TV screens in dozens of languages flashed the IPC countdown clock and quite a few producers had the same idea as Stasi: using churches, cathedrals, mosques, and synagogues as evocative props for their stories.

These looped reports combined with frequent live cut-ins to news chopper shots of the expanding humanity at the Bolz farm in Nebraska and the hapless road blocks keeping only the least-determined out.

There were new angles too. Many news crews in unmarked cars and vans simply drove off-road onto the farm, hitting holes in the FBI perimeter and joining the congregation. There, armed with cameras, satellite dishes, and battery packs they embedded themselves and roamed the dirt of New Rising City, interviewing anyone who'd talk to them and turning long lenses on the federal agents staking out the other side of no-man's-land. Erik Bolz was a plum target and occasionally he obliged; but the ultimate "get" was Alex Weller, who remained elusive, preferring the controlled medium of his own web videos.

The FBI set up its command center in the cafeteria of Rising City Elementary School. Public schools were shut down and parents were keeping their kids at home or sending them to relatives elsewhere. Led by Bob Cuccio, the FBI team, manned mainly by Washington and Quantico people, was supplemented by agents from the Omaha field division. The ever-expanding field perimeter was patrolled by agents and U.S. Marshals from contiguous states.

Cyrus and Emily arrived for Cuccio's morning briefing from their Super 8 Motel in Columbus about twenty miles north of Rising City.

In the parking lot she asked, "Are you sure it's okay for me to go to this?"

"Bob was impressed by what you had to say yesterday. You're on the team."

"This is a new experience," she said, taking in the sea of police and FBI vehicles.

"It's a new experience for everyone."

Cuccio had played college basketball and still had a beanpole body. Set against the diminutive tables and chairs of the elementary school cafeteria he looked whimsical, like an elongated giant; but no one was sniggering. Cuccio's message to the packed room was sobering.

"The president, the attorney general, the secretaries of Homeland Security and Defense, everyone, and I mean *everyone* has us under a microscope, ladies and gentlemen," he began. "We're sitting at T minus three days on the IPC clock and the closer we get to zero the more this situation turns into a tinderbox. Now we've all seen the theories about Weller's intentions when the clock winds down. I know some think it's a publicity stunt and nothing of substance is going to happen but we have to play out all the scenarios. The president, I know—because he's told me directly—is concerned about worst cases, something apocalyptic, some call to violence or destruction or social disruption. Frankly, no one sitting in the White House Situation Room has the inclination to sit back and wait to see what transpires."

One of Cuccio's aides fired up a projector and another pulled down a movie screen commandeered from the school's audiovisual department. The photos, taken at dawn that morning, revealed that the farm population had swelled even further overnight. Estimates were that up to 10,000 people now occupied the farm—and that in three days, with all the publicity, those numbers could go much higher. He mentioned Woodstock, invoking the prospect of 400,000 people.

"Here's the main house," Cuccio said, pointing at the roof. "We suspect Weller's there but we have no direct evidence. We've tried to spot him in aerial crowd photos but it's like trying to find Waldo. Even though it's private property, I'm certain there's a laundry list of illegal stuff going on in that farm including narcotic use, child endangerment, even—look at this shot from yesterday afternoon—burying bodies without a permit! But Weller is our primary target and we've got a federal capital murder warrant to back us up. We have to decapitate the IPC and that means taking out Weller. The clock hits zero Sunday morning at ten o'clock, central time. We're under direct orders from the DOJ and White House not to let that happen. I'm going to recommend to my superiors that we continue our efforts to engage him in negotiations and urge his voluntary surrender but absent that, we enter the farm at eight-fifteen A.M. on Sunday and capture Weller by force, if necessary."

For the next hour, a succession of speakers from the FBI Hostage Rescue Team, the U.S. Marshal's Service, and the Nebraska State Patrol discussed tactical options, and every speaker began and ended their talks the same way: We don't want another Waco.

Yet to Cyrus, sitting beside Emily in the middle of the cafeteria, his legs wedged under a child-size table, none of the tactical plans held water. Alex Weller was not going to allow himself to be taken. There would be bloodshed, tremendous bloodshed. Waco would be dwarfed. Rising City would be the new national stain.

The last man to speak came to the front from the side of the room where he'd been standing by the American flag. If he weren't in uniform, his mild, unassuming appearance would allow him to pass for a middle-aged, midlevel executive.

"I'm Brigadier General Evan Kates, Fifty-fifth Wing Commander of Offutt Air Force Base. I know my presence here might be seen as controversial. Believe me, I know all about Posse Comitatus, I know all about the military's supporting role in Waco and the second-guessing that followed, but Rising City is a special situation." His voice cracked with emotion when a photo was projected of the four Apaches parked on one of Bolz's fields. "And damn it, this is personal with us."

Emily nudged Cyrus's shoulder and whispered, "What's Posse Comitatus?"

"The law banning the military from engaging in police actions within the United States," he whispered back. "But wait for it: we're going to see them dance around it."

The general talked about the firepower of his Apaches and the experience of the pilots who deserted. "If they decide to take to the air and become hostile," he said, "their thirty mm autocannons and machine guns and their Hellfire missiles have the capability of over-whelming any conventional civilian law enforcement measures. That is why there are, I believe, active discussions at the highest levels of our government to find a lawful way for the U.S. military to provide materials and men to assist you folks in your operational plans. I'm going to follow orders that if and when issued, will come down a long chain of command that goes up to the secretary of defense and the commander in chief. Those are my men who illegally took these helicopters and it'll be men and women under my command who take them back."

After the briefing, Cuccio kept Cyrus and Emily waiting for an hour. When he was ready they went to the principal's office, which he'd commandeered.

Cuccio had them sit and joked, "I'm at home here. When I was a kid I spent a lot of time in this kind of place."

Cyrus didn't feel like bantering. "Bob, you don't know Weller the way we know him."

"That's why you're here," Cuccio said.

"Good. I want you to hear Doctor Frost's assessment of what he's likely to do."

"Go ahead," Cuccio told her.

"Alex has severe narcissistic personality disorder," she began. "Even before he discovered Bliss he was preoccupied with power and pres-tige. His salon, the Uroboros Society, was a temple to all things Alex.

I attended once and was unsettled by how self-centered and control-ling he was. Around the hospital he had a reputation for brilliance and arrogance in equal measures. The wild, unimaginable success and influence of his Inner Peace Crusade will have had the effect of pour-ing kerosene on a raging fire. My guess is he's feeling omnipotent, like a king or a czar or even a god. I wouldn't be surprised if he's taken on some paranoid features, and that would make him particularly dan-gerous. He won't surrender. He'll want martyrdom. Bliss has probably made him completely unafraid of death."

Cyrus jumped in. "If we raid the farm, there're going to be mass casualties, Bob. I think you know that. There're likely hundreds of guns on that farm and you heard what I heard about the Apaches' capabilities. And maybe if Weller sees himself going down, he acceler-ates his countdown clock, sends out whatever message he intends to send out earlier, and we get the same apocalyptic result anyway. We think there's another way."

"I'm listening," Cuccio said.

"Let Doctor Frost and me go in and negotiate with him directly. We both know him. He was my daughter's doctor. It may be a long shot, but we've got a finite chance of being able to persuade him that he'll be held in even more esteem by his followers if he walks out of that farm and prevents bloodshed."

"If he agrees to let you in, you'd be sitting ducks. He could intro-duce Bliss into your food or water. That's in his bag of tricks."

"We can bring our own provisions," Cyrus said.

"He could take you hostage. If you don't succeed and we get a go decision from the White House, it won't matter that you're in the line of fire. I'm telling you that straight."

"I understand."

"Do you understand, Doctor Frost? You're a civilian. You'll be in harm's way."

"I fully understand," she said firmly. "I want to go with Cyrus."

Cuccio reclined pensively in the principal's chair. "Let me run it up the flagpole," he said.

That night, while Alex was having dinner with Jessie, Sam, and Steve, there was a knock on the kitchen door.

Erik Bolz came in clutching his cell phone.

"The FBI called me again."

Alex laughed. "No, I still won't talk to them."

"It was a different fellow this time, a guy named Cyrus O'Malley. He said to tell you he's with Doctor Emily Frost and the two of them want to come here to talk to you."

Alex dovetailed his fingers, slowly put his hands behind his neck and leaned into them. "Now that's interesting," he said with a satisfied look.

"He scares me," Jessie said. "It's some kind of a trick."

"Well, he doesn't scare me," Alex said. "You call him back, Erik, and tell him I'll sleep on it."

54

I DAYS

Alex played cat and mouse with Cyrus and it wasn't until Friday night that he agreed to let him and Emily come to the farm on Saturday afternoon.

It was a bright day, unseasonably warm, and Cyrus adjusted the Ford's air vents for comfort. He could tell from Emily's stiff posture that despite her denials, she was apprehensive. For his part, Cyrus had no trepidation about entering the belly of the beast. He wanted Weller so badly he could taste the rage in his mouth.

His only fear was for Emily's safety. He'd spent the morning wildly second-guessing his own better judgment, trying to change her mind about coming. He began to argue with her as they were lying in bed and he continued while she was putting on makeup, then over breakfast, and throughout the journey to the farm; but she was adamant. She wanted to see it through and held fast to her assertion that her help could be critical in dealing with Weller.

The state road leading to the farm was deserted in both directions beyond the roadblocks. He turned at the Bolz mailbox. Men with rifles were waiting.

He took a deep breath. "Here we go."

Cyrus got out first. A large bearded man approached.

"I'm Steve. I'm with Alex. We need to frisk you, check your car, check your stuff."

"I know," Cyrus said. "I agreed to that. No weapons. No cell phones. As advertised."

Steve patted down Cyrus and another man had him open the trunk of the car.

Emily scowled as Steve swept his hands over her chest and up and down her jeans, finishing before Cyrus could witness the maneuver. "Isn't it customary for a woman to search another woman?" she whispered angrily.

Steve snorted. "Nothing's customary around here."

Their backpacks were thoroughly searched.

Steve laughed out loud at their provisions. "You don't trust our food?"

"We didn't want to impose," Cyrus replied.

Steve led the way to the farmhouse but he stopped on the porch.

"So how do I know you don't have a microtransmitter that shows your location?"

"Why would we bother?" Cyrus asked. "They know we're here." He pointed to the helicopter overhead. "We figure Weller's staying in the house. If he wants to go sleep in one of the barns or a tent or a hole in the ground, it's okay with us."

Steve shrugged and opened the door for them.

Alex was in the kitchen at his usual spot at the head of the table. He'd taken to wearing his hair untied and flowing, the way Jessie liked it: very Christlike, she gushed. He rose and greeted Cyrus and Emily as friends, exuding the warmth of a generous host.

"Hello Special Agent O'Malley! Do I still have to call you that? Couldn't it just be Cyrus? And hello, Emily. I was very surprised you were here. I really can't understand why you're involved with this but I'm sure you'll explain. Come and sit."

Cyrus glowered but Emily smiled sweetly and shook his hand. "Hello, Alex. It's a long way from Children's Hospital."

"A very long way," he replied, sitting back down. Cyrus and Emily took chairs at the table, joining the others. "I want you to meet my inner circle. This is Jessie, the love of my life; Sam, our computer genius; and Steve, whom you've met, my guardian angel. It's smaller than it used to be thanks to your work in Bar Harbor. Steve's girl-friend, Leslie was taken. My brother was killed."

"You took my daughter. I rescued her," Cyrus said simply.

"How is Tara?"

Cyrus took a breath to control his rage. "She's dead."

"I'm very sorry to hear that."

"Are you?" Cyrus asked.

"Yes, I am."

"Why did you take her?"

"I wanted you to leave us alone. It didn't work."

"The trauma sped her passing."

"We took excellent care of her. It was her brain tumor, not me, Cyrus."

"Fuck you," Cyrus seethed, almost coming out of his chair. He'd agreed with Emily's admonition to try to keep his emotions in check but it wasn't possible. "You're under arrest. I want you to come with me and end this."

Alex responded with a forced smile. "I don't think that's going to happen. Tomorrow's a big day. I wouldn't want to miss it."

Emily shot Cyrus a cautionary look and deftly jumped in, "Alex, do you recall that I went to one of your salons once?"

"I remember. I was sorry you didn't continue. You would have brought a lot to the table."

"I'm not much of a joiner but it was fascinating. I do want to tell you that I think your discovery of Bliss is an incredible achievement. If you'd stuck to the science side of things, it's the type of insight that wins Nobel Prizes."

"That's kind of you to say that, Emily, but I'm not interested in prizes. So tell me, why are you here?"

"I took care of Tara. Cyrus and I became friends. I offered to help."

"By profiling me? By psychoanalyzing me and finding my weak spots?"

She smiled and shook her head. "Mainly, by trying to prevent him from trying to strangle you."

Alex laughed at that and even Cyrus let his facial muscles relax.

"So, Cyrus," Alex said. "You came like Daniel into the lion's den. I admire that."

"Daniel survived."

"And you will too. You and Emily can leave anytime you want. But if you decide to stay to see the clock strike zero, you're welcome. You can stay in the downstairs guest room. We'd love to have you."

Steve agreed. "And if you're here, there's less chance they'll lob a missile onto the house."

"Steve has an active imagination," Alex said lightly. "Can I offer you something to eat or drink?"

"They brought their own stuff," Steve said.

"Do you think we'd poison you?" Alex asked.

"You tried before. My partner's dead because of you."

"Is he? What happened?"

"He killed himself."

"A lot of people choose that once they've seen what lies ahead. Well, I'm going to have more coffee. Help yourself to whatever's in your bags."

Emily took a bottle of water from her pack but Cyrus kept still.

Jessie poured Alex a coffee. He sipped it and said, "Just so you know. In case there is an attack on the farm, all we have to do is push the Enter key on one laptop computer and the clock accelerates to zero. Isn't that right, Sam?"

Sam spoke for the first time. "That's right."

"And then what?" Cyrus asked.

"And then, you'll see," Alex said.

"What are you trying to accomplish?" Emily asked.

"You haven't seen my videos?" he said with a slightly hurt expression.

"Of course I have. I wanted to hear it from you."

"It always sounds so pretentious," Alex said, shaking his head, "but this movement, our Inner Peace Crusade, is attempting to point the world to the solutions that lie within our own souls. I've got a favorite quote from Carl Jung. 'As far as we can discern, the sole purpose of human existence is to kindle a light in the darkness of mere being.' It's amazing. Jung, who was this incredible genius, had this sense of the truth long before the Bliss era. Everyone has the power to change his or her life. Collectively, we have the power to change the world. We're approaching a tipping point."

Emily nodded. "But Jung also said, 'Every form of addiction is bad, no matter whether the narcotic be alcohol, morphine or idealism.'"

Alex clapped in appreciation. "Bravo! I'm blown away."

"I knew you liked Jung," she said slyly. "I looked it up before I came."

Cyrus looked disgusted. "So, in the name of saving the world, you're willing to give people Bliss against their wills? You're—" He was about to level the murder accusation, but Emily had urged him to hold that in abeyance, especially in front of his supporters. "You're threatening the world and scaring millions with this melodramatic countdown?"

"As a doctor, I know that curative therapies often have side effects."

"So tomorrow at ten, you're going to be announcing the cure," Cyrus said contemptuously.

"Something like that."

"I'll stop you."

"You can't, Cyrus. It's unstoppable. Bliss is unstoppable. You shut down Miguel Cifuentes and guess what? A dozen Miguels took his place. From the moment I discovered it, as long as man now exists, Bliss will exist too. Come on, it's a beautiful day. Let me show you around New Rising City."

Cyrus was struck by several things during their afternoon walkabout. The first was the adoration for Alex. Being at his side was like walking with the Chosen One. People tumbled out of their tents and campers, scrambling to speak to him, touch him, be touched. A crowd of children followed wherever they went and their parents happily let them.

Then there was the encampment. It was orderly and peaceful, not the crazed lawless affair that Cuccio and others were postulating. You couldn't glean from the air that most everyone on the Bolz farm was salt of the earth: working people; families. This wasn't a Woodstock by any stretch of the imagination. There wasn't even a scrap of litter!

Lastly, Cyrus was sobered by the raw, animal power of the Apache helicopters resting on a patch like buzzards sunning themselves. The crews, polite and earnest, gave him a tour of their armaments and avionics. Their squadron leader, Major Thomas, told Cyrus, "I never thought I'd do what I did but after Bliss, all my old ways of thinking changed. I hope they don't try anything. I don't want to shoot at my friends—but if they come, I will take to the air and I will defend Alex Weller."

Emily hung back and strolled with Jessie at first, trying to get her to talk about herself and her relationship with Alex. Jessie, though, was uncomfortable around Emily and reticent, as if scared to open up. All she'd repeat was that she loved him very much, trusted him completely, and would follow wherever he led; and then she begged off and said she had to go back and start seeing to dinner.

Emily walked alone for a while until Sam drifted to her side and smiled at her.

"Hi," he said, his cheeks dimpling.

"Hi. So what did Alex say, you're the computer guy?"

"I guess so."

"How long have you known him?"

"I met him just before he discovered Bliss."

"You were interested in his salon?"

"Not at first. I followed a girl, Erica. She was in Bar Harbor. She was one who got killed."

"I'm sorry."

"Don't be. She's on the other side. She's happier than we are, that's for sure."

"You're not happy?"

"There's a lot of tension. The farm, the countdown, you know?"

"What's going to happen tomorrow, Sam?"

"Please don't ask me that."

"I'm sorry," she said quickly. "I won't ask again. I imagine you've taken Bliss."

"Tons of times."

"And your experiences are profound?"

"Amazing."

"And who's there for you?"

"My father."

"When did he pass away?"

"When I was a kid. He was robbed and knifed on his way home from work."

"How terrible, I'm sorry."

"It's okay, I love being with him when I'm on Bliss."

"But you've never contemplated suicide."

"Doesn't appeal to me, but I'll do what I have to do."

"Meaning … ?"

"Meaning nothing. I don't know why I said it that way."

"Do you have brothers and sisters?"

"No, just my ma."

"Does she know you're a big wheel in the IPC?"

"Yeah, she knows. She didn't like it before."

"Before what?"

"Before she took Bliss herself."

"She wanted to see your father too?"

"She didn't want any part of it. Alex put some in her tea."

She stopped walking. "Really!"

Sam sighed. "Yeah, that's what he did."

"How did that make you feel?"

"I was pretty mad, but as usual he was right. She changed her mind about Bliss after taking it. Like Alex says, with Bliss, the end always justifies the means."

In the guest room Cyrus and Emily took off their backpacks and lay on the bed. The walls were thin and they could hear Alex and the others talking excitedly in the kitchen. They kept their own voices low.

"I think this is pointless," Cyrus said. "He's not going to surrender."

"It's not likely," Emily agreed. "He's got himself a flaming God complex going."

"Maybe I should grab a steak knife and just kill the sonuvabitch."

"That's so not you," she said wearily.

"If you weren't here, I'd be considering it. Look, if we don't make any headway this evening, let's get out of here by ten and report back to Cuccio tonight."

"Alex is too far gone, but Sam and Jessie—Sam especially—might be vulnerable to reason. That's where we should press. I want to get Sam alone again."

"Go for it," Cyrus said. "Do your magic."

Jessie knocked on their door at dinnertime. They took sandwiches, fruit, and water from their backpacks and slid the bags under the bed.

The beef stew and boiled potatoes smelled good but Cyrus and Emily chomped on their dry sandwiches and listened to Alex's animated speculation about what great men of history might have thought about Bliss.

After dinner, Emily tried to let Jessie help her with the dishes but she shook her long fiery hair and said, "I don't want to talk to you, okay? You only want to hurt Alex. Leave me alone."

Alex hoisted a bottle of wine and insisted that everyone assemble in the sitting room for a surprise that anticlimactically turned out to be a long piano concert by Erik Bolz's wife, who had a serviceable repertoire of Bach, Mozart, and Chopin.

Cyrus spent the next hour fidgeting with his watch and playing out in his mind how an assault on the farm would go down. He knew he wouldn't be part of the entry team but he looked forward to being asked to identify Weller's body when the time came.

Emily sat next to Sam, who seemed to enjoy the attention of an attractive woman. Classical music clearly wasn't his thing, and when he asked her if she wanted to take a walk she jumped at the chance.

It was the time of year when daytime warmth quickly dissipated and the nights were still frigid. He gave her his bomber jacket.

She waved toward the gaslights and cooking fires stretching into the fields. "So many people," she said. "It makes me incredibly sad."

"What does?"

"That many of them might die tomorrow."

He looked startled. "How did you know?"

"I was talking about the loss of life if Alex doesn't yield and the authorities storm the farm. What were you talking about?"

"Nothing."

"Sam, what's Alex got planned for tomorrow? Please tell me. I won't say a thing to him, I promise."

"There's going to be a call to action."

"What kind of action?"

"Mass suicide. Alex thinks millions will do it if he asks them to."

"Christ," she whispered.

"Yeah, it's heavy stuff."

"What will you do?"

"If Alex goes, I'll go too. I wouldn't mind hanging with my dad."

The air was filled with laughter on the wind. "What about all these people?"

"They're here because they want to be here and everyone who offs themselves will do it because they want to do it. No one's going to force them."

"What about the children?"

"In my mind that's a little tricky," Sam said. "But you know, ends justifying means? Remember?"

They went back inside and sat on the braided rug. Cyrus pointed to his watch and flashed his palms twice: he wanted to leave in twenty minutes. She nodded vigorously.

Cyrus got up to use the bathroom then went to the guest room and retrieved his backpack. There was one water bottle left, safely sealed. He cracked the cap and gulped at it, missing the glue-sealed puncture wound on the bottle neck.

Steve and Alex were following him with their eyes when he came back to the sitting room. Steve couldn't suppress a grin at the sight of the three quarters–empty bottle in his hand.

Cyrus bent over Alex and said frostily, "We're leaving soon. There's no point in staying."

Alex looked miffed. "Stay till LuAnn's finished playing. You don't want to hurt her feelings."

"Fifteen minutes," Cyrus said.

While she was midway through Mozart's Rondo in A Minor Cyrus's head began to feel heavy and an overwhelming urge to sleep overtook him. He tried to fight it, tried to stand. He got halfway up.

Emily screamed when he hit the floor and then the music abruptly stopped.

55

DAY ZERO

Cyrus awoke in Emily's arms in the small hours of the night. They were alone in the guest room.

She audibly exhaled with relief when his eyes opened and she told him that she was there for him.

Tears pooled in his eyes and spilled from under the lids. He lay motionless, staring at the ceiling. "Tara," he choked. "I was with her. She was jumping up and down the way she always does when she's so excited she can't stand it. I wanted to lift her up and hold her and tell her I love her but I couldn't get to her, Emily. I couldn't get all the way across."

"Oh, Cyrus," Emily said, stroking his hair. "Oh, baby."

"I've got to get back there. I know she's happy, but she's all alone." He stopped to think. "Well ... not completely alone. There was something else there. I couldn't see it but I felt it ... it felt like God."

There was a knock on the door and Alex came in.

"I heard voices. You're back! How's my patient?"

"Leave us alone," Emily said angrily.

"No, stay," Cyrus said, sitting up. "I saw Tara."

Alex smiled. "How was she?"

"Beautiful ... and healthy."

"That's good, Cyrus, I'm happy for you."

"I want more."

"More Bliss?"

"Yes."

"You can have as much as you like." He unzipped a fanny pack and tossed a handful of sticks on the bed. "You might want to wait till the morning. You took a fairly heavy dose. I didn't know how much of the water you'd drink. Looks like you were thirsty."

"It's unconscionable," Emily spat. "You're despicable, Alex."

"I like you Emily," he said. "But I respectfully disagree. Ask Cyrus what he thinks."

"I don't care about him," Cyrus said. "I want to be with my little girl."

"I'll take that as an endorsement," Alex said, leaving. "See you bright and early. It's going to be a fine day tomorrow."

"We should go now," Emily told Cyrus. "I can drive."

Cyrus dropped back onto the pillow. "No, I want to stay," he said weakly.

He moved his hand and found the pile of Bliss straws.

"No!" she shouted in alarm. "I'm not going to let you do that!"

"I can't let her be alone. I've got to get to her."

She grabbed both his hands and with unexpected strength pulled him to a sitting position then dragged his feet over the side of the bed. She stood over him, tilted his chin up, so he had to look her in the eyes. "Cyrus, listen to me. I've never taken Bliss and I don't want to, but I don't doubt the power of the experience you've just had."

"It wasn't an experience, it was real."

"I'm not saying it wasn't and I'm not saying there's no afterlife, and I'm not saying there's no God. What I *am* saying is that children can die but their parents have to go on and live their lives for the sake of themselves and other people who love them. Your time will come, Cyrus, hopefully when you're old, after an amazingly full life, full of love and books and poetry. And Tara will be there waiting for you, the same pretty little girl. That's the way it's meant to be."

"Why wait?" he asked in a tone just above a whisper.

"Damn it, Cyrus!" She shook him. "Because of me. Because I love you and I don't want to lose you. I'm begging you. Choose life. Choose me."

He said nothing for half a minute but stared at her determined face and burning eyes. He sighed heavily. "If it weren't for you, Emily Frost ..."

She let him lie down and covered him with a blanket.

"Sleep now," she said. "I'll be next to you all night."

Sunday morning began with a dawn as rich and beautiful as anyone could remember. Most of New Rising City was up, watching the rosy spectacle and watching the clock.

Emily hadn't drawn the curtains that night, relying on the sun to wake her. Cyrus was curled on his side, breathing smoothly. She whispered close to his ear, "Cyrus, you've got to get up now."

After a moment of disorientation, he asked, "What time is it?"

"Seven-forty. Cyrus, I need to tell you what Sam told me last night before they gave you the Bliss. At time zero a message is going out from Alex calling for mass suicides. Millions are going to die."

He stood on wobbly legs. "We don't have much time."

There was an air of controlled chaos in the elementary school cafeteria. FBI personnel wearing headsets were stationed at computer terminals where live feeds from the helicopters were superimposed on map grids.

Bob Cuccio shouted to everyone and anyone, "Any word from O'Malley?"

In the silence that followed, he swore and said, "I shouldn't have let him go in."

"You made a command decision," said General Kates.

"The wrong one. He could be dead already."

"We've got thirty-five minutes till eight-fifteen," Kates said. "When are we getting the final go decision from the White House?"

"At eight. Is everything set on your end?"

"I've got twelve Apaches airborne, holding over Columbus. They'll take out the stray birds, hopefully while they're still on the ground. We've got four M1A1 tanks positioned on the compass points around the farm, about a half mile from the perimeter, and sixteen Bradleys. The tanks and Bradleys are operated by DOJ personnel because of Posse Comitatus but I've got my combat engineers in the vicinity if we need their support."

"There's a presidential finding in place authorizing your Apache pilots."

The general nodded but then added, "Whatever happens, I think you and I are going to be spending the rest of our careers testifying before Congress."

"The only thing I care about is getting through today," Cuccio said.

The kitchen smelled of bacon. Jessie was slicing freshly baked bread; Sam was scrambling eggs. Steve was nervously looking out the windows at the sky—and Alex was sitting serenely at the table as if he had no cares.

"Good morning!" he said when Cyrus and Emily came in. "Sleep well?"

Cyrus silently nodded.

"Have some breakfast. I swear to you there's no Bliss in it. That mission's accomplished."

They were hungry and thirsty but they refused. It was 7:55. They had quickly choreographed their plan while Cyrus dressed and now had precious short time to make it work. If it didn't, Cyrus was determined to get Emily out before Cuccio and the army moved in.

"You enjoy manipulating people, don't you?" Cyrus said.

Alex looked surprised. "I enjoy enlightening them. Weren't you enlightened?"

"The truth?" Cyrus asked.

"Why not?"

"Yeah, I was."

"So, once again, the end justifies—"

Cyrus cut him off. "That's bullshit. You're a manipulative self-serving son of a bitch."

Steve stepped forward, his hand on the butt of one of the guns stuffed in his belt.

"It's okay, Steve. Cyrus is just being his argumentative self. Bliss doesn't make everyone see the light."

"I want to say something to you," Cyrus said, controlling his anger, "and I want your friends to listen carefully. Now that I've taken Bliss I understand you better. You've got an edge over other messiahs and prophets. Most of them are delusional or frauds. Bliss is real. And it's made you so hopped up on a power trip that you're willing to make decisions on other people's lives. And today you want millions of people to honor your self-imposed status by killing themselves."

"Who told him?" Alex asked sharply, surveying the room. Sam looked away. "It's okay, Sam. It doesn't matter now. Throughout the ages, prophets have always been attacked."

"If I chose to appoint myself a prophet I'd be preaching a different message," Cyrus said.

"And that would be?"

"That we're here on earth for a purpose. What that purpose is, I don't know. But when we've lived the best lives we could, we haven't come to the end. Something follows, something good that's going to answer all the questions we've been asking ourselves our whole lives."

Alex scoffed. "That's the same tired message that's been dished out over the centuries by people who operated on the basis of faith rather than proof. Now that Bliss proves that the afterlife is real—and not only that, but that it's glorious—there's absolutely no reason to wait."

Cuccio snapped his cell phone shut.

"General Kates, I've just received the authorization. I'm going to tell my people to proceed on the farm. You can do the same with yours."

Kates nodded. "May God help us."

"You wanted your proof," Cyrus said softly. "There was nothing you wouldn't do to find that proof, was there?"

Alex looked at him blankly.

"You murdered Thomas Quinn, didn't you?"

"He committed suicide. I happened to be there. I've told everyone what happened."

"Suicide? Did you tell them you caved his head in and stuck a needle in his brain?"

Jessie had been quiet, staring at her unfinished breakfast. "He was injured?" she asked, looking up.

"And did you tell them you picked up five innocent women on the street, five young prostitutes—a couple of them teenagers—whom you strangled and drilled their skulls while they were still alive?"

"Alex?" Jessie said.

Cyrus pressed. "That's how you discovered Bliss, isn't it? And you were going to do that to my little girl too, weren't you?"

Jessie pushed her chair from the table and stood with a glassy, confused look. "Is it true, Alex? Did you kill Thomas? Did you kill those women?"

Alex stood up. "They're all in a much better place than the one they came from. I helped them get there."

Cyrus and Emily rose too. "Do you know how sick that sounds? Has there ever been a sorrier justification for murder?"

Alex flushed with anger. "Murder … suicide … accidents … disease … they all lead to the same place. And it's a bloody amazing place."

"Murder is different, man," Sam said sadly.

Alex boiled over, his face beet red. "You want to call me a murderer, Cyrus?"

"I am calling you one."

"And you want to punish me?"

"Yes."

Alex pointed to Steve. "Give me your guns."

"Why, Alex?" Steve asked.

"Just give them to me!" he screamed.

Alex took both and handed one to Cyrus. "Then punish me," he said. "Go ahead and shoot me."

Cyrus clicked off the safety. "I only want to arrest you."

Alex was six feet away. He pointed his gun at Cyrus's head.

Emily screamed, "No!"

Cyrus raised his gun in response, chest-level.

"I said shoot me! You don't have a choice. I'm in control here," he bellowed, "not you!"

"Alex, no!" Jessie yelled.

Cyrus held his arms out in firing posture. "You don't have to do this."

"I like my position because I can't lose. Sam, when I'm gone, you have to take over. You know what you have to do."

"Alex," Sam moaned.

"Just do it, Sam. I'm going to count to five now, Cyrus. Then I'm going to kill you unless you kill me first." He glanced at Jessie, mouthed *I love you*, then shouted, "One!"

Cyrus felt the weight of the gun, the hardness of the trigger against his finger.

"Two!"

Jessie began to cry.

"Three!"

"Please, Alex, don't," Emily said.

"Four!"

Cyrus lowered his aim and fired into Alex's abdomen.

Alex groaned and doubled over then sank to his knees, letting the gun slip away.

Jessie ran to him.

Cyrus didn't see Steve coming. The big man charged like an enraged bull and knocked him flat, then violently stripped the gun from his hand, aiming it at his head.

"Don't kill him," Alex said, through gritted teeth. Jessie was pressing her hand against his wound, trying to staunch the bleeding. "He did what I wanted him to do. Sam, push the button."

Sam's laptop was on the counter near the stove.

His finger hovered over the Enter key.

Emily's voice rose over Jessie's sobs. "Sam, this is extremely important. Pushing that button will kill countless impressionable but good people: people who shouldn't die today."

Alex was struggling to talk. "Don't listen to her. Push it."

"You have a mother, Sam. She loves you. She needs you."

"What about my father?"

"Carry your love for him inside you. When your time comes, he'll be there. You know he will."

Sam began to sob uncontrollably. He slowly closed the laptop until it snapped shut and then he sank to the floor.

Cyrus was looking into the gaping barrel of a pistol. "Steve, it's over. You're not a bad guy. Your girlfriend's going to need you. Put the gun down."

Steve looked to Alex, who was on his side, breathing hard, his eyes staring ahead. Blood was oozing from his mouth. Steve began to blubber like a child, his big chest heaving. He lowered the gun and gave it to Cyrus.

Cyrus got on his feet. "Sam, I need you to go online and send out a message that the countdown's been canceled: that Alex had a change of heart, that he just wants people to live good, full lives. Something like that, okay? Then get on your bullhorn and tell all these people to go home peacefully. Can you do that, Sam?"

"Yeah, I can," he said numbly.

"Then do it now. Hurry." It was 8:10. "And for Christ's sake, someone give me a phone."

Bob Cuccio's mobile rang. He didn't recognize the number.

"Bob, it's Cyrus! It's over. I shot Weller. You've got to stand down! You've got to abort!"

Cuccio looked at the clock and rubbed his eyes. "Thank God." Then he began to yell orders at his people like a man possessed.

Emily knelt beside Alex, checking his pulse. It was weak. His shirt was soaked through. "I'm sorry, Jessie," she said. "I don't think he can be saved in time."

Alex's lips were moving. Jessie leaned over and put her ear close.

His chest stopped moving.

Jessie slumped onto her rump, her jeans staining with Alex's blood.

"What did he say?" Emily asked.

Jessie looked at Emily, her voice pitifully tiny. "He said, *come with me*"—and before anyone could react, she picked up the gun near his body and shot herself through the temple.

Alex felt himself floating like a wisp of a feather on an air current. The kitchen was bloody … but the sight of his and Jessie's bodies wasn't disturbing; all that was over now. He was ready for the journey.

And when it began it was as wonderful as always. Even better.

The tunnel seemed blacker, the sparkles of light more intense, the light ahead the purest white imaginable.

He was running with childhood abandon to the green horizon. When it came into sight the luminous river looked more beautiful and sounded sweeter than ever before. He wept.

His father seemed mad with joy to see him: his arms waving so hard Alex thought they'd fly off.

He was halfway across, easily navigating the stepping-stones.

"You've made it!" Dickie shouted. "You're here for good!"

He pushed off the last stepping-stone onto the bank and threw his arms around his father's neck, felt the man's stubble against his cheek. "Hello, boy," Dickie sobbed.

Then came the moment Alex had been waiting for most of his life. He felt his father's strong arms around his shoulders, felt his chest being crushed in a loving embrace.

"Dad."

"My Alex."

"I've missed you."

"I know you have. Come on. Let's walk together."

The green plain was vast, the horizon, unbounded. Alex felt an unalloyed, powerful force out there that filled him with exultation. They followed a path, darker green than the rest of the plain, reminding Alex of trodden grass.

They walked, hand in hand, as they'd done when he was little.

Then Dickie slowed and came to a halt.

"Why are we stopping?" Alex asked.

Dickie said nothing but his eyes looked sad.

When Alex looked ahead he saw it.

They'd come to a fork. The path split in two, each branch running its own course toward the infinite horizon.

EPILOGUE

Crocuses pushed up from the rich mound of dirt in front of Tara's grave. Spring was coming.

Cyrus brought her a stuffed bear. Emily had a bouquet of spring flowers.

Emily started to cry first and that set him off. They both placed their offerings against her headstone and sat down on the black granite meditation bench Cyrus had installed.

"God, I miss her."

The bench was small and Emily was pressed against him. She took a pack of Kleenex from her purse, dabbed her eyes and handed him one.

He took it and said, "I'm going to be with her again."

"I know you will. But my job's to remind you every day why you should keep on living. I love you too much to lose you. And you're too stubborn to let Alex Weller win, aren't you?"

He put his arm around her. "You're right. I am."

They went back to Emily's apartment. Her roommate was on duty and they had the place to themselves. They made love and afterward lay on top of the bed holding hands. She got a text message. One of her patients had been readmitted and the parents wanted her to come. She dressed and told him she'd be back by dinner and kissed his forehead.

When she was gone, Cyrus put his clothes on and poked around her living room. Thanks to him she had a small collection of Shakespeare in the bookcase.

He knew exactly what he wanted and went straight for a passage in *Macbeth*.

> To-morrow, and to-morrow, and to-morrow,
> Creeps in this petty pace from day to day
> To the last syllable of recorded time,
> And all our yesterdays have lighted fools
> The way to dusty death. Out, out, brief candle!
> Life's but a walking shadow ...

He left the book on his lap and felt inside his pocket.

There was a single stick of Bliss.

He untwisted one end and let the crystals fall onto his tongue, where they melted like the final snowflakes of the season falling onto warming ground.